MW00637311

DEBTS UNSETTLED

A MYSTERY ACROSS TIME

HOLLIS OLIVER

DUSTY RAIN
PUBLISHING

This is a work of fiction, all characters, events, and organizations portrayed are either products of the authors imagination and purely coincidental, or used in a fictitious manner.

Debts unsettled – A Mystery Across Time
www.hollisoliver.com

Copyright © by Hollis Oliver

All Rights Reserved. No part of this publication may be reproduced, stored, in any type of retrieval system, or transmitted in any form or by any means, electronic, mechanical, photocopying, recording, or otherwise, without prior permission of the author and the publisher.

DUSTY RAIN
PUBLISHING
Washington, USA

ISBN 978-0-578-66781-2 (Trade Paperback)
ISBN 978-0-578-66780-5 (eBook)

First Edition: April 2020

Printed in the United States

0 9 8 7 6 5 4 3 2 1

I dedicate this book to Suzy

You have been the love of my life longer than most people have lived.

I invite you to sign up for my mailing list. I will not send out frequent emails, only those that announce a new release or an offer. Also, I will not share your email address with others; it's between you and me. I am producing a recording of the song I wrote for this book and will use the mailing list to notify you when you can go to my website to listen to it. That notification will only be sent to people who are on my reading list. I will also be offering deleted scenes, and a Novella related to this story. They will not be for sale; again, these are exclusive to only those on my mailing list.

Sign up today: https://www.hollisoliver.com

"There are no foreign lands. It is the traveler only who is foreign."
— Robert Louis Stevenson

1

~

Present Day, Portland, Oregon – Thursday, October 3rd

For over 30 years, Michael Mays had lived with, even accepted, the unsolved murder of his mother.

That alone was not why he sat in a waiting room that day.

After losing his job with a large L.A. law firm, and everything else to his ex-wife, he was smart enough to know he may need help.

Dr. Downing stepped out of her office, holding the door to allow a teenage girl to pass through. The woman opposite Michael, stood and met the doctor and the girl at office entrance. She hugged the girl. "How are—"

The girl interrupted her mother in a whisper, "Can we talk later?" She glanced at Michael, then back to her mother.

"Of course." The mother turned toward the doctor. "Thank you, Dr. Downing. We'll be back next week."

"You'll love Dr. Hardy. He has my notes and I'll brief him before I go on sabbatical." Mom nodded and glanced at Michael. She and her daughter rushed through the door.

"Michael, give me a few minutes please."

"I'll be here." He said, as he looked at her and nodded.

He re-adjusted his position in the chair. His 6'4" frame, even though relatively lean, didn't combine well with waiting room furniture.

After the promised few minutes, the doctor stepped out. "Please come in, Michael."

Her office breathed and exhaled harmonized femininity. A whiff of cinnamon and vanilla pulled him in to see bouquets of flowers, floral-patterned fabrics, and well-placed art and furnishings. Classical music played in the distance.

A sofa was set next to a built-in bookcase; in the bookcase, someone had placed books at random positions. Michael saw the books as wrestling against conforming with the rest of the office.

The doctor shook his hand and motioned him to have a seat in a floral chair that faced the bookcase.

Dr. Jennifer Downing, approximately the same age as Michael, dressed like her office, everything neat and in place. But not cinnamon or vanilla, her scent was a hint of gardenia.

She sat in a matching chair facing him. Michael saw the books behind her back, wrestling against her.

"Michael, when we first met, I noticed you took in my entire office before sitting, as you did today."

"Your office is calming and peaceful," Michael said, "but it's foreign to how I decorate."

"Does it make you uncomfortable? Are you having second thoughts about seeing a female psychologist?"

Michael shook his head. "No, both of my law firm partners, men, recommended you. But I am fascinated by the emotions I have when we meet."

"Do you sense *why* you have those emotions?"

Michael thought for a few seconds. "I have two *whys*. First, when we shake hands, I pick up a trace of gardenia. That's a strong memory I associate with my mother. I was 12 years old when she was murdered. She loved that perfume. I still have the last bottle she was using."

"Should I not wear it next time we meet?"

"No, it's a great memory, please wear it."

The doctor smiled. "Okay, what's the second *why?*"

"The woman who raised me, my grandmother, decorates with a similar feminine touch. An older, Victorian style, but feminine."

"We haven't discussed your grandmother. Is she still with us?"

"Yes, 90-years-old and *very* much alive."

The doctor nodded. "Your response makes me want to meet her. When we last met, we discussed your mother and father. We *didn't* discuss you being 12 when your mother died, or who raised you. So, is your mother's mother, the woman who raised you?"

"Yes."

"How has she dealt with her daughter's death?"

Michael lowered his gaze. "If you had a daughter who was murdered, how would *you* deal with it?"

Dr. Downing shook her head. "My question was clinical, wasn't it? I apologize."

Michael leaned toward her and stared into her eyes for a few seconds. "Doctor, my grandmother is the most important person in my life. If I could do one thing for her—to pay her back for how she loved and raised me—I'd choose finding who killed her daughter, and bring closure before she dies."

After considering his response, she gave a soft smile and nodded in agreement. "If I could help you with that I would, but I'm far from being clairvoyant or a detective.

"During our last meeting, I sensed you have a goal of discovering why your father abandoned you. Is my takeaway from that conversation correct?"

Michael put his hand to his chin. "You're more of a detective than you know. I guess you could say *I too* need closure, on both my mother *and* my father."

She made a note on her notepad. "So, it's *not* just your grandmother who needs closure."

Michael tilted his head, looked at her for a few seconds, then shook his head. "I guess not."

"Any hope of achieving either, or both?"

"None I can see."

"Maybe we can discover a way to bring closure for *you.*

* * *

Willamette State Penitentiary, Oregon – Same Day

Daniel Wygal entered the prison library and scanned the room. Hushed clicking met him, along with the odor of confined men. His face conveyed the disgust he had for wasting over 30 years in that hellhole, filled with nothing but losers.

Everyone in the room, including the guard, avoided eye contact.

He spotted an available computer in the far corner and sauntered across the library's linoleum floor, his shoes squeaking on the waxed surface.

All eyes followed his movement by watching his feet pass over 12-inch squares of black and gray.

The State of Oregon moved the penitentiary—'hellhole'—in 1866, where it stood desolate in the fields and woods surrounding it.

Over the years, while on his daily walks in the prison yard, Daniel saw fields succumb to commercial buildings, and woods become housing developments.

But progress was unsuccessful in intruding upon Daniel. He avoided newspapers, television, and most of the internet. He held no interest in knowing what he had missed outside the prison walls, except for how his investments were doing.

Instead, he read classic novels, and never tired of re-reading his favorite authors: Louis L'Amour and Wilbur Smith.

After 30 years in prison, Daniel's heart was still the heart of a killer—a serial killer.

He worked out daily and looked as lean and fit as he was the day he walked into the hellhole.

Upon first meeting him, people found his pockmarked face, weak chin, and thinning—but brilliant—white hair in conflict with his arrogance and swagger.

Prisoners *and* guards knew him as deadly smart and ruthless. They feared him *and* his network.

Thirty years fed his bitterness, not lessened it. Each year, August 8th came and went without occasion to take vengeance upon the appropriate gender.

Six times during his 30-year stay, Daniel waged his lethal anger on men who identified as women. It did not quench his hate.

But Daniel saw hope: A parole hearing the next day.

He took a seat in a metal chair in front of an HP desktop computer.

Watching the computer fire up, he marveled at how comfortable he had become with that technology. It had been less than six months since attending computer training. His know-how was more like that of a 16-year-old than a 60-year-old, but he continued to avoid current news and social media.

He found the computers *most* useful in managing his trust fund investments. Prison staff and inmates knew he was wealthy. They did not know that he was one of the wealthiest people in the State of Oregon.

Daniel had an idea. He wondered if it was driven by a guilty conscience, remorse, or morbid curiosity. While considering the three, morbid curiosity brought a slight smirk.

He opened Google and searched for personal information on the woman the State of Oregon convicted him of killing.

The discovery of her having a daughter piqued his curiosity. He searched archives in several on-line sites and found information about the sons and daughters of the four women police suspected he had killed.

One committed suicide, several had drug and alcohol related arrests, and most had failed marriages.

But the son of Deborah Mays, one of the four murder victims they suspected him of killing, took a different path. Michael Mays became an attorney.

What put this kid's life on such a different track?

He found Michael's law firm's website and clicked on, "Our Team."

"What the—" he yelled out and slammed hard against the back of the metal chair. The sound reverberated in the concrete and metal room.

It brought attention from everyone, including the guard.

Daniel moved his hand to his lower back and grimaced at the guard, "Muscle spasm."

He leaned forward and studied the computer screen.

It's the guy from over 30 years ago.

That confused and shook Daniel. Several times while stalking Deborah Mays, a 12-year-old Michael, her only child, was with her.

This guy… this grown Michael was there too. How is that possible?

He leaned back, with his hands behind his head. His mind went back three decades. Back to when he and the adult Michael confronted one another, even clashed physically.

Daniel wondered, *Is this the same guy? Will I get to face him again? If so, this time he stays down.*

He was at a complete loss over the implications of his discovery and sat motionless for an hour running history through his mind.

* * *

Dr. Jennifer Downing's Office – Still the same day

"Okay, Michael, let's continue last week's discussion. We discussed the loss of your job and your failed marriage. Since that session, and in reviewing my notes for today's session, I've wondered about communication between you and your ex-wife. How would you characterize it?"

Michael stared at her for a few seconds, then leaned forward, elbows on his knees his hands out. "If we were going out to dinner, just the two of us, I'd ask a question, which took about a quarter of a mile. Her answer, three miles. Her follow-up question, a mile. My answer turned the car back toward home."

Dr. Downing hid a smile. "Is that your experience in conversations with your friends?"

"No. We joke and jab one another sarcastically, but it causes laughter, not anger."

The doctor made a note. "Since we're there, tell me about your friends?"

He looked at her, tilted his head, and pursed his lips. "What do you mean? I guess I don't understand the question."

"It's not a trick question. I want to hear your perspective on your relationships with friends. Let's start with two."

Michael looked down while resting his chin between his index finger and thumb. He looked back up. "My grandmother—"

The doctor cut him off. "A friend who's not a relative. She's your friend because she raised you and, because she's your grandmother."

"Okay," Michael sat up straight and crossed his arms. "My friend Matt. We went to law school together."

"When did you last spend time with him?"

"A month or two after Gwen and I divorced."

She flipped two pages back and looked at her notes. "You and Gwen divorced two years ago?"

"And, life gets in the way."

"In your way, or his way?"

"In *everyone's* way."

"Did you reach out to him?"

"No, like I said, life got in the way."

Dr. Downing looked at Michael for a few seconds before making a note. "Okay, tell me about another friend?"

Michael turned his head away for a few seconds, closed his eyes, then looked back at the doctor. "Kenny."

"Describe that relationship."

"We play golf in the men's club at the golf course where we're members."

"When was the last time you talked to him?"

Michael sighed through his nostrils. "It's been about a month."

"When will you see him next?"

"Spring of next year, when golf season begins." Michael slid forward in his chair, elbows on his knees and hands spread. "What do Matt or Kenny have to do with why I'm seeing you?"

Dr. Downing did not say a word. She allowed their conversation to percolate through his mind.

It was a full minute before she interrupted Michael's thoughts.

"Michael, it's important we end at this point. Between now and our next session, I want you to journal observations about your friendships and relationships. At minimum, the two that first came to mind. They sound more like acquaintances, yet you cited them as friends. If they're available, get together with them and use the skills that make you a good attorney. You recovered after your experience in California. In your current law firm, you made Partner in less than three years; don't ignore that accomplishment."

Michael gave a weak smile.

"At the end of each day, I want you to journal what you learned from that day's personal interactions. Is that okay with you?"

"Ending the session, or friends being more like acquaintances?"

"Ending the session and journaling your daily thoughts and observations."

Michael clasped his hands and rested his chin on his thumbs while looking down. He shook his head, then looked up. "Yes."

Dr. Downing leaned forward. "Your mouth says yes, but your body language tells me it's not okay with you?"

"I was hoping you'd have *some* answers today. Instead, I feel like I'm being accused of something."

"Michael, I'm making no accusations. But I will help guide you through a self-discovery process. Then we can discuss answers, or more accurately, the actualization of mitigating your discoveries."

He stood. "And people think attorneys use cryptic language."

She smiled. "I'm out of town the next six weeks, so you'll have plenty of time for reflection. I look forward to discussing friendships, or better yet, relationships. All right?"

"I heard you tell the woman in the waiting room she would see your associate next week?"

"Different situations. Overall, you're functioning well. It will be good for you to use the six weeks to consider relationships as you're living them."

Michael nodded and shook her hand. "I'll see you in six weeks."

Michael drove toward his office, feeling like his thoughts were being tossed around in a blender, and his emotions were bleeding like they were being untangled from blackberry brambles.

He jabbed his assistant's number on his phone's *Favorites* screen. His car's speakerphone came to life.

"This is Trevor, Mr. Mays' assistant. How may I help you?"

"Hey, Trevor, Michael here."

"Hi, Mr. Mays."

"Trevor, I have no appointments until after lunch, right?"

"That *was* correct, but your late afternoon partners meeting and your 2 P.M. meeting were both canceled, so other than three phone calls to return, your day is free."

"Text me the phone messages. I'll see you tomorrow."

"Okay. Have a great afternoon."

"Thanks, Trevor."

Given he had six weeks to work on his journal assignment, his immediate priority was to regroup from the doctor's insights. The prescription, driving to Sisters, Oregon, to have Halibut fish & chips for lunch. The result would be six hours behind the wheel. Side effects may include the recognition that he sucks at maintaining relationships. He considered that possibility as he merged onto I-5 Southbound. A random thought interrupted.

She's taking six weeks off?

He finished the phone calls before he was thirty minutes down the road. One led to interesting, even challenging work. The other two were not profound issues.

Intellectual Property Attorney 101 level.

His calendar, during his first two years with the L.A. firm, overflowed with 101 assignments.

The third year, Michael's cases became more stimulating. By the end of that year, his former wife caused the firm's Partners to ask him to leave.

Move on. I will not spend 5 ½ hours with that cyclone in my head.

He ousted those thoughts by replaying his conversation with Dr. Downing. By the time he'd passed through Salem, and turned onto the highway to Sisters, the realization the doctor was correct smacked him. Other than his grandmother, he found few relationships. And, those few were surface only.

A roadside sign announced an exit in a fourth of a mile.

No reason to spend four more hours on the road rehashing what I know is true.

The exit would take him back to Salem, near the Capitol building, to a restaurant he loves.

I have better relationships with restaurants than I do with most people in my life.

He realized how pitiful that sounded.

While taking the exit, he looked to his right, across an open field. The Willamette State Penitentiary loomed behind chain link and razor-wire fencing.

His stare locked onto the prison, causing him to nearly run off the road.

Life could be worse.

2

Willamette State Penitentiary, Oregon – Still the Same Day

After lunch, Daniel told his cellmate what he had found.

The cellmate stepped back and sat on the edge of his bunk. "What difference does it make, Daniel?" He grabbed his pillow, placed it on his lap and began rubbing one of the pillow's corners between his thumb and index finger.

The cellmate was a big man, scary-ugly and smart enough to fear Daniel and his network of enforcers. Or, as Daniel called them, part-time employees. Scary-ugly was also a part-time employee.

"*Someone* helped the police put me here… it must be him. He's the same guy who hounded me, over *30 years* ago. He carried a device I'd never seen, or since; I believe he used it to take pictures of me."

Scary-ugly became wide-eyed, looked at the floor while slamming his hand on the top of his bald head. "That means, somehow he traveled back in time. That ain't possible, right? Maybe it was his daddy you seen. I mean, I seen sons who look just like their daddy."

Daniel stood, paced, and talked out loud to himself. "That could be, but why was he always on the sideline? Each time, he was watching Deborah Mays and her son from a distance."

"Maybe his daddy was shy. Maybe he wanted to keep an eye peeled but didn't like crowds, or people."

Daniel's gaze slashed at Scary-ugly. "Stop interrupting my thoughts."

But Daniel's thoughts were taking him nowhere. He leaned against a wall and gazed into the past. "I guess I'll never find out short of time travel being discovered."

Scary-ugly recoiled, wishing he could take back his comments. While withdrawing farther onto his bunk, Daniel's last sentence registered. He blurted out, "Hey, there's a dude in here who says he's innocent—"

Daniel cut him off. "Don't we all?"

Scary-Ugly hugged his pillow tighter and pleaded, "Let me finish, Daniel. It might *be* something." He retreated farther onto his bunk until the concrete block wall stopped him. "This dude claims he used a book to travel back in time. It's a *convincing* story, man. Most dudes laugh at him, but I've listened to him tell it, probably ten times. It never changes."

"A book?" Daniel's full attention fell on his cell mate. "Michael Mays, or whoever it was, had a book. What's the guy's name?"

"Russell. I never heard his last name."

Daniel swung his feet up onto his bunk and laid back. "Point him out at dinner."

As Daniel drifted off, clanking sounds startled him. "Get up, Daniel. The Warden wants to see you." Again, the guard hit the cell's doorjamb with his baton.

Daniel sat up, placed his feet on the floor, and glared at the guard. "Hit the doorjamb *again*." The guard backed away.

While walking through his cell's doorway and into the hallway, Daniel put on his shirt. The guard pulled out handcuffs.

Daniel scowled. "Lead the way." He buttoned his shirt as he followed.

Approaching the Warden's office, the guard pointed to an oak banker's chair outside the office doorway. Daniel glanced at him but continued walking straight through the Warden's open door. The guard moved to stop him. The Warden held up his hand. "It's okay, Jim. Please close the door."

The Warden's office had two large bookcases stuffed with books that showed no signs of wear. In the bookshelf closest to his desk, well-worn policy manuals occupied a full row, at the ready, waiting to pounce. He'd lined his walls with framed certificates of training participation, his college diploma, and years-of-service awards.

The warden sat behind his desk, tapping the edge of the file folder in his right hand against the palm of his left hand.

Daniel sat, not waiting for an invitation.

The Warden stared at Daniel for a few seconds. "Daniel... *we* have a problem."

"What problem do *you* have, Warden?"

The Warden remained calm. "You *know* controversial material isn't allowed on our in-house computers."

Daniel did not break eye contact or respond.

"Our IT people searched the library server and found *disturbing* photos in a file you created."

Daniel still did not break eye contact or respond.

"Your parole hearing is tomorrow, right?"

Daniel's head lowered and his eyes narrowed, but his stare held.

The Warden stood and opened the file folder. He pulled out photos and laid them one-by-one on the desk until there was no room for those remaining in the folder. Daniel did not shift his glare.

The Warden held up a photo of a partially clad woman who died from traumatic, disfiguring injuries. He slid the photo back unto the envelope and pulled out a photo of a naked woman with similar injuries. "What will the Parole Board think when they see this? Should I continue? Do you believe they will view you as rehabilitated and grant you parole?"

Daniel did not speak. Instead, he reached next to one of the photos on the desk and picked up a pad of yellow sticky notes. With a pen from a wooden "Years of Service" award pen holder, he wrote on a sticky note, peeled it from the pad, and stuck it to a photo.

The Warden removed it.

He fixed his gaze on Daniel and raised the note until it came between them.

For a few seconds, he stared at the note.

Lowering it, his face went pale.

Panic leapt into his eyes. "Where did you get this?"

Daniel snarled. "It doesn't matter where. But if the Parole Board sees *those* photos," again, lowering his head while maintaining eye contact, "I will have my employees—*on the outside*—pay your family a visit."

His face contorted into a twisted smile. "Imagine *your* family's photos among those on your desk."

Without another word, Daniel stood, walked to the door, opened it, and walked out while waving to the guard. "Let's go, Jim."

The Warden continued to stand, staring back and forth between the yellow sticky note and the photos on the desk.

That evening, Scary-ugly pointed out Russell.

As Daniel walked toward the table, he made eye contact with the inmate sitting across from Russell and gave a side nod.

There was no hesitation, he was up and gone.

Daniel placed his food tray on the stainless-steel table surface, sat on the attached stool, and considered Russell for a few seconds. His impression was that the guy looked slippery. A pretty-boy, and everything about him screamed huckster.

"I take it you want to talk?"

"Yeah," Daniel said, as he smeared margarine on a piece of bread and took a bite. "Someone told me pieces of your story." He chewed, wiped butter from the corner of his mouth with the back of his hand, and used his knife to level the butter on the bread. "I want to hear it for myself."

"I know who you are, Daniel. Your reputation precedes you."

Daniel dumped ketchup on his meatloaf. He cut off and speared a piece with his fork. "My reputation is what I want it to be." Looking back up, he shoved the meatloaf into his mouth. "I have people who build it and protect it *for me.*"

Russell studied Daniel for a few seconds. "Do you want details, or the Reader's Digest version?"

"The whole story—but hold on—you're willing to tell me without bargaining? No one in here does that."

Russell lifted his fork. Sickly colored, gelatinous gravy oozed through the fork's tines. "Either I tell you the story… or eat this crap." He studied it without emotion, then looked at Daniel. "If I keep telling it, someday, someone will believe me and help me get out of here."

A metal food tray slammed against the concrete floor.

The clatter caused Russell flinch.

Daniel gave a slight smile. "I'm listening; I might be that someone."

Russell told of being convicted of murder and losing everything, including his wife and son.

He moved on to how he had found the book. "When I was in high school, my mother told me a story about my grandmother Doris finding my grandfather James shot to death in their garage. When she found him, he was holding a blood-soaked book.

"Not long after my mother told me the story, I was searching my grandmother's attic, looking for stuff I might turn into beer money. One thing I found was the blood-stained book. I took it and kept it. It was my only connection to my grandfather."

After describing the exterior of the book, he told Daniel how he discovered its powers. He told of how he had used it to travel back in time, but on one adventure left it behind by mistake.

He ended his story with, "Well, that's it. Do you believe me?"

Daniel re-positioned the piece of apple pie on his plate to make it easier to cut with his fork. "I've never been one to believe in things like time travel, and your story hasn't convinced me. But I've learned to be careful in rejecting something out of hand, without considering it further."

Daniel crammed pie into his mouth and told Russell what he had discovered during his on-line search.

"I don't understand how I'm related to that story?"

Daniel did not allow excitement to overcome calm. "I'm not convinced you are, but the man on the law firm's website, Michael Mays, carried a book *identical* to the one you described.

"How's that possible? I lost the book."

"That's *one* question, isn't it? But first, I have to figure out if Michael Mays *is* the man from 30 years ago. The only way I can do that is to get *out* of this hellhole.

"And when you get out, I expect you to help *me* get out."

Daniel ignored Russell. He took on the look of a wolf approaching its prey. A wolf with pie crumbs on its face. Russell leaned away and retreated to the rear edge of the stool.

"If I find it *was* Michael Mays, and he *has* the book you described, I will destroy both him and the book!"

3

Willamette State Penitentiary, Oregon – Friday, October 4th

Prior his parole hearing, Daniel met with his attorney in a small holding room. A four-by-four-foot metal table and two metal chairs sat stark in the room. The furnishings were surrounded by four concrete block walls and a metal door which held a small wired-glass window at eye level.

As his attorney walked in, Daniel's first thought was, *They sent me a high school student?*

Sunlit red-wine lipstick—which matched her fingernails—emphasized her full lips. Her cropped hair was platinum blonde with a hint of violet and appeared wind-blown.

Gray-violet eyes threw Daniel into a turmoil.

Or, was it the black suit jacket and skirt, tailored tight, stressing she was young and fit.

Either way, it was a feeling he had not experienced in over 30 years.

Her fragrance made him want to grab her, bury his face in her hair, and breath in… slow.

As he studied her, he fantasized adding her photo to the Warden's desktop.

"Daniel, my name is Sam Grant." She removed her backpack and placed it on the floor next to the door. She pulled out several files, turned, looked up and caught Daniel staring at her backside. As he raised his eyes, his lecherous smile caused her to step back. She tried to hide her fear, which pleased Daniel.

"Daniel…" she faltered, "I can… I can help you," as she shook his hand with a grip strength that did not represent the weakness she felt in her gut. She looked at the files trembling in her hand. "I've reviewed your case and personal history."

With none of the confidence she'd walked in with, she said, "I believe you'll be out of here soon."

As she laid out her strategy, her phone buzzed, causing her to jump.

Nervous as a schoolgirl. Daniel mused.

"Excuse me, I have to answer this text."

Daniel saw no use for phones. His parents were long gone. No brothers or sisters. Maybe he'd find a use for one if paroled.

She held up her iPhone. "I apologize, my office sent a message I had to answer."

As she lowered it, something caught Daniel's eye. "Hold it."

Sam saw he was looking at the back of her phone. Almost dropping it, she turned it over as if expecting a black widow spider.

Daniel leaned forward. "The shiny thing. Looks like an apple?"

She pointed to the back of the phone. "Oh." She let out a deep breath. "That's Apple's logo. It's on all of their products."

"Does it do more than make calls?"

"More than we have time to discuss."

"Does it take pictures?"

"Yes, great photos."

"When were those phones first made?"

Sam tilted her head and furrowed her brow. "My brother bought one of the first models while I was in my sophomore year in college. So… 2007?"

"Sam, I can tell these questions sound strange to you, but I've been in here 30 years. I know nothing about phone technology."

"How is it possible you've avoided smartphone technology?"

"I've avoided all technologies, except for our library's computers. And people know I avoid it, so they are *very* careful with their conversations around me."

The puzzled look on her face suggested she thought that was an odd arrogance.

She considered that comment for a few seconds. Daniel saw the fear return to her eyes. She looked at the file folder. "Well, let's get you paroled so you can catch up."

Sam impressed Daniel as he listened to her speak to the Parole Board. The five-person Parole Board, made up of four men and a woman, sat on metal chairs behind a metal table. It was a cold, sterile room, and the Board's demeanor reflected the ambiance of the room.

Sam presented Daniel's record as a model prisoner. She made a convincing argument that the evidence used against him 30 years ago was sketchy, and that he was no longer a danger to society. As she made that statement, she gave a nervous glance Daniel's way.

Daniel watched the body language and facial expressions of the Board. He suppressed a smile, her ability to charm the Board amazed him.

She's pulling it off.

After a brief interview with Daniel, they excused him and his attorney.

As Sam and Daniel sat in the holding room, they discussed the hearing.

She looked at her notes. "Their body language suggested they agreed with my points. When they reinforced me quoting from the Department of Corrections report, emphasizing you're a model prisoner, I sensed we had them."

"Sam," Daniel placed both hands on the table, "do you believe I'm no longer a threat to society?"

She struggled to maintain a businesslike demeanor. "It's… it's not my place to judge, but to represent you to the best of my abilities."

Daniel stared at her with the same look she'd caught when she had stood and turned from her backpack. "I admire your abilities."

"Thank you." Sam responded as she looked at her watch and found a reason to step out of the conference room and make a phone call.

The Parole Board called Daniel and Sam back into their meeting room. They reviewed their deliberation and informed Mr. Wygal, parole was being granted. Daniel using his most sincere voice, thanked them. But it smacked of flattery more than sincerity.

Daniel and Sam met back in the conference room. She reviewed with him the conditions of his parole and gave him a copy.

She shook his hand and turned toward the door. "Sam... hold it." He continued his effort to be sincere and appreciative, but flattery didn't give way. "Thank you. We make a good team. Let me take you to dinner after I'm released."

She gave an uneasy smile. "You're welcome, Mr. Wygal. My firm has a strong policy against fraternizing with clients." She opened the door and rushed through, hoping the guard was a fast walker.

While waiting for the guard to return, Daniel sat dejected. But, upon pondering his Monday morning release, he took heart.

There are plenty of sweet young things out there who'll appreciate a wealthy, older man.

At dinner, Daniel described the hearing to Russell, including his release and his plans.

"I've decided to give your story a chance. Understand this, if I get the book, and try it as you've explained, and it doesn't work—" Russell winced. Daniel smiled.

"I won't stop till I find the book. I'll try it as you described, then destroy it.

"My *only* lead is Michael Mays and I'm counting on you letting me know if you come up with, or remember, *anything* that might help me.

"I'll buy a phone Monday afternoon and get the number to you."

"Daniel, I'm trusting that when you find the book and try it, you'll use it to get me out of here... and give me the book rather than destroying it."

Daniel tilted his head and gave a lopsided smile. "Of course."

Saturday, October 5th

Saturday afternoon, laying on his bunk, Daniel recalled stalking Michael's mother. He remembered the two houses she had frequented. One was easy to figure out. It was her home, where she lived with her husband and son. The second house took an investigation to sort out.

The second house belonged to Michael's grandmother and grandfather.

He recalled talking to Michael's grandmother as she worked in her front yard.

In her late fifties, Daniel remembered her being an attractive woman. She wore jeans and a plaid flannel shirt which must have belonged to her husband. Leather work boots and gloves protected her feet and hands. As she weeded flowers, which lined both sides of the walkway to her front door, strands of silver-streaked brown hair hung over her vivid blue eyes.

Daniel introduced himself; she introduced herself as Louise.

He turned the conversation to her daughter. "Louise, I live around the corner. On one of my walks, I stopped here and talked to a young woman as she was getting out of her car with, I assumed, her son. We didn't talk long, just made introductions. She was a nice young woman."

Louise pushed back the strands of hair. "Yes, that was my daughter Deborah and her son Michael. She may have been dropping Michael off while she headed to a meeting, or a doctor's appointment, or some such thing. She knows I love spending time with my only grandchild."

Daniel remembered smiling. "What makes your time with him so enjoyable?"

He recalled Louise tilting her head and pursing her lips while she thought for a few seconds. "Michael is such a nice young man, polite and smart. He loves to play board games and card games. He always wins, no matter what we're playing... I *don't* let him win.

"For example, he's never lost to me when we play Clue... I've seen nothing like it. Only 12 years old and he beats me every time. He has a knack for putting clues together and coming to a conclusion. But he always makes excuses for me losing and then encourages me. I love that young man."

Daniel remembered complimenting her again on her yard work while saying goodbye. That was thirty-two years ago. It was the last time he saw Louise.

I wonder if she talked to her daughter again.

4

~

The rest of the weekend, Daniel continued putting his computer skills to work. He did a property records search on The City of Portland Development Services website. Michael's grandparents, Ben and Louise Nelson still owned the house; he wrote their address in a small spiral notebook.

First, I pay Michael's grandparents a visit.

Sunday, October 6th

That evening, after lights out, Daniel lay in his bunk talking with his cellmate.

"Daniel, I heard Big Ben bad-mouthing you this afternoon. He called you a coward and said you're lucky you're being released tomorrow. He claimed you wouldn't have survived another week in here."

Daniel chuckled. "He's been a pain for 20 years. I want you to deliver a parting gift to him. The gift of freedom."

"My pleasure. I'm tired of him too. He's done nothing but make fun of me and talk trash to me in front of his buddies. I'll catch him when they ain't around."

"Great. My only disappointment is that I won't be there to enjoy the gift giving."

Monday, October 7th

Daniel breathed deep as he walked out of the penitentiary, then threw his head back and let the Fall sun warm his face for a few seconds. He was unsure about what he'd do with the rest of his life, but getting the book, and trying it as Russell described, was his priority.

If it didn't work, Russell is dead.

Michael is dead no matter what Daniel discovers.

He realized he was sifting vapor, but if Russell's story is true, he could change history. A history where his life was on his own terms, not restrained by concrete and steel.

Guards closed the gate behind Daniel.

The air tastes good.

Daniel stepped off the bus in Portland. His first order of business was to buy a cell phone, a van—his vehicle of choice—and find a place to live.

He entered the bus station, approached a ticket window and got directions to a phone store, which was only blocks away.

Cell phone purchased; he approached a taxi driver. "Hey, I need to buy a van. Any used car lots nearby?"

The driver asked in an accent Daniel couldn't place. "How new do you want?"

Daniel shook his head. "I don't care, as long as it runs well."

The taxi driver pushed back his faded Seattle Mariners baseball cap. "My uncle has business on 82nd Avenue. I'll take you there. He can help you."

Daniel climbed in the back. "Lead the way, and find a Wells Fargo Bank."

"I know of one."

With Wells Fargo holding his Trust Fund, it was easy to get them to issue him a Visa Card.

Excited about his possible release from prison, Daniel got an Oregon ID card from the Department of Motor Vehicles. The bigger challenge was the fake ID, but when in prison with a thousand criminals, most with outside connections, it wasn't the challenge Daniel anticipated.

The cab driver stopped at the bank. Daniel went in, showed his Visa card and his DMV ID, and withdrew $20,000 cash. While Daniel was in the bank, the cab driver called his uncle.

With newfound energy, Daniel leapt back into the cab. Freedom energized him.

No guards telling me what to do, where to go, and when to move.

After 15 minutes of driving, the cab driver drove into his uncle's car lot.

Daniel bought the first van they showed him. The waving of cash resulted in a quick transaction.

After signing the paperwork and getting the keys, the uncle and the cab driver thanked Daniel and waved goodbye.

While walking toward the van, he slipped on a pair of work gloves he'd lifted as he left the car lot's office.

He climbed into the old, but serviceable white Ford van, started the engine and headed for the exit.

It's early, I might as well visit the grandparents.

He stopped the van, removed one glove and pulled out his spiral notebook. He entered their address into Google Maps.

There you are granny. It worked just as the phone store girl showed me.

Daniel slipped the glove back on, put the van in gear, and exited onto the street.

He parked in front of the house and sat for a few minutes planning his approach while sipping a cup of coffee he'd bought along the way. Coffee gone and plan in mind, he walked to the front door and knocked.

I'll remember that coffee joint. Been a long time since I've had a good cup of coffee.

An hour later, Daniel walked out of Michael's grandmother's house. He'd gained far more information than he'd hoped for. Most helpful was hearing grandma describe Michael's weekend routine—coffee shop and used record store—every Saturday morning.

It amazed him that she welcomed him right into her house. Her husband's dead and she lives alone.

She invited me in. Stupid old lady.

Daniel shifted his focus to finding a place to live. He spotted a hotel near a mall he'd hung out at as a young man. The name "Residence" hooked him.

After an early dinner, Daniel relayed his new phone number to Russell.

Wednesday, October 9th

Wednesday afternoon, Daniel sat on the edge of his bed experimenting with his new computer. He'd never used a notebook computer. He liked it.

His phone interrupted him. "Yeah?"

"Daniel, it's Russell. My ex-wife visited me this morning to bring my son to see me—"

"You're calling me to share *family* moments? Don't waste my time. Call me when you can tell me where I'll find the book."

"Wait, Daniel, that's why I'm calling. As she was leaving, she told me she's having a yard sale this weekend. She claims she has the book and will sell it, or give it away, she doesn't care which. It's too much of a reminder of the past; she wants it gone."

"At first, I wasn't buying her claim to have the book. She refused to tell me how or where she got it, but I'm now *convinced* she has it."

He traced a memory out loud. "I left the book behind while paying a visit to her sister, so somehow..."

Russell's voice trailed off as he considered the possibilities.

"I hope you convinced her *not* to sell it."

Russell's voice stammered. "I... I begged her... to bring it to me, but she... she refused."

"What's her address, maybe I can buy the book for us."

"I don't know... she moved... years ago, and she didn't give it to me. I'll try again. I promise."

Daniel ended the call. As he laid the phone on the bed, the Apple logo caught his eye. He was struck by the irony of Gutenberg and Apple playing roles in his imprisonment.

Saturday, October 12th

In a neighborhood restaurant, eating breakfast on the morning of the yard sale, Daniel's phone buzzed. "Yeah."

"Daniel, it's Russell. I called a friend I haven't talked to in years. He told me she hasn't moved."

"What's the address?"

As Russell recited what was once his home address, Daniel wrote it in his notebook.

He looked at his watch; his voice raised. "Russell, *it's 8:15*. She's opened the yard sale by now. You're not taking this serious dude. If that book's gone, it's on you. Those walls won't protect you. They didn't protect Big Ben."

"I know, I heard that. I'm trying—"

Daniel hung up before Russell finished. He grabbed his coat, the notebook, and left money on the table. He decided to first go to the coffee shop Michael's grandmother mentioned. Daniel's plan was to see if Michael has the book. If he does not, Daniel will head to the yard sale. Either way, he will destroy the book. And, if that requires killing Michael...

Everyone needs a hobby.

Something about his plan troubles him. *Not* the part about killing Michael, but that he has bought into Russell's story.

If it's a fool's tale.

5

Portland, Oregon– Saturday, October 12th

Finished with his shower and shave, Michael Mays was drying his face when his phone rang.

"Michael here."

"Michael, it's Gwen—"

"If I'd have recognized the number, you'd be talking to my voice mail now. I'm surprised you're up this early, Gwen. *Especially* on a Saturday morning. What do you want?"

Gwen, Michael's ex-wife, the same age as Michael, was smart, but without his drive, character, or work ethic. Her parents generously indulge her through financial support.

"Michael, I know how bitter you are—"

"Bitter, you must mean how much *better* I am, without *you*."

"Michael, I need something—"

"Let me think, the court gave you our house, everything we accumulated, even my Blazer season tickets —"

"Michael, *stop*. It was a fair deal. You got three years of great experience in a large Los Angeles law firm."

Michael scoffed. "Yeah, and because of you, that experience ended too soon."

"I was only trying to help you get a raise. I sensed you weren't sticking up for yourself. You *wanted* to work there… an area *way* too expensive for your entry level salary. One of us had to pressure them."

Michael pulled the phone from his ear and strangled it and shook it.

"And you did, *repeatedly*. Even after I asked you to stop… *repeatedly*."

"Well, if you would have succeeded, I wouldn't have kept trying. During that time, *I* supported us, *and* supervised construction of the house on property *my parents* gave *me*.

"Every time we speak, Gwen, we get nowhere. This time you need something; what more could you want?"

"I know I agreed to you keeping our collection of 19th century novels, but I miss them. Can I have them?"

"Seriously, Gwen? You convinced the court that everything else we owned was because of you. Move on, *please*. Live your life and stay out of mine."

He ended the call without waiting for a response, opened her contact information and added her number.

Next time, her name on my screen will warn me.

He threw his phone on the bed. It bounced, ricocheting off the headboard onto the floor. He picked it up and got dressed.

Out of his apartment building and on the sidewalk, Michael realized how fast he was moving. The sound of Gwen's voice, making frivolous requests, drove his legs and feet like a locomotive engine. "Let me have it, give it to me, let me have it, give it to me."

Two blocks from his apartment, a yard sale sign pointed to a side street. It was not part of that morning's plans, but he needed a diversion; time to cool off before heading to The Coffee Shop, where he had planned to ask Stephanie Clark out for dinner.

Michael wanted Gwen out of his head. But kept hearing, "Let me have it, give it to me."

Michael knew he was being petty and unrealistic, but he hoped to find a 19th century novel to add to *his* collection.

At the yard sale, he found a table lined with over 50 books. He began sorting through them.

The yard sale kid had Michael in his sights as he circled a table made of an old interior sliding door on top of two, even older, wooden sawhorses. He picked up three Matchbox cars that were parked on the table.

While juggling the cars, he walked to the folding table where Michael stood.

"We've got a ton of stuff scattered around the driveway and the yard. Some of its crap, but most of its good stuff." Still juggling the cars, he twitched his head to keep hair out of his eyes. "My mom says our crap may be another person's treasure. See anything you like?"

Michael did not raise his head. He held up a book. "How much for this?"

The kid glanced away from the circling cars. "My mom said a buck, but it's worth more."

Michael looked at the book and snapped at the kid. "For this, *why*?"

Michael's response startled the kid, but he continued juggling. His friendliness turned argumentative, "Because she told me to give it away if I couldn't sell it. She doesn't give stuff away. I figure it's *something* she wants to get rid of, but *something* she won't throw away. *Something's* worth more than *a buck*."

"What's your name?"

Back off, the kid's not Gwen.

"My name's Jacob, what's yours?"

"Michael, I live around the corner. How old are you, Jacob?"

The kid's voice became nasally and sarcastic. "Twelve, how old are you?"

Michael looked down and chuckled. "Forty-four... and, Jacob, I apologize. I wasn't making fun of you for being young. I meant it as a compliment to your reasoning skills. My attitude this morning stinks and I took it out on you. I'm sorry."

"Oh, thanks, Michael. I guess I read it wrong."

"No, you read it right. I was being a jerk."

"Yeah, I guess we both were," Jacob said, as he caught two of the matchbook cars in his left hand. He circled his right hand behind his back, releasing the third car up and over his left shoulder. He caught it in his left hand, but it struck the cars he cradled there and bounced away.

Jacob looked at Michael with a wide grin. "Almost," as he brought his right hand back around and shook Michael's hand. "I'll keep trying 'til I get it."

"Won't be long and you'll have it perfected."

Michael turned his attention back to the book. The book's title, 'Making Pictures Come to Life,' had caught his attention.

The clear packing tape that bound the book piqued his curiosity most.

Why keep it from being opened? The stains on it, wine, blood?

"All right, I'm interested in photography, so I'll give you two bucks for it, but that's it." Jacob was about to counter. Michael made a stop motion with his hand. "That's 100% more than your mom wants for it."

Jacob's eyes widened, he grinned and couldn't help but give a small fist pump. "Okay, it's yours," Jacob said, as he placed the Matchbook cars on the table. From the waistband of his Portland Trail Blazers gym shorts, he pulled out a plastic Walgreens sack and dropped the book into it.

Before paying, Michael asked, "Hey, Jacob, I collect vinyl record albums. Do you have any?"

Jacob mouthed, "vinyl record albums." As if it was a foreign language.

Michael handed Jacob $2. "That's okay, Jacob. Good doing business with you. And I enjoyed meeting you."

Jacob arched to see Michael's face. "You too, thanks." It was not because Jacob was small for a 12-year-old. Most people looked up when talking to Michael.

When they did, they found he had dark brown hair, green eyes, and chiseled facial features. Women considered him handsome and single men viewed him as competition. Although he wasn't as lean and fit as he was in his college sports days, he was still strong and agile.

Monday through Friday, Michael dressed in either a suit, or sport coat and slacks. On weekends, his choice was to get out of his "uniform" and into denim and un-tucked flannel. That morning, he also carried a rain jacket.

After the yard sale diversion, Michael set out for the first of his two Saturday morning destinations, The Coffee Shop. Not a clever name, but there is no doubting what they sell.

The Coffee Shop was on a corner. During the 1930s, the building was a drug store and soda shop. The two floors above the business still housed renters. Or, as The Coffee Shop's owner called them, "built-in customers."

The owner refinished the original oak cabinets and counter. Customers enjoy sitting at the counter and talking with the baristas.

On the two exterior sides of the shop, the original wood casement windows stretched from the ceiling to table height.

The builder had set the front door in the building's corner where the two windowed walls met. Customers entered the door from two sidewalks.

Every time Michael entered The Coffee Shop, it reminded him of waking up to the good-morning aroma of coffee in his grandparents' house.

He ordered coffee, and a chocolate filled croissant, then wound past several tables to a window table he had spotted when he entered. He placed his things on the table and returned to the counter. His grandmother came to mind as he waited for his order. She had not allowed him to drink coffee until he was a senior in high school.

I've more than made up for what I missed.

Back at the table, he ate his croissant and placed his lips on the rim of the cup, blew, and sipped. The coffee cooled as he made his way through the mid-week Oregonian newspaper, which he'd saved for that morning.

He had access to the daily on-line editions, but enjoyed holding the real thing, snapping it open, and taking in the fusion of ink, newsprint, pastry and coffee.

Smells like weekend mornings.

Tomorrow morning, he would be back having coffee and a chocolate croissant with *Sunday's* Oregonian, the second of the two weekly printed editions.

He opened the sports section first and read a report on the latest Blazer game.

That was a good game, Blazers 111, Kings 108.

He recalled hearing a co-worker say with sarcasm, "Just give each team 100 points and two minutes on the clock. The results would be the same."

While sipping his coffee, he looked out the window. The dark, threatening skies brought Gwen to mind. He loves basketball and wished he could have seen that game sitting in his season-ticket seats.

But that ended with Gwen's divorce settlement, or as Michael said too often, "Gone with the Gwen." He told his mind to go elsewhere, nothing good to see in that territory.

His mind jumped.

Why is that book taped shut? Jacob is a sharp 12-year-old, I'm impressed. Blood or wine stains?

Coffee and croissant gone, he checked his phone. It was 9:50, 10 minutes until the record shop opened.

Most Saturdays, he left his newspaper on the table for the next Saturday morning coffee junkie. But the skies were getting darker and more threatening. He folded the newspaper in half and placed his yard-sale sack between the fold.

Might need an improvised umbrella.

Michael stood and turned to leave. He noticed Stephanie Clark sitting at the table behind him. His face lit up.

Stephanie was in her mid-thirties. There are people who would say she is plain. Michael found her attractive. Freckles crossed the bridge of her nose, and her cheeks dimpled when she smiled. She was always up and positive, although sarcastic, which Michael enjoyed.

"Hey, Steph, I didn't see you come in. How goes your morning?"

She looked away from the window and smiled. "Great."

Without a doubt, that smile could push aside my search for old vinyl records.

"Even better now," her smile growing. "When I walked in, you were engrossed in your newspaper. I hoped you'd look around before you left."

Stephanie's auburn hair was pulled back and fell over the hood of her rain jacket.

"You're prepared for what the sky's threatening—beautiful color," as he pointed to the rain jacket.

"It's called 'Wild Geranium'."

"Whatever it's called, you make it look good. Auburn hair and blue eyes against wild geranium… stunning."

Her face became the color of her jacket. "Be still my heart."

They hurried into their typical small talk.

Though not unusual for a professional photographer to carry, Michael pointed to the camera on the table. "I don't think I've seen you with this camera."

"It's new. I bought it to use with a 300 MM, f2.8 lens… blah, blah, blah," as she waved her hand as if brushing the camera off the table.

"I think I mentioned I'm teaching a Saturday afternoon photography class."

"That's right, you told me that two weeks ago."

Well, the vinyl record search is back on.

"Today, I'm teaching my final session. I meet my students downtown for lunch and give them feedback on the photos they've shot during the past week. Then we'll be on the streets of downtown Portland until dark.

"I'm hoping the rain holds off, but then rain can make for interesting shots. I have to walk back home to get my car. So, just in case, I'll grab an umbrella."

"I hope it goes well for you, rain or no rain."

A white-haired man approached them. "Excuse me."

Stephanie and Michael both looked up. "Hi."

He smiled and shook their hands. "My name's Joe. I'm leaving and wondered if you could help me?"

"We'll try," Michael said, as he glanced at Stephanie.

Stephanie jumped in and covered Michael's lack of introductions. "Hi, Joe, I'm Stephanie and this is Michael. How can we help you?"

"Thank you. But first, what a good-looking couple you are. Do you have the same last names?"

"Well, we're… we're… not a couple." The words stumbled out of Michael's mouth.

Stephanie jumped in again. "But we are good friends. We see each other here most Saturdays. And, no, my last name is Clark and his is Mays."

"Hmm, fooled me. I think you should rethink your relationship."

Stephanie and Michael both blushed, then Stephanie said something that left Michael speechless.

She looked at Joe and cocked her head while making a slight nod of agreement. "You might be right, Joe."

Joe said, "I'm not from Portland, I'm here on business. I hear there's a used record shop in this neighborhood. Do you know where it's located?"

"Yes," Michael said, then gave him directions. "That's my next destination, maybe I'll see you there."

"Thanks. Yes, I might still be there." He winked at Stephanie as he turned and went back to his table to gather his coffee and coat.

Michael recovered from Stephanie's response to Joe. "Anyway, I'd love to see the photos you get today. Will you be here *next* Saturday?"

Her response both disappointed and pleased Michael. "And, I'd love to show them to you, but I'm going to the East Coast on assignment. So, I'll be out of town the next four Saturdays. But when I get back, buy me coffee and I'll show you the photos… and… I'll throw in the best of those I shoot back east."

"Deal, and I'll throw in a pastry of your choice."

"Thanks again," Joe said, as he walked by with his coat on and coffee in hand.

"Goodbye, Joe," echoed both Michael and Stephanie.

Stephanie added, "Good luck finding what you're looking for at the record shop."

Walking toward the door, Joe lifted his arm and waved. "Thanks,"

* * *

Michael and Stephanie had no idea the man they'd just talked to would as soon kill them as talk to them. Outside the shop, white-haired Joe—AKA, Daniel Wygal—thought, *Michael hasn't realized it yet, but we've met. I'll make sure he never realizes it.*

Just a folded newspaper in his hands; wrapped around a plastic bag, the book could have been there… or not.

Daniel couldn't take that chance. If Russell was telling the truth, keeping

Michael from using the book motivated Daniel to do whatever it takes, including killing him.

After meeting Michael face-to-face and hearing his voice, Daniel had no doubt Michael was the same guy from 30 years ago.

6

After saying goodbye to Joe, Michael wrote his cell number on one of his business cards. "Call me when you get back in town. I have a better idea than coffee and croissants. I'll take you to dinner and you can show me photos and tell me about your trip."

"You're on. I'd love that."

Michael gave her a hug, "Have a great trip; I look forward to seeing you when you get back."

Her blue eyes smiled. "Likewise."

Michael headed to Vinyl Grooves. A vinyl junkie for as long as he could remember, he had always admired his mother for resisting the transition to compact discs in the early 80s. During the first 12 years of his life, the only music she played was from vinyl records. His earliest memories were of sitting on the floor with her as she interpreted lyrics. Michael believed his vinyl habit was a tribute to his mother—keeping her memory alive by rescuing old vinyl albums.

He walked into Vinyl Grooves. The familiar musty odor that permeates used record stores met him. To Michael it was the aroma of a quest, even an adventure.

After half an hour, he gave up his search. He was not enjoying the search. Stephanie leaving was on his mind.

But he made a great find. Left Banke's 1968 album, 'Left Banke Too' in excellent condition.

"Thanks for the directions, it was easy to find."

Michael looked up, "Hey, Joe... did you find something you can't live without?"

"What I found *I can* live without." Michael tilted his head and his brow wrinkled as he looked Joe in the eyes while considering his response.

Joe turned to leave, "Good to see you. I hope I run into you again."

"Yeah, who knows, Joe. We might cross paths again."

Michael headed to the cashier counter. The attractive, pierced and tattooed young woman rung up his sale. "That will be $15. Do you know there are tracks on this album that have a young Steven Tyler, pre-Aerosmith, as a backing vocalist?"

"Yes." Michael marveled as he pulled out his wallet. "I am stunned. We're probably the only people in Portland who do."

"Well, I read anything that discusses the history of rock. I love both power and baroque pop, both were Left Banke's genres. We sell new and used music magazines, and reference books too. I enjoy reading when business is slow."

"Okay, you've elevated yourself in the world of my favorite music genres."

She handed him five dollars change. "I'm glad."

He put the five in his wallet and moved to pick up his newspaper. As he did, the book slid out of the bag. She looked at the newspaper and book, then at him. She pulled out a big plastic bag from beneath the counter. "Those, along with your album, will fit into this."

"Thank you, again. Please don't take this as me hitting on you, but you have a beautiful, friendly smile."

"Thank you, I appreciate your compliment. Truth-be-told... guys hitting on me *all day long* wears me out—tiresome."

"I bet it does."

She looked down, placing his album and book into the Vinyl Grooves bag. "You've been in here before, right?"

"I come in almost every Saturday. You're new, aren't you?"

"I've only been here a month." She smiled and considered Michael for a few seconds. "Are you an attorney?"

"I am, how did you know?"

"A friend, well more like an acquaintance, mentioned you last week as we talked music.

"She told me you come here every Saturday after visiting The Coffee Shop. I told her I'm in a band that plays the same genre of music as on the CD she bought. She asked me if our band plays original songs. I told her, yes, but I'm the only member who writes."

The salesclerk handed Michael his bag. "She recommended I ask if you'd be willing to give me copyright advice over a cup of coffee... I'll buy."

"First you try to impress me with your knowledge of power pop music, then you invite me to have *coffee* with you. You're right, it gets *tiresome* being hit on, even by a *beautiful* woman." That caused them both to laugh, and her to turn red. "What's your friend's name?"

"Stephanie. I don't know her last name, but she comes in and buys CD's. She's been in at least once a week since I've been here. We've connected, so if I'm not busy we talk for a while."

"Isn't Stephanie *great*. What's your name?"

She reached out her hand. "Leanna Jones."

"Leanna, my name's Michael Mays. I'd be happy to sit and talk over coffee. I can steer you in the right direction."

"Wow, that would be great, *thank you*."

"My pleasure. I'll be back next Saturday."

As Michael turned to leave, Leanna said, "Oh... Michael. Yesterday, the guy you were talking to a few minutes ago was here asking about you."

"*What?* Did he give you a name?"

"Yes, Joe."

Michael turned his head and looked out the windows. "Hmm, did he say why he was looking for me?"

"No. Just that he was an old friend and hasn't seen you in years but wants to reconnect. Which struck me as odd—if he hasn't seen you in *years*—how did he know to come to this shop? Even more so now; I couldn't help but hear your conversation. There was no indication he's an old friend."

"Wow, that is odd. I met him minutes ago at The Coffee Shop. He stopped and asked for directions to *here*."

"But he was here yesterday? And before you came in this morning, he walked around, but didn't look at anything, other than me. Several times, I caught him staring at me. It was creepy."

"Yeah, I bet it was."

Michael pondered what Leanna told him as he wrote on one of his business cards. "Here, I've written my personal cell number on the back. Call me when you're ready to meet."

"I will... thank you."

"I look forward to meeting with you, Leanna." Michael started to turn but stopped. "Before I head home, I'll walk around the block to make sure he's not lurking outside."

"I appreciate that," Leanna said. "See you next week."

He walked out of the shop with both Saturday morning treasures protected, and the possibility of a future client. He stopped and, on his phone, noted Leanna Jones' name, along with the date and location where they met.

As he walked around the block, he stopped at each corner. His survey included cars parked on both sides of the street.

There was no sign of Joe. Back at the entrance to the record store, Leanna was watching him through a window. He smiled, gave her a thumbs up and waved. She returned his smile and wave.

As he headed home, his thoughts returned to Stephanie, and how their Saturday mornings are the closest he's been to dating since his divorce.

Pitiful.

After walking a block, something at the corner of his eye caught his attention.

A white van was coming right at him while increasing speed.

It swerved into him.

Michael jumped.

But the van's rear quarter panel hit him hard, sending Michael flying.

The van sped away as Michael tumbled twice. His left hip slammed against the curb, stopping his momentum.

Blinking his eyes, he sensed he'd just regained consciousness. Before trying to stand, he assessed the seriousness of his injuries. His clothes were dirty and there was a blood-soaked tear in the right knee of his jeans. The lump on the back of his head throbbed, and there were bloody scrapes on both elbows.

Sloth-slow, he moved his arms and legs.

They're okay.

He stood, picked up, and checked the plastic bag. The book and record album were okay. His phone was lying five feet away. It still worked. The time stamp on the note he'd made about Leanna told him he could have only been unconscious for seconds.

He looked around and saw no witnesses, but spotted his jacket draped over the curb. He carefully bent over and grabbed it.

That was not an accident. But my cat-like reflexes saved me. Or maybe my grandmother is right when she says, 'cat-astrophic like reflexes.'

Michael limped across the street. He stopped at the corner and called 9-1-1.

7

Daniel pounded the steering wheel, snarling and cussing as he looked in the side mirror. "He's getting up."

He had hoped to back up and check Michael's body for the book.

With Michael getting up, Daniel's hope changed: If Michael had the book, his injuries would sidetrack him and delay the discovery of its abilities.

But… if Michael hasn't bought the book….

Daniel set out for the yard sale to buy it if it's still there.

* * *

"9-1-1, what is your emergency?" Michael told her his story.

"Are you injured, sir?"

"Only a few scrapes and a bump on my head."

"I'll transfer you to a dispatcher; they'll dispatch medical help."

"No… no it's not serious, but I want to report a hit-and-run." He didn't tell her he sensed his hip seizing-up and the lump on the back of his head is now bleeding.

She took his information and told him an officer would contact him. "Sir, due to heavy call volume, we have no officers available in your area to respond. We can only respond to in-progress emergencies."

He told her he understood and thanked her.

* * *

Daniel pulled over and entered the address of the yard sale into Google Maps.

Only six minutes away.

After a minute of driving, a young woman turning left onto a side street caught his eye. She was sipping coffee, while protecting a camera in the crook of her left arm.

Michael's girlfriend, Stephanie.

Daniel remembered her telling Michael she was going home before heading downtown.

Knowing where she lives might come in handy later.

Turning, he pulled over and watched until she went into her house. He stopped in front of her house to note her address.

While driving to the next intersection, the Google girl kept screaming at him to make a U-turn.

Daniel stopped at the intersection, added the street's name to his notes, then headed for the yard sale.

After thirty years of not driving, the freedom and elation, coupled with the possibility of getting the book, caused him to push past the speed limit. As he turned onto the yard sale's street, he ignored the stop sign. The van's tires squealed as he barely slowed.

* * *

As Michael limped home, he admired the craftmanship of the old Queen Anne and Craftsman style homes that make up his neighborhood. His apartment was the entire top floor of a three-story Queen Anne-style house. There were two bedrooms—one he'd turned into an office—1½ baths, a kitchen with a pantry and a breakfast nook, a dining room, and a large living room.

An ambulance speeding by interrupted his thoughts. Emergency lights blazing and siren wailing. He heard more sirens, he estimated them to be a quarter mile away.

Michael brought his thoughts back his apartment. Although nice, and he appreciates it, it is not where he thought he would be at 44 years old. Gwen brought with her a hurricane that was nowhere on his radar.

One thing Hurricane Gwen took in her path was the dream house they designed and built together. The dream included growing old in the house together.

The skies darkened. He picked up his pace as much as his tumbled body allowed.

Not even 11 A.M. but feels like evening.

Before he finished that thought, Michael lifted the plastic bag above his head and looked down to avoid rain pelting his face. After limping a few more blocks, a white Honda Accord's brake lights came on as it passed him. It stopped, causing Michael to raise his head.

The car in front of the Honda was stopped. It stopped because there was a fire engine, with emergency lights flashing, parked in the street. A police car, emergency lights also flashing, blocked the entrance to a street two blocks from Michael's apartment.

The yard sale was held in the cul-de-sac at the end of that street.

He was curious. He walked to the street's entrance.

The darkened skies allowed the red and blue flashing lights to dance around in the wet leaves of the huge maple trees lining the street. It gave the street a whimsical, parade-like feel, betraying the probable seriousness that lay ahead.

Police strung yellow barrier tape from curb to curb, blocking the street's entrance, but not the sidewalk. Michael limped past the emergency vehicles and tape barrier.

At the end of the street, more emergency vehicles added to the parade-like ambiance. A police cruiser, fire engine, and an ambulance parked in the cul-de-sac, each with emergency lights flashing. The stance of each was toward the yard sale house.

He walked past the fire engine.

The yard sale sign lay crumpled on the ground.

It was in the path of the white van that had smashed into the house.

Yard sale items, broken tables, and wood siding lay scattered, destroyed and splintered around the van.

As Michael moved closer to the van, he came to an abrupt stop.

He stared at a Matchbox car lying crushed in the tire tracks on the grass.

His gut tightened.

On the other side of the van, paramedics were providing care for a person on the ground.

He couldn't see the patient.

His attention shifted to two firefighters who were covering yard sale tables with clear plastic sheeting.

Police officers were talking to a woman whose arm hugged Jacob.

Michael let out a sigh and walked over, getting as close as he could to listen.

The two firefighters cut a piece of the plastic sheeting from a roll and walked up behind Jacob and the woman. The firefighter closest to the woman, said, "Excuse us," as they each handed her and Jacob a corner of the plastic sheet. They thanked them as they pulled it up and over their heads.

One of the police officers said, "Ma'am."

"Please, it's Linda."

"Thank you, Linda… one more thing. Officer Pratt, the first arriving officer, said your son told him there was a loud noise. The noise caused him to look up in time to jump out of the way."

"That's what he told me, too."

She's his mother.

Officer Pratt, Michael assumed, walked up and entered the conversation. "A neighbor who was walking his dog, told me the van came down the street fast, then into your yard, not slowing until it crashed into your house."

The officer skimmed his notes. "Your neighbor said the driver—a white-haired man—struggled to get out of the van. His forehead was bleeding and he limped away on crutches."

The first officer jumped back in, "Ma'am—" she corrected herself, "Linda, did you see the man driving the van?"

Linda shook her head. "I heard someone yell, 'Slow down,' then there was a loud thump and scraping sound, which must have been the van jumping the curb. I realized that whatever it was, was coming right at me, so I jumped."

The kid has good genes.

"It passed behind me. I heard the crash, but my focus was checking on my son. Please, I need to know, how is the injured woman?"

"She's in critical condition. Paramedics will be transporting her to the hospital soon."

"Do you know where they're taking her?"

"No, but I'll find out for you."

"Thank you. Officer, you mentioned the driver left on crutches." She turned and pointed. "He used the old set of wooden crutches that were for sale. They were leaning against the house, close to where he crashed."

Linda's comment caused Michael to turn his attention to the van. He moved as close to the van as he could. He saw where the impact of his body caved-in the left rear quarter panel. That convinced him that it was the van that hit him.

He approached the first police officer, who was walking away from her conversation with Linda. He told her he had more information about the van. She pointed to the police car parked at the cul-de-sac entrance. "Our Sergeant is standing by that car. He'll help you and take your information."

"Thank you." Michael walked to the police car.

"Sergeant, my name is Michael Mays."

"How can I help you, Mr. Mays?"

"Sergeant," Michael pointed to the van, "I believe that van hit me 30 minutes ago. I sensed he intended to kill me."

The Sergeant looked at the van. "What makes you believe that's the van?" He looked back at Michael. "And why do you think he was trying to kill you?"

Michael described his observations of the van. "I don't have a clue why he'd try to kill me. But I *know* he veered into me while increasing speed. I saw the van in time to jump and avoid more serious contact.

"Also, I contacted 9-1-1 and reported the incident."

The Sergeant finished writing notes. Michael gave him a business card. "Please contact me if you have questions or any information that will help me make sense of this. I'd appreciate it."

"I'll do that. Thank you, Mr. Mays."

Michael limped away.

Why would the van's driver want to kill me… or Linda and Jacob?

He considered the appearances of a white-haired man.

Joe at The Coffee Shop, Joe at Vinyl Grooves, and now the white-haired man limping away on crutches.

Too much to be a coincidence.

8

Crouched among a cluster of landscape bushes a few blocks from the crash site, Daniel Wygal called one of his henchmen. He began barking orders.

"BTH, come get me, *now*— Aghhh."

"What's wrong, boss?"

Daniel wiped his hand on the grass behind him. "Dog crap. I need you to take me to a hospital, somewhere *far* from Portland." He described his injuries to BTH. "Bring towels, and ice… and sanitizer to clean my hand."

He gave him the cross streets of the intersection near where he hid. "I'm at the NW corner of the intersection, behind the big bushes. Make it quick; I'll be watching for you."

"Got it, boss, I'll be there right away. Boss, you know I don't like BTH. Why do you keep calling me that?"

"Stop the whining, BTH. Come and get me *now*. Don't open the car's door until you're sure there's no cops around." Daniel hung up.

While trying to clean off his hand on the lawn, he thought back to his childhood and growing up in the same Portland neighborhood as BTH.

Not unlike this one… we even spent time in the joint together. He's not the sharpest crease in the closet, but loyal to a fault.

He couldn't remember when he first called Bob, BTH. But he remembered why. Bob heard one of his teachers use the word henchman. Later that day he asked Daniel what it meant.

"It's what you are, Bob, you're Bob the henchman."

Bob thought it must be a term of endearment until someone told him others interpreted it to mean flunky—another arrangement of letters Bob hates.

BTH arrived at the intersection and parked in front of the bushes. He jumped out of the car and walked to the corner of the sidewalk. He looked in all directions and returned to the bushes. "Boss... it's Bob. No sign of cops."

Daniel took a deep breath and shook his head. "BTH, I told you *not* to get out of... Another deep breath. "Never mind. Open your back door and help me get in."

BTH helped Daniel get into the back seat and lay down. He placed the crutches in the trunk, then helped arrange the towels and ice on Daniel's ankle and forehead. He opened the container of sanitizing wipes and helped Daniel clean his hand.

"Okay, now make your way to I-5 North. We're heading for Olympia, Washington."

"Man... that's two hours away? An *elongated* drive."

Daniel shook his head but refrained from correcting BTH.

"What's with the whining today, BTH? Just drive. I can't take a chance with local hospitals. The cops will check them."

As they were heading north, BTH broke the silence. "What happened, boss?"

"Let's just say a certain cab driver will suffer far more than I am. He'll pay for selling me a van with bad brakes. They failed under the first hard braking."

"You want me to take care of him for you."

"Yeah, my injuries will lay me up a while. Be sure he knows why you're visiting him."

Daniel plowed through the trash on the rear seat's floor. He came up with a crumpled Burgerville sack. He smoothed the paper and wrote the name of the taxi driver, and name and address of the used car lot. "For bonus points, you can *thank* the car lot's owner too; the taxi driver's pudgy, pizza-breathed uncle. But first I want you to visit a yard sale... today."

He tossed the sack over the back of the front seat and shook his head,

"Your car's a frickin' mess, Bob. I wrote the info you need for both on that piece of the mess."

BTH smiled as he looked in the mirror. Daniel had called him Bob.

After dropping Daniel off at the Capital Medical Center Emergency Room in Olympia, BTH drove away with his marching orders: retribution and discovery.

9

Michael unlocked the apartment house front door and limped up the stairs to his third-floor apartment. The stairs ended at his door.

As he fumbled with his keyring, he saw a package at the base of the door. Until today's encounter with the white van, he'd never considered the possibility of a bomb on his doorstep.

Get a grip, Michael.

The package was light.

A bomb would weigh much more.

A golf umbrella, in the ceramic butter churn next to the entry door, served as a cane to help him limp to the kitchen.

He took the book and record album out of the bags and set them, along with his UPS package, on the kitchen table.

His priority was ibuprofen from the pantry, and lemon/lime-flavored club soda from the fridge.

"Crazy morning," he said to himself, and tossed both plastic bags into the recycle bin.

After he'd showered, changed clothes, and cleaned and bandaged the injuries to his knee and elbows, he returned to the kitchen. Ibuprofen on board and the soda half gone, he grabbed two cold packs from the freezer. He stuffed one between his hip and his waistband. The other he held against the back of his head.

He read the UPS package label address out loud. "Lewis & Clark College Bookstore." Relief set in. He had ordered a Lewis & Clark fleece vest and a matching Pennant. "Go Pioneers," he said, half-heartedly waving the pennant.

I AM a nerd.

But he will be one of thousands of nerds wearing and waving orange and black in the Griswold Stadium this football season.

During their high-school senior year, Gwen and Michael applied to Lewis & Clark College in Portland. The college accepted both.

Michael subsequently earned a Jurisprudence degree in Intellectual Property Law from the Lewis & Clark Law School.

Gwen majored in music and earned a Master of Music Composition degree. He used to joke, "You create the music and I'll make sure it's protected and royalties are paid—team effort."

Team effort. She fractured our team when she assumed, we had an open marriage.

The no-win Gwen situation and the crazy morning's events caused Michael to seek a diversion. He picked up the Left Banke album, walked to the living room, and placed the record on the turntable. Its first track, "Goodbye Holly" filled the room.

Another band influenced by the Beach Boys—love it.

Michael walked back to the kitchen and picked up the photography book. He chose a paring knife from his cutlery block to cut the packing tape. The tape was what stirred his curiosity enough to offer Jacob twice as much as his mother wanted.

Michael's hope was that he could remove the tape without damaging the dust cover. Even with tedious coaxing, it had been on too long to avoid serious damage. Instead, he folded each half of the tape toward the inside of the front and rear cover boards.

He returned the knife to the block.

A wedding gift.

The divorce judge's voice fueled his imagination; he could hear him saying, "But wait Michael… as a consolation, we have for you this beautiful set of knives… and, for safe storage, it includes a magnificent block of slotted wood."

Move on.

He headed to the living room sofa and sat, placing the ice pack on the end table.

First, he considered the book's front cover. There were two photos of an attractive young woman. One pictured her looking through the camera's viewfinder. Below it was one of her smiling—looking at him.

What does she see through the viewfinder that puts such a big smile on her face?

His mind conjured up several scenarios before jumping to Stephanie.

She's downtown right now, attractive and smiling as she looks through her new camera's viewfinder.

He opened the book, thumbed through two pages and saw it was published in 1943. There was a dark reddish-brown stain on the outer edges of half the pages. The stain bled in about ½ inch. He fantasized that it looks like dried blood, but realized he's trying to make an old book on photography more intriguing.

He closed the book and turned to the back cover. It was a marketing vehicle for the Eastman Kodak Company.

He opened it to the first chapter—*The Proper Equipment for Making Good Pictures.* By the third page, he was struck by what digital photography has done for the photographer.

Most two-year-old's have more pictures stored on their parents' hard-drive than were taken of me in my entire 44 years.

At the bottom of the page 6, someone handwrote in ink, "*KEEP READING.*"

There was a knock at the door. His thoughts jumped to white-haired Joe.

Come on… this guy will not rule my life.

He walked to the front door, book in hand, and looked through the wide-angle viewer. It was Tony, a neighbor who lived on the 2nd floor. Michael opened the door. "Hey, Michael," Tony said, "how goes it?"

"It's going well, how about you?" Michael answered with no expectation of fact.

"Doing good. I'm going out of town for the night, headed to my son's birthday party in Seattle. Would you mind checking on Max tomorrow morning?"

"It would be my pleasure."

While making small talk about the upcoming World Series, Tony's cell rang. He looked at the screen. "Excuse me, Michael, it's my son, I have to take this." He turned and walked toward the stairs.

Michael called after him, "Later." Tony raised his hand and Michael closed the door.

He enjoys looking in on Max, a golden retriever.

He's just happy to be alive, even happier if there's a human who appreciates what he offers.

First, he offers his head, then his hind quarter, then lies on his side. Michael can almost sense him saying, "yep, yep, yep, right there, oh yeah, you got it."

As he turned to head back to the sofa, his mind went to the upcoming World Series. That thought triggered him to look at his Little League team photo hanging on the hallway wall.

A warm wind buffeted him from every direction.

What the... He looked around and realized he was standing among a crowd of smiling, laughing people who were picking up lawn chairs, small coolers, and saying goodbyes.

Straight ahead, he saw a team of young baseball players being photographed.

"What the heck?" he wondered again, but out loud this time.

A woman walking past said, "Oh, I'm sorry, I didn't mean to block your view."

He ignored her, and said aloud, View... what's the view? And where's the view... and when... how?

Did bumping my head on the street knock me crazy?

He turned to the man standing next to him, who was staring at Michael with his head cocked and eyes narrowed. "Do you know the address of this park?"

"No, I don't, but the name of the park is, Woodstock."

"Thank you." He remembered playing baseball here. "I'm sorry, but another question, What's today's date?"

"May... 17th." The man maintained his look of confusion.

Michael ignored the look. "Thanks."

The baseball field was lined on each side with majestic evergreen trees, which helped maintain the City Park's atmosphere, but also served to stop wayward baseballs.

Michael returned his attention to the team being photographed. A few of them looked familiar. He looked at the parents but recognized none of them, until a woman photographing the team lowered her camera and said something to a woman next to her.

She turned and looked toward the area where he stood. "Mom... that's my mom!" He whispered, as tears welled.

He limped toward the photographers; eyes fixed on his mother.

This is not possible—not possible, but that's my mom.

He kept moving toward her.

On the previous Mother's Day, Michael had scanned a photo of her his grandmother had given him. He posted it on Facebook.

Even the same clothes.

"Deborah Mays?" Michael mumbled as he drew near.

She turned. "Yes... hi, do I know you?" A young boy in a uniform ran up to her. "Mom, we need to go. The team's leaving and heading to the pizza place. You told Mrs. Blake you need to follow her."

That young boy was 12-year-old Michael.

Mouth ajar and eyes wide, he looked at his younger self.

This can't be, but...

Michael's mom looked at him. "I'm sorry, we have to run."

She looked him in the eyes for a few seconds. Then looked down at the 12-year-old looking up at her. She looked back at Michael, eyes widened, and lips parted.

Michael sensed she recognized him.

She was shaken.

He couldn't blame her for turning with his younger-self hugged close and walking fast toward the parking lot.

She looked back once, causing her to walk faster.

Michael stood there, confused.

Not a clue what to do or where to go.

So, he followed his mother.

As he trailed behind, he looked around.

Did my dad ever come to any of my games? Not this one.

At the edge of the parking lot, he stopped and watched his mother and his younger self get into a Ford Thunderbird. Michael recognized the car and wondered what will happen to it in three months.

Did dad sell it?

The warm omnidirectional wind hit him again. He was standing back in the hallway, staring at his Little League team photo.

Shook-up, he forced himself back to the sofa, where he fell back into the cushions.

He exhaled hard. "What was that?"

Michael placed the book on the end table next to the sofa. He let his head fall against the sofa cushion. "Ow!" The pain reminded him he had slammed hard against pavement. He picked up the ice pack from the end table and re-applied it.

He closed his eyes, hoping when he opened them, he would be waking from a crazy, incredible dream.

That hope vanished when he opened his eyes. He sat thinking about the warm wind, the parents, the ball field… and his mom. In his heart he knew his mother recognized him.

He didn't doubt it was real, but he could come up with no rational explanation.

Was I gone for a long time, or was it just a flash of time in the present?

He grabbed his phone and called Tony.

"Hey, Tony, I have what may seem a like strange question, but would you mind checking your recent call screen to see what time your son called?"

"Sure. That's a question I've never been asked. Okay… here we go. It says: 12:35."

"Thanks. it's something I put in the oven. I was about to set the timer when you knocked. I walked away without setting it. Have a safe trip to Seattle."

He lied, but he couldn't tell Tony the real reason for asking.

The clock on Michael's phone read, 12:45. His calculation came up with six minutes gone. "Not long," he said to himself, "but the most incredible six minutes of my life."

A vague recollection struck him.

I think there's a date on the back of the Little League picture.

He walked back, removed the photo from the wall and took it to the kitchen table. He removed the metal brads and cardboard from the,. The handwriting on the back of the photo read: "May 17, 1986." Less than three months prior to someone murdering his mother.

My mother's handwriting.

Before putting the picture back together, he removed the photo from the frame and took a picture of both the front and back of the photograph.

He put the photo and frame back together and re-hung it.

Back at the sofa, he picked up his soda and downed the remaining half. He looked at the book and considered reading more… the young woman on the cover was still smiling at him. "Sorry, but I'm not in the mood. I need lunch and a nap."

After a ham and swiss on rye and a ten-minute nap, he returned to the living room, shut off the turntable and returned the record to its dust jacket. He spent the rest of the afternoon reviewing a case. He was representing a writer/client who was suing another writer for plagiarism.

But his mind kept turning back to the most extraordinary day in his life.

* * *

The rain stopped as daylight faded. After removing the protective plastic sheeting from the yard sale tables, Linda and Jacob boxed up the sale items.

"Jacob, while I begin taking these boxes down to the basement, fold these tables and stack them against the house."

Jacob wiped away a raindrop that hit his cheek. "Will do, mom."

He turned as he heard a voice behind him. "Hey, kid."

Jacob saw a skinny old man, not much taller than him. "I'm sorry, but we're closed. My mom said to try back next weekend."

"What's your name, kid?"

"Um... it's Jacob, what's yours?"

"Bob. Hey... I was here early this morning. I found a book I wanted, but got an emergency phone call and had to leave. There was no one here to require my money, so I put the book down and left."

"Require your money?"

"Yeah, you know, make me pay." Jacob just tilted his head and stared at the little man.

Bob saw himself as charming. But years of sucking in nicotine and carcinogens—and the lack of dental hygiene—resulted in excessively wrinkled skin and wretched teeth. Creepy, rather than charming.

"I don't remember you, Bob. I was here all morning until someone crashed into our house. You must have the wrong yard sale."

"Nope, it was here, and the name of the book was, 'Making Pictures Come to Life.' I came back to acquire it."

Jacob bent his neck to the side. "That was one of the first things I sold this morning. How could you have looked at it?"

Bob gave an intimidating sneer. "Doesn't matter, kid, who did you sell it to?"

"We don't keep a list of who bought what."

"Tell me what you remember about the person who bought it."

"My mom doesn't want me giving out information about customers."

Bob drew close to Jacob and pulled back his jacket to reveal a holstered pistol.

"Kid, I know your dad's in prison, and all you have is your mother. Tell me what you remember, or there won't be a father, *or a mother* to take care of you."

Jacob stammered, "I... I don't... all he told me was his name, Michael."

Bob put his hand on the gun. "You sure that's it, kid?"

Jacob motioned in the direction Michael had pointed. "He said, he lives around the corner. I promise, that's… that's all I know."

Linda came out of the house. "Is everything okay, Jacob?"

"Sorry, ma'am," Bob said. "just checking to see if you're still accessible."

He turned and speed-walked back to his car, which was parked around the corner.

Linda called Jacob to come into the house.

After he stepped inside and she closed the door, she hugged him, "Jacob, you're shaking, what happened?"

Jacob told her the story. Linda immediately called 9-1-1. Without a description of the little man's vehicle or license plate number there was nothing they could do. But the Call-Taker promised to send an officer to Linda's house to interview Jacob.

* * *

"Boss, the kid only knows the first name of the guy who bought the book… it's Michael."

"That's all I need, BTH. Now go to the address I gave you, pack up my stuff, and bring it up to me. The plastic card I gave you will get you in."

"One more thing, boss. The kid told me Michael lives around the corner and down the street. He pointed east."

"Okay, but for now, bring me my stuff."

"Boss, I'm tired. How about I reside the night down here in your room? I'll bring your personal effects tomorrow."

"Yeah, it'd be too late to get much done, and I'd have to pay for a hotel room. Get up here by noon. We have plans to make."

"Will do, boss."

"BTH, a question before you hang up."

"Render it, boss."

"I've noticed a change in your vocabulary. What's going on?"

"Just trying to convalesce myself. I'm going through the dictionary finding words I like. I'm inaugurating them into my talking. I have an abundant list in my notebook. I'll keep adding to it as I grow."

"Okay BTH. Good luck with that."

10

Sunday, October 13th

Stretched and wrenched muscles protested as Michael got out of bed. His entire body ached.

Hot water from the shower helped; it would be his friend for days to come. As the hot water warmed his muscles, he considered heading to church.

Michael grew up going to church, but his attendance faded in high school. It disappeared by the end of Law School. He gave his grandmother hope by making appearances on holidays.

Must be a holiday somewhere.

Michael chose to ride his bike. The Fall morning sky was vivid blue, but light frost clung to the grass and to shaded roadway surfaces. Michael watched for those areas as he rode but—as much as his knees and hip would allow— let loose when the roadway was clear.

He thought back on how his Grandmother influenced him. Her encouragement and the accountability she demanded caused him to smile.

At the same time, she supported his grandfather through his wildest schemes. He was an attorney and an entrepreneur, not a good or successful entrepreneur, but he was consistent.

After someone murdered Michael's mother, his grandmother didn't hesitate stepping forward to help his father raise him. She was devastated, yet she pushed her grief aside for Michael.

Michael scoffed at associating his father with helping his grandmother raise him.

Didn't happen.

His father's job as an advertising executive kept him on the road. Michael didn't have a clue whether his father enjoyed most, his work or the traveling, but as a 12-year-old, he sensed they were both more important than him.

He locked his bike to a fence, which was close to the steepled white church's entrance.

As Michael passed through the sanctuary door, the beautiful stained-glass windows, telling stories through their depiction of biblical scenes, impressed him. The artwork on the walls portrayed none of contemporary culture's progress. Michael stopped just inside the door and considered both the church's interior and the peace it brought.

It is a sanctuary.

No need to scan the room for his Grandmother, she was sitting in her usual seat. He hoped her 90-year-old heart could take the shock of realizing it was him who sat down next to her.

As he sat, she looked at him, smiled and wrapped her arm around his. It felt good, like home, a peace he had counted on since the day his mother was murdered.

Mid-service, his mind wandered back to when he was a 12-year-old sitting here between his father and grandmother. His grandfather to her left. He thought back to the Pastor eulogizing his mother, which included the senselessness of her death. Michael remembered wondering, *So, there might be a way mom's death could make sense?*

Thirty-two years ago, his 58-year-old grandmother, held onto his arm just as she was that morning.

As Michael and his grandmother walked out of the church, they stopped often. His grandmother introduced, or re-introduce him to lifelong friends, who'd been there for her many times.

One gentleman, who was Michael's grandmother's age, looked at him.

"Pleased to meet you, Michael, my name is Marvin. We have a common interest."

Michael looked at his grandmother, then back to Marvin. He raised his right hand, palm up and chest high, pursed his lips, and shook his head. "Umm…"

"Your grandmother…" Marvin laughed, but his eyes, staring into hers, were not joking.

"I keep asking her for a date, and she keeps saying, 'We'll see.'"

Grandma wrapped Michael's arm in hers, touched her head on his shoulder, then looked at Marvin. "We'll see, Marvin, we'll see."

"Louise, I'm a retired ophthalmologist. I can help you see clearer."

She waved him off. "Oh, Marvin."

Michael retrieved his bicycle and pushed it alongside as they walked. "Grandma, if I didn't know better, I'd say you became giddy and blushed a little when Marvin joked about your relationship." She looked up at him, smiled, and gave a tug on his arm.

"What do you say we stop at Ella's café on the way home?"

She stopped and turned toward him. "Well… there *will be* friends there who've never met you. They may think I'm out painting the town with a young stud, but it is my favorite restaurant, so I'll take that chance."

"Grandma, message received. I'll work at being here more often. I don't want your friends to catch on to your moral depravity."

"I appreciate that, Michael. My reputation has taken 90 years to build."

The café was small and welcoming. White clapboard siding, with dark green trim, and matching dark green flower boxes attached to the bottom of the shuttered windows. Plants with red and yellow flowers—still hanging on in the Fall weather—filled them. Shrubs grew between the sidewalk and the café's foundation.

A young woman greeted them. "Louise, so good to see you. Who's this handsome man with you?"

Michael shook her hand. "I'm Michael, Louise's grandson." Louise beamed as she watched.

"Glad to meet you, Michael. I'm Kelsey. Follow me, I have a nice table for you."

She led them through tables with green and white checkered linen table clothes. A flower arrangement was placed in the middle of each. Michael's grandmother stopped several times to say hi to friends and introduce Michael. Kelsey smiled, and patiently waited each time.

After they finished breakfast they reminisced. Out of nowhere, Louise said, "Oh... I had a very nice conversation with an old friend of your mother's this past Monday evening."

"Who was that, Grandma?"

"His name is Joe."

Michael came on point.

"I can't remember a friend of mom's named Joe. Can you describe him?"

She looked away for a few seconds, then back at Michael, "Oh... he was young... mid-50s, though his hair was white... but everyone looks young to me. I wondered if he might have gone to college with your mother. He said he met your mother long ago, and that he'd talked with you twice."

Michael had no recollection of a longtime friend named Joe. "Did he mention how he knew mom, or where he met me?"

"No. Just said he was in town and that he hadn't seen you in years. He wanted to get together to find out how you're doing. And, that he might have a few stories about your mother you haven't heard.

"Such a gentleman. There was something familiar about him, so I invited him inside. We talked for at least an hour. He enjoyed the photos I have of you in the—what did you call it—electric picture frame?"

"Digital photo frame."

"Yes, that's it, digital photo frame. It fascinated him to watch you at various ages, and the different sports you were involved in. He said he was happy you adjusted so well after losing your mother.

"He told me he was leaving town on Saturday—yesterday—and asked how to contact you. I gave him your phone number. I hope you don't mind."

Michael lowered his eyes. "Grandma, never let a stranger into your house.

I don't care how nice he seems. And, please don't give my phone number out without asking me first."

"I'm sorry… but he was so nice and friendly and had a genuine interest in you."

"I admire your hospitality, Grandma, but the world has changed."

She smiled. "He asked if you'd be available before he left town. I told him you work *way* too much during the week—"

"Grandma, I've told you many times… I love my work."

"Well, you work *too* much. Anyway, I told Joe you have a Saturday morning coffee routine and maybe he can meet you there. He laughed and said, 'I always saw Michael as predictable, even as a kid.' I agreed. Then he asked, 'What routine has Michael got himself doing on Saturdays?'

"I told him about the coffee shop and your love for old records."

"Grandma, I had a brief conversation with a man with white hair yesterday morning, who introduced himself as Joe. Then minutes later, I ran into him at the record store. But he didn't mention we'd met before. Did you tell him which coffee shop, or the record store's location?"

"Yes, I told him you have coffee at a place called 'The Coffee Shop.' But I couldn't remember the name of the record store. I told him they're only a few blocks apart."

Michael leaned forward with his arms resting on his inner thighs and hands clasped. "Your description fits the guy I met this morning. Did he park a car out front?"

"Yes, he parked it in the street. I watched him walk to it when he left. But it wasn't a car, it was a van… a white van."

Oh boy, here we go again.

"Grandma, did Joe ask questions that seemed odd to you?"

"No… well yes. His interest in whether you ever thought of doing your own investigation of your mother's murder?"

Michael concealed his concern. "Did he ask anything else about mom, or dad?"

"Only how I handled your mother's death."

"Did he say how he found out she died?"

"No, I didn't ask."

The server brought the check. Michael grabbed it. "It's on me, Grandma."

She smiled, stood, and walked ahead of Michael to the front desk. Michael paid the check, then walked her back to her house.

"I have to go, Grandma. I have a case I must work on—"

"It's *Sunday* Michael. You should take time for yourself. Find the girl of your dreams and live. You work *too* much."

"Grandma—"

She smiled and squeezed his arm again.

"Grandma, please promise me you won't invite strangers into your house."

"I promise, but only if you promise to come to church more often *and* buy me breakfast at Ella's."

Michael strapped on his helmet. "You're on." They hugged, he kissed her cheek, and waved as he got on his bike and rode off.

I love that woman.

As he processed the discussion between him and his grandmother, he realized his hip and knee were loosening. He peddled faster and faster, not paying attention to his direction, He needed to work off his stress and confusion around white-haired Joe. He knew no one named Joe, nor could he remember his mother having a friend by that name.

But… there was the white-haired Joe from yesterday.

* * *

Daniel lay in a hospital bed in Olympia, Washington.

Is it revenge or a pre-emptive strike? Doesn't matter… both call for an end to Michael Mays's life.

The doctor walked in and broke Daniel's hateful thoughts. "Mr. Wygal, you're a lucky man." He blew hard through pressed lips. "To survive that fall at your age…" The doctor looked at the digital x-ray image on a monitor. "Your ankle's fracture is serious. How did you make it here? You must have an incredible tolerance for pain."

"Well… I used crutches to get to the taxi. I guess when you have a good enough reason, a person can do extraordinary things. My family's important.

I don't want to disappoint my grandchildren.

"If I'd called my family for help, it would have ruined their memory of the tree house I'm building. Now they'll visit me, happy the surgery went well, and not associate it with the tree house."

"I get your point. But next time, call 9-1-1 *and* your family."

Not too hard to fool doctors. Prison doctors are even easier.

Got me out of work details.

Through glasses sitting near the end of his nose, the doctor looked at Daniel's chart. "Surgery is scheduled for tomorrow afternoon. The surgeon will be here in the morning to evaluate you. Healing time for this injury is 6-12 weeks, then rehab will be close to that."

He continued scanning Daniel's chart. "You're diabetic," he said and looked up, "that complicates the healing process. Your recovery time may be longer. Daniel, you won't enjoy hearing this, but I'm having you transferred to a nursing home for your extended recovery. The ankle and the forehead laceration, plus a broken rib and being beat up in general, will lay you up for quite a while." He consulted his clipboard again. "Your paperwork says you live alone. We can't keep you in a hospital room, and I can't send you home without live-in care."

"Do what you have to do, Doc. I want to get back on my feet as soon as possible." Then, with the sincerest face in his collection, "Gotta finish up that tree house for the grandkids."

The doctor removed his glasses. "I'll have the arrangements made. I suggest you call someone to finish the tree house."

Daniel smiled.

Yeah, while I'm making arrangements for Michael Mays.

* * *

Michael put his bike in the basement storage cage, not in the mood to work.

I'm as excited to work on the plagiarism case as I am about volunteering for a root canal.

He was prepared, and confident the case was on solid ground. Kicking back and finishing Left Banke's album, while reading a few chapters of the book, was more appealing. But he could not lay aside the question: Who is Joe?

After putting side two of the Left Banke record on the turntable, Michael sat, picked up the book and the TV remote control.

He loves watching sports and listening to music, so muting the TV allows him to satisfy both passions. The previous week, he heard a broadcast special on past World Series' would be aired that morning. He had set the satellite box to record it. A few clicks and he found the recording and pushed play. He read while listening to Left Banke.

He glanced up now and then to check which game they were showing. He'd set the TV to display closed captioning, allowing him to keep up with the commentary.

As the sports commentators were discussing the play, a black & white photo came up of Enos Slaughter making a slide into home after his 'Mad Dash' from first base.

Michael spoke out loud. "1946, Cardinals versus the Red Sox." He went back to reading. The author of the book stated, "If you get one outstanding photo per roll of 36 exposure film, you are doing well."

Doesn't apply anymore. I keep shooting, frame after frame, and then delete those I don't want. Like the score cards of some of the people I play golf with.

While finishing that thought, he looked up to see Carlton Fisk waving his ball into fair territory, running and jumping, realizing he'd hit the winning home run in the 12th inning of the 6th game of the 1975 World Series.

There it was again: the warm omnidirectional wind. Michael stood watching Carlton Fisk running and jumping.

Michael raised his arms, with fist's clenched.

Fenway Park... 1975 World Series... game six!

11

"Hey, watch it, where did you come from?" the big biker said, as he bumped into Michael. The biker wore Levi's, with a black leather vest over a white t-shirt. The back of the vest, above the motorcycle club's logo, read: "Fugitives." Beneath the logo: "Everywhere."

Michael gave an awkward smile. "I'm sorry, I didn't see you coming. I got caught up in the moment."

The biker, his Red Sox hat knocked lopsided, gave him a side glance. "Yeah, whatever. You caused me to spill my beers, klutz."

The biker grunted and elbowed his way past.

"Hey, I apologized, and I may have done you a favor."

"What favor?"

"Your breath and stagger suggest you've had *more* than enough to drink."

The biker turned.

With his jaw set, he glared at Michael. He stepped up two stair steps and dumped both cups of beer over Michael's head.

Michael wiped his eyes.

The biker dropped the cups and shoved Michael hard.

Michael fell back onto people in seats behind him.

They pushed him back up. Michael closed the book, gripped the edges, and held it up to deflect the biker's punch.

The book deflected the punch from his face, but the energy transferred to his arms and knocked him back onto the people pushing him.

A few men sitting near the biker stood, jumped up, grabbed him, and tried to calm him.

His biker buddy, a few rows away, ran up and helped hold him back. Holding onto his friend's arms, he said, "Calm down, man. You can't afford this trouble."

Michael stood shaking his head in disbelief. "Friend… you're in *desperate* need of anger management counseling." Then turned and walked away.

The biker strained against those holding him. "I'll be waiting for you outside… I'll *show you* some anger management."

Michael walked away wondering, *If he showed me, would I go back to my time injured? If so, he'd be an old man. When healed, I could find him…*

He knew he wouldn't beat up an old man. He told himself to let it go.

Forcing his attention back to the ball game, he's seen replays of this home run since he was a kid. He was hearing it, seeing it, touching it, and he was soaked with beer.

No doubt it's real.

On the stairway landing, he took in everything. To his left was the Lone Red Seat. Ted Williams hit a record setting home run there in 1946. The ball landed on the head of the man sitting in that seat, crushing his straw hat. Williams' record still stands.

As he pondered that, he looked at his phone. He had a few minutes left. In front of him, by the railing, stood a yellow shirted hot dog vendor calling out: Get a dog to go *here!*

He had time to get a Fenway Frank.

Michael maneuvered his way through the swarm of fans and approached the vendor. "Hey, I'll take one of your dogs."

"You got it. Mustard or ketchup?"

"Mustard."

"That'll be a buck."

Michael handed him a $20 bill.

The vendor held the twenty at eye level. "Hey, buddy, what's this? I've been doing this for 25 years. People like you tryin' to pass off your funny money." He slapped it into Michael's palm. "Take it and get outta here before I call a cop."

Face red, Michael walked along the railing. Fans, who heard the vendor, gave dirty looks to, even elbowed past, the man with the beer-soaked hair and shirt. Michael stopped and turned toward the field while, again, squeegeeing his hair with his hands.

What was that about?

His mind churned until the recollection hit him. *Oh man, The Treasury Department redesigned the $20 bill... somewhere around the year 2000.*

To the vendor's 1975 senses, it was either counterfeit, or play money.

He slipped his wallet back into his pocket, leaned on the rail, and took in the players and the park.

Phenomenal.

The warm, omnidirectional wind took him back to his sofa.

Michael expected to be at Fenway Park for six minutes. But he sensed he'd been there longer. Re-opening the yard sale book, he found the page he was on when he looked up and saw Carlton Fisk celebrating his home run.

Page 10.

He turned back to page 6 where, at the bottom of the page, someone handwrote, "KEEP READING."

Michael realized the time spent in the past relates to the number of pages read. "Wow... learned something."

He closed the book, set it on the end table, and ran the information through his mind—going through the details of each scenario,

I was on the sofa, reading the book each time it happened. No... I wasn't on the sofa the first time? Okay, I was reading the book in both instances and still holding it when I arrived in the past. This makes sense, but at the same time, it makes no sense.

He felt his brain melting. He walked around the apartment, running the Red Sox game through his mind. In his bedroom, he took off his shirt and smelled it.

Yep, no doubt that's beer.

He needed a shower and clean clothes.

As he dressed, Michael considered what he'd learned; he didn't like his conclusion.

So, from now on, when I look at a photo, watch TV or go to a movie, the book will transport me back to that moment? That's a curse.

He lowered his gaze as he walked toward the bedroom door.

Near the doorway hung a framed photo of his Law School graduation ceremony.

Still looking down, he stopped and stood in front of the photo. He braced himself. "Okay… here I go."

He looked up, nothing. No warm wind, no audience, or graduates around him. Just Michael, standing near the his bedroom door, confused.

He knows he had not hallucinated. To compound his confusion, his mind landed back on the World Series TV special.

Carlton Fisk wasn't the first scene I looked at while reading the book. It was Enos Slaughter making his slide into home. So… why Fenway Park and not Sportsman's Park?

He grouched out loud, "Come on, Michael, figure this out."

Okay, I know the book took me back to my 1986 Little League game. Will it do it again?

He walked to the hallway and looked at the team photo. Nothing. "Come on, recreate the scenario."

Back at the sofa, he picked up his phone, opened the clock app and selected stopwatch. With the book and cell phone in hand he walked to the Little League Team photo. Looked at it again. Nothing.

Okay, what's different?

He replayed the first event.

When I got up from the sofa to answer Tony's knock, I closed the book… wait. I closed the book around my index finger to keep my place. It was open.

He opened the book to page 10 and looked at the Little League team photo. The warm omnidirectional wind engulfed him.

He was standing in the same spot had landed on his previous trip.

Okay, the book must be open.

He touched Start on his phone's timer.

Michael wondered if he would return to his apartment if he closed the book.

I closed it at Fenway Park to block the big guy's punch.

Closing it, he stayed.

Not wanting to frighten his mother again, he stood where he had previously materialized. He took a few photos of her and the team, unsure if they would still be in his phone's memory when he arrived back home.

Overwhelmed during his first trip, he had not paid attention to his mother's appearance.

She's beautiful.

Much thinner than he remembered her. But he bases his memories of her on photographs.

Again, his father came to mind. He wondered if he had overlooked him during the first trip.

Michael swiveled his head, sweeping the ballpark, His father was not there.

He looked around to find if he recognized anyone else. Something to his mother's left caught his eye. A man, he guessed to be 30, was standing near her. Michael thought he too was photographing the team. A curious action caught his attention. The man turned and snapped a quick picture of his mother. He did it several times. Each time from a different angle.

That's odd.

Then he remembered his mother was the team's secretary. Each year, she put on a slide show at the team's end-of-the-season pizza party. He and his teammates loved it.

Maybe he's also taking pictures for the party.

Michael walked closer to the team to see if he recognized his teammates.

Yep, there's Adam Norris with his fingers in a Victory sign behind my head.

Michael took a photo of the team.

He lowered his phone. The man who had been photographing his mother was staring at Michael's phone. His gaze shifted to the book under Michael's left arm. The man's puzzled look increased. Michael understood how a Star Trek character visiting a strange, less advanced planet would have felt.

He walked to the tree-lined perimeter of the ball field and sat on the grass next to a Douglas Fir. He watched his mother and wanted to run to her and hug her.

The photo session ended, and the team began to leave. His kid-self ran to his mother and hugged her.

Well… I got the hug I wanted.

Michael's kid-self pointed toward the parking lot. Michael knew he was telling her they need to get going so they could follow Mrs. Blake to the pizza shop.

The timer on his phone read 8 minutes and 45 seconds.

His impulse was to stand and walk toward his mother, but the man photographing her caught his eye again. The camera now pointed straight at Michael.

Out of nowhere, a man appeared behind the photographer.

His intentions became clear when he looked right at Michael and raised a rifle.

Michael fell back bringing his knees toward his chest.

He rolled left behind the Douglas Fir.

Two consecutive gunshots rang out.

He heard the first bullet strike the ground somewhere beyond where he had sat.

The second bullet struck the edge of the tree trunk, sending bark and splinters past Michael's head.

Crouched behind the tree, Michael looked around him. People were running everywhere, shouting warnings, or screaming.

He considered his options. Other than running to the tree behind him, there were not any. He stood and turned and was about to lunge forward.

"Are you okay?"

He stopped and looked. There was an older man walking away from the tree he had been hiding behind.

"Yes, but *get down* before you're shot."

"The shooters gone."

Michael peeked around the tree trunk. "What do you mean *gone?*"

"Like I said, he's gone. I glanced around the tree... he disappeared right in front of my eyes."

Michael began to respond—the warm, omnidirectional wind hit him.

While gathering his thoughts from the past 10 minutes, he looked down at the fir needles and dirt covering his clothes. To avoid shaking off the debris, he shuffled to the bathroom. He made it to the bathtub without leaving much of a trail.

As he was brushing off in the tub, on his right pant leg, just above his knee near the outside seam, he saw something that gave him chills: two bullet holes

The bullet passed through a fold in the denim. He pinched the fold together and put his finger through the holes.

The shooter was good. If I had hesitated a fraction of a second, the bullet would have found my chest.

After changing his clothes, he went to the living room to sort through his thoughts. He sat on the sofa with more insight.

I can travel back to where I've been, and it'll be a new event.

He smiled.

Must have blown the old man's mind, seeing two people disappear before his eyes, within less than a minute.

Michael wrestled with the notion that somewhere in the future, there's someone with a copy of the book. But more curious was, why do they want to kill him?

12

At dinner, Michael pushed his food around the plate with his fork. Few forkfuls made it to his mouth. Food had no appeal to him.

What do I do with this shooter?

He could not get his mind away from the idea someone *from the future* wants him dead.

To divert his thoughts, he opened his calendar. The upcoming week was full and hectic. But he had little interest in work; someone wants to kill him.

He forced himself to think about the next week's top priority: A plagiarism case.

But the book forced its way back into Michael's mind. He wants to dedicate next Saturday to exploring the book's abilities.

With little time during the day, he committed to read each night before turning out the light.

The book was small: 5 ½ inches wide by 8 inches tall, with 240 pages. He'd read 10 pages. His goal was to read 10 pages per night. By Saturday, 70 minutes would be available for each exploration.

Tuesday, October 15th

In bed, he looked up to consider a point in the book. Michael's eyes caught the graduation photo he had looked at earlier. Warm omnidirectional wind— he was standing in the Lewis & Clark College Pamplin Sports Center, at the rear of his graduation ceremony—wearing nothing but his boxer shorts.

Oh man… how long will I be here?

Michael was standing in one of the alcove doors that exits from the gymnasium's floor.

Everyone on the riser seating could see him.

Confusion and concern marked the eyes of those close by who had noticed him.

Two men stood and hurried down the bleachers, toward Michael.

Michael walked backwards until he felt the door's panic-opener hardware. He pushed open the door and slinked through.

The two men rushed to follow Michael.

Three groups of people stood in the hallway.

One group turned. A young man broke from the group. "Hey... are you okay?"

"Yeah, everything's okay. I got confused."

Michael looked around and saw a men's bathroom sign.

He hurried through the door, locked himself inside a stall, and sat waiting to go home. He had read to page 35.

The two men walked in. "Anyone in here? Is something wrong?"

"Yeah, I'm in here; got my doors mixed up."

They looked at each other, shrugged and left.

Back in bed, Michael thought, *That was an important, but embarrassing lesson.*

Saturday, October 19th

Michael was ahead of his reading schedule. He had read 116 pages and now has an hour and 56 minutes for each block of time travel.

He looked forward to a weekend of exploration. A box of family photographs stored at his grandmother's house came to mind. Like him, she was an early riser. He called her and asked if he could come over.

"Grandma, I want to go through the box of photos stored in my former bedroom's closet."

"Oh... I don't know if it's a good time, Michael. What with my Saturday morning calendar full and people lined up on my doorstep... of course you can come over."

Michael laughed. "I'm on my way."

He grabbed the book and headed to Grandma's. When he arrived, the box was out, opened, and his grandmother was sitting on her sofa looking at pictures. Tears streamed down her face. He hugged her. "Hi, Grandma."

"Oh, Michael, I haven't looked at these photos in years."

Michael thought, *I've never seen a smile so sad.*

"I remember taking this one of you and your mother. The date on the back is only days away from—"

Michael pulled her to him and hugged her. For a few minutes, neither of them said a word.

"Grandma, we should stop. This isn't a good idea."

She held up the picture. "Michael, this is my daughter, I have to do this. I do it in my head every day. I'm refreshing memories of my beautiful child. I don't want to lose sight of who she was."

She recounted memories for him as she held up various photos. Michael asked her about photos that cued his interest.

He discovered the envelope containing the shots his mother took of the Little League team. There were also photos of team members eating pizza at the after-game party.

It was the same Little League pizza party where his mother and his kid-self hurried off to on May 17, 1986.

He set aside one of the pizza party photos and continued searching. He selected a couple more from the envelope. One was a picture of Michael and his mother standing in front of an ice cream shop. His mother had one hand on his shoulder. In her other hand was an ice cream cone. She tilted her head to lick the side to prevent it from dripping. As Michael stooped to pet a kitten, his scoop of ice cream fell from the cone.

Michael held the picture up for his grandmother. "Perfect timing, grandma."

"I love that photo. The ice cream fell at the same time I snapped the picture. While the ice cream shop owner refilled your cone, the kitty feasted."

"You caught the scoop in mid-air, that's great. Can I borrow this and make a copy?"

"Your mother was so engrossed in *her* cone she didn't notice I was taking a picture. Take it and keep it. You should have it."

"Thanks, Grandma, I love it." He looked at it again, then put it in his pile.

She held up a picture of her daughter in uniform. "Your mother was so proud of making the cheerleading squad. And I was proud of her. She practiced in her room every night to a song called… I don't remember hearing the name of the song, but it said something about a pony eating macaroni, giving mashed potatoes to an alligator. I never understood the song or knew who sang it."

Michael lowered a picture he was looking at, while suppressing smile. "The artist was Wilson Pickett, Grandma. The name of the song is 'Land of a Thousand Dances.' I still have the album, along with her other albums. You let me bring them with me when you and grandad took me in."

"Oh, well, it doesn't matter who he was or what he was talking about, she loved it and convinced the squad to do a half-time dance routine to it. I wish I would have had a movie camera to film it."

"Grandma, I know the song well—I can see her dancing."

"Now that you mention it," she winked, "I remember, more than a few times, hearing you listening to that song in your room."

He looked at the photo again, admiring how beautiful his mother was. He gave it back to his grandmother. "She's beautiful, takes after her mother."

She looked down at the picture. "Oh, Michael…"

Grandma dropped her hands to her knees and looked up. "I didn't even offer you a cup of coffee. I'll go make us a pot."

"Thanks, Grandma, but I have to go. Who knows, I might be in church tomorrow."

She smiled but framed it in sarcasm.

Michael began packing the pictures he had not selected back into the box. "Please, leave them out," grandma said, "I want to continue going through them."

"Okay, but with the tears you're shedding, I should get you a glass of water. I don't want you to become dehydrated."

She waved him off. "Get out of here." He gave her a hug and said goodbye.

At The Coffee Shop, he ordered his usual—coffee and a chocolate croissant. No newspaper reading this morning. He focused on eating and heading home to experiment with time travel.

On his way home, he slowed as he came to the street of the yard sale. He could see the work crews repairing the house. He turned right and made his way into the cul-de-sac.

The yard sale lady stood on the sidewalk talking to a neighbor. The memory of her asking the police officer to call her Linda came to him.

He pulled over to the curb, near where she stood.

Michael got out of his car and walked toward her. "Hi."

She looked at him. The neighbor said something, then walked away.

Linda was unpretentious; pretty, but didn't know it. Late thirties, 5 and a half feet tall, dark brown hair, dark complexion and an athletic physique.

She wears those medical scrubs well.

But her countenance hinted sadness.

Michael put out his hand. "Hi, my name's Michael Mays. I live two blocks away."

Linda, tilting her head, squinted, and accepted his hand with caution.

"Michael… I'm Linda. Have we met?"

"It's nice to meet you, Linda. We haven't met… but I believe we're connected." Michael turned his head toward her house. "They're making progress in getting your house back in order."

Still guarded, she folded her right arm across her chest and placed her left palm on her cheek. "Yes, but I'm not worried about the house repairs. My son and I are *still* shaken. *We* need to get back in order."

"That's understandable. Linda, a week ago, I was on my way home from The Coffee Shop. The emergency vehicles and the commotion here caught my attention. I walked near to where you stood talking with the police and, I confess, eavesdropped on your conversation. My apologies for that, but I'm sure the van that damaged your house—as well as damaging you and your son—hit me earlier that morning. I'm certain he intended to kill me. I told the police captain about my run-in with the van."

Linda's eyes widened. "Yes… now I recognize you. Are you okay?"

"My injuries were minor. Stiff and sore the next few days. Bumps and bruises, but like you and your son, Jacob's his name, right?"

"Yes." Linda said, while tipping her head to the side and narrowing her eyes.

"Like you and Jacob, I'm still shaken up and wondering what happened."

She was warming to the conversation. "Besides the white van incident, we have something else in common."

She scrunched her brow. "What's that?"

"I was a customer at your yard sale that morning. I bought an old book on photography from your son."

Her body language changed. Even though still standing in front of Michael, her body was in motion to leave. "Look... I'm tired. I need to go. I've been up all night. I only stopped to check on the progress of the repairs."

He looked in her eyes, opened his mouth to question her about the book, but hesitated. "Linda... I understand you need sleep... but would you walk to The Coffee Shop with me? I'll buy... I have a few questions. I'm trying to figure out of why someone wanted to hurt, or kill *us*, and... destroy your yard sale? Maybe together we can solve this."

She looked away and shook her head. "Okay, but it will have to be decaf."

As they walked, he asked, "Is Jacob here with you?"

"No, we're staying with friends while our house is being repaired. He's with them."

"I'm impressed with Jacob. We haggled over the price of the book... that's how I know his name."

"I wondered. Yes, Jacob is smart, sometimes too smart for his own good. He can't help himself, or I should say, his mouth. I love him to death, but he can be a challenge for a single, working mom."

"I noticed you're wearing scrubs. Where do you work?"

"I'm an RN at Legacy Emanuel Hospital. How about you?"

"I'm an attorney. I practice Intellectual Property Law. It always strikes me funny when I say it like that. I can defend another person's intellectuality, but I'm not always so good at practicing it."

She laughed. "We all have *that* DNA."

As they walked, Michael changed the subject. He commented on houses they walked past and how his appreciation of them has grown to where he hopes to buy one someday. She warmed to the discussion, which caused her to loosen up. She too expressed her love for them.

They walked into The Coffee Shop. He went straight to the counter and ordered. Linda found a table. Before beginning the conversation, they each took a bite of their croissant and had a sip of coffee.

Michael raised and looked at his croissant. "My second one today. But in my defense," he looked at Linda, "it's your fault because you asked for one first. I'd have been rude to let you eat alone."

"I've heard that it's been the woman's fault from the beginning."

"Thank you. I might have a third."

She shook her head and took another bite.

"I don't want to keep you from sleep, so I'll get right to it. The only connection we have—that might link us to the man in the white van—is the yard sale and the book. Is there any reason either of those might link us together?

Linda looked at her plate and breathed deep, as if preparing herself for pain. She looked at Michael for a few seconds before responding. "I don't see how either of those could link us together. But I'll tell you my story; maybe you'll recognize a connection. But be warned, it's a long story."

"Okay, I'm warned."

She began telling a story that blunted any future telling of his 'Gone with the Gwen' story.

13

"My former husband is in the Willamette State Penitentiary… convicted of murder."

"Who did he—"

"Please," she pleaded, "I haven't told this story to *anyone* since the courtroom trial. If you want to hear it, let me get through it the best I can. So please, no questions."

Michael held his hands up in surrender. "Go ahead."

"My former husband's name is Russell; I call him Russ. We met on our first day at Clark College, which is across the river in Vancouver. I've always been a science nerd and Clark College has a great Biological Sciences Associate Degree Program. We married right after graduation. Soon after, I got a job as a Lab Tech here in Portland.

"We were married five years before Jacob's birth, but we struggled. It started with petty jealousy… on my part. I sensed Russ had a thing for my younger sister Liz, and she played along. I thought it was a young girl teasing an older man thing.

"Someone murdered Liz three years after Russ and I married. The crime went unsolved for two years. The police arrested Russ a month before Jacob's birth; they charged him with my sister's murder.

"From the beginning, my father believed Russ killed Liz. But Russ had what appeared to be a rock-solid alibi, a Seahawks game. He claimed he was at the game and spent the night in a Seattle hotel with friends, and that's where I thought he was.

"Early in the investigation, the police questioned his friends. They insisted he was with them. One even showed the police a group photo taken in a Seattle tavern, and swore their server took the picture the night of the murder.

"The killer raped Liz and strangled her with such force it broke her neck. The forensic people had a rape kit performed, hoping to find a viable suspect.

"My father couldn't let go of his belief that Russ killed Liz.

"One evening, my dad watched a special on TV about DNA. The reporter discussed how DNA was becoming more prevalent in forensic police work.

"Dad followed up by doing research in the downtown Portland Library. After he felt comfortable with his research and the knowledge he'd gained—

"Michael… I'm sorry I'm spitting this story out rapid fire. But… it's like a bad taste I'm trying to get out of my mouth. It's hard for me to tell."

"Linda, as an attorney, I'm accustomed to hearing people communicate bad memories in this manner; you're doing great."

"I appreciate that, but I feel like I need a shower."

"I can't imagine the pain this memory brings."

She wiped the sides of her face with both hands and sighed. "Where was I… oh yeah… dad completed his research. He asked a lifelong friend, a Captain with the Portland Police Bureau, to meet him for lunch. Dad asked him for a favor.

"After hearing how Liz's unsolved murder, and his suspicions about Russ, were making Dad crazy, the Captain agreed to help. Dad told his friend there was only one way he could get past his suspicions: have the rape kit from Liz's murder investigation tested against a sample of Russ' DNA.

"The Captain agreed to take it forward. He received permission to run the test.

"Dad collected hair from the headrest of the driver's seat in Russ' car. He took Russ' toothbrush from our bathroom and cigarette butts from an ashtray on his workbench in our basement.

"The Oregon State Police Forensic Services Division found that Russ' DNA matched the evidence in the rape kit. Multnomah County Court issued a warrant for his arrest. They charged him with murder."

"Wow—" Michael inserted himself into the conversation.

She held up her right hand's index finger and cocked her head. "No interruptions, remember."

"Sorry, Linda, sometimes I can't help myself. I guess Jacob and I are alike. Maybe that's why I liked him."

Michael saw the corners of Linda's mouth raise.

She continued her story. "Throughout the trial, Russ maintained he didn't kill my sister. He admitted he and Liz were lovers until we got married. He claimed they ended the relationship a week before we married but rekindled it the night of Liz's murder.

"The prosecuting attorney questioned the Seattle Seahawks alibi Russ had used during the investigation.

"He told the court he *was* in Seattle that night. But it wasn't *the him* that was in Seattle that slept with Liz that night. The prosecuting attorney threw an astonished look to the jury.

"Russ claimed he traveled back in time to see if he could coax Liz into a one-night stand. He claimed the book gave him the ability to time travel.

"Now, as an attorney, you can imagine the looks on the faces of everyone in the courtroom. This time, the prosecuting attorney grimaced as he looked over at the jury, then moved in closer to Russ.

"He asked Russ to produce the book and show the court how it's used. Russ said he accidentally left it in Liz's bedroom and didn't know what became of it.

"The prosecuting attorney was having fun. He asked Russ to tell the court how 'the book' worked its magic.

"Russ explained how he stole the book from his grandmother Doris' house. It was in her attic, stored in a box along with other books and various items. His mother told him his grandmother found his grandfather, James, shot to death in their garage.

"When she found James, he was holding a book covered with his blood."

I suspected wine or blood.

"He took the box home and found the book inside. It was the blood-stained book his mother mentioned. He kept it and claimed he gave the rest of the box's contents to the Goodwill. Which, I couldn't imagine.

"Russ, taking time to make a trip to Goodwill, to make a charitable donation? Beyond belief.

"Anyway, Russ explained how he discovered the book's powers by chance."

I can relate to that.

"It took him two years to figure out how to use it. The prosecuting attorney asked Russ what 'use it' meant.

"Russ explained that the time he spent in the past related to how many pages he'd read. He first experienced time travel via the book after he'd read 22 pages.

"The defense attorney objected. He told the judge the prosecutor's line of questioning was neither necessary nor related to the trial. The judge denied the objection. He wanted to hear more.

"The prosecuting attorney asked, 'So, you got to page 22, and you showed up somewhere?' Russ explained that the first time it happened he was reading the book while sitting in his recliner. Without thought, he looked at a photograph on the coffee table; the next thing he knew he was *in* the photographed scene.

"The prosecuting attorney asked him if he considered traveling back to see if Oswald acted alone. At that point, Russ sensed that the attorney was playing with him.

"He became frustrated and told the prosecuting attorney he found he couldn't go back farther than his birthdate."

Answers my confusion over not being transported to Enos Slaughter's slide into home base. Long before my birth.

"The prosecuting attorney asked Russ what he did on his trips through time. He confessed he traveled back and committed theft and robbery. What he held onto, money, jewels, etc., came back with him."

Another piece of helpful information.

He wanted to jump in and ask what happened to the things Russell brought back, but Linda had warned him twice.

"Russ insisted he never committed murder or even hurt anyone.

"With dramatic astonishment, the prosecuting attorney looked at the jury.

'Stealing another person's money and property *doesn't hurt* them?'

"The defense attorney stood and objected that the prosecuting attorney's comment was badgering.

"The judge warned the prosecuting attorney.

"Without missing a beat, the prosecutor apologized. He turned and walked toward the jury. 'So... let's go back to something the defendant mentioned earlier. He had *sexual relations* with his sister-in-law.'

"He turned back to Russ. 'Mr. Curt... you stated earlier the night you went back, the night the *other you* was in Seattle, you had sex with your wife's sister. That was her 20th birthday, isn't that correct Mr. Curt?'

'Yes, that's correct.'

"The prosecuting attorney told Russ that a yes was sufficient. 'You stated earlier that you and your wife's *little* sister had sexual relations while you and your wife were dating. Up to, and until, you married Mrs. Curt. Isn't that correct?'

"Russ looked down. The prosecutor embarrassed him, but he hadn't picked up on where this was going. He answered, 'Yes.'

"The prosecutor asked, 'How many years did you and your wife's *little* sister engage in sexual activity before you married your wife?'

'I'd guess from about two months after I met Linda... until we married.'

'Mr. Curt, have you heard the term, age of consent?'

'Yes.'

'Then I'm sure you realize that the age of consent in Oregon is 18 years old.' He didn't give Russ time to answer the question. 'Now, let me understand this—your wife's sister Liz, died on the night of her twentieth birthday. That was three years after you and your wife married. And you had sexual relations with Liz for two years before you married. Isn't that correct?'

"Russ answered, 'Yes.' The prosecutor's point began to dawn on him.

"The prosecuting attorney walked over to his table, picked up a pad of paper and wrote as he walked back in front of Russ. 'So, if my math is correct, Liz—the *little* sister—was only 15 years old when you first had sexual relations with her. I'm wondering Mr. Curt, that night... did Liz threaten to tell your wife and her family you had sexual relations with her *multiple* times, when she was just a *child*?'

"The defense attorney jumped up and objected. The judge agreed and upheld the objection. Again, the prosecuting attorney apologized and stated he was only offering a motive for murder.

"Again, the defense attorney stood. 'Your Honor, please!' The judge gave the prosecutor another warning."

Shaken, and in tears, Linda paused. Michael placed his hand on top of hers. "Linda, do you need a break?"

"Yes. I need to get up and compose myself. Earlier, I said I've never told this story out loud. That last part was tough."

"I understand. While you do that, I'll get us another coffee."

"Thank you. It's clear I need to talk about this. I'll be right back."

"I'll be here."

14

As BTH approached the taxi, he slipped on a pair of thin leather gloves. He opened the back door and slid onto the seat.

The driver looked in the rearview mirror. "Where can I take you?"

"To the parking garage on SW Clay."

The driver pulled away from the curb. "You got it. Just get off the bus?"

"No, I parked in the garage earlier, and ran errands. A few minutes ago, I was hurrying back to my car and stepped off the curb across the street. I slipped on something and sprained my ankle. Man… it hurts. I'm afraid it's more than a sprain."

"Do you need me to take you to hospital?"

"No, I've called my doctor. She can fit me into her schedule if I get there within half an hour. Hey, your accent, where are you from, Europe?"

"Eastern Europe. Would you like to hear my story?"

"No, just probing." The cab driver looked in the rear-view mirror, head tilted, and his brow creased.

BTH did not notice. "I figured you're not from around here."

"No, a long way from here. I noticed limp as you approached, but I didn't want to ask and offend you."

"No offense taken. Is this your full-time job?

"Part-time. I work mostly at selling used cars."

"Do you find customers for the car lot's owner while doing this job?"

"I do. I can make a bargain because my uncle owns the lot. Well, here we are. Are you first level?"

"No, second level. If you take me to my car, there'll be more gratitude."

"OK, just guide me to the spot."

The driver pulled up and stopped at BTH's parking spot. "Hey, remember the van you sold to a white-haired guy a week or two ago.?"

"Oh yes, Joe was his name."

"That's right. The van's brakes *failed,* the *first time* he braked hard, now he's in the hospital."

In the rear-view mirror, BTH saw the driver's eyes widen. "Hey, I gave him good deal and told him we sold van as is, no guarantee."

BTH looked around; no one was in sight. "Joe wants me to show his appreciation," he attached a silencer to his pistol. "and *guarantee* you don't give anyone else one of your good deals."

* * *

Linda returned from the restroom composed and refreshed.

"Okay, where was I?"

"The judge gave the prosecuting attorney a warning for suggesting Liz threatened him that night."

"Oh, yes… the prosecuting attorney continued, asking him why and how he ended up at my parents' house on the night of the murder. Russ told the attorney we had a framed picture of Liz on our bookshelf, taken at her 20th birthday party. He remembered me discussing the picture.

"Michael, I'll never forget how Russ glanced back at me during the trial. The look never suggested he was apologetic. It was a look of guilt, like a child caught hitting his little sister for no reason.

"My parents were out of town the week of her birthday, and our friends had left. I picked up my camera to put it away, but noticed a great photo-op.

"It was a candid shot of her looking at her birthday cake." Linda smiled at the recollection. "The expression on Liz's face was, 'I can't believe we ate that much cake.' She was holding her hands out, with fingers spread." Linda added, "Liz never missed an opportunity to be dramatic.

"He knew he would appear behind me—and that everyone else had left—so he wasn't worried about being noticed.

88

"Liz's cell phone number was in his contact list, so he made sure he took his phone with him.

"Arriving behind me, he snuck up to Liz's bedroom, and after I left—"

Linda interrupted herself, "Doesn't this sound crazy, Michael?"

"It does," Michael said, as he pursed his lips and nodded. "Can we back up? What did you mean by, 'Russ knowing he would appear behind you'?"

She chuckled, and said, "I'll allow your interruption."

"And I have so many more—"

"I understand, but I need to keep going. Russ claimed he always appeared behind the photographer. He said, he never figured out why one time he'd be five feet behind the photographer, then the next time 100 feet behind them. But there was never a barrier separating them."

More useful information.

"You can imagine the courtroom scene. Anyway, Russ said he didn't want to scare Liz, so after I left, he called her phone. When she answered, he teased with her, telling her he had a birthday surprise for her upstairs; she ran up the stairs.

"Michael, his depravity is beyond comprehension. He knew the picture was one of the last photos taken of Liz alive, and that she died *that night*. Let's pretend he didn't kill her." Linda picked up her napkin and spoke through sobs. "But he traveled back, *knowing* she died that night. Who could do that?"

Michael reached across the table and again put his hand on hers. "Linda, that was unconscionable. I know I'm violating my agreement, again, but did he suggest he thought by being there it might save her?"

"No." She said, drying her eyes with her napkin.

"Okay, I didn't realize how raw my emotions still are after 13 years."

"And again," Michael said, "you're doing great."

Linda nodded her head while wiping her eyes. "Thank you."

"Russ said, after they had sex, he and Liz laid on her bed talking about her future. He was almost out of time. He told her he had to leave.

"In a rush, he dressed as he left her bedroom. When he reached the stairs, he claimed a warm wind transported him back to his future time.

"When he arrived back home, he realized he'd left the book on Liz's dresser. He again emphasized that my sister was very much alive when he left."

I can leave behind the book and I'll still return to my time.

"The Jury saw through his unbelievable story. They convicted him of murder and sent him to prison for life.

"Our family believed Russ was telling the time travel story hoping to make an insanity plea. Obviously, it didn't work.

"After they imprisoned Russ, I returned to school—The University of Portland's School of Nursing—I earned a BS in Nursing. I mentioned that I work as an RN at Legacy Emanuel Hospital. I don't think I told you I work in the Level I Trauma Center."

"No, you didn't... tough job."

"Yeah, it can wear you down."

Linda took a sip of coffee, then cradled it in her hands while staring into it. Michael sensed she was done. "But you had the book. Did you test it to find if it had the powers he claimed?"

She looked at him as if he'd asked the most ridiculous question possible.

"I have *no* interest in trying to help him. I told you what he testified. He had an affair with my *underage* sister... then killed her. He robbed and stole money, jewels and who knows what else, he is not a good man, Michael.

"Whatever you may find out or discover about the book, please keep it to yourself. I'm sorry, you may think I'm cold-hearted, but I have no love for Russ. None. I still believe he killed my sister."

"Linda, I understand. I am humbled and appreciate you sharing the story with me."

As they walked back to the house, Michael asked, "Linda, did you tape the book shut?"

"No, that's how I found it. My father died last year. I found the book while cleaning out his house before putting it on the market. He'd sealed it in a U-Haul storage box along with other books. I recognized it from Russ's courtroom testimony and sold it, along with other items from my dad's estate."

"When did you last meet with Russell?"

"The week before the yard sale. He'd asked me to bring Jacob to visit him. Russ hadn't seen him in six months, so I agreed."

"Did you tell him you found the book?"

"Yes. But looking back, I shouldn't have. I knew he'd tip over when he heard I planned to sell it, so I waited till the end of our visitation time.

"Russ pleaded with me to bring the book to him. I told him no; I wouldn't contribute to his crazy fantasy. As I predicted, he blew up. Guards came in and restrained him. With my arm around Jacob, we left while Russ screamed and cussed. I swore I'd never go back."

"Linda, why didn't you throw the book away?"

Startled, she stopped and looked at Michael. "Russ asked the same question. To be honest, to throw it away felt like I'd be agreeing that the book had powers. That I could rid the world of those powers by burying it in a landfill. I don't believe it does. I sold it as a regular, old interesting book, as I did the rest of my father's books."

Michael nodded. "I understand your logic."

They continued walking. "One last question, if I may. In your recount of the story you never mention your mother?"

Linda shook her head while looking at the sidewalk ahead. She looked back at Michael with her arms waist high and palms up. "What happened to her is a mystery to us. Two years after Liz died, we found out my mother had malaria.

"She'd been sick for a while but hadn't told us. By the time her doctor diagnosed malaria, it was too late.

"She wasn't a healthy person—heart issues and type 1 diabetes—the P falciparum strain of malaria was a death sentence for her. The doctors couldn't figure out how she contracted malaria."

"Tragic," Michael sympathized. "Is your mother's poor health condition the reason you stay fit?"

Linda went red. "You noticed. I *think* I appreciate that."

Michael realized the embarrassment he caused. "I apologize, Linda. I'm a man… it's in our DNA."

"Yes, it must be. But thank you, and yes, the results of my mother's poor health practices helped shape my health-related habits.

As they approached Linda's house, they stopped near Michael's car.

"Again, thank you for trusting me with your story. I promise I won't discuss the book again, unless you bring it up. But we must talk more about the white van." Michael teased. "*That's* not a taboo topic, is it?"

Linda laughed. "No, that we can discuss."

"Linda, can I ask a favor?

"Sure."

"After hearing your story, I'd love to see that picture of your sister."

"And, I'd love to show it to you, but I never got it back from the court. The prosecution used it as evidence. I suppose they used it to show the absurdity of Russ' claim. But there's another I took right after taking that photo. I put it in the empty frame. I can show you that one."

"Yes… *please.*"

"Okay, let's wind our way through the construction."

"Lead the way," Michael said, and followed her through the maze of construction materials and workers.

In her living room, they walked to a built-in maple bookshelf. She picked up the picture—looked at it for a few seconds—then handed it to him as tears came to her eyes. "Excuse me, I need a tissue."

Michael nodded and gave a gentle smile. She rushed away.

He pulled out his phone and took a picture of the photo. Linda rounded the corner, tissue in hand, as he was returning the phone to his pocket.

"She was a beautiful young lady."

"I know, and I miss her so much. I like this photo because it captures her joy and her playful spirit."

Michael looked at the photo again. "Her smile is infectious. Looks like she was enjoying the evening."

"She was. What you can't tell by looking at the photo is that she was telling me how much she loved me, and that she was glad we're sisters." Linda used the tissue again.

"Thank you for showing me the picture and telling me your story."

Linda only nodded and used the wadded-up tissue.

"Here's my business card. If you hear from the police or discover any related information, call me. Together, maybe we can answer this white van question."

She thanked him, then asked, "Do you have another card?"

He pulled out a card. "Sure."

Linda picked up a pen lying on a nearby table. "I'll give you my cell number. Please pass-on whatever *you* discover."

"I'll do that."

He moved to shake her hand and to his surprise, she hugged him. "Thank you, Michael."

She walked him back out.

As they approached his car, Michael said, "Okay, I lied... one more question."

Linda laughed, put a hand to her temple and shook her head. "Okay, what is it?"

"I'm an only child and had a father who was never there for me. That hurt. I'm sure it hurt other relationships. And, it caused resentment I've tried to bury."

"I can understand that."

"Linda, I liked Jacob. You have a smart son, everything points to him being a good kid. But, as you said, I can see how he'd be a challenge for a working single mom... or dad."

"You were listening."

"Yes, and maybe I can help."

"I like the sound of that. How?"

"I'm an avid golfer, played on my college team and love the game. Jacob's a thinker, so I believe he'll like the game. Would you allow me to take him to the driving range? I'll give him a few lessons. If he likes it and wants to continue, I'll coach him."

"Wow," Linda replied, "I believe he'd love that, and *I* can use an occasional break. What about the equipment he needs?"

"I have golf buddies; I'm sure we can put together what he needs. What's best, weeknights or weekends?"

"Weekends. On weeknights, homework is his priority."

"Done deal. I'll contact my friends. If I can come up with the equipment, he'll have his first lesson this weekend."

"You have my phone number. If you come up with the equipment call me. Jacob will be thrilled."

"Great, I'm excited to help him, and you."

"Here," Michael said, as he picked up the pen Linda placed back on the table, "let me write my cell number on the card I gave you."

Linda said, "Thanks."

As Michael was driving off, Linda lingered on the sidewalk. He put his arm out the window and waved. She waved back, and he headed to his apartment.

Inside his front door and about to hang up his jacket, he remembered the photos he'd selected from the box at his grandmother's house. He stuffed the book under his arm, removed the envelope from the jacket's pocket, and hung it in the hall closet.

He sat at the kitchen table, removed the three photos, and laid them out in front of him.

The first photo he considered, was one of him at a table with his teammates, eating pizza and being as cool as 12-year-old's can be. He studied the photo for friends other than Adam Norris, again, giving the victory sign behind Michael's head.

A face in the shadows caught his attention. He used a magnifying glass to check the face. It was the same man who was taking photos of his mother at the game. He was staring at her as she photographed the team eating pizza.

Michael wondered why he was standing in the shadows rather than hanging with the rest of the parents? He picked up the photo and the book. He was off on another adventure.

15

The warm, omnidirectional wind took Michael to a doorway leading from the pizza restaurant's main dining area, to a banquet room. He saw his mother's back as she was photographing him and his buddies demolishing pizzas and guzzling pitchers of soda. He set his timer for 1 hour and 54 minutes and slid the phone into his rear pocket.

The pizza restaurant had an old-school Italian ambiance. Red & black velour wallpaper on two walls, and Mediterranean style dark wood accents around the room. Someone had used corked empty wine bottles as part of the ceiling's décor.

Michael walked the banquet room's perimeter until he came to a small group of parents. They were standing, eating pizza, and talking while keeping a protective eye on their kids.

"Excuse me, my name is Michael. I provide security for the restaurant." They smiled and returned his greeting.

"I watch for odd behavior, or if there's someone who doesn't fit in with the rest of the group—"

A man jumped in. "Well, you caught me." The rest of the group laughed and agreed.

Michael laughed. "As the saying goes, it takes one to know one, or in this case five. I have a question for you. I won't point him out, but do you recognize the man standing in the emergency exit alcove to our left?"

"I don't," a woman said, "but I noticed him."

The rest agreed with her.

The woman looked at the man, then back to Michael. "And, I believe I've seen him at our baseball games."

"Thanks. Typically, these are non-issues. Most likely he's someone who's with the next group and arrived early. But I'll continue to watch him. Thanks for your help. I hope you enjoy your party."

While working his way around the room, Michael avoided being seen by his mother. He got within 10 feet of the stranger and pulled out his phone. To free his hands, he tucked the book under his left armpit. After Michael took a few shots, the stranger turned and looked at him. Michael turned to his left to give the impression he was taking photos of the entire room.

He glanced to his right. The stranger was staring at his phone with the same puzzled look he'd shown at the ball field. Michael continued scanning to the left.

He lowered his phone and worked his way to the opposite side of the room.

Michael sat at several tables making small talk, but always mindful of the stranger's movements. Several times, he spotted the stranger watching him.

The stranger caught on. He looked around, stroking the side of his face, while compressing his lips, then left in a rush.

Michael followed him at a distance until the stranger went out through the front door.

He squeezed between a window and a table nearby. "Excuse me, I thought I saw someone messing with my car." He watched the stranger get into a VW camper van.

The man at the table pointed to their pizza. "We have plenty, you might as well join us,"

They shared a nervous laugh.

"I appreciate that, but I ate."

Michael took a few photos as the stranger drove away.

There was an empty table against a wall. He sat, took the book from under his arm and placed it on the table.

Within seconds a server appeared. "Good afternoon, sir, something to drink?"

"No thank you, I'm with the group in the back. I need a few minutes of quiet."

"I understand. But here's a glass of water in case you get thirsty while taking your break."

"Thank you, I appreciate that."

"Would you like something to eat?"

"No, I'm not hungry enough to eat an entire pizza."

"That's ok, since you're with the group in the back, I'll bring you two slices at no charge. We have cheese, pepperoni, and combination pizza by the slice."

"Thank you. I'll take pepperoni."

"You got it. I'll be right back."

The server was back in less than a minute with two slices. "There you go, anything else?"

"No, this'll do it. Thank you."

As Michael ate the pizza, he opened photos and skimmed through the ones he'd just taken. There were four photos of the VW van. He enlarged the second one he took and found the license plate's numbers were readable.

"Excuse me." He looked up at the 30-something woman who'd told him she'd seen the stranger at their ball games. "I came out to find you. Can I sit?"

Michael put his phone in his pocket. "Sure, my name is Michael."

She shook Michael's hand. "Hi, I'm Jen."

He pointed to her t-shirt. "I see you're a supporter of the team."

"Yes, my husband and I own the business that sponsors the team."

"Good for you, Jen. I'm happy to meet people who give back to the community."

"Thank you. We enjoy it."

"What can I do for you?"

"I've been thinking about the man you pointed out. Looking back on this season, I've seen him taking pictures of Deb Mays several times, which struck me as odd.

"After you moved on to the next group, I watched him. It was obvious he was tracking Deb."

"Yeah, I noticed that too. I saw him leave and tried to catch him, but he left in a hurry."

"Kind of creepy if you ask me."

"Yes. I'll be watching for him."

"Me too."

Michael's phone alerted him.

Two minutes left.

He pulled two dollars out of his bookmark envelope and laid it on the table. "I'm sorry, Jen, but I have to go. I appreciate your concern *and* the information."

"Thank you, Michael. You should come to one of our games."

"I promise to do that. Do you mind if I take a photo of you? I'll tag it with your name. I'll look for you and your husband next season."

She struck a left-knee forward pose, while using both hands to stretch the t-shirt to show off her business's name. "That's the smallest camera I've ever seen."

"Isn't it great. They haven't released it yet, but I was able to get one."

"Hmm, never seen such a thing. I look forward to seeing you next season."

"Thanks, Jen. I'll be there."

Back in his apartment, Michael jotted notes and thoughts on what he'd learned from his trips back in time.

He wanted to spend the rest of Saturday exploring the book's ability to cause time travel, but he'd scheduled a 4 P.M. meeting on Monday with a potential client. He needs to decide whether he'll take the case.

The potential client is a Portland band named "Hauler." The members claim they wrote a song titled "Beaten Path," two years before it became a worldwide hit by an acclaimed band named "Jimi's Daze." Revenues from royalties were most likely in the six-figures.

Jimi's Daze lead singer/guitarist—Mac "Truck" Cailen—claims he wrote the song. He denies knowing the band Hauler, or ever seeing or hearing them.

Hauler heard that Truck Cailen was at one of their shows and stayed through their last set. The set began with "Beaten Path."

After his first meeting with the band's members, Michael agreed to look at the case.

Is there convincing evidence Cailen committed a crime? That's the question Michael must weigh. He told them he will decide, then discuss the decision at Monday's meeting.

He feels great about their integrity and believability. They have reputable jobs in the Portland area. Two high school teachers, a successful executive chef, a graphic designer with an upscale marketing firm, and a designer for Nike.

But we need better evidence.

Michael asked the band to look for photos taken of Cailen that night. An email to their fan mailing list produced one photo. It was Cailen, but the location was unclear. The photo showed Cailen sitting at a table talking with two young couples. But it could have been any club, anywhere.

Michael wanted to spend time exploring the book's abilities. It was a perfect opportunity.

His phone's timer was still set for 1 hour and 54 minutes.

Far more time than I'll need.

He opened the book to page 116 and looked at the photo.

The warm wind took him to a spot near the stage, behind a woman photographing Cailen.

He started the timer and found a vacant table near Cailen's.

A young woman in tight jeans, a Beatles tee shirt, and pink sandals approached him. "What can I get for you?"

"Do you have an IPA on tap?"

"We do." She flicked a coaster on the table. "Comin' up."

"Thanks, but before you leave, when does the next set start? The band's name is Hauler, right?"

She looked at her watch. "Yes, Hauler is the band's name and they'll be out for their last set in, fifteen minutes." Michael thanked her; she turned and left.

She was back within a minute, impressing Michael. He paid and tipped her. He leaned back, took a sip, trying to get a feel for Cailen.

Arrogant.

Cailen sat with his arms crossed. When a fan approached for an autograph, he let out a heavy sigh and avoided eye contact. While scribbling on whatever they handed him, he ignored them, checked his phone, and re-crossed his arms.

As Hauler walked on stage, Michael took out his phone and began videoing Cailen. Cailen watched Hauler, while listening to the people at his table.

The lead singer strapped on his guitar and walked to the microphone. "The first song in this set is one we put on our EP CD earlier this year." The audience knew the song. They stood and applauded.

"Thank you. It's a special song to us. I had the idea after my sister's boyfriend—" he took a deep breath— "beat her to death." He paused, watched his hand strum a chord, then wiped his eyes. "Still gets to me. Discussing it with the other guys in the band," he looked at his band mates, "we discovered that each of us know someone who is, or was in an abusive relationship, so we wrote it together."

"The song title, 'Beaten Path,' comes from a time I was trying to convince her to leave her boyfriend. As she turned to walk away, she said, 'It's the path I've chosen.' I never saw her alive again."

The keyboardist played a haunting, atmospheric intro. The lead singer sang while strumming his guitar.

> We all make choices[1]
> We don't *always* hear the voices of those who love us
> Whenever we met, we'd cry, but you'd run to avoid my hug
> Could I have loved you better, I've loved you your whole life
> Even when you shoved me aside...

---

[1] Beaten Path' © Dusty Rain Music – Hollis Oliver

The chorus built in intensity.

You chose a path, said it's the only path you knew
Rejecting all attempts I made to walk beside you
If I could go back I'd die, to block that dead-end path
Paved with hope that he would change, oh… but his truth was fists and lies
No matter how hard I tried, or how much I begged and cried
You stayed on… the beaten path

How did you make those choices?
I can't imagine the voices, you must have heard
But you were not hearing mine, did you even hear one word
Was there a way to say it clearer, oh… I tried
But no matter how hard I tried…

You chose a path, said it's the only path you knew
Rejecting all attempts I made to walk beside you
If I could go back I'd die, to block that dead-end path
Paved with hope that he would change, oh… but his truth was fists and lies
No matter how hard I tried, or how much I begged and cried
I lost you… on the beaten path

Let's stand opposed to those who choose to hurt the ones we love
Let's call them out… shout it out, oh… scream it out and raise a fuss
Try until we die… to block their beaten path

Don't choose the beaten path, it is not your only choice
I promise I will shine a light and always be your voice
Don't walk my sister's way, turn now and leave today
Your way is hoping he will change, oh… but his truth is fists and lies
No matter how hard you try, no matter how much you cry
He'll keep you on… the beaten path

The song was ending; Michael realized it had mesmerized him and he'd lost track of why he'd came. He hoped he'd kept his phone steady.

Truck Cailen held a small digital recorder. Michael looked at his phone's screen to assure Cailen was still on the screen.

He swung around to Hauler, then stood and walked 20 feet back from where he'd sat.

Panning the club, he included the bar, and zoomed in on areas that identified the club. Next, he aimed the phone at Cailen's back, making sure he included Hauler on-stage.

He walked closer to show it was Cailen who held the recorder.

The band finished the song. Everyone in the room stood and applauded. Most had tears in their eyes.

Michael swung back to Cailen, who was turning the recorder toward his face. He pushed two buttons, put the recorder to his ear, and smiled.

He looked up and saw Michael. "Get out of my face." Michael did not. He kept recording.

Truck set his recorder on the table and stood. Michael looked up. *This truck's an 18-wheeler.*

Cailen took a step forward with his elbows bent and his knuckles white from the skin being tightened over them. "I *said*, get out of my face." Again, Michael did not. The 18-wheeler slipped into gear and shoved Michael hard, knocking the phone from his hand as he slammed against the table in a booth behind him.

Two guys standing in front of the booth put out their arms, trying to lessen Michael's impact. Michael straightened up from the table. He walked back toward Cailen. The two guys grabbed him. One said, "Let this go dude, it's not worth the pain."

A young woman picked up his phone and handed it to him. "It's broken."

Michael looked at it. The impact shattered the screen and the phone would not turn on.

"Are you going to phone a friend?" Cailen taunted.

Michael raised his arm and showed Cailen his phone's broken screen. "If I wanted to, I couldn't. Mr. Cailen, you've bought yourself an assault charge and a lawsuit."

Cailen smiled crooked. "Oh, I suppose I'll be hearing from your attorney tomorrow, huh?"

"No, I am an attorney. It will be *me* drawing up the papers you'll receive."

Cailen's jeering stopped. "I'll tell you what, first, I'll buy you a beer." He lifted his backpack from the floor and put it on the table. He looked over at the pink sandaled server. She understood and hurried off to get Michael another IPA.

"How much will it cost to replace your phone?"

"Mr. Cailen," Michael's voice dripped with sarcasm. "I don't track iPhone prices. I don't have a clue." Michael was done with Cailen's arrogance and condescension.

A young man offered, "Last week I bought the latest model 64 gig iPhone for $750."

Truck pulled 15, $100 bills from his backpack. "Okay, here's 15 hundred bucks. Should cover a new phone and the time you'll spend getting it." He threw the bills on the table, picked up his recorder and backpack, and turned to walk out. "I'm done here."

"I'm not done, Mr. Cailen," Michael said.

Cailen turned. "What?"

"My time spent searching for a new phone is worth far more than that, so you're still getting sued."

Cailen returned to the table and pulled out 35, $100 bills and added them to the pile.

Michael said, "We're getting closer… but we're not there yet."

Cailen was fuming. He pulled out 20 more $100 bills and laid them down.

Michael picked up the money. "That'll do it." He turned his back on Cailen and returned to his table.

Cailen slammed his backpack over his shoulder and stormed out.

The band played an up-tempo song, which refocused the audience back to them.

One thought Michael considered as he sat, was the incongruity of Truck Cailen having a hit with that song. It was more likely he would be the one taking the woman down the beaten path.

Michael picked up his phone and pushed the power button for a few seconds. Still nothing, which meant no way of knowing how much time he had left. He stood and moved to an empty booth in a darker corner of the room. He placed a $100 bill on the table for the server, then sat listening to Hauler's music, while nursing the beer Cailen had bought him. All he could do was wait for the warm wind to take him home.

Back at the kitchen table, with the beer glass still in his hand, he believed his firm's IT people could salvage the video from his phone. He stood, walked to the sink and dumped the remaining beer down the drain. He set the glass in the sink, returned to the table, and plotted an action plan. Two things struck him as he reviewed notes from the first meeting with the members of Hauler:

They love their chosen careers and have no interest in becoming touring musicians.

They want to become more serious in their songwriting.

Their goal is to pitch songs to national and international artists.

Michael's goal was to recoup their rightful royalties and collect punitive damages. He would include his law firm's fees on top of the settlement.

Experience told him that Cailen's attorneys will settle out of court. It will not save Cailen money, but if his attorneys are smart and tough, they will convince him that, from a PR perspective, he will be way ahead.'

16

Monday, October 21st

Michael was sitting at his desk when he received the email from the IT people. They had attached the recovered Cailen video. He watched it and smiled.

We're on.

He walked out of his office and gave Trevor the go ahead to begin the lawsuit paperwork. He also asked him to call Hauler to confirm the 4 P.M. meeting.

As he walked back into his office, he recalled his conversation with the psychologist about the difference in their offices. He inherited the office from a former law firm partner who had died in a nursing home. Michael looked at the dark wood paneling that lined all the walls. The bookshelves blended with the paneling. The wood floor was a continuation of the theme and the color ran up onto his desk.

He decided it was time to redo his office.

Old school, gloomy and boring.

The Hauler band members arrived just ahead of the scheduled time. They walked in apprehensive, but by the end of the meeting they were elated.

On the way home that evening, Michael reflected on the meeting.

They don't realize what may be on the table.

Tuesday, October 22nd

While sitting at his desk discussing the Hauler lawsuit with Trevor, Michael's cell phone rang. The ID came up as Matt Hindler, the long-time friend from college he'd mentioned to the psychologist.

"Trevor, give me a minute."

"Sure." He stood and walked out.

"Matt, good to hear from you."

"Hey, Michael, you too, it's been too long. I received your email requesting youth golf clubs?"

Michael gave Matt a quick overview of Jacob and Linda's history. "Jacob's a smart, good-natured kid. Transitioning from a 12-year kid to a young man is tough. Maybe I can help him."

"Michael, I'll tell you what, MJ outgrew his clubs, after only *a year*. Crazy how fast he's growing. But they will serve Jacob well. Sounds like the kid and his mom could use a break. Is there something else in there that you're not telling me? Are you interested in the mom?"

"She *is* smart, beautiful, and down-to-earth, but I haven't got *there* yet; leave it to you to come up with it."

Matt laughed. "Yeah, well, when your primary practice is Divorce and Family Law you have a skewed perspective of life."

"That's a sad statement, isn't it?"

"You have no idea, Michael."

"Can I pick them up sometime this week?"

"How about this? I'll ask Carrie which evening this week works to have you over for dinner. We can catch up and you can take the clubs home with you."

"I'd love that, thanks... and tell Carrie hi for me and that I'm looking forward to seeing her... talk to you soon."

Michael called Trevor back in and told him what was going on with Jacob and his mom.

Trevor is a 25-year-old African American man, with the build of a long-distance runner. He's one inch short of six feet. His brown eyes convey he's hearing and tracking every word Michael speaks. He has an incredible grasp of nuance, and a work ethic that guarantees his success.

"Mr. Mays, I haven't mentioned this, but a single mom raised me."

"Tell me about that. I'm interested in hearing how she instilled such a great work ethic in you. And please, call me, Michael."

Trevor grinned. "I'll try, but I can't promise I will; my mother taught me well."

"I can relate to that, except it was my grandmother who taught me."

"My mother had high expectations and held me accountable for my studies *and* my time. She encouraged me and believed in me. She didn't allow me on the path many of my friends took. When I gave the Valedictory speech at my high school graduation, my main point revolved around my mother's influence."

Trevor graduated from the University of Washington with a degree in Criminal Justice and Criminology. His sights were on becoming an FBI agent and had one more year of night school to complete his law degree.

Michael wanted to jump in but held back.

Trevor told him his father had shot and killed an FBI agent. Several FBI agents struck up conversations with him during his father's trial. Their professionalism and kindness both surprised and impressed him. That's when he began pursuing a career with the FBI.

"Wow, Trevor… thanks for telling me your story, I'm interested in your progress. I'll be cheering for you. I'd love to see you work here, but I understand and respect your choice."

"Thanks, Mr. Mays."

Michael smiled, looked at him, and nodded his head. "We better get to work. Okay, where were we?" Michael looked at his notes. "The last thing is finish up the paperwork for the official notice of the Cailen lawsuit."

"I'm on it, Mr.… Michael."

As Trevor walked out, Beth, the law firm's receptionist, knocked and asked if Michael had a minute. "Sure, Beth."

"I received a strange call. A woman named Linda called and asked if you're an attorney here."

"I hope you told her yes."

She laughed. "I told her I've never heard of you... which you know... is me kidding right?"

"Right, Beth. Did Linda say why she's asking?"

"Yes. She's considering allowing you to spend time with her son. She wanted to make sure you're legitimate. I assured her your father married your mother before you were born. Which is me kidding—again—I'm sorry. Sometimes I can't help myself."

"And sometimes, it's good to add humor to our day. Thank you, Beth. Oh, her last name is Curt, right?

Beth looked at a pink piece of paper in her hand. "Yes. It's Curt, C-U-R-T, Linda Curt."

"Thanks."

"You are welcome."

Michael pulled out his iPhone, and the business card on which Linda had written her cell phone number. He created a new contact with her information, which caused him to pass her story through his head. What came out was an idea. "Trevor," he called via phone paging, "come back in please?"

"I'll be right there, Mr. Mays."

Trevor entered Michael's office. "Yes, Michael?"

"I want you to file a visitation application form with the Willamette State Penitentiary. The visitation will be with an inmate named Russell Curt... C-U-R-T."

"I'll get on it."

Michael's cell phone buzzed. It was Matt. "Hey, long time since we last spoke."

Matt Laughed. "How about dinner, at our house, Thursday evening?"

"You're on. What can I bring?"

"Carrie said to bring wine and crusty bread."

"Deal. Tell her, considering her culinary skills, she's selling herself way short, but I'll take it."

"Great, be here by six and bring your clubs."

"My clubs? Fall—shorter days—even though you live on a golf course, there's no way we can get more than two holes in after dinner."

"Michael, trust me, bring your clubs, the bread and wine."

"Okay, I'm trusting you, and I have my shopping list. I'll see you at six o'clock on Thursday—"

"Hold it, Michael." He could hear Carrie in the background.

"Michael, I told Carrie, Jacob and Linda's story; she wants them to come to dinner with you. MJ and I can present Jacob with the golf clubs, and Linda can share in the surprise. What do you think?"

"Great idea. I'll ask and get back to you."

"We're looking forward to seeing you, and meeting Linda and Jacob."

17

Thursday, October 25th

Michael arrived at the Hindlers' with his clubs, and his shopping assignment well-filled. Matt opened the door, but Carrie rushed through to give him a hug. "It's so good to see you, Michael."

She took the wine and bread and hurried off toward the kitchen. Michael called after her. "But not as good as seeing the wine and bread."

Without slowing, she looked back over her shoulder. "We all have priorities, Michael."

Carrie is an attorney. Michael recalled her once saying: "The kitchen is my favorite room in the house. After a full day of prosecuting bad guys, I can come home and lose myself in preparing a great meal."

Carrie is a Deputy District Attorney. She is likely to become the next Multnomah County District Attorney.

She bears a striking resemblance to actress Halle Berry. Michael doesn't say it, but he would prefer Carrie over Matt on a golf tournament team.

Matt gave Michael a hug. "Bring your clubs and follow me."

While Michael succeeded in golf at Lewis and Clark College, Matt was a gifted athlete in both track and football. Though not as tall as Michael, he was lean, strong, and fast. Running is still part of his daily routine. Carrie refers to him as her "Hot Chocolate."

As they neared the top of the stairs, he asked, "Do you remember that unfinished bonus room above our garage?"

"Yes. So, we'll play ping pong with our golf clubs?"

"Nope, the ping pong table is now in the garage," Matt said, with a laugh as he opened the door.

"No way." Michael paused in the doorway. "Matt, this may be the coolest man-cave I've ever seen... wow."

"I know. Isn't it incredible? But it's a *family*-cave. Carrie and MJ use it as much as I do."

At the far end of the room was 12-foot by 10-foot projection screen for the golf simulator. Theater-style curtains flanked it. "Wow, even leather sofas on both sides of the tee box."

"I can't express how fortunate we are. We appreciate it and use it every day, even for movie nights.

"Wow, I love it. So, where are we playing tonight?"

"How about Pebble Beach?"

Michael delivered a challenge. "After dinner, you're on, my friend."

Matt and Michael descended the stairs blustering about their ability to take each other to school on the golf course. A whiff of Italian food and bread warming in the oven, quickened their steps. They stopped when they realized Carrie and MJ were in the foyer talking with Linda and Jacob.

Michael raised his arm and sprung down the stairs. "Hi, Linda, hey, Jacob. I see you've met Carrie and MJ." He turned to Matt, who was on the last three steps, and motioned to him. "This is my good friend, Matt Hindler."

Matt walked over to Linda and gave her a hug. "Welcome, Linda." Then, turning to Jacob said, "Jacob, I'm so glad you and your mom could make it tonight." He shook Jacob's hand. "Let's go eat." Jacob high-fived Matt, and said, "yes."

Dinner was superb. Even more so was Matt, Carrie, and MJ meeting Linda and Jacob. They both fit in and the Hindlers welcomed them as friends.

Linda talked Carrie into allowing her to help clean up the kitchen. Jacob and MJ sat in a corner talking video games while Matt and Michael caught up in the family room.

After 20 minutes, Carrie walked in. "Okay men, we're ready. Where's this Pebble Beach match you promised us?"

Matt jumped up. "Follow me Jacob and MJ. Ladies don't forget to bring your favorite adult beverage."

As they entered the family-cave, Matt stopped everyone and pointed to his right, "Linda and Jacob, your team, I'm sorry, but the losing team, will sit on that sofa. Carrie and MJ, the winning team, is on that sofa. Carrie did you bring plenty of tissues for the losing team?"

Michael chimed in, "Matt, maybe you should have installed a floor drain beneath your team's sofa to catch the copious tears Team Hindler will shed by the end of the match."

Carrie laughed. "Some things never change do they, Michael?"

Michael looked at her, while shrugging his shoulders. "Longtime friends, we can't help ourselves."

She and Linda looked at each other, shaking their heads.

"Before we begin," Matt motioned Jacob and MJ to join them on the tee box.

"Jacob, golf is a great game. A wonderful sport. Our family thinks it's the perfect way to hang out with friends and family, while enjoying God's creation.

"Michael told us he talked with your mother and asked her if he could teach you how to play the game. I understand you agree. Is that correct?"

"Yes," said Jacob, as he looked at his mother for validation.

Matt turned to Linda. "And, Linda, is it true you've done a thorough background investigation and reference check, and gave Michael permission to indoctrinate Jacob into the world of golf?"

Almost spitting out a mid-sip of Chardonnay, Linda covered her mouth while laughing. "Yes—"

Matt picked up a golf bag from behind team Hindler's sofa, "Jacob... Carrie, MJ, and I want you to have this set of clubs. MJ used them for just over a year, but has grown to where he needed longer shafted clubs. He'll agree that they are excellent clubs with plenty of great golf shots in them."

Jacob gave a huge smile and accepted the clubs.

Matt looked at Michael. "Jacob, I haven't told Michael this yet, but we want you guys to use this family-cave golf simulator to practice, anytime you want."

Linda put her wine on a side table, got up, walked over and hugged Carrie, MJ and Matt. "Thank you."

Michael sensed he needed to get Linda and Jacob out of the spotlight. "Okay, tee it up buddy."

They had a great time playing the Pebble Beach Course. Contrary to the seating assignments, team Hindler suffered a humiliating loss.

After scheduling Jacob's first lesson, Linda and Jacob thanked Matt, Carrie, and MJ, and turned to say goodbye to Michael.

Michael's phone rang.

No caller ID.

He looked at Linda. "Don't leave yet, I have a call. I'll make it short." He stepped out onto the porch. "Michael here."

"Well, Michael—I didn't put you down with the van—but I will put you down."

"What, who is this? Put me down?"

"I'll do whatever it takes to get the book you bought at the yard sale. If you refuse, I'll get to you by first cutting a deadly path through your friends and family.

"If you haven't given me the book by then, as I said... no... let me make it clearer, I *will* kill you.

"Michael, I know where your girlfriend Stephanie lives, and where Granny lives, such a *lovely* old lady. I know where you are *tonight*. Don't be surprised when you find I know where *you* live. You *will* give me the book if you want these folks, including yourself, to live long and die of natural causes."

"You have the wrong number." Michael ended the call. He turned and walked back into the house.

Linda's brow wrinkled and she placed a hand on Michael's shoulder. "Michael, what's wrong?"

"Matt... Carrie, can Linda and I speak with the two of you?"

Matt said, "Sure. Let's go into the den. MJ, take Jacob upstairs. Explain the difference between each golf club and how they're used."

"Sure dad. Come on, Jacob."

In the den, Matt motioned for them to take a seat. "What's going on, Michael?"

"The phone call I just received was from the man who, Saturday before last, tried to kill me. Then, only 15 minutes later, destroyed Linda's yard sale—"

Carrie interrupted, while rubbing her forehead. "Wait... what are you talking about?"

Michael and Linda told the story, including appearances by the mysterious white-haired Joe.

Carrie looked intently at Michael and Linda while crossing her chest with one arm and placing the other hand on the side of her face. "You told us you met just last weekend. But the week before you met—within minutes—this man was *purposeful* in his attacks on both of you?"

Michael said, "I believe a book I bought at Linda's yard sale, is the connection between Linda, Jacob, me, and the man threatening us. I suspect there's a link between him, the book I bought, and Linda's husband."

Carrie looked down and shook her head in confusion.

"Carrie, let me tell you my story," Linda said, "it will help you understand why Michael suspects the connection."

Linda told Carrie and Matt an abbreviated version of the story she told Michael.

Carrie leaned forward, crossed her arms, and rested her elbows on her knees as she listened to the story. When Linda was done, Carrie placed her chin and cheek in the palm of her hand and shook her head. "Crazy story... wow." She looked at Michael. "Not much we can do with this."

"No," Michael said, "but I want you aware and watchful until we get a handle on this guy. Linda and I will let you know if we find out more about him."

Matt put his arm around Carrie. "Thanks for telling us your story, Linda.

And, Michael, thanks for the warning." Carrie agreed.

Linda stood. "Well, we better get going. MJ and Jacob have school tomorrow."

"Yes," Carrie responded, "we need to get MJ started in the process, He's an expert at drawing-out 'getting-ready-for-bed.'"

"Jacob isn't at the expert level yet, but he's aiming for it."

Linda called for Jacob, thanked, and hugged the Hindlers again. She turned to Michael. "Thank you. Jacob and I appreciate what you're doing for us." Both she and Jacob hugged him and said goodnight.

Michael thanked Matt, Carrie, and MJ for their kindness and hospitality, and for their offer to use the practice facility. Matt said, "So good to reconnect, Michael. See you soon."

"Yes, great to see you guys too. Goodnight, and please be watchful. The man is dangerous and said he knows where I am tonight."

"Thanks, we will be careful," Carrie said, as she looked at Matt.

18

~~

In his car, heading home, Michael reflected on how great the night was. Until the phone call.

Gwen and Michael often went out to dinner with Matt and Carrie, even vacationed together. After the divorce, life got in the way, and the friendship drifted apart.

I can journal: The relationship is back.

He parked his car and climbed the stairs to his apartment, golf bag over his shoulder. While climbing the last flight of stairs, he looked up and noticed his door was ajar.

His step stopped mid-air.

No sounds were coming from the apartment.

He lowered his foot and climbed the two remaining stairs.

A sound, like that of a keyring tossed onto a hard surface, stopped him.

Approaching his door, he stopped and listened. Nothing.

Michael removed his 5 iron from the golf bag.

He pushed the door open, slow.

What?

The sofa was upside down.

Books were thrown from the bookshelf.

Papers were scattered everywhere.

Everything was in disarray.

He put his golf bag on the entry floor and replaced the 5 iron.

A baseball bat he kept in a ceramic butter churn near the door would serve him better.

He raised the bat and began his search.

As he walked into his bedroom his peripheral vision caught movement to his left.

He turned while swinging the bat, slamming it against the right forearm of the weaselly guy who was charging him.

The weasel cried out, grabbed his arm, then bent over to dodge behind Michael.

He aimed for the front door while using his left arm to clutch his right arm against his stomach.

By the time Michael recovered from the swing, the weasel was on the second-floor landing.

Fast weasel.

Michael dialed 9-1-1, which he realized fell in the wrong order of decision-making.

While waiting for the police, Michael wandered around his apartment amazed at the havoc one weaselly guy could do. Other than dishes, there was little breakage. Still, clean up would be labor intensive.

He pulled out his cell phone. "Siri, call Linda Curt."

Linda laughed as she answered. "Michael, miss us already?"

"Well… I enjoyed tonight, so yes, I do. But that's not the reason I called. I arrived home tonight to find my apartment broken into and in shambles."

"Oh no. Are you okay?"

"I am, but the burglar isn't. I used my baseball bat to deliver a home run swing across his forearm. There's no doubt the bone broke. But he got past me and out the door before I could go after him."

"Wow, what can we do to help?"

"Nothing tonight. The police should be here soon. This leaves *no doubt* that we're targets; I needed to know that you guys are okay."

"We're fine, Michael. We're at the friend's house I mentioned. They're home, but I appreciate the heads-up. Take care; let me know if you need help."

"Will do. Thanks, Linda."

As he moved to hang up, Linda said, "Michael, didn't you say the man on the phone warned not to be surprised when you find he knows where you live?"

"Yes, but I didn't expect he'd hit me tonight."

"Well, he's serious."

"No doubt. Let's talk more tomorrow."

"I look forward to it."

"Goodnight. You and Jacob be careful. And I'll text Carrie to let her and Matt know."

"Good idea, Michael. Goodnight."

Michael sent the text and was wandering around surveying the damage when the Police arrived. "Mr. Mays, Portland Police."

He rushed to the front door, greeted them, and shook the hands of both officers.

He spread his arms wide. "You can see, I have a mess to clean up."

"You do," the female officer said.

Michael thought, *She's a gym rat.*

Small, but judging her physique, he didn't want to face her mad side.

They interviewed him and took his information. Michael knew the Portland Police Bureau could not put serious effort into break-ins. They said they'd put out word to hospitals asking them to report broken right forearms.

The gym rat asked a series of standard questions. One resonated with Michael, "Can you think of anything he might be looking for?"

Michael couldn't tell the truth without sounding crazy. "No, I don't keep cash, jewelry, guns, any of those types of things here."

Interview complete. Michael thanked them and they left. He locked both locks on the front door.

The Weasel must have picked the locks.

He remade his bed and leaned his baseball bat against the nightstand. The Officer's question stuck in his head, "Is there anything he might be looking for?"

He'd experienced the book's powers.

It's something a bad guy will hurt, even kill to get. I'm glad I kept the book with me.

It was in the front pocket of his golf bag

I need to find a better way to keep it close… and, talk with Linda's ex-husband.

Tomorrow morning he'll see if prison officials can speed up his application to visit Russell Curt.

* * *

Daniel answered his phone. "Daniel, it's me. I tore the guy's place apart. He ain't got the book."

"He has it. I guarantee it."

"Well—maybe—but it's not in the apartment. I tore it apart, and all I got was a busted arm."

Daniel snapped back. "What? Are you at a hospital?"

"No, but I need one. The pain is excruciating me."

Daniel shook his head. "How did you break your arm?" He left off the word, 'fool.'

"The dude came home when I was gettin' ready to leave. He's a big guy—"

Daniel cut in. "Everyone's bigger than you BTH, that's why you're good at what you do."

"Still, my only choice was to try knockin' him down. I tried, but he hit me hard with a baseball bat. He smacked my right arm, but I got past him and escaped."

"Do you think he knows your arm is broken?"

"Yeah, the bone snapped loud and he couldn't have missed me yellin' out in pain."

Daniel warned, "Don't go to a hospital in Portland. If he called the police, hospitals are on the alert for broken arms."

"I have to get this fixed."

"Okay, here's what you do, come up here—"

"But it *really* hurts, Daniel."

Daniel lost patience. "Man up, BTH. Stop and get a bag of ice to put on your arm. Once it's fixed, you can go back to Portland. I've got another job for you this weekend. I want you to pay Michael's girlfriend's parents a visit. Write this down."

"I can't, my right arm's busted."

Daniel gave a huff. "I think I've got this texting thing figured out, so I'll send their address to your phone. You need to get the girlfriend's contact information; come up with a story why. Her name is Stephanie Clark. Once you receive her contact information, call me. But for now, get up here."

19

Friday, October 25th

Prior to lunch, Trevor came into Michael's office. "Okay, you're approved to visit Mr. Curt under the professional visitor guidelines. Should I schedule a time?"

"Let's try for early next week. It's an hour's drive, and I'll need an hour with him."

"Will do. I'll get that posted on your calendar today."

That kid's good. I'd love to have him working here... as an attorney. Wonder what it will take to get him to stay?

At noon, Michael headed home to work on his apartment. He scheduled a 1PM appointment with a locksmith. An upgrade to his apartment's security was in order.

While cleaning, repairing, and bringing order back to his apartment, he received a text from Trevor. "*Russell Curt: 9 A.M. Tuesday, the 29th. I blocked out your entire morning.*

He texted back: *Great. Thanks.*

Michael continued to wrestle with the idea that someone wanted the book. More so, the book's powers.

But why would someone from the future want me dead?

Then he wondered, *Is the man from the future, who shot at me in the park, the man who tore my apartment apart last night?*

Does he kill me in the future to get the book?

That thought shook Michael. He sat on the end of his sofa and processed his adventures with the book, but one thought kept returning:

Who's the guy in the background at the Pizza restaurant and taking pictures of my mother at my little league games?

It hit him.

The man wasn't photographing for the team slide show. He was using a Polaroid camera.

Michael hadn't seen a Polaroid in years, but he knew they didn't use slide film.

He returned to the kitchen table to get the envelope containing the three photos he'd selected from the box at his Grandmother's house. They weren't there, so he looked to the floor. Flour and splotches of peanut butter were scattered over the kitchen and dining room floors, along with cookware, dishes, and silverware.

The peanut butter puzzled Michael and caused him to wonder if the Weasel fixed himself a sandwich. He imagined the weasel entertaining himself by flipping dollops of peanut butter on the floor while he ate. There's no way Michael would use the rest of the peanut butter in that jar. He threw it in the trash.

After stepping carefully and moving pots, pans, and assorted bakeware, he found the envelope on the floor.

Michael returned to the sofa and pulled the pictures from the envelope. The first one was the after-game pizza party. The next picture was of a young woman he didn't recognize.

He looked closer.

My mother's target wasn't the young woman; it was the man behind the young woman.

The man faced his mother and held a Polaroid camera, but he was looking to the right. Michael assumed he looked away after realizing he'd been busted.

He opened his briefcase, got the book, laid the photo on the end table, and opened the book to page 116.

Warm-wind and he was standing 15 feet behind his mother as she was taking the picture. He looked around and discovered he was standing in the

Oregon Museum of Science and Industry, better known as OMSI. His phone's timer was still set to 1 hour and 54 minutes from his last trip. He started the timer.

Michael didn't know if this was before the pizza party or afterwards. If after, the man with the Polaroid camera would recognize him. Shoving the book in his back waistband, he turned and walked away.

He came to a plexiglass enclosure that contained two sets of human lungs. He remembered seeing the display as a kid. Its impact on him stuck; Michael never smoked.

The use of human lungs had fascinated him. He remembered standing there, studying the extreme difference between a non-smoker's healthy set of lungs and those of a long-time smoker.

It more than fascinated him, it affected his life. He took a deeper than normal breath, then exhaled... slow.

Thank you, OMSI.

It occurred to him he was not in the new OMSI. It was the old OMSI, next to the Portland Zoo complex.

Much smaller than the current building.

He moved behind a display wall, finding a position that gave an unobstructed view of both his mother and the Polaroid man.

Michael's mother turned and walked toward a group of adults talking and watching their kids. The Polaroid man photographed her, then moved to another exhibit. The group smiled as they saw her walking toward them.

She joined them, and as the Polaroid man walked by, she said something to them. They shook their heads. Michael assumed they responded that they didn't recognize him. They continued watching him as he stopped in front of an exhibit.

One man broke from the group and walked toward him. Though Michael couldn't hear the conversation, the body language of both suggested it was confrontational.

Michael made his way to another exhibit wall 10 feet from the two men.

"You're kidding me," the Polaroid man growled back at the man who had confronted him. "I'm here minding my business—and a princess—flattering herself, thinks she's worth my time and attention? Get out of my face, old man."

"Listen," the old man said, "I've known her my whole life. She's never been one to flatter herself or make crazy assumptions. I'm telling you, stay away from my daughter."

"Well, *old* man," the Polaroid man mocked, "I'll go where I want, when I want to, and I don't have a problem with knocking an old man to the floor. So, get out of my face."

Michael caught the threat, but his mind was still back on, "my daughter." The old man was his grandfather.

He looked at the group. She was 30 years younger, but he recognized his grandmother. She was paying no attention to the men arguing. Her hand was on her daughter's shoulder, comforting her.

Where's my father?

Michael pulled out his phone and took a photo of his grandmother and mother.

He'd lost track of the conversation between his grandfather and the Polaroid man until the Polaroid man yelled. "I warned you, old man."

Michael looked over as the Polaroid man swung, hitting his grandfather in the face.

His grandfather fell.

The Polaroid man wasn't done.

He stepped toward the grandfather to kick him.

Michael shoved the phone into his back pocket and, in two running strides, covered the 10 feet separating him from the Polaroid man.

He tackled him.

The Polaroid man's camera flew from his hand, smashing on the linoleum.

As they hit the floor, the Polaroid man rolled out, stood and pulled a knife.

Michael jumped up, looked to his left and picked up an unused cordon stanchion.

Michael raised it as if it were an axe. "You sure you want to do this?"

The Polaroid man looked around at Michael's grandfather, his mother's group, and other visitors who heard the noise and had gathered.

Incensed, he took a step toward Michael, then thought better.

Turning and muttering expletives, he re-sheathed his knife, picked up the shattered camera, and walked away.

Michael looked at his grandfather, now standing with the group. His grandfather's nose was bleeding, his hair stuck out at odd angles, and he held his broken glasses.

A bystander asked, "Are you okay; should we call 9-1-1?"

"No, I'll be okay," his grandfather said, "just shook up and confused as to why he *attacked* me?"

Michael's grandmother and mother came alongside and put their arms around him. His grandmother was checking her husband's injuries.

Michael looked into his mother's eyes. She tilted her head and silently pronounced, "Michael?"

He wanted to make sure Polaroid man had left, but struggled to pull his eyes from his mother's. With a tender smile, he turned to follow the Polaroid man.

Michael caught up with the Polaroid man and watched as he left the building. He followed him through the parking lot until the man reached a VW van.

The same guy, in the same van.

The Polaroid man started his van, looked up and saw Michael watching him.

He glared at him; the same look he'd given Michael's grandfather.

This guy MUST be connected to white-haired Joe, or is he Joe?

Michael made his way back into OMSI. He looked at his phone's timer.

Ten minutes left.

He found his mother and grandparents. His twelve-year-old self had joined them.

Michael followed them at a distance as they walked out of OMSI and into the parking lot. Grief overwhelmed him as he watched them drive away.

They're only weeks away from our lives being devastated.

Because of the drama and excitement, Michael forgot about the book. He wiped his eyes and checked his waistband.

The book was not there.

He panicked and ran back into OMSI.

He continued running until he came the spot where he'd wrestled with the Polaroid man.

It was not on the floor.

He got on his hands and knees and began looking under exhibits.

A voice came from behind. "Are you looking for this?"

Michael turned to see a young woman holding the book. "Yes, thank you. Where did you find it?"

"My son and I were here when you stopped the man from attacking the older man. When you left, I walked over to see if I could help. There was nothing I could do, so I turned to get my son and leave. He was standing behind me, holding and looking at your book. I asked where he got it. He told me 'The man who jumped on the floor dropped it.' We were walking to the front desk to turn it in when my son said, 'There's the man,' as you ran past us. I knew where you were headed, so here we are."

Michael shook her hand. "Again, thank you." He got down on one knee. "And thank you—" He looked up at the mother.

"His name is, Lucas."

Michael smiled, nodded, then looked back at her son. "Thank you, Lucas. That's a nice Blazers warm-up jacket you're wearing. I bet you love it, don't you?"

"Yes, I got it for my seventh birthday."

"So, it's important to you… right?

Lucas nodded his head and looked at his mother, who was smiling.

"Lucas, in the same way your jacket's important to you, this book is important to me. Can I shake your hand?" Lucas smiled, looked to his mother again, then he nodded. Michael took Lucas' hand in his. "Thank you, Lucas."

Walking toward the exit, Michael turned and waved to Lucas and his mother. They waved back as he exited out into the parking lot.

While walking around in the parking lot to kill the remaining minutes, Michael resolved to buy a backpack.

He began rehearsing in his mind what his next move would be.

What he'd been hearing as background noise intensified as the VW bus downshifted and sped up behind him.

His senses came on-point.

He turned in time to jump aside.

Mid-jump, he felt the warm wind around him as the book transported him back to his living room.

He sat on the sofa trying to wrap his mind around what had just happened. There was only one explanation, the man in the past *is* white-haired Joe.

Michael's gut told him it's not about gaining the ability to experience history, it's about gaining the ability to change history.

20

BTH parked in front of the house and double checked the address.

Standing on the porch, he pushed the doorbell button while pumping two shots of breath spray.

The door opened. "Hi," a woman said, as she looked down with eyes squinted. "Can I help you?"

"Ma'am, are you Ms. Clark?"

"No... I'm sorry, she's not home."

"My name is Bob. I'm a friend of Michael Mays. I'm trying to get in touch with Stephanie."

"Oh. Why do you want to talk with Stephanie?"

"I'm here with bad news. Michael asked me to let Stephanie know."

"How can I help?"

"Michael's injured and wants me to get in touch with her to explain why she hasn't heard from him. Are you willing to confide Stephanie's contact information?"

Karen tilted her head and gazed at Bob for a few seconds, then looked at his cast. "Were you hurt in the same accident?"

"Yes, but my injury's nothing compared to Michael's. He cares for Stephanie extensively and wants her to comprehend."

Karen again tilted her head for a few seconds to consider Bob's comments. "I'm sure Stephanie would want me to help you. I'll be right back." She closed the door; the lock clicked.

After a few minutes, Karen opened the door and handed Bob a piece of paper. "Here's the information I have, including the name of the hotel where she stayed last week. But she's moved on and hasn't given us new information." Karen furrowed her brow. "I'm sorry, but what's your name again?"

"It's Bob."

"Bob, her cell phone number is on there, but she doesn't like interruptions while she's working; her phone is off far more than its on."

"Thank you, Mrs. Stephens, Michael will esteem this."

Karen paused again. "Please give Michael our best. Tell him he's in our thoughts and prayers."

"You have my vouch, thanks again."

Karen closed the door, placed her fingertips at her temple, while shaking her head.

While walking to his car, BTH called Daniel.

"What do you have for me, BTH?"

As BTH got into his car, wind caught a cheeseburger wrapper he'd stuffed next to his seatbelt, blowing it across the street. "Boss, I'm leaving the parents' house. The address you gave me was advantageous."

"What…? Never mind. Tell me how it went and please don't tell me you screwed it up."

"Screw it up?" he protested, "It was an Academy Award winning exhibition."

Daniel muttered, "I can't imagine which category, but you're making me wish this was a *silent* movie."

BTH ignored the comment and began describing his conversation with Mrs. Stephens.

"Tell me what you found out. Give me the abbreviated version."

"Boss, I've gotta process these things. So, let me convey it… okay?"

Daniel shook his head. "Get on with it."

As he began telling the story, Daniel interrupted. "You told her your *real name?*"

"Yeah, but she don't know it is."

"BTH—, never mind. Go ahead."

After he finished, BTH said, "It shook her up. That's how good my performance was, boss."

Daniel replied, "Don't break your other arm patting yourself on the back."

"Boss, I should have gone into legit sales—could have made a fortune."

"BTH, with a fortune, you'd be dead in a week."

BTH gave no response.

"Okay, I want you to head to the airport. I set up a flight for you on a private jet.

I'll text you the address and the number to call."

"Wow, boss, I'll be a jet-setter."

"For what this will cost me... you better be a Michael's girlfriend-getter."

"You can count on me, boss."

* * *

That someone wanted the book to change their history was a turning point for Michael.

The book gave him the means to investigate the crime, or crimes, white-haired Joe must have committed. And to uncover the past he wants to avoid.

Michael began brainstorming items he needs in order to spend time in the past. He first wrote: "80's clothing, but remembered the Fenway Park hot dog misfire. He wrote: 80's money, above the clothing need.

Of his options to get the money, VanPort Acres Horse Racetrack was the strongest.

On eBay, he found a 1982 photo of Jockey Gary Stevens. The photo was of him on a horse, being congratulated on his win at VanPort Acres.

That'll work.

He photographed the photo on the screen.

His plan was to travel back and stay for the race following Gary Stevens' win.

I'll note who won, who placed 2nd and who came in 3rd, and return to bet on those three horses.

Michael remembered two, 1953, $10 silver certificates stashed with his childhood coin collection in a box in his bedroom closet.

He researched and determined that by picking three horses on a trifecta ticket—and betting $20—he'd win $1,600, or more, depending on the odds the horses are given.

Finding his mother's murderer won his internal ethics wrestling match. He'd rectify the ethical issue later.

Near his bedroom closet, he found the opened coin collection box. The contents were spilled on his bedroom floor. The two $10 bills were still there.

The weasel must have been in a hurry.

He picked up the $10 bills and used them as a bookmark in the book.

My apartment will be here when I get back; I'm going to the races.

He opened Photos on his phone and found the photo of Gary Stephens.

Michael stood in VanPort Acres, looking at Gary Stephens sitting on the winning horse.

This will never cease to amaze me; even something as ordinary as a person being photographed on a horse.

He started his phone's timer and wandered off to mix with the trackside crowd. Kids were picking up the tickets that disappointed race fans were throwing to the ground. Michael imagined that in the children's minds they *knew* they'd find a ticket worth a fortune.

He saw people studying race programs. Some were making marks in them, others held them while heading for the ticket windows.

Watching the different activities, he overheard a group of men next to him bantering with one another.

Long-time friends.

He turned to the one closest to him. "Excuse me, first time here. Where do I find the race programs?"

The man answered, "You must have missed them when you came in, but you don't need one. I can show you a better way to pick your horse."

His friends laughed, one of them said, "Run away. Go get a program, a hot dog, a beer, anything to get you the heck away from being sucked into the Jimmy Feller School of Horse Race Betting."

Michael laughed. "Now I have to hear this. There's no way I can pass up

Jimmy's expert betting advice." Michael shook Jimmy's hand. "My name's Michael."

As his friends continued the taunting, Jimmy said, "Step over here into my classroom. Let these losers stew in their jealousy of my *superior* knowledge and skill."

One friend said, "*Jealous*? Michael, don't say we didn't warn you."

After walking 10 feet from Jimmy's friends, Michael asked, "How do you find time to study the Jockeys, the horses, and their stats?"

"I don't, I use peanut M&M's."

"What?"

"Like you said, who has time for the research? But I enjoy hanging out with my friends and watching these powerful animals run. We make a day of it. We joke with each other, as only good friends can do."

Michael smiled at the thought of spending time on a golf course with his buddies. "I can appreciate that."

"Okay, Michael, here's what I do: On my way to the track, I buy a big bag of Peanut M&M's. I only bet $2 on each race. Before going to the ticket window, I shake three M&M's out of my bag. I pick a horse and jockey whose silks… do you know what silks are?"

"I assume it's the jockey's clothing?"

"Right, I pick a jockey that has any combination of those colors. Then, while waiting in line to buy my ticket, I eat the three M&M's.

"I spend five hours here, eat 30 M&M's and bet $20 total. Plus, we make side bets among the five of us. I think I do as well as people who spend their lives researching statistics. Cheap entertainment."

"Here, you try it. Put out your hand." He shook three M&M's into Michael's hand.

"Okay, you have red, blue and yellow. Your priority is to make a perfect match, all three colors. White and black are wild; you can use them with any of the colors.

If you can't find a jockey to match your three colors, you try combinations of them with the wild black or wild white. If still no match, you blend colors. For instance, a jockey came out in red, white and green, that's your next choice. Your blue and yellow combine to make green, plus your red, and the wild white. That gives you a match for the red, white and green silks.

"Are you with me?"

"I think so. Let's say a jockey comes out with white, blue, and orange silks, and I have no match with the other jockeys. He's my bet."

"Okay… explain it."

"I have no perfect match and no combination match, even with my white and black wild colors. I'll use my blue, and blend my red and yellow, which gives me orange. Adding my wild white, I have a match with the Jockey's white, blue, and orange silks."

Jimmy cocked his head and looked at Michael. He grabbed him by the elbow and led him back to his group of friends.

As they approach, Jimmy called out, "Gentlemen, may I have your attention please. Our new friend, Michael, graduated with honors from the Jimmy Feller School of Horse Race Betting. I want each of you to give him two dollars as a graduation present. He'll use your gift—and the education *I* gave him—to bet on the next race."

Jimmy's four friends whined, but he persisted until they each handed Michael two $1 bills.

Michael had to hang around until the end of the next race, so he said, "Okay, if I win, beers around, on me." That turned their whining into cheering.

Jimmy shook out three M&M's into Michael's hand, yellow, blue, and red. Michael used his two wild colors and came up with a match. While waiting in the ticket window line, he ate the three M&M's.

Tickets in hand, Michael returned to stand with Jimmy and his friends. Without missing a beat, Jimmy's friends ridiculed Michael's choice to win. At the end of the race—even though they cheered against him for all they were worth—Michael's horse won.

Jimmy boasted of his superior method, while his friends called out their beer orders.

Michael cashed in his four winning tickets, bought six beers, then stood enjoying a beer in the company of five new friends. He checked his time. He turned and removed his phone, shielding it as best he could with the book.

Thirty-three minutes left.

"Michael," Jimmy said, "I've never seen someone carrying a book here. Did you bring it, or did you find it?"

"This is my first time here. My intention was to hang out and people-watch while reading, but I got sidetracked by the Jimmy Feller School of Horse Race Betting."

Jimmy placed his hand on Michael's shoulder. "You didn't get sidetracked, you got educated. We're here most Saturdays; you're welcome to join us, anytime. And you won't need to bring a book."

Michael thanked Jimmy for the lesson, and his friends for their *encouragement.*

One of them said, "Well, I guess that's not one of our strengths." The others laughed and agreed.

"Gentlemen, I've had fun, thank you. But I must find a restroom and head home."

"Good to meet you, Michael. Come back, join us again." Jimmy said and pointed him in the general direction of the restroom.

After using the restroom, he wandered around the track, then climbed the stairs to the highest point in stadium seating area. He sat a few rows from the top, took two photos, and waited.

At the end of the race he walked to the reader board and photographed the first, second, and third place winners.

Back from VanPort Acres, Michael walked to the kitchen and found a small mailing envelope. He placed his racetrack winnings, along with the two $10 bills, in the envelope.

New bookmark, and I didn't have to use my money. Okay, no one else will clean up this mess.

A half-hour into his task, his phone rang. Linda's name was on the screen. "Hey, Linda, what's going on?"

"Hi, Michael. Jacob got home from school and asked if I'd heard anything new about the guy who broke into your apartment. Since I hadn't, I'm calling to get an update."

"Nothing new, but my case is a low priority for the police. I'm here cleaning and arranging, bringing order to this mess."

"Hold on a sec." Michael could tell she'd muted her phone. "Jacob and I are free. We want to come over and help. I'll even spring for a pizza delivery."

"Wow, I'd love your help, and pizza sounds fantastic."

"Text me your address. We'll be over soon."

The three of them made tremendous progress getting Michael's apartment cleaned and in order. They worked up a hunger and devoured the pizza.

"Jacob, you're a hard worker. I'm impressed."

Jacob leaned and picked up the last piece of pizza. "I guess I get it from my mom. She's a hard-working, single mom, you know."

Linda laughed. "You need new material, Jacob." She gave him a shove. He pretended to be on the brink of falling off the sofa. His eyes opened wide; he cradled the pizza with both hands. "Whoa."

"With that," Linda said, "it's time to get back to work." Michael agreed. Jacob gobbled up the pizza.

They finished around 9 P.M. As Linda and Jacob were getting ready to leave, Michael said, "Jacob, I'll pick you up at 9 A.M. for your first golf lesson. I'm looking forward to it."

"Me too. I've been checking out golf videos on YouTube. I think I'll like golf."

"Great. I believe you will. Thank you both so much for the help, the pizza, and the company. I enjoyed it."

"Me too, Michael. We'll see you in the morning." She gave him a hug.

As she was turning to leave, Michael said, "Linda."

"Yes?"

"The person responsible for this, I don't think he knows about our friendship, yet. But please, keep an eye out for things that look iffy."

She turned and hugged him again. "We will. Thank you."

21

Saturday, October 26th

Michael arrived at Linda and Jacob's temporary home. Linda greeted him at the door, with Jacob close behind with his golf bag slung over his shoulder like a pro.

Jacob smiled and put out his hand. "Hey, Michael."

"Good morning, Jacob. Here, let me take those. I'll put them in the car with mine."

"Ok, I'll run up and get the rest of my stuff."

Linda swatted Jacob's butt as he ran up the stairs, then turned to Michael. Jacob yelled, "Child abuse!"

Linda looked at Michael and shrugged her shoulders. "I'll walk out with you, Michael."

"Thanks again for helping and feeding me last night."

"You're welcome. Jacob and I had a great time. At least... that's what he told me ten times or more before we got home."

"Did you agree with him?"

"Every time."

"I had a great time too, and I look forward to more." Linda turned her head toward him and smiled.

"Okay," Michael said, "on to a different subject. Are you okay with me buying something for Jacob?"

Linda lowered her head and squinted. "Well, that depends on what you want to buy him?"

"Nothing dangerous."

"Thank you, but as a nurse, I need clarification on your interpretation of dangerous." Linda tilted her head and gave Michael a look he thought only his grandmother could give, then said, "*Far* more men are treated in our trauma center than women. Men who didn't consider their activities dangerous, until too late."

"So, a homemade-pipe-bomb kit, or a set of throwing knives are out of the question?"

Linda gave him the look again. "I hope they were never *in* the question."

"Hard-working, single moms are tough."

"It's part of the job description."

Michael said, "Okay, change of plans." Linda elbowed him.

Michael put his hand on his side, stopped and turned toward Linda. "I hadn't realized how *abusive* you are."

Linda raised and spread her hands. "Only to 12-year old's, Michael."

"Verbally abusive too," Michael said, as he placed Jacob's golf bag in the rear. "Back to my question," Michael picked up two items from the car's rear floor." Golfers need golf shoes..." he held up one of his shoes, then lifted the other hand, "and a golf glove. I want to stop by a sports store and get him equipped."

Linda reached out and touched the polyurethane spikes on the golf shoe. "Well, I don't want him embarrassed because he slipped and fell or blistered his hands. What kind of a mother would allow that to happen?"

"Not a hard-working, single mom trying to protect her only son."

Linda slugged his shoulder.

Michael rubbed his shoulder. "You and Carrie both... hitting me. Do I come across as someone who needs to, *repeatedly*, have the crap beat out of them?"

"Maybe it's because you invite it... or... you're like my old flashlight. Sometimes I had to hit it a few times to make the light come on."

Michael winced. "Wow, I'll take Jacob to the bar to drown our insecurities, coffee bar that is. It's a medical fact that chocolate croissants help diminish pain, both physical and psychological."

Linda put her fingertips to her tightened lips. "I think I did read that in a medical journal. Back to your question, I'm fine with you outfitting Jacob. Thank you."

"My pleasure, he's a great kid. Turned out good for being raised by a hard-working... ow." She slugged his shoulder again.

Michael rubbed his shoulder. "I don't know if I can swing my clubs today."

Jacob came running up, "I'm ready."

"Okay, jump in the car. Let's get outta here before I have to get a restraining order against your mother."

Linda laughed, waved goodbye, and called out, "I'll see you guys in a few hours."

Inside the car, Jacob looked around while running his hand across the dash. "This is a cool car, Michael. Mini Cooper?"

"Thanks. Yes, it's called a 'John Cooper Works Clubman.' Fun to drive and easy to park in downtown spaces."

"Cool, Michael."

Jacob and Michael walked into The Coffee Shop. Jacob found a table while Michael placed their order. Walking toward the table, Michael's phone buzzed. The screen read "No Caller ID."

"Jacob," Michael said, as he walked past the table, "I paid for our order and put it under your name." He held up his phone. "I have a call coming in?"

"Sure, Michael."

"This is Michael."

"Michael Mays?"

"Yes."

"How much do you care for Stephanie?"

"Who is this?"

"You've forgotten me? We had a nice conversation Thursday evening. That hurts, Michael. And we were becoming such good friends. I assume our conversation was accidentally cut off that evening. But I'm wondering, how much do you care for Stephanie? You need to decide how much, or what, you'd give to save her life."

"Okay, that's enough, I'm hanging—" the caller ended the call before Michael pushed the button.

He stood outside the Coffee Shop staring at his phone.

Jacob opened the door and stepped out. "Michael, are you okay?"

"Yeah, I'm fine. A confusing call."

"I got our order. It's on the table."

"Okay, I'm ready to *attack* it." Michael knew in his gut the voice on the other end was white-haired Joe, AKA, his mother's stalker. And the decision he wants is for Michael to give him the book.

He was trying to get into my head, it worked, he's there. More so, Stephanie's there.

* * *

"Hi mom, it's Jacob."

"Jacob, are you okay... where are you, are you still playing golf?"

"I'm fine, mom. We're at the Hindler's house. We finished my first lesson and MJ asked if I could stay for a couple of hours to play a new video game. Michael said, it's your call, not his. Can I... please mom?"

"Well, I'm okay with it if MJ's parents are."

"They are. Michael wants to talk to you."

"All right. But first, how did your day go?"

"It was great. Michael bought me new shoes, a glove and a towel to hang on the side of my golf bag. It's for cleaning my golf balls and clubs."

"How did you play?"

"Oh, I didn't, Michael taught me about the game, the rules, and how you strategize stuff as we followed Matt, Carrie, and MJ. We were behind them in a golf cart for nine holes and watched them play. They gave me a waterproof notebook and pen to take notes."

"Did you take notes?"

Jacob responded in a patronizing tone, "Yes, mom, I took lots of notes,

I'll explain them to you when I get home."

"Did you eat?" Linda asked, having fun at Jacob's expense.

"Yes, mom. Matt and Carrie bought us all cheeseburgers and fries at the golf course—I should go, mom—MJ's waiting."

"I'll pick you up in two hours. Love you."

"Love you too, mom. Here's Michael. Later."

"Hey, Linda, are you sure you're okay with this?"

"I'm fine. Took me by surprise. I'm glad you guys had fun."

"We did. Jacob's been great. Linda, I need to talk with you, not about Jacob."

Linda exaggerated exhaling. "Had me worried for a moment."

"No, like I said, he's great. I can come and pick you up or, if you'd prefer, meet you at The Coffee Shop?"

"The Coffee Shop sounds good. I'll meet you there. When do you want to meet?"

"If you're ready now, I'll say goodbye to Matt and Carrie and head that way."

"I'll be ready to leave in five minutes."

22

Michael arrived first, used the restroom to wash up, and found a table as Linda arrived. She spotted Michael, smiled, walked to the table, and gave him a hug. "What can I get you, Linda?"

"Coffee's fine. You had your chocolate croissant this morning, didn't you?"

"Yes, but I better get us each one. I won't be able to concentrate if I'm coveting your croissant."

They ate their croissants and sipped coffee while Michael answered questions about their day on the golf course. Linda finished her croissant and wiped her hands and mouth. "Okay, you invited me here, what's on your mind?"

"Well, I wanted to tell you something that I don't want you hearing second hand,"

"Okay…" she said, drawing out the word and looking at Michael with her head tilted and eyebrows lowered.

"I'm meeting with your husband next Tuesday morning—"

"What! Why in the world would you meet with *him*?"

"Let me explain. I hope my logic will make sense to you."

Shaking her head, she again drew out the word, "Okay," not liking Michael's idea.

"It's been spinning in my mind, trying to fit the pieces of this puzzle together. Why does the white-haired guy, in the white van, want to harm us? Now, here's the crazy thing, he's escalating the threats he made Thursday night."

"What do you mean?"

"This morning, after Jacob and I arrived here and placed our order, my phone rang. The voice on the other end asked what I'd give to save Stephanie?"

"Who is Stephanie? Have I met her?"

"No, she's a friend who has a routine like mine. Whenever she's in town, she has coffee here on Saturday morning. Over time we've struck up a friendship, never dated, but we catch up and talk photography, she's a professional photographer."

Michael described their encounter with the white-haired man.

"Are you with me so far?"

"Yes," Linda said, "so you're convinced the white-haired man is the guy in the van?"

"I am, and here's the thing, he introduced himself to us as Joe. The Monday before your yard sale, a white-haired man visited my grandmother and introduced himself as Joe. I don't understand how he knew who she is or where she lives. She invited him into her house, can you imagine doing that?"

"No. Not something I'd recommend."

"She means well, and she's meant well for 90 years. She promised not to do that again."

"She doesn't realize his capabilities."

"No, she doesn't. So, we have this white-haired Joe showing up, asking my grandmother questions—keep in mind—this was earlier in the same week someone attacked us.

"Then, we have white-haired Joe in The Coffee Shop asking for directions and eavesdropping. Next, he was at the record store I frequent. We talked for a few minutes and he left. The record store clerk told me he was in the store earlier that week asking questions about me. Minutes later, I was rolling on the ground after being hit by the van. A few minutes after that, a white-haired man was seen limping away from the van that crashed into your house.

"Then today, I received a call asking me what I'd give to save Stephanie's life? Do you recall me saying our only things in common are the yard sale and the book?"

"Yes, but—"

"Hold on, let me lay this out."

"Go ahead."

"Let's assume the book is the motivator, whether the story Russell told is true or not. If he told *his* story to someone in prison, and they believed him, what would a criminal do to gain a book that could change his past?"

Linda turned her head slightly, her lips parted while staring at Michael.

"I know this is hard for you, Linda, but I cannot come up with any other motivation for what's happened to us. That's why I'm meeting with Russell. I'll ask him if he told his story to anyone else? If so, did they show interest beyond what he expected."

Linda raised both hands shoulder high. "Michael, that triggered a memory. I can't believe I forgot this."

She told him about the small man who threatened Jacob on the afternoon of the yard sale.

"Michael... he had a cast on his right arm."

"It was the weasely guy who broke into my apartment." Michael put his chin in his hand. "Why does he want the book?" Before she could answer, "Because of the powers he's convinced it has. Are you seeing what I'm seeing?"

"*Yes*. The little man asked Jacob about the book, by its title. Maybe I've been in denial. It is so *farfetched*, that I don't want to believe it. Please tell me you haven't tried the book."

"Linda, I promised I wouldn't discuss the book. I think it's best we stay on that track. Again, the reason I'm telling you, is so you don't hear second hand that Russell and I met."

"And I appreciate that, but I have so many things running through my mind right now and, it frightens me, and it brings on anxiety."

"I understand being frightened. Why are you anxious?"

"The way you answered my question tells me you *have* tried using the book, and that it worked. And, if it worked, Russell is innocent of murder and the real killer is out there, living in freedom with no ramifications for what he did to my sister."

"Linda, please allow me to play this out. I'm good at what I do. I'll meet with Russell to find out if he can identify someone who fits white-haired Joe's description."

"Michael be careful. As I've told you before, Russ is not a good person. He'll lie to you if it serves his purpose and he'll use *you* to his advantage."

"I appreciate the warning. Do you want me to keep you updated, or keep it to myself until I find something concrete?"

"I'll wait."

"Alright. I will *never* intentionally harm my friendship with you and Jacob. I love our time together, and the friendship we're developing."

"We do too."

Michael put his hands over hers. "We can do this, together, okay? What I'm asking is for you and Jacob to trust that my goal is to stop this guy, not to harm you."

"We believe that, Michael."

"Thank you. Okay, do you want me to pick up Jacob and bring him home?"

"No, I'll do that. I want to see if Carrie has a few minutes to chat. I liked her and I want to develop that relationship."

"That is an excellent choice."

Michael gave her Carrie's cell phone number and started to say goodbye. She pulled him to her and hugged him tight. "Thank you for being our friend."

"It is my pleasure."

Michael went home to catch up on work. The Hauler case was at the top of his list. He called the lead guitarist/lead singer to check-in.

"Hey, Ian, Michael Mays. I hope it's okay to call you on a Saturday. How are you?"

"No problem, Michael. I'm doing well. What's the latest?"

"We've sent Cailen's Los Angeles based attorney our intent to sue for damages. I expect she'll get back to us soon. She's most likely an excellent attorney and will understand the seriousness of our claims. She'll want to make this go away.

"When they see the video we've uncovered, they'll become queasy. I believe there will be an offer to settle that day. In our notice, we prepared them by mentioning we will seek $2.5 million in royalty recovery, plus punitive damages. On top of that legal fees, which will be equal to 25% of the monies awarded to the band. The total we presented to them is $3.125 million. Who knows what a jury will do with punitive damages?

"Cailen's attorneys will counter with $1,000,000, or more likely, far less."

Michael heard Ian whisper. "Unbelievable."

"That's when I review the issues. Mr. Cailen will repeat that he's never seen Hauler. He'll claim you're the ones trying to take credit for a song *he* wrote. Then, well, it should be interesting."

"Wow. My band mates and I haven't thought in terms of millions. What we were hoping for is our song... to be our song."

"Ian, Truck Cailen has taken in a fortune from that song. To make it your song, you deserve recognition as the songwriters, and to receive the royalties due to you."

"I'm overwhelmed, Michael. Let's get the meeting scheduled and move forward."

"I'll work to get one scheduled within the next two weeks."

"Thanks, I'm looking forward to hearing from you soon."

"Thank you for trusting me to represent you. I'll keep you updated."

Michael spent the rest of the afternoon planning his Tuesday meeting with Russell Curt. He outlined his questions. His primary goal: Get Russell to identify white-haired Joe.

* * *

"Daniel here."

"Boss, it's Bob."

"Have you found the girlfriend?

BTH answered with a tone suggesting, 'you expected less?' "*Yeah*, boss. They must pay her well. This is a swanky joint. I followed her to her floor, then hung back. I pretended like I was fumbling with my room's keycard, a few doors from where she discontinued."

Daniel shook his head, again. "Okay, hang around. I want you to take a picture of her and send it to me. I'm going to text it to Michael to prove we have her in our sights—no forget that, never mind. If I'm right, he could use that photo to travel to her hotel—I'd be helping him rescue her."

"What?" BTH responded with disbelief. "Use a photo to travel to her hotel... *boss*?"

"Just do as I say. I'll fill you in later. Keep track of her until I get back to you with instructions. Do *nothing* till I tell you."

"Okay, boss, you got it. Hey, it'll be way easier for me to stay on top of her whereabouts if I get a room in this joint. What do you think?"

"Yeah, fine, but don't go to the bar. I need you clear-headed."

"Thanks, boss. You can trust me."

* * *

That night, while eating Chinese takeout, Michael pondered the craziness that's become his life. His reflection began with the morning he stopped at Linda's yard sale. It seemed like years, not weeks, since his life went from planned, even methodical, to chaotic. He sensed it would never return to what it was.

Okay, enough of that. Time to get the Trifecta money.

23

Michael materialized in the top section of the racetrack viewing stands. He was sitting in the same seat, still holding his phone in the photo taking position.

This answered whether a photo taken on his phone works. And, he discovered he replaces himself—the photographer—when he returns.

Michael stood and walked down the stairs to ground level while considering the book's powers.

Is it a new event, or only from the photo forward?

He made his way through crowds of people studying race programs, and couples arguing over which horse was the best bet. While looking to his right and considering the crowd, a man studying his race program ran into Michael from the left. Ashes from the man's cigar fell on Michael's shirt. Not knowing if the ash was hot, Michael brushed them off quick, hitting the man's cigar. It fell to the ground. The man glared and his jaw muscles flexed. "*Hey*, watch what you're doing."

Michael stepped on the cigar. "Me, watch what *I'm* doing? That thing's too dangerous for you to carry around. Think beyond yourself and your race program."

The man stood looking up at Michael, now clenching his fists and his jaw. He spit near Michael's feet, looked back up, mumbled and walked away.

Michael shook his head and walked to the betting lines. As he waited in line, he found the photo he'd taken of the 1st, 2nd and 3rd place horses.

The three horses Michael bet on, crossed the finish line in the succession.

A person could become wealthy using this book… crazy.

Michael toyed with the notion that wealth could be white-haired Joe's motivation.

May be a connection, but I'd bet on him wanting to change history.

He collected his winnings, which were more than he'd expected. The ticket lady said, "Four tickets with a long shot for your 1st place pick… you better keep buying, today's your lucky day."

"It seems so; I may stop on the way home and buy a lottery ticket."

She removed her glasses and nodded. "That's what I'd do."

A voice came from behind. "*Mister*, you got your money. Kiss her and move on."

Michael turned to see a short woman in her 70s, 50 pounds overweight, with a cigarette hanging from her mouth. He feared her spandex pants might explode if she took one more bite of the hot dog gripped in her hand. She flung her head back. Smoke escaped her mouth as she spoke. "See the line behind me? Move it."

He looked at the line, started to respond, but turned back to the ticket lady. "I'll take one ticket on each horse in the next race, please."

She put her glasses back on, smiled and, in no hurry, punched in numbers for each horse and took the money one ticket at a time.

Michael thanked her, checked his timer and turned to the woman behind him. "Looks like you're up."

She moved forward while muttering smoke clouded expletives.

Plenty of time for one more round with my new friends—unless it's a new event—they may not be my friends… yet.

He headed to the concession counter.

The five friends stood in a circle. The friend facing Michael looked up and yelled: "Michael." They turned to look, and another friend yelled: "Beer."

It's a new event from the moment I take the picture.

Jimmy put his arm around Michael's shoulders. "Michael, I thought you left us?"

Michael continued to pass out cups of beer. "Well, I knew you'd miss me, so I'm back."

Jimmy shook Michael's shoulder as if he was shaking his hand, slopping both of their beers. "Glad you are."

The four friends picked upped where they left off and jabbed Michael about listening to Jimmy. Michael held up his cup. "Well guys, the proof of Jimmy's method working is in our hands."

They looked at their beer cups and laughed. The 'beer' guy looked at his friends. "Well brothers, he's got us there." They all agreed, while Jimmy gloated.

Michael turned to Jimmy. "What do you guys do for a living?

"We're Portland Police Lieutenants."

"Seriously? Next time I'll bring donuts."

The two friends who'd yelled: "Michael" and "beer," high fived and yelled: "Donuts." "And beer." They high fived again.

Jimmy looked and laughed at his two friends. "No, you did good. Today is the one day we indulge ourselves, but this will be our last beer for the day… two's our limit. A DWI wouldn't sit well with the Police Bureau. What's your occupation, Michael?"

"I'm an attorney, —"

"Drink up boys," said the 'beer' guy. "Michael's an attorney; he can get us out of the ticket." After everyone laughed. "I'm kidding, Michael," the beer guy said, "we love our jobs too much to take that chance."

"Good. DWI's are *not* my field of expertise. But I could use the expertise the five of you have."

"What can we do to help you, Michael?"

Michael turned toward Jimmy. "Years ago, someone murdered my friend's mother. It's gone unsolved, and he's asked me to help him. I want to dig through the reports on the crime scene and the resulting investigation. Can you help me with that? I'm an Intellectual Property attorney, and not familiar with the required procedures."

Jimmy pulled out a business card and gave it to Michael. "I'm happy to help you."

"Thank you."

"I speak for all of us when I say, we're here for you."

"Thanks again guys for letting me hang out with you. Jimmy, a special thanks to you for teaching me the Jimmy Feller Method of Horse Race Betting. And to the rest of you… thanks for showing me how not to bet."

The 'Beer' guy threw up hand. "Hey, you caught us on a bad day. Most Saturdays Jimmy's begging us to tell him which horse *we've* picked."

"Right," said Jimmy. "Truth be told, we're here for the camaraderie, not hopes of winning big. Most of the time our wallets are lighter when we leave." His friends agreed.

"Well, this time *I am* leaving."

"Michael, come back and join us. You're always welcome. Call me when you want me to help you with those investigation reports."

Michael shook their hands. "Thanks, gentlemen."

Michael materialized back in his apartment, tired. He went to bed early but couldn't sleep. The question by the man on the phone kept running through his mind: "What are you willing to do to save Stephanie's life?"

What will I do?

Michael knows she's somewhere in the southeast, but has no idea how to contact her?

Do I surrender and give him the book?

He couldn't shut off his mind, so he finished the book.

Sunday, October 27th

Michael crawled out of bed groggy. He considered surprising his grandmother by showing up at church, but needed to come to grips with the threat on Stephanie's life.

He stood in the shower, letting hot water bring him back to life while considering the book.

Now I'll have 4 hours… plenty of time.

He needed caffeine and sugar from the Coffee Shop.

Halfway there he felt his phone vibrating.

No caller ID. Here we go.

"Michael Mays here."

"Michael, what will you do, or *give*, to save Stephanie's life?"

"The question is, what will I do to stop you from harming her? Let's say I have what you want. And don't care if I ever use it again. But I can't give it to you. Then suppose I use it to start the charcoal in my outdoor grill. Are you willing to take that chance?"

"So, you're willing to gamble. I'm not a gambling man, Michael, and I don't bluff. Whether you refuse to give me the book or you burn the book, Stephanie will be dead. The only way this ends with her alive is for you to give *me* the book. Will you hand it over?"

"No, I will *not* give it to you."

"Not a good decision, Michael. I know where she is. Do you? I have my man standing by, waiting for my orders to take her. Who do *you* have protecting her? Oh, that's right, you don't. It never entered your mind, did it? The way you fawned over her in the Coffee Shop, I thought she's someone you cared for... hmm... my mistake."

The caller ended the call. He was right, Michael didn't think Stephanie was in danger. There's no doubt now.

Michael's mind raced.

Okay, what I told Linda was correct, it's him. White-haired Joe is the guy who asked for directions, and he overheard Stephanie tell me she was leaving town, but how did he discover her location?

He realized there was only one way. Somehow, Joe found and talked with her parents. Michael abandoned his quest for caffeine and sugar.

24

Michael turned and retraced the route to Stephanie's parents' home. He had walked her home one morning, using his umbrella to protect her from the rain.

There's no way I can tell them about the book, they'd think I'm crazy.

He needed to cook up a scenario.

Stephanie's father opened the door while clearing his throat. "Hi, can I help you?"

"Hi, my name is Michael Mays—" Michael saw that hearing his name changed Stephanie's father's appearance.

He had tilted his head and paused. "Did you say, Michael Mays?"

"Yes, sir. I'm a friend of Stephanie's."

Her father held up his index finger and turned his head. "Karen, can you come to the front door." A few seconds later, his wife came rushing to the door.

"Honey, this man says he's Michael Mays. Didn't you tell me Michael Mays is in the hospital, in critical condition?"

Karen stared at Michael in disbelief. "Yes, I did."

Michael raised and spread his hands at shoulder height. "Well, I'm not in the hospital and I'm not in critical condition. Where did you get that information?"

Stephanie's mother tugged on her blouse as she looked at her husband, then turned back to Michael, while bringing her hand to her cheek as her brow furrowed. "Your friend Bob stopped by to get Stephanie's contact information. He wanted to tell her you're in the hospital. There was a cast on his arm; he said the same accident caused the injuries to his arm."

Michael pulled out his wallet, gave them a business card and showed his driver's license. "Can we talk?"

They said in unison, "Please, come in."

Michael followed them into their living room. He puzzled over a comment Stephanie once made. She mentioned that one reason she moved in with her parents was to help them do things they can no longer do.

I guess she's planning—for the distant future?

While walking to their living room, the contemporary furnishings and décor surprised him. He had assumed her parents were elderly and expected to find traditional style furnishings like those in his grandmother's house.

They were both, at most, mid 50s and fit, even athletic.

Stephanie's father motioned to a wood and leather lounge chair. "Please, Michael, have a seat."

"Before I sit, allow me to re-introduce myself. My name is Michael Mays and I'm a friend of Stephanie's, and I'm healthy and uninjured."

Stephanie's father laughed as he stepped toward Michael. "Nice to meet you, Michael, I'm Stephanie's father Mark." He shook Michael's hand.

Michael walked over and clasped Karen's hand in both of his. "Very nice to meet you, Karen." She scrunched her eyebrows and glanced at Mark, then back to Michael.

Michael sensed her confusion and said, "I heard Mark call out your name from the front door."

"Oh, that's right, nice to meet you too. Even though we haven't met, Stephanie has told us about you, and how much she enjoys her time with you at The Coffee Shop."

"You guys did good. Stephanie's a gem."

Karen and Mark made quick eye contact as they took a seat shoulder to shoulder.

Michael sat. He placed his elbows on the chair's arm rests and clasped one hand over the other while leaning forward. "I have a troubling situation I need to discuss with you."

Mark looked at Karen and he too leaned forward. "Is Stephanie okay?"

Michael glanced at the geometric patterned area-rug and the maple hardwood floor. He looked up while clearing his throat. "I'm concerned for her safety."

Mark looked at Karen again. "Not what a mother and father want to hear."

"And, not news I want to bring. I assume Stephanie told you I'm an attorney."

Karen nodded. "Yes, she did."

"My field of practice is, overall, free of revenge. We handle copyright violations, theft of intellectual property, and such. But sometimes, a case will involve a tremendous amount of money, and crazy people.

"That's what's causing my concern. I won't go into detail, but a man is in prison for murder. He stole an idea and design from his associate, which turned out to be very profitable. So much so he killed the associate to cover his theft.

"The law firm I'm with, represented the family of the slain associate. My investigation, and the related testimonies I gathered, were key in his conviction. We recaptured only a small portion of the money he gained. The rest is most likely hidden offshore. He's wealthy *and* vindictive.

"What that means is, he can reach out from prison and hurt me, and those close to me. He has people on the outside who do his dirty work. Karen, the person who talked with you is one of those people."

Karen jolted back. "Oh, no."

"Don't blame yourself. He would have got the information somehow. They want to find Stephanie so she can be used as part of his revenge on me."

Mark put his arm around Karen. The living room became quiet. She reached up and put her hand on top of his. They glanced at each and nodded before looking at Michael. "Karen and I understand."

Michael leaned farther forward, put his elbows on his knees and linked his fingers. "This morning I received a call from him. He told me he *will* kill me. But first he'll hurt my friends and family. He knows Stephanie and I are friends."

Karen gasped and looked at Mark. "Honey—" Her chin quivered; she couldn't speak.

Mark removed his arm from Karen's shoulders and leaned toward Michael. "Michael, we hear the seriousness of the threat, and we believe you. How can we help?" He wiped a tear from his eye and slid his hand to cup his chin and left cheek.

"As an attorney I investigate, gather information, and draw a conclusion. So, I need your help."

Mark's voice trembled as he let out a heavy sigh. "Anything."

"Do you know where Stephanie is? The hotel, the town, something that will help us find her?"

Karen wiped her eyes. "No. She doesn't have an itinerary. The company she's working for wants her to discover, attend, and photograph events for a travel brochure they're creating for the State of Georgia.

"She calls us every few days to check-in but doesn't talk much about herself, just wants to know how we're doing.

"I gave the man with the broken arm the name of her most recent hotel. And, I gave him her phone number. But Stephanie warned me that many of the places she'll visit have poor cell reception. And, she turns off her phone while she's working; she only turns it on when she calls us. She's old-fashioned that way."

An idea came to Michael. "During one of our conversations, Stephanie told me that when she's on assignment, at the end of each day, she downloads that day's photographs to her computer. Then uploads them to a cloud account; can you get into that account?"

Karen leaned in with a touch of hope in her voice. "I can. Stephanie knows I'm her biggest fan; that I enjoy looking at her photographs. She gave me her password and I go in every few days to see what she's photographed."

"When was the last time you checked?"

"Not for two days."

"Let's go check them."

Karen stood, turned, and rushed toward the staircase. "Follow me."

As Karen was signing in on her computer, Michael looked at Mark. "I need photos from the last few days loaded onto a flash drive. Do you have one I can use?"

Mark opened a drawer in the desk where Karen was working. "Yes." He removed the drive from its packaging and handed it to Karen.

"Tomorrow, I'll have our I.T. people check the metadata in the photos you give me. They should be able to come up with *something* to help locate her."

As the photos downloaded, Karen swiveled in her office chair. "Michael, shouldn't we contact the police?"

"That's up to you, but until we have a clue to where she is, the police have no place to look. She's not a missing person, so I don't know what they could do at this point. Keep trying to phone her. If we can discover the town or county where she's working, we can help the police find her."

Karen unplugged the flash drive and handed it to Michael.

As Michael was leaving, he hugged both Mark and Karen. "I'll contact you as soon as I get an answer from our IT people. Should be tomorrow, mid-morning. Would you search Stephanie's room to see if you can come up with her employer's phone number or email address? If you do, contact them tomorrow. They may have her current location."

"I'll begin searching right away. If I find it, I'll call you."

"Great. Thank you, Karen."

Karen hugged Michael. As she let go, he took her hands in his. "I am so sorry that Stephanie's caught up in this mess. I'll do everything I can to protect her."

Mark placed his hand on Michael's shoulder and squeezed, while trying to smile. "We trust you will."

Michael hurried home, dodging standing water on the sidewalk and jumping over street storm drains clogged with Autumn leaves.

He arrived at his apartment building soaking wet. Making his way up the stairs, Joe's threat came to mind, which caused his senses to detonate.

White-haired Joe knows where grandma lives!

Michael pulled out his phone and called his grandmother.

It went to voice mail.

He tried to stay calm. "Hi Grandma, please call me as soon as you get this message."

After drying off, he combed his hair, changed his shirt, wiped moisture from the book and placed it in a large zip-lock bag. He grabbed a dry jacket from the hall closet and hurried to his car.

Michael needed to get her to a safe location. He headed to her church hoping to catch her there.

25

Michael parked in the church's parking lot. In front of the church, groups of people huddled under umbrellas, some red, a few blue, but most were black. He recognized one person and ran toward her. "Mrs. Edwards." She turned to look.

"I'm Michael Mays."

She waved. "Oh yes… hello, Michael. Haven't seen you in a while. How are you?"

Michael stopped and stood with his shoulders hunched and head leaning forward, water running down his neck. "I'm doing okay, but I need to talk with my grandmother. Have you seen her this morning?"

"Yes, church got out," she looked at her watch, "half an hour ago, and we talked afterwards. She introduced me to a nice young man who's new to our church. She was taking him to Ella's café. Your grandmother loves that place. She's everyone's friend, and hospitable, to a fault."

Michael moved the conversation along. "Yes, she is. How long ago did she leave?"

"It was right after she introduced the young man to me."

"Thank you, Mrs. Edwards."

"Come back and visit us soon, Michael," she called out as he ran back to his car.

He waved above his head and answered without looking back. "Thanks, Mrs. Edwards, I will."

There was no parking near the cafe. He made a left turn and found a tight parking spot two blocks away.

Michael sprang from his car and ran to Ella's. On a street behind the café, he launched off the curb trying to clear a six-foot-wide puddle caused by leaf-plugged storm drains. He didn't make it. Now his feet were soaking wet.

So much for changing into dry clothes. There's a reason I never made the track team.

Grandma waved at Michael as he came through the door.

She patted the seat of a chair next to her. "Michael, what's going on? I saw you run past the window. My first thought was, you wouldn't be running unless someone's chasing you.

Sit and drip dry.

"I want to introduce you to a new friend. Michael, meet, Curtis. Curtis, meet my grandson, Michael."

Curtis offered his hand, which Michael accepted. "Hello, Michael."

Michael folded his arms across his chest and glared.

There's maliciousness in that smile.

"Do you live in this neighborhood, Curtis?"

"No, just got into town. I'm a god-fearing-man and thought it good to find a church while in town."

Never the linguist, Michael couldn't make out his accent.

African, Caribbean...?

Michael moved his left hand's thumb and index finger to his chin. "God fearing... huh? What do you fear... that He'll reveal the man you are and blow your cover?"

Grandma slapped her hand on the table.

People at neighboring tables jolted and looked.

"Michael, I didn't raise you to talk like that."

As grandma chastised, Michael kept his focus on Curtis. Malice manifested itself in Curtis' bold stare and insolent smirk.

"Grandma, you're correct, you did not raise me to be rude. Curtis, I apologize."

Curtis, enjoying the apology, maintained his smirk and stare.

"Grandma, please excuse Curtis and me for a minute. We need to talk?"

"Michael... behave."

"I'll do my best, Grandma."

With an air of superiority in his swagger, and a smug smile on his face, Curtis followed Michael to the front door. Even his clothing portrayed his confidence. Tailored loose enough for comfort but close-fitting enough to reveal his excellent physical conditioning. As his arms swung with confidence, his rose gold watch flashed against his espresso skin.

They stood under the entry awning, which was the source of a waterfall curtain between the sidewalk and them.

"Curtis, there is nothing I value more in this life than that woman. I'll do whatever it takes to protect her. Do you understand?"

"I understand it would require you to be with her 24/7. Will you take her to work with you? Or out of the country? Protecting her is quite simple. Give my friend what he wants. He's asked you nice, but how long will he maintain nice? When he tells me to not be nice, I can be very un-nice, Michael. This should frighten you: he's given me the go-ahead to be un-nice at my discretion."

"It's time for you to leave, Curtis."

"Michael, this will not end well."

"Our time together ends now. Leave, Curtis."

"Have it your way, Michael. I assumed you'd be smarter than you are demonstrating."

Michael walked back in and sat across from his grandmother.

She placed both hands on the table and gave a look Michael knew well. "Where's Curtis?"

"He had to leave."

"*What* did you do, Michael?"

"Grandma, he's not the man you think he is."

As much as Michael hated lying to her, he retold the story he told Stephanie's parents, adding that Curtis works for the man in prison.

"He's threatened Stephanie and now he's threatening you. I'm doing my best to protect both of you, but you must help me, grandma. Is there somewhere safe we can send you until I get this resolved?"

"Michael, I'm too old for this, are you sure this threat's legitimate?"

"Yes, I'm sure the danger is real."

"Okay… I trust your judgment. I'll need you to help me get to my sister's place in Redding, California. But first, let's call her to see if she can help."

"Do you know her number?"

"No, we need to go to my house and get it from my phone list."

"I'll pay the check while you put on your coat."

"You don't have to, Michael. I invited Curtis to lunch, so I should pay."

"Consider it making up for my rudeness."

She smiled and squeezed his hand.

As they walked onto the sidewalk, she stopped. "Hold on, Michael, I'll put up my umbrella."

There was a gunshot.

Michael felt the water spray as the bullet passed through the awning waterfall.

"Michael, help me," his grandmother said as she fell.

He caught her and wrapped his arms around her.

He lowered her to the sidewalk and continued to hold her.

She looked up at him and tried to smile but could only wince. "I guess it *was* a legitimate threat."

The water from the awning was turning red as it ran off the sidewalk and into the gutter.

He pressed his hand against her right shoulder where blood was flowing.

"Stay with me grandma."

He looked up at a man coming out of Ella's restaurant. "Call 9-1-1."

Michael heard that vague foreign accent spoken close to his ear. "Oooh, that must hurt. You better have that looked at." He laughed with the same malice that poisoned his smile. "I gave you fair warning, Michael." His shoes splashed as he ran away.

* * *

Daniel's phone rang. "Yeah, Curtis, how'd it go?"

"He's not going to cooperate. I warned him consequences awaited, but he wasn't having any of it."

"Did you give him a stronger warning like I told you?"

"I shot her. But I don't think she's dead, but I guarantee he gets your message."

"Okay. Get out-of-town now. Head south."

"Will do. I'll stop when it's someplace sunny and 80 degrees."

"I may need you again, so don't go too far south."

"Only as far south as I need to. You call me and I'll be here."

* * *

The Paramedics arrived and did an excellent job of getting Michael's grandmother stabilized, loaded onto the gurney, then on her way to the hospital.

As Michael was watching, a Portland Police Sergeant approached him. "Sir, are you related to the victim?"

"Yes, she's my grandmother." He couldn't take his eyes away from the rainwater, still tinted by blood. "My name is Michael Mays."

"Mr. Mays, my name is Sergeant Romero." She shook his hand.

Michael told Sergeant Romero a short version of the lie he'd told his grandmother and Stephanie's parents. He gave her a brief description of Curtis. "I believe he's working for someone I helped convict years ago. But I have no tangible evidence to support my suspicions."

"Mr. Mays, please come to this address." She handed him her business card. "We need a thorough description of the suspect."

"Sergeant, first I'm going to the hospital and check on my grandmother. If she's stabilized, I'll come in right away. If not, I'll be in after they've stabilized her."

The Sergeant considered what he said. "I understand. But the sooner, the better."

"I want to help catch the guy, but I won't be able to concentrate until I find out how she's doing."

"Again, I understand. We'll see you at that address soon."

"As soon as I can." They shook hands and he ran off.

Michael parked in the Emergency Room parking area and ran into the waiting room. He identified himself to the receiving nurse. "I'll let the doctor know you're here. He'll talk to you as soon as he's out of surgery."

"Is he working on my grandmother now?"

"Yes, they took her into surgery right away."

"Thank you." He found a seat in the waiting room.

Forty minutes later, the nurse signaled him back to the counter and pointed. "Go through that door. The doctor will talk with you now." She handed him an I.D. lanyard. "Please wear this."

He nodded and turned to the door, pushing it open as he placed the lanyard around his neck. The smell of phenol and alcohol hit him as stepped into the hallway.

The doctor approached. "Mr. Mays?"

"Yes, please call me Michael."

"Michael, my name is Dr. Haskel. Your grandmother is very fortunate, the bullet struck her right shoulder and passed through. It involved no major arteries or bones. But she lost a lot of blood, and she's 90 years old. If she were a 30-year-old woman I could tell you she should mend and recover. I can't give you that news, but I can tell you she came through the surgery much better than expected."

"Thank you. She is tough and more than a little stubborn."

"Well, she's stable now, but I'm keeping her sedated for the night. You can step in and see her, but she won't know you're there."

"Thank you, doctor I'll do that, then I'm going to the police station to give them a more thorough description of the man who shot her. How long before she'll be conscious?"

"Tomorrow morning."

"Is it okay if I come back and stay with her during the night?"

"It's best you go home and get some rest. Come back tomorrow morning."

"I'll come back and check on her after I meet with the police. Then I'll go home. Thank you, doctor."

"You are welcome. It was nice to meet you, Michael."

Michael approached the striking Asian woman at the police precinct's reception window. "I'm here to meet with Captain Romero."

A cast on her right wrist accessorized her police uniform. She saw Michael noticing the cast and smiled as she held it up. "Responded to a domestic disturbance. I blocked a husband's attempt to hit me with a lamp. I'll be on modified-duty for a while."

"I've heard they can be dangerous calls."

"Yes... ugly... your name?"

He handed her the Sergeant's business card. "Michael Mays."

She pushed a few buttons on her desk phone. "I have a Michael Mays here to see you. Thank you, Captain.

"Have a seat, Mr. Mays. She'll be out in a few minutes."

Five minutes later a door opened next to the reception window and Captain Romero motioned him to come in.

She took his statement and supervised a composite sketch session with a forensic artist.

"Thank you for coming in, Mr. Mays. That's all we need from you today. We'll keep you posted. If we get a hit with this information, I'll let you know."

"Thank you, Captain."

"How's your grandmother doing?"

"The doctor thinks she will recover but, due to her age, gave an official disclaimer."

"I wish her the best. I hope we can find this guy. It might comfort her if she knew he's not still out there.

"*Me too*, thanks."

On his way home, Michael stopped at one of his favorite local burger joints. Curtis and a bullet had preempted lunch.

* * *

Sunday afternoon, BTH called Daniel to check in. "Hey boss, Bob here."

"Bag Michael's girlfriend, I need her for leverage."

"You got it, Boss. This is my third day tailing her at this festival. I think she suspects I'm up to something."

"She might have pictures of you. Destroy the film."

"There's no film, boss. I'll get the storage card in her camera and destroy it."

"Yeah, I forget about this digital crap. This might have to get ugly. He's refusing to give me the book. Move on her when she gets into her hotel room; if he continues to refuse, I'll have you rough her up. We might have to send him a photo of her to encourage him to cooperate. You have a gun, right?"

"I don't leave home without it, or I get one when I get to where I'm going, so yeah, I've got a gun.

"Boss... you don't have to tell me every step to take. This isn't my first rodeo."

"Yeah, but maybe I can help make it your first rodeo with no screwups. So, do what I say... you might get through this." Daniel paused, BTH did not respond.

"If he forces us to the point of sending him photo proof, without warning he'll appear behind you. I want you to kill them both, grab the book and get out of there. Wear gloves the entire time, leave no evidence that can tie you to her or the room. As soon as you take the picture, turn around with your gun ready. If he's determined not to give me the book, he'll try to save the woman. Put him down."

"What are you talking about boss, turn around after I take the picture? You're worrying me."

"Never mind. Do what I pay you for, BTH. Have I ever given you a bum steer?"

Bob hesitated. "No."

Haven't I always made it worth your while on the other jobs?"

"Yeah, you have boss."

"If I get the book and he doesn't show, you can do whatever you want with the woman to make her disappear for good."

"You can count on me, boss. You're not gonna want to hear this… but you're coming across like you've got a screw loose."

"I don't pay you to analyze me, BTH. That's way beyond your abilities— just do what I tell you to do."

26

Stephanie Clark finished the day's photo shoot. She got into her rental car not wanting to say goodbye to the Mountain Moonshine Festival and Car Show. She kept glancing in her rear mirror as Dawson, Georgia faded out of sight.

So far, the best day of my trip.

Another rental car had pulled out behind her, maintaining a strategic distance.

Stephanie had excellent photo opportunities at the three-day show and enjoyed learning about its car culture and moonshine history.

The people were great to work with and the variety of activities kept her camera clicking. Where else would one find a legal moonshine distillery under the same roof as the City Hall and the Georgia Racing Hall of Fame? Sunday's activities included sampling whiskey and a church service.

She came away in love with a car. A 1961 Ford Starliner. Chrome, lots of chrome, on jet black paint. The owner had the interior done in red Italian leather. While photographing the car she talked with the owner, finishing her conversation with, "I will own one of these someday."

The car's owner, mid-sixties, bald, and resembling a fire hydrant in a Hawaiian shirt, gave her his card. "When you're ready, call me. I have connections and can help you find the right one."

She looked down at him. "Thank you."

Stephanie wanted to try a Cracker Barrel, even though Portland metro area has several, she has yet to try their food. She pulled out her phone and

Googled to find the nearest one, which was not too far from her hotel. On a good day, the drive back to her hotel was an hour, but the traffic in Atlanta…

Who knows?

She pushed "Directions" and began her drive back.

I will visit Dawson again… when I'm not working.

Stephanie turned into the Cracker Barrel parking lot and parked. BTH slammed his palm hard against the rental car's steering wheel as he swore and grumbled. "I was hoping for room service at the swanky hotel."

While continuing to monitor Stephanie, he found a parking spot.

After she began walking toward the restaurant, BTH got out his car and followed her. When she neared the restaurant's front door, he waited until she entered, counted to 15, then walked in and milled around the gift shop until they took her to a table. He walked past the counter, ignoring the receptionist's effort to help him.

He found a vacant table behind Stephanie and took a seat. A young man in a Cracker Barrel polo shirt approached him with a couple following close behind. "Excuse me sir, but this table is for *this* couple."

BTH replied with a hiss in his voice and a smirk on his face. "You've made a miscalculation. This table is mine."

Confused, the young server, not wanting to cause a scene, turned to the couple, pointed to a table a bus boy was clearing. "Would y'all mind sitting at that table? It'll be ready in no time."

The man glared at BTH, who looked up while putting on his unnerving smile. "No problem," the man said.

Seated at her table, Stephanie considered her menu choices. She noticed the little man walk past her. Via a framed wall-mirror, she followed him as he walked to the table behind her. She recognized him from the Moonshine Festival and watched him try to be sly while waiting in the gift shop.

After hearing the little man argue with the server, she switched to her table's opposite chair. She now faced him. As usual, her camera is with her— she's never off duty—always on the lookout for interesting shots.

She picked it up and aimed it at him, taking no care to be discreet. Her first couple of pictures were of him looking into the camera's lens. He looked away, which allowed her to take a profile shot.

She got up, walked to BTH's table and sat across from him.

Her camera on her lap, held with both hands, she leaned into him. "Look... I don't know what you're up to, but you are *lousy* at stalking. Over the past couple of days, I've photographed you multiple times at the festival. So, whatever you're thinking, rethink it. I attached your photos to an email and sent them to my office. In the email, I told them you may be stalking me. You've blown whatever you've been trying to cover up or carry out. Back off, or next I dial 9-1-1."

Stephanie walked back to her table and signaled to the server. "I'm ready to order please."

Shook up, BTH rushed out of the dining room.

* * *

BTH sat in his car, dreading the call he had to make.

"Boss, she made me, she took pictures of me and sent them off to her office."

In anger, Daniel went off. "Why am I paying you, BTH? First you get caught searching Michael's apartment and end up with a broken arm. Now you blow your cover on the other side of the country."

BTH whined, "But I fooled her parents and got the information we needed."

With restraint he reserves only for BTH, Daniel replied, "Okay, here's what you do. Tomorrow, follow her to see if she moves on to a different location. If she does, let me know ASAP. Then get back to Portland as quick as you can, we need to set up a solid alibi for you. I'm sending in another player. Maybe *she* can get the job done."

"Do I get to fly in the private jet again?"

"Be at the Atlanta airport by tomorrow night. I'll send your flight information to you."

Daniel ended the call muttering, "Frickin idiot, I can't trust him to do anything."

* * *

"Katrina here."

"It's Daniel, I need your help."

"Hello, Daniel my dear, how can I help you? Whatever it is, I guarantee it will cost you *way more* than you pay your low-life convict friends."

"I don't have convict friends, Katrina, so the amount I pay them is zilch. I'm liking your fee."

"Well, Daniel, I'm guessing your fee isn't bringing you the results you want, so you're calling someone you know who will."

"Okay, you got me there. I need you in Atlanta at once. Write this down." He gave Katrina his phone number. "I'll have more information by the time you get there."

"Are you going to give me a hint, or do I make stuff up when I get there, then bill you for my vacation?"

"You'll *have* the information when you get there. Some things don't change, Katrina, and you're one of them. Trust me, you will enjoy this one. And I trust you'll pull it off well. At the airport pick up a photography magazine and read it, ads and all."

"Sounds like a fun job. But are we in agreement on my phenomenal fee?"

"Your reward will equal the results. If the results are phenomenal, your reward will reflect that."

Katrina was small for a hit-woman, and dangerously attractive. She'll lure you into her web of charm faster than a bullet leaves the barrel.

"Does my husband know about this, Daniel?"

"What happens in Atlanta, stays in Atlanta. Besides, you know he won't miss you, and I have no plans to see him. The Willamette State pen is the *last* place I'd visit.

"Katrina, as I've said before, we should take our relationship to a level higher than phone calls and emails. Dump that guy, we'd be good together."

"I don't think I'm good with anyone. Although the few times we saw each other across the room on visiting days, I liked what I saw."

"A casual relationship is okay with me, Katrina."

In her best southern accent, Katrina said, "Daniel, you make a poor girl's heart flutter."

"With the fees you charge, Katrina, you're far from poor. You'll have a text with directions waiting when you land in, Georgia."

"We have a deal then. I'm looking forward to meeting my *mystery* date."

Daniel opened his mouth to come back at Katrina's dig, but held back. "Don't forget to buy, and read, a photography magazine."

"It's on the list I'm making as we speak.

"Good; later."

Again, in the southern accent, Katrina said, "I am so looking forward to it, Daniel."

27

~

Monday, October 28th

Before going to the hospital to visit his grandmother, Michael stopped by his office to check-in with Trevor.

At his desk, he took a few minutes to reflect on the past three weeks, the only descriptor he could come up with was, "Amazing."

Michael pushed the intercom button his desk phone. "Trevor, come into my office please. Bring with you what will kill me if I don't deal with it now."

Trevor chuckled. "I'll be right there, Mr. Mays."

It took Trevor a few minutes to check and gather the information. "Good morning, Michael. It's still awkward for me to not call you Mr. Mays, but I'm working on it."

"It'll get easier with practice." Michael saw Trevor held a few folders. "Let's move to my conference table."

Trevor went over the information he had brought in, most of it was signatures needed. He did an excellent job of summarizing each before Michael signed. "Last, but not least, we received a response from Kassidy Frank, Mr. Cailen's attorney. She's requesting a meeting, but asking for several dates to help her find a fit with Mr. Cailen's touring schedule."

"Give her two dates, both with early afternoon times. Should be enough leeway for her and her client to get to our office."

"Will do. Is there anything else?"

"Yes." Michael handed him the flash drive. "Get this to IT and ask them for whatever metadata they can retrieve from the photos? Tell them I need it last Friday."

"I'll shoot for this afternoon."

"Thanks. I'll be out for an hour. I don't recall any appointments being scheduled this morning. If I do, please reschedule them to this afternoon or later this week."

He told Trevor what happened to his grandmother. "I'm so sorry to hear that, Michael. I'll clear your morning."

"Thanks."

Michael approached a woman sitting in the hospital Information-Kiosk. "Hi, my name is Michael Mays. My grandmother, Louise Nelson is a patient here. Please check her room number."

After entering information into the computer, she looked up. "I show Louise Nelson as being checked out."

"That can't be. A man shot her yesterday, followed by surgery yesterday afternoon?"

"Dr. Haskel signed her release an hour ago."

"Is he still in the hospital?"

"I'll check. Give me a few minutes please."

"Sure," Michael said, as he walked off, running his fingers through his hair as he circled the Information-Kiosk.

Did white haired Joe get to the doctor? Did he threaten him… or buy him off?

She waved him over as she hung up the phone. "Dr. Haskel is still in the hospital and asked that you meet him in the second-floor Chapel in 15 minutes."

"Thank you. I need a cup of coffee. Is there someplace close?"

She pointed directly behind him. "Down the hall to the left there's a small coffee shop."

"Thank you."

Coffee in hand and following the signs, he made his way to the second-floor Chapel.

The doctor was there, seated and waiting for him. "Hi, Michael, I'm sure you're confused."

"That's an understatement, doctor. Help me understand this."

Dr. Haskel handed Michael an envelope. "This is for you." Michael did not say a word. He set his coffee cup on an end table, accepted the envelope, opened it, and read:

> *"Michael, I know you're upset that I'm not here when you returned. Doctor Haskel is a long-time friend and agreed to honor my decision. I told him about the threat we face. He too is a friend of Dr. Marvin Malcom, the retired Ophthalmologist you met as we left church the last time you visited.*
>
> *Marvin agreed to take me in and care for me. Dr. Haskel knows Marvin well and trusts his ability to do that. I felt very vulnerable being in the hospital.*
>
> *I'll contact you soon, but I believe this is best and takes pressure off you.*
>
> *Please don't be mad at me, or Dr. Haskel. Again, we both believe it is best for you and me.*
>
> *Love,*
>
> *Your Grandmother."*

As Michael looked up, the doctor said, "Michael, your grandmother was gaining strength far faster than I could have imagined. Her injury is no longer life threatening. Dr. Malcom is a fine physician and surgeon, albeit surgeries related to the eye, but I trust him to give Louise excellent care, and I'll continue to check on her daily."

"Doctor." Michael wiped his face with his hands and rested them on the sides of his neck. He took a deep breath. "Are you sure this is a good idea?"

"Michael, I wouldn't have agreed with your grandmother if I thought this move is detrimental. The move will be good for her emotionally. And, it will lessen her risk of infection."

"Well, I know my grandmother better than anyone. At this point it doesn't matter what I think. She's decided, and I trust her judgement. Thank you, doctor." Michael stood, shook the doctor's hand, and headed back to his law office.

* * *

BTH was in the atrium-themed hotel coffee shop hours before he would have chosen to get out of bed. He wanted to make sure he didn't miss Stephanie or disappoint Daniel again. His gut told him she would check out, so he did the same.

He sat eating the Breakfast Special. His table was behind a partition that allowed him to see the front desk while being discrete. After finishing his omelet and hash browns, he spread two individual containers of Orange Marmalade on his last half-piece of toast. After admiring his ability to spread the marmalade evenly, he looked up and saw Stephanie approach the front desk.

He shifted behind the partition until only his left eye viewed Stephanie.

By the time she completed check out, he'd finished his toast and washed it down with the last gulp of orange juice. He left a $10 bill on the table and made his way to the lobby.

After Stephanie exited the front doors, he hurried to the doors but stopped to check before walking out. She wasn't there.

He stepped through the doors and looked to his right.

She was walking into the parking lot.

He ambled across the registration parking area, then kept his eyes on her while ducking behind vehicles until he found his car.

* * *

Stephanie locked her doors and sat in her car reviewing notes from the day before.

Ah, there it is.

It was the name and address of the cabin she reserved during lunch on her last day at the Moonshine Festival and Car Show.

A couple she shared a table with, talked about an Oktoberfest they'd left that morning. They said the festival ran until next weekend.

After they introduced themselves and heard what Stephanie was doing in Georgia, the wife said, "Oh, honey, it's the cutest little town. Perfect for the brochure you're working on... don't you think so, Sam?"

"Stephanie, I agree with Gloria. It's a quaint Bavarian Village and a great Oktoberfest. There's outdoor recreation—"

Gloria burst into the conversation: "And it has over a hundred shops for... *shopping.*"

Sam laughed. "And, she *did* some shopping, while I played golf on an outstanding golf course. Rooms in town are hard to find. But when we checked out, a man at the golf shop told us the cabin we stayed in, on the golf course complex, is available. That was five hours ago. If you're interested, I can call and check."

"I'm *very* interested, Sam, thank you."

Sam called and talked with the golf course representative while Gloria recommended her favorite shops to Stephanie.

Stephanie heard Sam say, "Great, I'll hand her my phone, she can give you her information."

She made a reservation, thanked Sam and Gloria, and said goodbye.

Stephanie opened her Google Maps app and entered the address the man at golf course gave her. It was just over four hours to Helen.

* * *

BTH followed Stephanie out of the hotel parking lot, but hung back, trying to always stay a few cars behind.

He didn't want to lose her or scare her into calling the police. His boss would have his hide.

28

After an early dinner, while heading home, Michael's mind churned the thought of being a target while at Woodstock Park in 1986. He was at a loss for explanation, but concluded the shooter traveled through time just as he does. And, the shooter used a picture taken of him by his mother's stalker.

The only thing he could do was to avoid being photographed by anyone, especially his mother's stalker.

There was something else gnawing at the back of his mind. His feelings toward his father troubled him. His trips back to the Little League game and OMSI, and seeing his mother, had uncovered resentment he's buried for years.

What happened to my father? What caused him to abandon me?

Michael's father turned his upbringing over to his grandparents and never looked back.

His grandmother told him, more than once, that his attitude toward his father seemed hostile. He had maintained that it was more disappointment than hostility.

Needing to shift his mind to another subject, the mess waiting for him at home in his office, came to mind.

I can't put it off any longer.

At his apartment building, he trudged up the stairs, and through his door. He walked into his office and turned on the light.

A complete mess... I never use it... close the door... call it a storage room.

But he knows he needs to do this.

He'd decorated the office with what little of his father's memorabilia he had.

Michael re-hung three pictures and the high school letterman jacket his mother framed for display. The stripes on the jacket's left sleeve declared his father's abilities in baseball. He was amazed the glass didn't break when the weasel flung it to the floor.

Michael returned two bowling trophies to the credenza, along with his father's framed Bachelor of Science degree in marketing.

It was a struggle putting intact lamps, books, and pictures back in their pre-disheveled positions.

He stopped, sat in one of his office's two overstuffed chairs, and pondered his purposeful avoidance.

Truth is, I don't want to put them back—they're the reason I don't come in here. I need to get past this.

Michael knows his grandmother is right. He's pierced through with hurt, anger, and resentment. But, since his father died 24 years ago, he couldn't sit and talk, man-to-man.

He was staring at a framed photo's glass, shattered from the weasel throwing it to the floor.

He leaned forward and, while letting the glass slide off onto the floor, pulled the photo from the broken frame. It was a picture of his father and his bowling team. Michael's grandmother gave him the picture when he moved out.

Until grandma gave me this picture, I didn't know he was bowler, let alone that he'd been on a team that won their league's 1988 championship.

Michael decided to cause an opportunity to talk to his father.

Walking to the living room, he removed the book from his briefcase, grabbed his phone and a jacket, then returned to his office.

He propped the photo against a lamp on the end table and set his phone's timer for 3 hours and 50 minutes.

That'll give me a ten-minute warning.

He opened the book and looked at his father's team photo.

Michael was standing close behind a group of people watching. They stood 10 feet behind the woman who was taking the team photograph. "Let me take one more. Smile… on three, then counted: 99, 98, 97." Everyone laughed, and she snapped the photo. After the camera flashed, they applauded.

A short, portly man, wearing tan khaki pants, a red and black bowling shirt, and a toupee, turned while still laughing and clapping. He bumped into Michael. "I'm sorry. You snuck up on me," which re-energized his laughing.

Michael gave him a friendly slap on his shoulder. "No harm done."

Re-directing his focus, he saw his father walking back to where his teammates were gathering. His dad reached beneath one of the plastic benches, picked up his bowling ball bag, sat on the plastic bench, and placed his bowling shoes and ball in the bag.

The back of his yellow and green bowling shirt read: Al's Nursery.

Above the left front pocket, it read: Gutter Garrett.

From a table overlooking the lanes, Michael watched his father talking with his four teammates. There was a sadness in his demeanor, even when he was joking with his friends.

He was disconnected and… sad, the only word Michael could make fit.

They ended their conversation with an idea that brought on high-fives and laughter.

The idea turned out to be a celebratory drink in the adjoining lounge.

Michael followed the team and sat in an empty booth beside them. He sat and slid over until he was right behind his father.

He signaled the server and ordered an IPA, which resulted in a confused look. "Is that a beer?"

He realized that in 1988, the craft beer movement wasn't in traditional bars yet.

"Yes… but I think I'll take an unsweetened iced tea instead"

"You got it. Iced tea coming your way."

He sat drinking his iced tea and listening to the five team members relive the past season and complement one another, over… and over… and over again, until they, one by one, said good night. Michael was waiting for his father to get up to leave so he could approach him and start a conversation,

That didn't happen. His father sat alone in the booth and ordered another whiskey straight up.

Michael finished the iced tea he'd been nursing. He stood and turned to face his father.

"Excuse me, but I couldn't help hearing you guys savoring your championship and wanted to offer my congratulations."

No response. "Sir... did you hear me? Sir?"

"Yes son, I hear you."

He called me son. I can't remember the last time he called me son.

Michael slid into the booth. "What's going on? Anything I can do?"

"There's nothing anyone can do."

"Maybe *I* can help."

"Are you a psychiatrist?"

"No, but I'm a good listener."

"Well, I'm a lousy talker. Even more so when I'm not in the mood, and I'm never in the mood. The last thing I want to do is burden a stranger."

Michael leaned forward. "What's your name?"

"Garrett... it's Garrett." He looked up and considered Michael for a few seconds. "Sorry I called you son, I thought you were younger." He held up his empty glass, signaling the server for another whiskey.

"That's okay. My name's Michael."

His father winced. "That's my son's name."

"Before I sat, you called me son. Should I call you dad?"

"No one's called me that in a long time, which should tell you I'm an even lousier communicator with family."

"Why is that?"

"Listen, I appreciate your concern, but this conversation is over."

"Again, maybe I can help—"

His father held his palm in front of Michael's face, cutting him off. "I *told you...* I am *not* good at this!" He tipped back his whiskey glass, downed it in one gulp. "*Leave... me... alone!*"

He turned his whiskey glass upside down and slammed it on the table. He grabbed his bowling bag and hurried away.

Michael felt like a kid again.

The server approached the table. "Excuse me, I heard Garrett yell at you; are you okay?"

"Yeah, I'm fine. You know Garrett?"

"Sure, when I started three years ago, he was a regular here."

"Did you meet his wife?"

"No, but after she died, he talked about her a lot, especially when he'd had too much to drink."

"What did he talk about?"

"How much he loved her, but when he'd been drinking, it was a different story."

"What changed?"

"He cried, and blamed himself for her death—"

The warm omni-directional wind hit him.

Michael was back in the overstuffed chair in his office. "What... that wasn't four hours?" He said, aloud while pulling out his phone to check the timer.

Only 61 minutes?

He wondered what went wrong. He read the entire book and should have had four hours.

Baffled, but time was insignificant at that point. He sat back and reflected on his conversation with his father.

After a few minutes, his conversation with the server came to mind.

My disappearing may have caused her to order herself a drink.

Her comment that his father, "... blamed himself for her death," bounced around in his head until his phone rang. Linda's name came up on his phone's screen.

* * *

BTH, hidden behind low-hanging branches of a Red Cedar tree, watched Stephanie as she returned from dinner. He called Daniel.

"Yeah."

"Boss, I'm watching the girlfriend. She just returned to her cabin."

"What cabin? And where?"

"She's staying in a cabin on a golf course in Helen, Georgia. I know you said you're gonna call someone else in, but I can take her with no problem."

"When did she check into the cabin?"

"We got here around 12:30 and—"

Daniel cut him off. "You've been there hours, and you're just now calling me? I told you to follow her and report back. That's all I wanted." He sighed. "We need you to have an alibi established when this goes down. Text me her address. Do you understand?"

"Yeah. You can make me do it, but you can't make me like it."

"I don't *care* if you like it. If you want to work for me again, head back here tonight. Send me the text now. Got it?"

"Yeah, I got it, boss, and I'm commencing back."

Daniel ended the call.

I've got to take his dictionary away.

* * *

Michael set the book on the end table and answered the phone. "Hey Michael, what's going on?"

"I'm putting my apartment back together. How are you and Jacob doing?"

"We're great. Jacob is still talking golf. You may have created a monster."

He took a seat in one of the overstuffed chairs. "I love it."

"We'd be happy to help if you need us."

"Thank you. Please don't take this wrong. Do you remember asking if I needed help with the room behind the closed door?"

"I do."

"That's what I hope you won't take wrong. When you asked me what I'm doing, it's something that I must do alone. I'm putting that room, my office, back together. It's not that the office is more complex or harder than the rest of the apartment. It's the *emotions* I'm working through. I don't use the office and it's becoming clear why."

Linda didn't respond.

Michael looked around. "The lack of memories associated with my father's memorabilia... it's like I bought a bunch of stuff at Goodwill and decorated my office with it."

"Do you want to discuss it, or process it a while?"

"I *want* to discuss it. But give me some time. I'm discovering I have more resentment, even bitterness, towards my father than I thought."

"Whenever you're ready to discuss it, I'll listen."

"Thanks, Linda."

Linda took a deep breath. "There's something we need to discuss."

"Okay, but my listening will be better than my discussion."

"That's okay Michael. I've been thinking about your meeting with Russell. I still believe he's guilty, but I'm asking you to promise me something."

"What can I promise you?" The conversation fell silent.

"I want you to promise me—" her voice broke, "that if you find Russell is not guilty—" She struggled to complete the sentence.

Michael cut in. "Linda, I once told you I'm very good at what I do. If I discover Russell's not guilty, I'll do everything in my power to bring the killer to justice."

A few more seconds of silence. "Thank you, Michael."

"I promise you, if that scenario plays out, I'll get Russell to agree to never contact you or Jacob again."

"I don't understand what that deal could be, but I trust you'll make it."

"Thank you. Okay, let's change the subject."

Linda sniffled and took a deep breath. "That sounds good. You sure you're okay to continue? We could talk tomorrow."

"No. Let's keep going. The weather forecast for next Saturday looks terrible, so I'll check with the Hindler's and see if their family cave is available. If so, I want to give Jacob his first golf lesson. Why don't you come and encourage him?"

"I'd love to. Jacob won't be *as* enthusiastic to have his mother come along, but count me in. Excuse me, Michael." He heard her set her phone on the end table and blow her nose. "Okay, I'm back."

"Let me call Matt and Carrie to see if it works."

"Great, let us know. Talk to you later," as she sniffled.

"I will and thanks again for trusting me."

"If you recall, I did a thorough background check."

"Yep, all the more reason I'm surprised you still trust me."

She laughed then hesitated. "Michael, one more thing. I'll say it again, please be careful. Russell is a liar and good at twisting his words."

"And, I'm good at untwisting them. But I will be careful."

29

Tuesday, October 29th

Michael headed to the Willamette State Penitentiary. Prior to leaving Portland, he stopped by his office to lock the book in a security file cabinet. When he walked in, Trevor looked up. "I thought you were out this morning, Mr. Mays?"

"I am. But I needed to stop by and take care of one item of business. I'll only be here three or four minutes."

"How's your grandmother?"

"She's okay. We can talk after lunch, unless my meeting gets cut short. If so, I'll update you when I get back."

"Oh, Mr. Cailen's attorney got back to us. There was a voice mail when I came in this morning."

Michael turned and walked back toward Trevor's desk. "Great, what did she say?"

"They can meet with you this Thursday, at 2 P.M."

"Okay, set it up and let the members of Hauler know. I want Ian and at least one other member at the meeting,"

"I'll get on it."

After stashing the book, Michael hurried to his car.

Michael walked into the Willamette State Penitentiary's check-in room and approached the window. The uniformed officer was 60ish, matronly and serious. "How can I help you, sir?"

"My name is Michael Mays and I'm scheduled to meet with Russell Curt."

"Just a moment while I check." She found his name on the approved visitor list. "Okay, there you are. You're an attorney, sir?"

"That's correct."

"What's the nature of your visit?"

"Reviewing his case."

"I'll tell the Guard's office to bring Curt to the visitation room. An officer will be here in a few minutes to escort you."

"Thanks."

Michael took a seat in an orange plastic chair set against the concrete block wall opposite the check-in counter.

The Guard arrived. "Mr. Mays, I'm Officer Morrow, please follow me." She was a taller version of the Portland police officer gym rat who investigated the break-in of Michael's apartment.

Could be her big sister.

As they walked, she said, "I'll be accompanying you and standing by as you meet with Curt. How long do you expect your meeting to last?"

"I shouldn't need more than an hour. Will it be a problem if it takes longer?"

"No, but we want prisoners to take part in lunch, which begins at 11:45."

Michael stopped at the door to the visitation room. "I'll make sure we're done in plenty of time for him to make it to lunch."

Officer Morrow smiled, turned her head, and unlocked the door. "As will I."

She pointed to a table. "Have a seat in the back corner."

"Thank you, Officer."

Michael opened his portfolio notebook and reviewed his notes. He stood when he heard the door being unlocked. Russell walked toward Michael, but his head turned to a table in the far corner of the room where an inmate was meeting with a middle-aged man in a tailored suit, whose leather briefcase sat open on the table.

Russel turned his head only enough to make eye contact with Michael. He lowered his head and raised his right eyebrow. His body language told Michael he did not want to be there.

"Mr. Curt, my name is Michael Mays, I'm an attorney. Do you prefer I call you, Mr. Curt or is it okay to call you, Russell?"

"You can call me whatever you choose."

They both sat. "But who are you and why do you want to talk?"

Russell was a handsome man, early 40s, with brown eyes, black hair combed straight back and a trimmed mustache. Tall, but three to four inches shorter than Michael.

"I'm an attorney, but the discussion I want to have with you isn't a legal matter. I want to discuss a book on photography."

In a heartbeat, the room went from being the last place Russell wanted to be, to the *only* place he wanted to be.

Russell placed his hands on the table and tapped his fingers. "What do you mean, 'book on photography?'"

"I met your wife, she told me your story."

Russell looked away and shook his head. "Why, who are you to her?"

"I'm a friend, and I bought the book from your son at their yard sale."

Russell sat back in his chair and rubbed his forehead with both hands, then continued his fingers up through his hair. He clasped his hands behind his head while squeezing his arms against the sides of his head and leaned forward until his elbows touched the table.

Russell looked up, his fingers slid apart, and his arms dropped. His eyes met Michael's. "What do you know, other than what Linda's told you?"

"Enough to believe your testimony—I've used the book—as you claimed."

Russell's mouth dropped open while closing his eyes and shaking his head. He sat studying Michael for a few seconds. His right hand rubbed his cheeks and chin as if he were stroking a beard. "Too many thoughts are going through my head. But I keep coming back to this, if you bought the book at Linda's yard sale, why would she give you background on it? She couldn't do that with every customer."

"Good observation, Russell. Which leads to the reason I'm here."

"I'm listening."

"Good. She told me the back story of the book, but I had to pry it from her. She only allowed me to pry because of something we have in common."

"What's that?"

"Someone, the *same* person, tried to kill both of us, and Jacob. He's threatening me to give him the book, or else he'll kill me."

Russell slammed his closed fists on the table. "He lied. He used me."

"Curt!" Officer Morrow snapped.

Russell swiveled his head and nodded.

"Who used you, Russell?"

Russell looked at the table, shook his head, flexed his fists, while giving a guttural growl. "I had no part in that, that's not what I wanted. There's no way I'd hurt Linda or Jacob."

Michael leaned forward. "Russell, you can't hurt them much more than you've done."

Russell squinted and lowered his head. "What do you mean?"

"Whether you killed Linda's sister or not, you had an affair with her while you were engaged to Linda. And again, after you were married. You don't think you hurt her *and* Jacob? Adding to the damage you inflicted, you had sexual relations with her sister on the night she died... *knowing* she'd die that night."

That stunned Russell, as if he'd never put that discrepancy together. "Yeah, but I meant I wouldn't beat them."

"Russell, help me. You'll be helping Linda and Jacob, and my family and friends. Tell me who this guy is."

"What do you mean, help your family and friends?"

"He's threatening to kidnap and hold a good friend of mine for ransom; he wants the book in exchange. And, one of his thugs shot my 90-year-old grandmother. I'm certain he meant it as a message for me."

With a tinge of remorse in his voice, Russel asked, "Is she okay?"

"She will be, but what kind of person would do that?"

Russell hung his head. "A terrible person, one who did 30 years for killing a woman, but they suspected him of killing more. His father left him money, a lot of money. Bad dudes in here work for him. They're paid to rough up and even kill fellow inmates. He has people who once worked for him in here, now working for him on the outside."

"Why rough-up people in here?"

"Because he *can*. If he told you he wanted the cake that came with your dinner, and you refused," Russell looked intently in Michael's eyes, "you *wouldn't* make that mistake again."

"You mentioned 'on the outside.' Why keep them on the payroll?"

"Cons in here have family out there. He ruled this place through threats and intimidation. *No one* crossed him. If they did, by the next morning, if they were still alive, they'd wished they weren't."

"You said he spent 30 years in here?"

"Right."

"That suggests he's no longer in here?"

"Yeah, they paroled him last month."

"How in the world could a guy who killed someone, was a suspect in killing others, and brutalized inmates, get paroled?"

Russell stared at Michael for a few seconds. "In the eyes of the Parole Board, he was a model prisoner. No one dared to say otherwise, not even the guards—they have family on the outside too—they'd suffer the consequences."

"Wow," was all Michael could say as he leaned back in his chair. He sat speechless for a few seconds. "Russell, maybe we can help each other."

"Yeah, how's that?"

"You tell me who this man is, and I'll protect your family,"

"Who'll protect me? He can reach back in here so fast... I'd be dead by morning."

"Okay, you give me his name and first I'll clear you of the murder charges."

Russell leaned back; fingers interlocked at his chest. He cocked his head and squinted. "How will you do that? Yeah—I get it—you're a lawyer, but the court didn't buy my story back then, for sure they won't buy it now."

"We're not talking new trial with the same testimony. I'll use the book to go back, find who killed Linda's sister, gather evidence and get you acquitted."

Russell jolted forward. "You'd do that for me."

"No, but I'd do it for Linda, Jacob, and my family and friends."

"Whatever you do, you better do it fast."

"Why is that?"

"Because Daniel will find out I met with you. You can't trust anyone in this joint. Daniel *will* find out."

"So, his name is Daniel?" Michael made a note in his notebook.

Russell pursed his lips and shook his head. "Yeah, I didn't mean to let that slip out yet."

"What do you mean, 'slip out yet?'"

"I wouldn't have given his name until you get the evidence to clear me."

"Really, Russell? How difficult will it be for me to find information related to men recently paroled?"

"Not very hard, I guess."

"Your guess is correct. There's no way I will put time and effort into clearing you without the name up front. I've promised you, and I'm a man of my word."

Russell looked at the wall behind Michael and shook his head. "Either way, in here or out there, I'm a dead man... shovel ready."

"What's his name, Russell?"

"Daniel Wygal."

"W-Y-G-A-L?"

"Yes."

As Michael wrote 'Daniel Wygal' in his notebook, he asked, "Are you still in touch with him?"

"Not since the first week after his release. He promised he'd stay in touch, but once he learned my ex-wife was selling the book, not a word from him since."

Michael opened photos on his iPhone. He zoomed in on a photo he'd taken at OMSI. "Is this Daniel?"

"Yeah, younger, but yeah."

"Okay, let's go back and start at the beginning. How did he find out about the book?"

"His cell mate told him how I used it as an alibi in court. That got his interest."

"What's his cell mate's name?"

"Billy Chapman."

As Michael took notes, Russell told the story of his relationship with Daniel, and why he wants the book.

Russell hesitated. "He told me if I helped him, he'd help me." He shook his head. "I was a fool to trust him."

Michael paused and searched Russell's face. "What caused him to become interested in me?"

Russell told him the story Daniel told him. Michael was spellbound by what he heard.

30

~~~~

Russell finished his story.

Michael shook his head and held his hand up, palm toward Russell. "Hold it. The police never found my mother's murderer. Are you telling me Daniel Wygal is her killer?"

"He never admitted that. But as I said, he searched for kids left behind by the women police *suspected* he murdered."

Michael leaned back, considering what he had heard. He wondered out loud, "So, I somehow find him in the past?"

"Sure sounds like you did."

"No, it sounds like I do."

Michael pondered that for a few seconds. "What brought on his interest in the *book*?"

"After I described the book's cover, Daniel told me he saw you carrying *that* book."

Michael put his hand on the back of his neck. "Wow. You mentioned you called his cell phone. So, you have his number?"

"Yeah."

"Do you have it with you?"

"No, it's in a notebook, back in my cell."

Michael gave him a business card. "Call me and give me the number as soon as possible."

Russell leaned forward, slammed both palms on the metal table.

"Curt!"

192

Russell looked behind him again and nodded.

"Last warning. Do that again and you're back in your cell."

"Yes, ma'am."

He looked back at Michael. "Dude, as soon as you call him, he'll figure out who gave you his number. I might as well cut my throat."

"Okay, you give me the number and I'll hold off calling him until we get you out of here?"

"You promise?"

"I promise."

"Yeah, well, Daniel promised too."

"I'm not Daniel. I keep my word."

Russell stared at Michael for a few seconds. "I guess I have no choice but to trust you."

"You're right, you don't. Let's discuss the book. I heard what you claimed during your trial. Some, I've figured out myself. But last night, something happened that confused me."

"What's that?"

"It was the first time, since reading the entire book, I'd used it—"

Russell interrupted mid-sentence. "You didn't have four hours, right?"

"That's correct, what happened?"

"While you've been working your way through the book you've had 10 minutes, 20 minutes and so-forth, depending on what page you read last, right?"

"Yes."

"And, it didn't matter what page you opened it to, the number of minutes you had were still connected to the number of pages you'd read."

Michael said, "I always opened to the page where I'd left off."

"You didn't have to. But now that you've read the entire book, whatever page you *open it to* is how much time you'll get. How much time did you get last night?"

"I believe it was 61 minutes."

"That means you opened the book to page, 61."

"Good information. It'll keep me from wasting time."

"Yeah, it does, and it kept me out of trouble more than once."

Michael let that pass. He wasn't interested in hearing Russell's stories.

"Did you go back to a point where someone else, from a different time, is using the book? For instance, what if I use the book to go back to the night someone killed Liz? You claim you left the book behind that night. That places the book in the same time and location with itself."

Russell's brow furrowed. "I never thought of that."

"Okay, another question, on a trip back to one of my Little League games, Daniel was there taking pictures of my mother, stalking her. He became suspicious of me and photographed me while I was sitting on the grass watching my mother. Out of nowhere, a man with a rifle appeared behind Daniel. He lifted the rifle, pointed it at me and fired. A witness said the shooter vanished before his eyes. Did that happen to you?"

"What, no." Russell said. "That means someone else has a copy of the book."

"Or," Michael speculated, "someone has my book."

Russell rested his elbows on the table and spread his arms. "Either way, why kill you? And, how did he find you?"

"There's only *one* way," Michael said, "When you showed up at your sister-in-law's birthday party, you appeared behind Linda, right?"

Russell's head leaned and his eyes squinted. "Yes."

Michael hesitated, then asked, "Why did you appear behind her?"

"Because she'd just taken—" As if a light came on, Russell said, "Daniel had just taken a picture of you."

"That's right, so the question is, how did the shooter get the photo of me sitting on the grass, next to a tree?"

"Wow," Russell said, "if Daniel is working with someone in the future, I'd run away and hide if I were you. What are you going to do with this?"

Michael shook his head. "I don't know. But it's all linked to Daniel."

"I told you, Daniel is a bad guy, but this doesn't make sense."

"To me either," Michael shrugged and rotated his palms up. "Okay, we won't solve that puzzle today. Let's talk about Linda and Jacob."

"What about them?"

"Two things. First, Linda and I have become close friends—not dating—not lovers, but Daniel's attempts on our lives has created a bond."

"Okay, what's second?"

"Jacob and I hit it off from the time we met at the yard sale. He impressed me as being smart, likeable, and a good kid."

"I wouldn't know, I wasn't there to watch him grow-up."

"And that was someone *else's* fault?"

Russell's face reddened, and he started to slam his fist on the table but stopped. "Go ahead."

"Linda is doing a great job. You can be proud of him. I lost my mother when I was Jacob's age. My father died eight years later. He wasn't a part of my life during those eight years."

"You think Daniel killed them both?"

"No, my dad disappeared from my life after someone murdered my mother. My grandparents raised me. Which brings me back to Jacob. I know what it's like to not have a father. I asked Linda if I could spend time with Jacob."

"You said your grandparents raised you; that means you had a grandfather?"

"He was in his late 60s, but still practiced law. A good man, but too caught-up in work, and crazy schemes and inventions, to give me much time. I was in college when he died. My *grandmother* raised me.

"Back to my point. I was on the Lewis and Clark College golf team and I still play. Linda's allowing me to teach Jacob how to play golf. So far, he loves it."

Russell studied Michael for a few seconds. "I guess that's okay."

"Russell, I'm not asking for your approval. I'm telling you out of courtesy." Michael sensed Russell not liking that and was ready to tip over. "I'll solve Liz's murder and get you cleared, on one condition."

"Yeah, what's that?"

"That you never talk to, stalk, bother, call on the phone, or communicate with Linda or Jacob again."

Russell stood and clenched his teeth. "That's too far, dude. There's no way I'll agree to that."

Michael closed his notebook and stood to leave. "Okay."

"What are you doing, man?" Russel looked back at the guard, then sat in his chair. "You can't leave without helping me."

"I can, and I offered. I hope you enjoy the rest of your life in prison."

"Wait. You'll walk out and leave me hanging?"

"Nope, you're leaving yourself hanging. You can be a free man, Russell, but you must agree to my conditions. And remember, I have the book. If you violate any of my conditions, I will use the book to put you back in here. And, if I even hear a rumor, or sense that you are working with Daniel Wygal, I *will* put you back in here. Do you understand? Do you agree with the conditions?"

Russell put both hands palm down on the table and bowed his head.

Michael slid his chair in, turned and walked away. "Wait—" Michael heard Russell whisper. Michael stopped and turned as Russell looked up. "We have a deal."

Michael looked him in the eyes, nodded, and left.

31

Katrina Kane answered, again speaking in her best southern accent. "Daniel, my dear, Katrina here."

"Cut the crap, Katrina, did you find the woman's cabin?"

Daniel could hear her breathing, then sigh.

"Are you there, Katrina?"

"Yeah, I'm here. There's never a how's your day, Katrina; I hope you're doing well, Katrina. It's always, extort him, Katrina; kidnap her, Katrina; shoot them, Katrina—

"Would it be that hard for you, just once, to ask me how I'm doing?"

"I *don't* need to ask how you're doing, Katrina. That's why I hire you and pay you top dollar. I assume you're doing well, and I trust you to do well."

"You are such a compassionate dear, Daniel, and you assume too much. *Yes,* I found the place and I'm here."

"Did you find a good photography magazine?"

"Two, and I learned a lot. One had a good article on the latest equipment. The other was more general information, not as informative, but I learned from it."

"What's your thoughts on a plan?"

"This is a quaint little town and, based on the background in your text, I assume she's here to do a story. So, tomorrow I'll be here bright and early to follow her. If I'm correct, I'll strike up a conversation and build a relationship with her. Then, what do you want me to do?"

"Her boyfriend has something I want, and I have no problem taking the most extreme measures to get it."

"So, hostage, threat of pain, which may escalate to serious pain. What if he still refuses?"

"Katrina, whether he gives me what I want or not, she ceases to be available to take the witness stand."

"Wow, whatever you want must be something precious to you. To make it worth my while, you can expect my fee to be much higher than *whatever* you'd planned to pay."

"Make it happen, I told you I'll treat you well." Daniel paused for a few seconds. "I don't trust Bob's assessment. She may have stopped for one night only and is heading out in the morning. Check out of your hotel in the morning in case she's off to another location."

"Bob's an idiot, Daniel. We've discussed this before. I don't understand why you continue to use him? How about I do a pro bono for you and rid you of that problem?"

"Katrina, I have experienced little loyalty or true friendship in my life. But, since we were kids, Bob's been a loyal friend. He's taken the bullet for me, even as kids, more times than I can remember. I talk rough with him and lose patience, but that's been our relationship since we first met. *Hear* me on this. Anyone who harms him won't survive that day, even if they think they're doing me a favor. Is that understood?"

"I understand, I disagree with keeping him around, but I respect your loyalty to him. It's a side of you I've never seen."

"Do your job, Katrina and leave Bob to me."

* * *

Katrina could not find a hotel vacancy, so she slept in her car. Trees near Stephanie's cabin concealed her night's sleeping quarters.

Wednesday, October 30th
Katrina's alarm woke her at 6 A.M., allowing her time to arrange herself as best she could.

Brushing my teeth with bottled water... again.

Stephanie walked out of her cabin; Katrina looked at her watch.

8:30, about freaking time.

As Stephanie turned to lock the door, she hesitated, then stepped back to the edge of the porch while removing her camera from its bag. After taking a few pictures, she looked at the Nikon's Image Review screen and smiled.

Katrina mocked.

She must really like the cabin's front door.

Katrina saw a man walking toward her. In a whisper she said, "What's this?"

Must be out for a morning walk and thinks I have car trouble.

She got into her car, backed out, and parked a quarter mile down the road waiting for Stephanie.

Stephanie stopped at a local restaurant for breakfast.

Katrina pulled in behind her and parked.

I'm not starved, but I should eat.

She guided the server to the table she wanted. Behind Stephanie and not too close. Her goal during breakfast: watch and listen to Stephanie's interaction with restaurant staff.

Her impression was that Stephanie was very amiable, approachable, and has a sense of humor.

After breakfast, Katrina followed Stephanie downtown. While Stephanie parked, Katrina drove two blocks past her and parked, then hurried on foot to follow her.

Stephanie approached a tall, handsome young man dressed in Oktoberfest tradition. Lederhosen with suspenders and all.

My first order of business is to find a printed schedule.

"You either work here, or you're really into this festival," she joked.

"Both." He extended his hand. "My family owns the bakery across the street, and I volunteer during the festival. My name is Peter." They shook hands. He placed his hand over Stephanie's and lingered in the handshake. "Do you need help?"

"Nice to meet you, Peter." Stephanie smiled as blood rushed to her face. "Yes. I hope you can help me. My name is Stephanie. I'm here doing a photo shoot for the State of Georgia."

"Oh… wow. Glad to meet you too, Stephanie. I am at your service. What's the purpose of the photos?"

"It's for a travel guide to unique and lesser known events; things that will draw tourists to Georgia. Is there a printed schedule of Oktoberfest activities?"

"I'll make sure you get a schedule, but," spreading his arms wide, "what do you want to see?"

"I'm interested in things that make your festival unique compared to other festivals in Georgia."

"There's *nothing* in Georgia like this festival."

"Great. Where do you recommend I start?"

"Where better to start an Oktoberfest tour than the beer garden and food court. Follow me."

Peter took off at a pace he realized may be too fast. "I'm sorry, Stephanie, I'm a fast walker and forget that other people don't always appreciate my pace."

"I need a good walk. This trip, I've been driving and sitting too much; I can use the exercise."

"Okay, let's go."

They hurried past food stalls that sold pretzels, gingerbread hearts, and soft drinks.

The aromas made Stephanie want to stop and just stand and take in the smells.

Following, Katrina picked up her pace while maintaining a discreet distance.

Peter lifted his arms waist high as they approached the beer garden. "Here we are."

Polka music was coming from multiple directions. But mostly from a huge blue and white striped canopy with people already beneath it dancing and drinking beer.

Stephanie asked, "Do you import German beer or use a local supplier?"

"Both." He pointed to the German brew pub in front of them. "This place brews my favorite beer. Are you interested in a tour of their operation?"

"Yes, I'd love that."

"Great. This way please."

Katrina sat inside the fenced-off area in front of the pub.

How do I get her away from this brewmeister dude?

A young woman dressed in Bavarian dirndl fashion, approached Katrina. "What can I get for you, ma'am?"

"Hi, you can call me Kat. I overheard a young man say this place brews his favorite beer. He passed by just moments ago, escorting a young woman into your pub. I didn't catch the name of the beer, but I want to try it."

"Sure, that was Peter, he orders the Bavarian Pilsner. It's fantastic and one of our most popular beers."

"Bavarian Pilsner sounds good. By the way, your apron is tied on the left side. That means you're single... right."

"Yes. Are you German?"

"No, just did a little research before I came?"

"Well... thanks, good job. I'll get that for you, at no charge, Kat."

"Thanks."

Katrina sat and sipped the Pilsner, admiring Peter's palate for beer. She was halfway through the glass when Stephanie and Peter walked out of the pub.

She overheard Peter ask Stephanie, "Will you allow me to buy you a glass of my favorite beer?"

Stephanie looked at her watch, tilted her head and looked at him for a few seconds. "You know, it's earlier than I've *ever* drank alcohol, but I'll take you up on that offer."

"Great, I'll be right back with a Bavarian Pilsner."

Katrina raised her glass. "Good choice; it's excellent."

Stephanie pulled out a chair at the table next to Katrina, placed her camera on the table, and sat. "I'm looking forward to it."

Katrina leaned over to get a closer look. "Is that a Nikon D500?"

"Yes. Are you familiar with it?"

"Only from afar. But yes, I've read reviews and seen work produced by it. You must not be a tourist."

Stephanie saw Peter approaching. "I'm being treated like a VIP tourist—"

Peter set the Pilsner in front of Stephanie, "Here you go," then sat across from her.

"Thank you, Peter. I was just telling —" Stephanie stopped and looked at Katrina. "My name's Stephanie, what's yours?

"Kat, nice to meet you, Stephanie."

"Peter, I was going to tell Kat you made me feel welcome. Not like you were just *doing your job.*"

"That was my goal, and I'm happy I succeeded."

"Kat, my name is Peter."

"Good to meet you, Peter."

"You too, Kat." He stood and placed a hand on each of their tables. "I hate to leave you two lovely ladies alone in this crazy place, but I sense you'll survive without me. But, I am doing my shift of volunteer work, so I better get back. Stephanie, I wish my real job was as enjoyable as escorting you."

"Thank you, Peter."

Real job?

He bowed, looked at Stephanie and handed her a brochure. "I found a festival schedule in the pub. I placed my family's business card inside. I wrote my cell phone number on the back, just in case you're free for dinner tonight. You've sampled my favorite beer, allow me to take you to my favorite restaurant."

Stephanie tilted her head, looked at him as the corners of her mouth crept upwards. "You just might receive a call from me, Peter."

Peter smiled, turned and as he walked away, jumped and clicked his heels together, took a couple more steps, turned and walked backwards with arms outstretched. "I'll be standing by."

Kat leaned toward Stephanie and teased, "I believe he's smitten with you."

Stephanie blushed. "The truth—I'm smitten with *him* — I got lost there for a minute. Back to your question about the camera.

"No, I'm not here as a tourist, I'm a professional photographer, shooting for a Georgia travel guide."

"Wow, I'm in the presence of greatness."

"Well, I'm good… but great?"

Katrina leaned over and put her hand on Stephanie's arm. "I'm talking about the Nikon dear."

Stephanie looked at her, then burst out laughing, as did Katrina. "I'm kidding," Katrina said, "I'm glad you have a sense of humor."

While finishing their beer, they sat and discussed their impression of the Oktoberfest. Stephanie finished her beer and stood. "Back to work—Kat—walk around with me, I'd love the company."

"And I appreciate the offer. Will I be a nuisance if I ask questions?"

"No, not at all, I'm used to it. On Saturday afternoons, I teach a photography class in downtown Portland, Oregon. Students walk with me while we shoot. I explain what I'm seeing, and coach them as they choose their subject and decide upon composition."

Katrina hooked her arm in Stephanie's. "Then, we're off."

A parade had begun since they had parked and walked in. People lined the streets watching Polka bands, Bavarian 'oompah' bands, and participants dancing in Bavarian garb.

Stephanie and Katrina walked back to where Stephanie first met Peter. "This is the main street," Stephanie said, almost shouting. "Are you up for walking to the end of town and back?"

"Of course," Katrina called back, "it should be interesting."

They walked a block and came to Helen's Bakery. "Peter told me his family owns this bakery, let's go inside."

Katrina patted her stomach and puffed out her cheeks. "I do like me some pastries."

"Ridiculous, Katrina, you have a cute figure."

Katrina pulled on Stephanie's arm and walked faster. "So, I heard permission to indulge myself."

While Stephanie used Peter's name to get invited into the back of the shop, Katrina used selecting a pastry as an excuse not to follow her.

* * *

"Daniel, Katrina here. I'm with the girl and she's eating up my charm."

"Okay, what's your plan?"

"Still working on that, but I don't sense there'll be any issues. She trusts me."

"I assume you'll move on her tonight?"

"Yes, and I'll call you as soon as I have her secured."

"Her boyfriend will want to talk to her to prove we have her. I'll let you know. You picked up a burner phone, right?"

"Daniel, why do you even ask."

"I always ask. I pay you to listen and do."

"We'll talk later, I better get off the phone."

32

Katrina made her choice from the pasty display. She took a few extras napkins and sat at a small table pretending to eat her pastry. She broke off a small piece, wrapped the remaining piece in two napkins and threw it away. She saved the one bite until Stephanie came out of the back. Katrina made a flourish of finishing. "I'm done. Don't want to keep you from your work."

As Katrina exaggerated wiping her mouth, Stephanie smiled. "That tour was very interesting. I'm glad we stopped. How was your pastry?"

"Wonderful. I could hurt myself if I stayed *here* any longer."

They walked and talked. When Stephanie saw something that piqued her interest, she explained to Katrina why it caught her attention and how she would compose the photo.

The last shop they stopped in front of was a quilt-themed shop. "Stephanie, take a few shots here. Every year quilting gets more popular. There's interest out there."

"You know, you're right. I've shot three shows on the west coast and always received positive feedback on them."

"Great, I'll follow you. Let's get something to eat after this."

Stephanie looked at her watch. "Wow, 1:30, let's do that. I saw a flyer at the bakery for a restaurant on the riverbank. I asked the woman who showed me around if she's been to the restaurant. She told me she has, and the food is great."

"I'm in and I'm buying. Consider it compensation for tutoring me."

"Deal, and don't forget you are in the presence of greatness."

"Your right, I'll buy the beer too."

"Heck with the quilt shop, Kat. Let's go."

"Nope. It'll only take a few minutes and I'm interested too."

"Geez. Pushy broad."

Katrina smiled and pushed Stephanie through the door.

You don't know the half of it.

As they finished their meal, Stephanie asked, "Is there something bothering you, Kat? You've become quiet since we came in here?"

"I'm okay. I've enjoyed hanging out with you *so* much today. I'm leaving tomorrow, but it's strange?"

"What's strange?"

"You and I hit it off, right away. I don't have many friends. Relationships don't come easy, but ours did, and I hate to lose that."

"So do I, but we don't have to lose it. In my line of work, I travel... sometimes too much. Every time I'm in your area—which I don't know where that is — I'll contact you and we can get together."

"That would be *great*, and I'd love you to meet my family."

"And, I'd love to meet them."

"My husband and children will love you. They'll welcome you as family. We live in Washington DC; my husband's an attorney."

"What's your line of work, Kat?

"I'm a meeting planner. I work out of our home, but I don't accept as much work as I did when I was younger."

"You must do a lot of traveling."

"I used to, but much less now. This past week, we were in Atlanta, where he was the keynote speaker at a conference. A conference I planned and oversaw. He had to get back to DC, but he knew I wanted to visit this festival, so, he told me to take the car while he flew back. 'Go experience the Oktoberfest.' He said, so here I am."

Stephanie looked at Kat for a few seconds. "Kat, I'll call Peter this afternoon and set a time to meet him tomorrow. You and I can hang out the rest of the day while I shoot a few more sites around town. I'll go back to my cabin and take care of work-related things—"

"I'd love to. Yes, I'm in," Katrina jumped in with enthusiasm.

"Great, but wait, there's more. You come over, say… 6ish. Do you like pizza?"

"I've never met a pizza I didn't love. Let's do *this*, you go back to your cabin and catch up. I'll pick up a pizza and get wine. Red or white?"

"I'm a white wine girl."

"Okay, I'm a red, so I'll pick up a bottle of each."

"Before we split up this afternoon, give me your address and I'll be at your cabin around 6, with pizza and wine and a treat from Peter's family's bakery."

"That will be a great evening. Kat, I have an idea. I want to include a few shots of the incredible views here. I have a beautiful view of the Alpine valley and neighboring mountains from my deck.

"We'll have a glass of wine and you could be in the photos. I'll shoot you holding the glass, leaning against the rail while taking in the view as the sun sets. What do you think?"

"That's a wonderful idea. You can get work done, while making me a star."

But wait until you discover who's shooting who.

Katrina waved the server over and asked for the check.

"Kat, I can put this on my expenses. Please let me get this."

"No, I said it's on me." When the server returned, Katrina waved off his attempt to return her change. "No change back needed."

"Thank you very much." The college-aged server said.

"Okay, Stephanie, onward and upward. Let's go shoot this place."

The server looked confused. Katrina laughed. "I didn't mean shoot *this place*," she said, while making her hand into a pistol.

Katrina placed her hand on the server's shoulder. "She's a photographer and we need to get more shots for her project."

The server gave a nervous laugh.

Stephanie touched his arm. "You've done a great job. Thank you."

Katrina thought: *Said the fly, while the spider kept spinning her web.*

* * *

After she and Stephanie parted ways for the afternoon, Katrina found a secluded spot near the river and pulled out her phone.

"Daniel, this is Katrina."

"What's in the works?"

"I'm going to her cabin tonight for dinner. I told her I'd bring wine and pizza, but I'll be serving zip-ties and bullets."

"Call me when she's secured."

"Won't be long."

* * *

As she walked into her cabin, Stephanie thought, *I'm beat, but there's still work to do.*

Her camera was uploading the days photographs to the cloud while she worked on her notes and observations.

After a quick shower, she put on her favorite hanging-out-around-the-house clothes: warm-ups.

The uploading was done. She placed her camera and notebook on the dining room table.

While walking out onto the back deck, the doorbell rang.

Must be Kat… Six o'clock.

Stephanie opened the door. Kat stood, head tilted forward, eyes looking directly into Stephanie's, and held a scoff, but no pizza or wine.

"Hey, Kat, right on time. Come on in… what's wrong?"

"Let's sit, Stephanie."

"Okay?" Stephanie said, and walked toward the sofa.

When she turned to sit, a gun was pointing at her chest.

Stephanie fell backwards.

"What's this about?"

"Well, tonight will not play out as two besties hanging, drinking wine, and chatting."

"So, you've been playing me the entire day?"

"And you played along so well my dear, and I like you—I do—which will make it harder if I have to kill you tonight."

"What, kill me? Why in the world do you want to kill me?"

"I don't *want* to, but I have a job to do and I always finish my job."

"So, you're some kind of hitman… hit person?"

"I prefer to call myself an 'agent of last resort.' And I'm superb at what I do."

"And humble."

"I am *not* humble. When you're this good, why try to hide it.

"Now stand, turn around and put your hands behind you."

Stephanie stood, turned, then heard Kat's shoes clicking on the hardwood floor as she approached.

When she judged Kat was close enough, she spun to knock her off balance.

Kat's gun hit the side of Stephanie's head halfway through her turn.

Groaning in pain as she fell, her head slammed against the arm of the sofa.

She laid there, semi-conscious.

This must be a dream.

But she felt Kat wrestling her arms behind her back and realized she could no longer move them or separate her feet.

She heard Kat talking with someone.

"Daniel, she's locked down."

33

In his office, Michael's cell phone rang. "This is Michael," he said, knowing who was calling from 'No Caller ID."

"Michael, we have Stephanie; there's a gun to her head. You have a life or death decision to make. Make the wrong one and she'll never again be available to meet you for coffee."

"And you have a life in prison decision to make. Without the book *nothing* changes, does it?"

"You have no idea what I would do or change."

"For as long as I can remember, I've had the ability to make sound assumptions from limited information. I've put together a scenario on why you want the book. So, you have an even bigger decision to make—let Stephanie go or there's no chance of ever getting the book—" Michael hung up and called Stephanie's parents.

Her mother answered. "Hello."

"Karen, Michael Mays here. There isn't time to discuss this, but I need you to look to see if Stephanie uploaded pictures today."

"I've been checking every hour since we talked. I'm looking at today's upload as we talk."

"Great, can you forward from her file?"

"Yes."

"Okay, I won't have time to look through all of the photos, so use your best judgement. I need a few that might give me a clue to where she's staying. Send those to the email address on my business card, ASAP."

"Sure… can you tell me anything?"

"I'm sorry, Karen, I have to take this call, but I *will* get back to you tonight."

"Okay—"

Michael abruptly ended the call and answered the incoming one.

"Never hang up on me again. It will mean sudden death for your girlfriend."

"Alright. Her life is worth more than the book."

"Now we're getting somewhere, Michael."

"Let me talk to her to."

"Oh, I'm sorry, Michael, but that won't happen."

"How do I know you have her, and that she's okay? Do you need to hang up and think it over? I'm not giving up the book on your word. I don't take you to be an honorable guy."

Michael heard the caller exhale hard.

"Stand by, you'll get a phone call soon."

Michael opened his briefcase and removed his notebook computer. While it fired up, Michael called Trevor, asking him to step into his office.

"Yes, Mr. Mays,"

"Trevor, get ahold of my four o'clock appointment, cancel it and reschedule."

"Will do."

"Thanks, and close my door please."

Michael opened his email and found the photos Karen sent. His phone rang.

No Caller ID.

"This is Michael."

"Well, the jilted boyfriend."

"Who's this, what do you want?"

"Like, I'll tell you my name. The way your girlfriend was flirting with a handsome young man today, I was preparing you for rejection. Here she is."

Kat held the phone to Stephanie's ear.

"Hello," Michael sensed she's dazed.

"Stephanie, it's Michael, are you okay?"

"I've been better."

"We have little time. Is there a clue in the photos you took today that will help me discover your whereabouts?"

Kat yanked the phone away. "Enough. I have her and she's okay—for now."

"Please, allow me to reassure her and say goodbye,"

Without a word, Kat jammed the phone against Stephanie's ear, causing Stephanie to let out a breathy "Ow."

"Are you okay, Stephanie?"

"Yes but get me out of here."

"A clue?"

"Butterflies."

Kat grabbed the phone again. "We're through—make it happen." The phone went dead. Michael opened the attachment Karen sent him.

* * *

"What's with the 'butterflies?'"

Stephanie shook her head and closed her eyes. "It's a term of endearment: Butterfly Kisses."

"Isn't that sweet. I hope your boyfriend cares enough to make this happen quick. Maybe you and I can still grab a pizza?"

Stephanie closed her eyes while shaking her head. "Make what happen?"

"Your boyfriend has something my boss wants, and he's willing to kill to get it."

* * *

Michael sorted through the photos. The third photo he opened was of butterflies on what appeared to be an exterior wall next to the front door. Something caught Michael's eye.

That's an address they've gathered on.

He zoomed in on the photo. There were three butterflies on top of the address, and several on each side. He saw three butterflies sitting on a 1, a 4, and the letter A.

Because of the other butterflies, he couldn't tell if there were more numbers or letters.

He printed out the picture and took the book from his briefcase. Both in hand, he grabbed his coat and headed out his office door.

"I'll be back in a half hour, Trevor."

"Mr. Mays, are you okay?"

Michael rushed by Trevor's desk. "Yes, but I have something to take care of."

He was out the door before Trevor could respond.

Michael headed to the building's underground parking lot, got into his car, locked the doors, and looked around.

Nobody in sight. I need only 10—15 minutes.

He turned to page 15 and looked at the photo of the cabin's door.

Michael was standing 100 feet behind Stephanie as she photographed the butterflies. He walked toward her, but noticed a woman standing to his left, who appeared to be hiding behind her car watching Stephanie. He slowed, veered from Stephanie, and walked toward the woman. She looked at Michael, jumped in her car, backed out from beneath the trees, and drove onto the road.

After watching her drive off, Michael turned his attention to Stephanie, but she was pulling onto the same road the woman had taken.

He couldn't catch her, so he walked to the porch. The butterflies scattered as he waved his hands above them.

14A.

He tried the doorknob.

Locked.

The curtain on the inside of the wooden door was drawn. He glanced back at the address. The butterflies were re-gathering.

Michael drew close to the brass letters. Condensation had formed on the letters overnight.

They're getting a drink.

He followed the driveway to the road the women took. After a quarter mile, he came to an intersection that had a street sign: "Bier Way."

He noted the address and walked back to the cabin, assessing what he'd learned.

The cabin number and street name are good only if I have the name of the town.

As he considered this dilemma, his weather app came to mind.

When I travel, it defaults to the local weather.

He opened his weather app.

So, Helen, Georgia?

He googled it and discovered Helen is in White County. Next, he googled White County, Georgia 9-1-1, which took him to the County's website where he found a tab for "Public safety."

The warm omni-directional wind hit him. Back in his car, he looked at his phone. It was still on the County's home page. He opened the Public Safety tab. The first thing listed was 9-1-1 Communications. Their page listed two options: Emergency Dial: 9-1-1, and the Dispatch non-emergency phone number, which he selected.

"White County Regional Communications Center, how may I help you?"

"My name is Michael Mays, please listen carefully."

"That's what I do, sir."

"I'm calling from Portland, Oregon. I'm an attorney here, with the Spiegel, Findlay & Mays Law Firm. If you need to contact our firm to confirm that I'm legit please call."

"Go ahead, sir."

"There is a hostage crisis taking place in your county as we speak, it's an emergency, but I'm unable to call your emergency dispatchers via 9-1-1 from here."

"Sir, I'll transfer you to an Emergency Dispatcher."

"Thank you."

"9-1-1, what is your emergency?"

He repeated the information he gave to the first call-taker. "A friend is being held hostage—I'm sure it's at gunpoint—at 14A Bier Way. I'm not familiar with your county, but it's a rental. Her captor is threatening to kill her if I don't meet their demands?"

"Sir, this is confusing. Her captor called *you*?"

"Yes, but a man who's threatened me for weeks, contacted me first. I told him I don't believe he's holding my friend captive and demanded to speak with her. A few minutes later I received another call, this time from a woman. She allowed me to talk with my friend, Stephanie Clark, a professional photographer, there on assignment. These people are extremely dangerous. They shot my 90-year-old grandmother."

"Sir, do you realize we can reverse-dial back to the reporting party? We can trace calls back to you. It is a crime to make fraudulent calls to 9-1-1."

"Please trace back to my phone, and call my law firm, Spiegel, Findlay and Mays, in Portland, Oregon. Call the Portland Police Bureau and ask if a 90-year-old woman named Louise Nelson was shot. Whatever you need to do to make you believe me.

"I'll stay on the line if needed, but please error on the side of safety. Send officers out to do a welfare check at 14A Bier Way… please."

The Emergency Dispatcher said, "Hold on sir."

After a brief pause, the Dispatcher came back on. "Please stay on the line. I've dispatched officers to that address."

"Please warn them the captor is armed and, I'm assuming, dangerous."

* * *

Six minutes later a City of Helen Police Officer pulled up to Stephanie's cabin.

A County Deputy Sheriff arrived seconds later.

They both announced their arrival to dispatch and met behind the Helen officer's car.

The Helen officer said, "Jen, cover me while I go to the door."

"I've got you, Rick."

"Okay, here we go," Rick said, as he climbed the stairs to the porch.

Standing off to the side, he knocked on the door.

Katrina peeked out of the cabin's front window.

Cops!

"Hold on, I'll be right there."

She went to the kitchenette, grabbed a knife, and cut the zip ties that bound Stephanie's ankles.

She pulled her from the sofa and shoved her against a wall in the hallway that leads to the bedrooms.

Kat checked Stephanie's wrist bindings. "Stay put. Don't make me kill anyone. But I will if I have to."

Katrina opened the door while looking up and squinting. "Hi, can I help you?"

"Good evening ma'am, my name is Officer Owens. Is Stephanie Clark available? I need to talk with her please."

"Stephanie's had a tough day, got in a fight with her boyfriend, so she had a glass of wine and is taking a nap. Please, come back in an hour."

"No ma'am, I need to speak with her before we leave."

When Katrina heard him say 'we' she looked to the driveway and saw the Deputy Sheriff standing sideways, with her right hand on her holstered pistol.

"I'll try to roust her—"

Katrina walked back and grabbed Stephanie's hands, pulling upwards hard.

Stephanie winced and moaned. "What do you want me to do?" Tears came to her eyes.

"You will tell the nice young policeman that everything is fine. I told him you had a fight with your boyfriend and that you wanted to rest and be alone."

Katrina used the knife to cut the zip ties binding Stephanie's wrists. "This gun in my hand," she jammed the barrel into Stephanie's ribs, "I know how to use it.

"Now go."

Stephanie threw her elbows back, arched her back and grunted as she exhaled hard.

She stumbled to the doorway. Tears streamed down her cheeks. "Officer—I'm Stephanie Clark—can I help you?"

"Ms. Clark, are you okay?"

Stephanie jumped to the right side of the doorway, out onto the porch while yelling, "She's got a gun."

Officer Owens grabbed her arm, using her momentum and the force of his body turning, he swung Stephanie behind him.

Katrina swung and fired, missing Stephanie, but hitting Officer Owens in the back.

He fell hard on top of Stephanie.

Katrina dove inside to her right and crouched behind the wall next to the door opening.

The Deputy Sheriff notified Dispatch that shots were fired and there is an officer down.

"Drop your weapon and come out with your hands up—*now!*"

"Why don't you come in and get me, beautiful? One girl against another... an interesting dual."

"Ma'am let's do this the easy way. They've dispatched more officers.

"You *are not* going to just walk away from here.

"I will not hesitate to put you down. *Now*, drop your weapon and come out with your hands up."

While the Deputy continued negotiating with Katrina, Officer Owens came to.

I'm thankful for my vest, but man that hurts.

The impact of the bullet, and the subsequent fall, stunned him and knocked him semi-conscious.

But he was regaining his breath and his senses.

He felt Stephanie trying to get up.

He looked at her, motioned with the palm of his hand, held his index finger in front of his lips, then sat up.

Turning, he leaned near the edge of the doorway and listened.

Kat's reflection was visible in one of the front door's glass panes. The dark curtain turned it into a mirror.

Katrina was sitting on the floor, leaning against the wall. She appeared to be staring off somewhere beyond the far-left corner of the living room, gun in both hands and pointed at the ceiling.

Officer Owens reached back and removed a pepper spray canister from his belt.

He slid his hand to the edge of the door casing, positioning it to spray into the Kat's face.

Ready to fire the pepper spray, he yelled: "*Hey!*"

She turned her head just as Officer Owens moved his hand six inches to the interior and fired while rotating his wrist.

Kat screamed and shot blind as she jumped to her feet.

Still screaming and cussing, she found the edge of the door and pulled herself through.

While turning to her right, she screamed. "I know you're there. Here's something to remember me by."

She lowered her arm, two shots sounded, she brought her arm up as she fell backwards, never to get up again.

Officer Owen looked around. The Deputy Sheriff stood at the bottom of the porch stairs, still holding her firing position, "Thank you Jen."

34

Stephanie sat in the cabin, shaken to her core. While the police continued their investigation of the shooting, she glanced over at Katrina's covered body. She broke down, again.

Paramedics evaluated Stephanie's condition and advised her to go to the Emergency Room. She declined and signed a waiver acknowledging their advice and her refusal.

After interviewing her, the police informed her she was free to leave the cabin, but not to leave town. They told her to come to the police station tomorrow morning to make a formal statement.

She began putting her belongings together.

I can't stay in this cabin.

Her first thought was to call Michael, but realized it was after midnight in Portland.

What could he do?

She remembered that the man she'd met today placed his card in the Visitor's Guide. She found it and called him.

"Hello, this is Peter."

"Hi, Peter, it's Stephanie, from earlier today."

"Hey, Stephanie. I was thinking of you when my phone rang. Tell me you've decided to let me take you to a late dinner."

"Peter... I doubt you've heard, but the woman sitting next to me today died tonight."

"Oh no. Were the two of you in an accident?"

"No, the police shot her when she resisted arrest."

"What… here in Helen?"

"Yes, but not in town. It was in my rental cabin, and it's a long story. I'll explain later. Peter, I can't stay here. Do you know of a bed & breakfast or a spare room I can rent for the night?"

"Let me call my parents, they have an extra bedroom. When I tell them your story, they will welcome you to stay with them. Are you sure you're okay?"

"No. But I'm better than I was an hour ago."

"That's understandable. Let me call them and I'll get right back to you."

"Thank you, Peter."

Stephanie thought of Michael again.

Even if I wake him and there's nothing he can do, he'll want to hear from me.

She went to her purse and found the business card he'd given her before she left Portland.

"Michael here."

"Michael, this is Stephanie. Sorry to wake you…" she sobbed uncontrollably.

"Stephanie, you didn't wake me. I've been hoping for this phone call. Are you safe? What happened?"

"Yes," she sniffled, as her breath stuttered. "I'm safe. Let's hold off discussing what happened. But, Michael, what caused this?"

"We can discuss it all later. You need to call your parents and tell them you're safe."

"They knew I was in danger?"

"I had to tell them, I needed their help to resolve this, which is part of the story I promise to tell you. But for now—please call your parents—they need to hear your voice."

"Thank you, Michael. I'll call them."

"Hello."

"Mom, it's Stephanie."

"Oh, Stephanie—" Karen began to cry. "Let me put you on speaker."

"Steph are you all right?" her father's voice wavered.

"Yes, I'm out of danger. I understand you guys helped Michael."

"We did, sweetheart," Karen said, "but it was his idea to use your photos to find you."

"It worked, but I can't imagine how. He told me he'd tell me later and insisted I call you first. If I'd known he'd contacted, you—"

"That's okay, Steph, we understand, and we appreciate Michael's sensitivity to us."

"Me too, dad."

"Are you heading back to Atlanta tonight or staying where you are?"

"After what happened here this evening, I can't stay in this cabin. I may have a place to stay, if not, I'll find one. Tomorrow, I'll finish this shoot, then drive back to Atlanta and fly out Friday as planned."

Her dad asked, "So, you'll be arriving here mid-day Friday?"

"No, I'm stopping in Washington D.C. for a lunch meeting, then on to Portland. I'll be home around 9 P.M.

"I know you're curious about tonight's events, but I ask that you give me time to process. Can we discuss it later, face-to-face?

"Sure. We understand, and we'll be there to pick you up," her father said. "Text us with your flight number and we'll keep track of your arrival time."

Stephanie's voice trembled. "Dad and mom—I love you so much. I can't wait to see you—and hug you."

Her dad said, "We are looking forward to it too."

Her mother added, "We love you, Steph."

"Thank you, mom and dad. You've always been there for me. See you tomorrow night."

Stephanie continued to put her belongings together. She was done by the time Peter called back.

"Stephanie, my parents want you to stay with them for the night. Give me your address. I'll come and lead you to their house."

"Thank you so much, Peter."

"I'll be there soon."

Stephanie followed Peter to his parents' house. When they arrived, Peter's parents welcomed her. After Peter introduced his parents—Garth and Helen—Stephanie hugged them all. Peter and his father took her bags to an upstairs bedroom, while Helen led Stephanie into their living room. "Please sit, Stephanie. Garth and I were just about to have a glass of wine. Can I pour you a glass too?"

"Helen, I would love that. Thank you."

Peter and Garth joined them. Helen called out to Garth, asking for help. "Excuse me, Stephanie." She gave a half smile.

Helen and Garth returned with four glasses and two bottles of wine, along with sliced fresh baked bread on a plate with butter, cheeses and fruit.

"Thank you," Stephanie said, "please don't be offended, but I don't have much of an appetite."

"No offense taken," Garth said.

Neither Peter, Helen, nor Garth pressured Stephanie, but she initiated the conversation and opened up about the evening. She relaxed enough to nibble on a few grapes and a piece of chocolate Helen had included on the plate.

After finishing her story, she said, "I appreciate your hospitality, but I am completely worn out and need to go to bed. I must be at the police station by 8 AM to make a statement."

"We understand," Garth said, "we're happy we could help you."

They all hugged and said goodnight.

As she turned, Helen stopped. "We're early risers, Stephanie. I'll have breakfast ready if you want to join Garth and me. You'd be welcomed."

Stephanie leaned into Helen again, hugged her tight and said, "Thank you, I know I'll need to eat something before I leave."

Peter jumped in, "I love my mother's breakfasts, so I'll be here to join y'all, and say goodbye."

Thank you, Peter. And thank you all for your help and kindness."

"You are welcome, Stephanie," Helen said. "Good night, dear."

Peter and Garth echoed goodnights.

As Stephanie climbed the stairs to her room, she thought, *I needed that time, but will time heal the damage from this day?*

35

Thursday, October 31st

Michael woke early and laid in bed worrying about Stephanie. After half an hour, he realized his worry was taking him nowhere. He needed to shower, shave, get to work and focus his mind elsewhere.

In his office, the first thing on Michael's agenda was to call Carrie Hindler and ask for access to Daniel Wygal's case file. Including any reports and photographic evidence associated with his mother's murder.

Michael told her of Wygal's hitman shooting his grandmother, and of Kat holding Stephanie hostage. Carrie agreed to give him access.

She made him promise that if he discovers solid evidence, he will allow the police to handle it.

"Carrie, whatever turns up, I will turn it over to you and the police."

"Okay, I'll have it for you tomorrow. My assistant will call you when it's ready. Michael, one last thing. Your mother's file will be graphic, and very disturbing. Are you sure you want to do this?"

"No, I don't *want to* see it, Carrie. But my grandmother deserves to find out who killed her daughter. And—before she dies—to know the killer received justice."

"All right, I'll see you tomorrow."

"Okay. Until then, thanks."

Prior to lunch, Michael helped Trevor set up the conference room for the 2 P.M. meeting with Cailen and his attorney.

At 1 P.M., members of Hauler met with Michael for a briefing. "Gentlemen," Michael began, "if you can't walk into the meeting room with confidence, then I ask you to wait in this room until the meeting ends. But don't display cockiness. I want them to see the genuineness you've shown to me."

The three band members looked at one another, then back to Michael and agreed with his expectations.

He laid out his strategy and warned them he will come hard against Cailen and his attorneys.

At 1:50 P.M., Trevor called Michael on his desk intercom, "Mr. Mays, Mr. Cailen and his attorneys are here."

"Thank you, Trevor. Show them to the conference room please."

"They are there and seated."

"Thanks."

Ian looked at his bandmates, then back to Michael. "*Attorneys?*"

"No surprise here guys, there's a lot at stake. They'll try intimidating us with their big city law firm."

"You're not intimidated, Michael?" Ian asked.

"Our case is strong. And, I worked for a big LA law firm for three years. We're all the same. We only differ in degrees of ego.

Michael stood. "You guys ready?"

Ian looked at his two band mates. "Let's do this."

While holding the door to the conference room for the band members, Michael surveyed the room. His eyes landed on Cailen, who had his feet on the table.

Michael looked at Cailen's attorneys. "Really? Mr. Cailen, please remove your feet from our mahogany conference table. Were you raised this way, or is this disrespectful behavior something you picked up from your rock star buddies?"

The female attorney touched his arm, Cailen looked at her, she nodded, and he removed his feet from the table, unclasped his hands from behind his head, and leaned forward.

As she turned back to Michael, he felt as though her eyes were penetrating his soul. Black-as-coal hair, vivid red lipstick and matching fingernails. Ivory skin framed her pale-blue eyes.

Spectacular

She was altogether reminiscent of classic movie actresses of the 1940s, and personified beauty, intelligence, confidence, and success. Michael sensed her competence was backed with substantial experience.

"I assume you're, Kassidy Frank?" Michael said, to the only female in the tri-team of lawyers.

She looked at the men around the table. "Good guess. And you must be Michael." Her smile exceeded the rest of her arsenal.

"Yes, I am. Ms. Frank—is Mr. Cailen's behavior the tone you're setting for this meeting—big-guy intimidation? If so, this meeting is over."

"No, I apologize. Mr. Cailen meant no disrespect by that—"

Michael spread his arms shoulder width and interrupted her. "Again, really? Let's move on, because we're off to a bad start. Ms. Frank, go ahead."

Michael sensed disappointment that her appearance hadn't intimidated him. But his response didn't throw her.

"I'll get to the point, Michael."

"Please do," Michael said, as he opened his case file folder.

"Your clients—Hauler, I believe is the name of the band—and I assume the three of you are band members?" She gave them a quick look. Not waiting for a response or introduction. "Your suit claims Mr. Cailen plagiarized the song 'Beaten Path,' is that correct?"

"That is correct." Michael responded.

She went on, "Our contention is that Hauler is claiming they wrote the song and have so stated from the stage. They have included 'Beaten Path' in their set list, and they have been playing the song without paying royalties to Mr. Cailen. Is that correct?"

"No, that is not correct, Ms. Frank."

Kassidy tossed her pen on top of her note pad. "You deny that?"

"Yes, we deny it. Your inference is that they are '*trying* to claim they wrote the song, when in fact, *they* wrote the song. And we deny they should pay royalties to the person who stole their song."

"And you—the band—hold to that position?" Kassidy said, while looking at the band members.

Michael leaned forward, placed his right elbow on the table, rested the side of his head on the fingertips of his right hand, while shaking his head. "That's why we're here. Why are you here?"

He leaned back while thrusting his right hand out and rotating his palm up. "You came all the way from LA to state your obvious position? Let's pack up and meet in court. This meeting is going nowhere."

"We came here to see if we could come to a reasonable agreement."

"Great, because I've yet to see a sign of reasonableness."

Kassidy leaned forward, picked up her pen and clutched it in her hand. "Mr. Cailen is a busy man. His tour schedule keeps him on the road. Taking time from that schedule—by canceling shows—will come at a high cost to him. We're here to make a reasonable offer to avoid that disruption."

Michael scanned the band members, then looked at Kassidy. "We're listening."

"In your suit, you've asked for 3.125 million dollars; that's absurd." Kassidy hesitated, expecting Michael to respond. Michael kept his hands folded, thumbs against his chin, while looking into her eyes.

Don't let those eyes suck you in Michael.

"We are prepared to offer, *today*, a $250,000 settlement."

Michael still didn't respond to her. He turned to Truck. "Mr. Cailen."

Cailen looked at Kassidy. She nodded, signaling it was okay to answer. "Yeah."

"Mr. Cailen, you've never met the members of Hauler or seen them play?"

"What reason would I have to watch club bands play. I'm a busy man? I can't find time to spend with my family, let alone hang out in clubs."

"That's not the question I asked you. So I'll ask it again, have you ever met Hauler or watched them play live?"

"No, I haven't."

Michael leaned forward, keeping his hands folded. "Well, if that were true, we'd have no case and your offer of $250,000 would be more than generous. Right?"

"Too generous, if you ask me," Cailen said. "I work hard, and I don't want to pay a penny toward this frivolous lawsuit."

Michael looked at Cailen's attorney. "Ms. Frank, you've coached him well, even gave him big words to use. But, there's a problem with your claim, Mr. Cailen," Michael said, as he lifted the remote control and pushed play.

The entire table heard Ian discussing his sister. Everyone in the room turned toward the 65-inch monitor on the wall at the end of the room.

The video panned from Hauler to Cailen, who was at a table talking to a couple sitting with him.

Michael paused the video. "This is interesting, Ms. Frank. I had the audio of the conversation between Cailen and the couple enhanced. Let's find out what the couple said to Mr. Cailen as the band was introducing the song, Beaten Path."

Michael pushed play and the same scene played again, only this time with the audio enhanced. "Hey Truck, this is the song we mentioned earlier— people always love this song—I think... *unintelligible voice...* maybe they'd let you."

Hauler began playing, Beaten Path.

Kassidy interrupted, "You're only validating what we're claiming, Mr. Mays—"

Michael held up his hand. "Hold on."

The camera moved, drawing close to Cailen's table.

Michael looked across the table. Cailen was watching himself hold up a digital recorder. He couldn't conceal his shock. His attorneys fidgeted with their notebooks and glanced at one another as the monitor displayed the video panning around the club.

Michael looked over to Ian and gave a slight smile.

The video panned to Cailen watching Hauler on stage as they ended the song.

Cailen pushed a few buttons and put the recorder to his ear and smiled. Michael paused the video.

Cailen's other attorneys looked at Kassidy. She looked at Michael. "Give us a few minutes, please."

"Let us know when you're ready." Michael stood and turned toward the door. Ian and his band mates followed him into his office and closed the door.

"Wow," Ian said, "Did you see Cailen's face?" Everyone agreed the video stunned him.

"Yes, he was," Michal said, "as were his attorneys. He's accustomed to getting his way. This is a new experience for him."

Ian said, "What do you think will happen next?"

"I expect them to argue that the video proves their point.

Ian said, "Are you concerned, Michael?"

"No, they've realized they're holding an empty bag."

"Let's take a break, get coffee, use the restroom, and stay calm. Again, do not walk back into that room intimidated. We have the power; let's play it well."

After 15 minutes, Trevor paged Michael's office, "They're ready for you, Mr. Mays."

"Thanks, Trevor." He looked at the band members, "ready guys?"

"We're ready if you are."

"I am. Let's go."

Michael asked as he and Hauler members entered the room, "Okay, folks— what's your decision?"

Kassidy looked at Cailen, then back at Michael. "Again, we believe the video you played, affirms our claim. Mr. Cailen was there gathering evidence to prove Hauler was claiming they wrote the song. So, to that extent, we are even considering withdrawing our settlement offer."

"And," Michael replied, "we are considering not accepting your offer and moving forward to letting a jury decide the outcome. Do you want to know why?"

Kassidy responded, as she looked at Cailen and her team, "Yes, we do."

"Ms. Frank, after watching the first section of the video, you jumped in and said your team wanted a caucus, and we agreed to leave the room. But we were not done with our presentation." In a condescending tone, Michael said, "Is it okay with you if we finish?"

Kassidy gave a side-glance to Cailen. "Sure... go ahead."

Michael brought up on the monitor screen a Rolling Stone magazine article in which they interviewed Cailen. Michael read a yellow highlighted section. "Truck Cailen discussed how he likes to go out to local venues at night, after his band's show finished."

"Mr. Cailen, that doesn't square with what you told us a few minutes ago," Michael looked at Kassidy, "Does it, Ms. Frank?"

Truck looked up and glared.

Michael read the rest of that section of the article, emphasizing, 'I keep my finger on the pulse of what's going on in other parts of the music world.'

"But, Mr. Cailen, earlier in our meeting you said you don't have the time to visit clubs or listen to other bands?" Kassidy looked at Cailen, now with a hint of disbelief.

Michael brought up a copy of an admission ticket to Jimi's Daze concert at the Moda Center in Portland. He asked, "Please note the highlighted date on the ticket."

He then brought up a copy of a flyer announcing Hauler playing at a local club. "Also please note the date of Hauler's show—the same night as the Jimi's Daze concert.

"Hauler's venue was only minutes away from the Moda Center. So last, but not least—" a photo of Hauler's promo-CD came up on the screen, "we will bring in the owner/engineer of the recording studio where Hauler recorded this promotional CD. I'll ask him to give testimony as to the date he recorded this CD, which was well before Jimi's Daze released it." Michael paused, allowing that to sink in.

"I believe you noticed the label on the promo-CD lists, Beaten Path.

"Ms. Frank, our research brought an interesting discovery. Two years ago, Jimi's Daze grossed over $75,000,000 touring to support their previous album. Not a bad annual income, even when divided between members."

Michael again hesitated for a moment.

"Now let's move to Jimi's Daze current tour, which promotes the release of their latest album. But more so, to capitalize on the success of the release of 'Beaten Path,' the first single from that album, which, as I stated before, became a world-wide hit."

"*So far*, in their current tour, Jimi's Daze has grossed over $125,000,000." Again pausing, to allow that number to marinate.

"What do you suppose a jury will attribute to that incredible jump in gross concert ticket sales when I show them this?" Michael brought up a YouTube video of Cailen, standing near the front of the stage, thanking the crowd for liking the song.

Cailen described feedback from people around the world. He swept his arm out in front of him. "The song is touching people, like you. They're sending us messages via our website, telling us how it has inspired them. How it has made them more aware of the abuse women face at the hands of boyfriends, husbands and others. Even inspiring them to support and work toward ending that pattern of abuse." Michael paused the video.

"Noble cause, yes?" No one could, or dared, answer.

"Mr. Cailen, you made the song the central theme of your concert tour… right? Cailen avoided eye contact with Michael.

"And, Mr. Cailen, we're not even considering your earnings from songwriter royalties.

"When we go into the courtroom, I will remind the jury of the settlement we're requesting." Michael scanned the eyes of Cailen and his team. Then I will compare that to the money Mr. Cailen is making from songwriter royalties associated with the song, *and* current tour revenue. A tour where 'Beaten Path' is the central theme. Mr. Cailen, isn't the name of your band's current tour, 'The Beaten Path Tour'?

There was no response.

"Then, I will finish by telling them *they* can award to Hauler, punitive damages commensurate with the crime Mr. Cailen committed."

Michael looked at Kassidy and her team. "So, here's the question I have for the big-city attorneys. I believe you to be smart, experienced and knowledgeable. How much do you think a jury will award, Hauler?"

Again, no response.

"After seeing and hearing our testimony, *you know* the jury will award Hauler a significant, if not a phenomenal amount in punitive damages."

Michael stood, pulled out his phone and touched the screen. "I'm setting my timer for ten minutes. We'll step out and come back when the phone's alarm sounds. We will consider your proposal. If it's not *far more* than what we originally requested… we'll see you in court."

36

The phone's alarm sounded. Michael and the members of Hauler walked back into the conference room. He removed two copies of a document from his folder and slid them over to Kassidy.

"Ms. Frank, during your first caucus, I asked my assistant Trevor to draw up a settlement agreement and attend this meeting to notarize it.

"The agreement stipulates we accept your offer of settlement. It includes a non-disclosure agreement and a withdrawal of our lawsuit.

"The agreement requires Mr. Cailen to cease claiming he wrote the song Beaten Path, and to remove it from his BMI Works Catalog, both as Songwriter/Composer and Publisher.

"Also, Mr. Cailen will pay in full within 30 days of the date we sign this document… which will be today. Failure on any point will negate our agreement. Please notice that Trevor left a space for you to write your offer. He made the space *large*. We will not be negotiating, so make your offer one that will motivate us to withdraw our suit.

"Today being Halloween, I suggest you choose treat rather than a trick."

Kassidy looked at Cailen, then to her associates, then back to Michael, who didn't flinch. She picked up her pen, wrote a number, signed and dated both copies. She slid them over to Cailen.

While looking at her in astonishment, Cailen slammed back in the chair. He made a threatening move against Kassidy. He turned toward her and spread his hands, as if aimed for her neck. Through clamped teeth, he hissed,

"That's over three times what we discussed minutes ago."

She nodded and shrugged her shoulders. She handed him her pen. He hesitated, took a deep breath, leaned forward, signed and dated both copies. He flicked them back to Michael and tossed the pen on the table.

Michael considered the offer. "I believe we have a deal." He signed and dated both copies, then handed them to Ian.

Wide-eyed, Ian looked at Michael. Michael nodded; Ian signed. Trevor notarized while Michael thanked everyone.

"Mr. Cailen, Ms. Frank, you've made a wise decision. Ms. Frank, Trevor will make copies of the document for your associates, and he'll give *you* one of the original signed copies. Good day."

Back in Michael's office, still in shock, Ian sat stunned. The two band mates asked what happened and what they agreed to pay?

Ian took a deep breath. "Twenty... *million*... dollars."

"Plus 25% legal fees," Michael added.

As the three bandmates did a group-hug, Ian reached and pulled in Michael. "The money is both shocking and great," Ian said, "but, we got our song back."

Trevor came in with the band member's copies of the agreement.

Ian looked at his copy and looked up at Michael. "Not in our wildest dreams did we expect this. Is this the norm?"

"No," Michael said, "this case is so egregious, that Cailen's attorney wanted the suit to go away.

"This isn't a typical plagiarism case where someone sues because someone else used parts of their song. Our suit would have proved Cailen *stole* your song verbatim. We have a video proving it. It's astounding that Cailen imagined he could get away with it."

"Well," Ian said, "thanks to you he didn't. And we appreciate you believing in us and helping us through this."

"To be candid," Michael said, "he got away with the millions of dollars he's making on this tour, which he wouldn't have made if it weren't for your song. But $20,000,000 in hand beats the risk of leaving it to a jury. Plus, *you* will get future royalties.

"As I came to know you guys, you were easy to trust; it was my pleasure. Thank you for entrusting me with your case."

After the band members left, Trevor stepped into Michael's office. "Mr. Mays, Kassidy Frank wants to meet with you?"

"Sure, send her in."

As Kassidy walked in, Michael stood and extended his hand.

"How may I help you, Ms. Frank?"

"Please, call me Kassidy. May I sit?"

"Of course," Michael said, as he too sat.

"Michael, I can call you, Michael… right?"

"Yes."

"Michael, I'm impressed with you and your abilities. Have you ever consider leaving Portland?"

"What are you asking, Kassidy?"

"I'm asking you to come to work for our firm in Los Angeles; I'd have to propose it to the other partners, but I can sell it."

"Are you asking me to become a partner in your firm or to come in as an associate?"

"An associate to start—"

"Kassidy, what sense does it make for me to leave here, as a partner, to become an associate in Los Angeles? I practiced in LA for three years and didn't care for it."

"I can convince them to promise, via contract, that you'd be a partner within two years."

"Very flattering, Kassidy, but I don't see myself leaving Portland. You and I both know your firm will not bring me in as an equity partner."

"Yes, but the annual income of a non-equity partner is much higher there, than an equity partner is here. And the range of your practice will increase and be far more interesting. You could use your skills and abilities in—"

"I apologize for cutting you off again, Kassidy. I appreciate your offer, but I must decline."

"Well," Kassidy said, "I knew 'no' was the answer if I didn't ask. As the old saying goes: 'Nothing ventured, nothing gained.'"

She wrote her personal cell phone number on her business card. "But, next time you're in LA, call me, I'll buy you dinner."

"Now that's an offer I *can* accept," he said, as he stood and walked her to the door of his office. As he shook her hand, she put her left hand on top of his right arm, looked him in the eyes and smiled that smile. "I hope you do, Michael." She lingered in his eyes for a few seconds, turned and walked away.

When she was out the front door, Trevor walked into Michael's office. "I have two wows for you."

"Okay, let's hear them."

"Wow, on the settlement, that was incredible. And, wow, she is a *beautiful* woman."

"Yes, she is, Trevor, and smart. She knows when to fold and cut her losses.'"

"Well, you had the high hand, Mr. Mays."

"Thank you, Trevor. You did a stellar job assisting me." He removed his overcoat from its hanger. "I'm done for the day. I'll see you tomorrow."

On the way home, Michael rehashed the day's events. His mind landed on his conversation with Carrie Hindler that morning. Which led to the promise he had made to Russell Curt of finding the person who killed Linda's sister.

At home, he fell back onto the sofa. Fifteen minutes later he jolted awake, surprised he had slept. After showering and putting on a change of clothes, he returned to the living room. While drinking a lemon-lime soda water, he opened his phone's photos to the photo of Linda's sister Liz.

How do I play this?

Several scenarios played out in his mind. The one most intriguing:

Can I stop the murder, and if I do, how will it impact Linda and Jacob?

Tough questions, but he could not imagine himself not intervening. What if it's a setup? Michael considered the possibility that Russell expects him to intervene, hoping he dies in the past.

I'll take that chance.

Michael remembered Russell claiming he carried back things he stole. He got up from the sofa, walked to the ceramic butter churn and grabbed his baseball bat.

Maybe I can take protection with me.

He realized he hadn't made a conscious decision to go back in time. It's becoming second-nature.

He removed a small tactical flashlight and a Leatherman tool from a kitchen drawer and stuffed them in the pockets of his Levi's.

In his office, he removed the book from his briefcase, set his phone's timer for one hour, and returned to Liz's photo. Just prior to looking at Liz's photo he realized he'll be visiting a murder scene. He went to the kitchen, grabbed a couple of vinyl gloves, and returned to his office.

He opened the book to page 60.

37

The warm Omni-directional wind took him to a corner of Linda's parents' living room. Linda was taking a photo of Liz.

He crouched behind an over-stuffed recliner, leaned against the wall, and peeked around the back of the chair while slipping on the vinyl gloves. Liz said something which caused Linda to lift her camera and take another photo.

The one they used as evidence and didn't return to her.

They exchanged goodnights and hugged. He watched Linda walk out and close the front door.

He shook his head.

This is crazy.

Liz's cell phone rang. The voice on the other end caused her to giggle and become giddy.

She ran up the stairs.

When she came to her room's door, she squealed with delight. Michael assumed it was Russell. Shoes thumped to the floor as they were kicked from their feet. The only other sounds were the voices of Russell cheating on his wife and Liz betraying her sister.

Without success, Michael tried making his 6'4" body comfortable as he crouched behind the chair. He had no choice but to tolerate the momentary discomfort.

The door to Liz's bedroom was open and, judging from the soft light coming through the doorway, Michael guessed they had left on a small lamp.

Out of the corner of his eye, Michael thought he saw movement on the stair's landing.

He tried to refocus by blinking his eyes and squinting.

Nothing.

He pushed it aside.

Maybe my excellent peripheral vision can even pick up my imagination's thoughts.

He heard Liz laugh.

Michael kept his eyes on her door.

A shadow drifted at the corner of his vision.

Something moved.

He tried refocusing again.

Still nothing.

Liz said, "No, don't leave me alone."

"I have to get going. I'm sorry, but I'll be back soon."

"Is that a promise, Russell?"

Okay, it's Russell, and he's lying.

Russell came hopping out of the bedroom, one leg in his pants, pulling up the second pant leg. He leaned against the bedroom's doorway and put on his shoes. "Yes, that's a promise." He buttoned his shirt as he hurried down the stairs.

Halfway down, he disappeared. Michael shuddered.

Done that—but haven't seen it done—creepy.

Michael stood to tuck the book in the back of his waistband. He tightened his belt.

That should hold it. I need to get a backpack.

He resumed crouching. With his baseball bat in his right hand, he waited.

His thoughts wandered back to the Hauler case that afternoon.

Liz's scream burst into Michael's thoughts. She calmed and said in frustration, "Oh, it's only you. What are you doing here?"

A man said, "It's *ONLY* me?"

He was both frustrated and angry.

"What am *I* doing here? What are *you* are doing here, Liz? Couldn't you have at least closed the blinds, so I didn't have to watch you cheat on me?"

"Cheat on you? You don't *have* to watch me, Eric. But you always do. You've never had the guts to come over. You've cheated yourself, Eric."

Eric yelled back, now furious.

"And you've always *enjoyed* putting on your show for me, haven't you? But this was too much, Liz. You knew I'd watch. Aand you did *this*?"

"No, Eric don't—" a fist hit flesh, hard.

Michael sprang and ran up the stairs yelling, "Stop."

As he made the stair landing, Eric yelled something unintelligible.

Michael looked up and saw him charging.

Big boy, was Michael's first thought.

He moved too fast for Michael to bring the bat into position.

Eric had the look of a madman. The sound coming from him was that of a wounded, trapped animal.

Michael anticipated the hit.

He dropped the bat and squatted while putting his hands behind his head.

The bat clattered on the wooden stairs as it tumbled toward the floor.

Eric stopped his momentum by grabbing the handrails on each side of him.

He kicked Michael.

Michael fell back while tucking his knees into his chest and rolled down the stairs.

At the bottom, Michael spread his arms trying to lessen his collision with the floor.

His head slammed against the wall, breaking through the lath and plaster.

Michael lay unconscious.

Eric returned to the bedroom.

When Michael came to, his head was four inches into the wall and Eric was walking past him.

Eric stopped and kicked Michael in the side.

Michael grunted as his breath rushed out.

"You're lucky I don't kill you too," Eric said, and walked through the front door, slamming it behind him.

Michael laid there, struggling. When he caught his breath, he reached up and pushed in the broken lath that was holding the sides of his head like a Chinese finger trap. He stood, but was lightheaded, and pinpoints of light floated in his vision.

His limbs functioned, but not without pain.

Tomorrow will be a different story.

He picked up his bat and put it to use as a walking stick. There was no reason to go upstairs. Liz was dead. Strangled and neck broken.

Just as Linda described... but she believes Russ is the killer.

Before walking out through the front door, he checked to make sure the book was still in his waist band. It was there, but he pushed it in a few inches.

He closed the door, staggered across the front porch, and down the stairs. He removed the flashlight from his pocket, turned it on, and limped to the back of the house.

Michael put together a mental image of where the stairway to Liz's room was located. He looked up. Light shone from only one window on the second floor. It was the same soft light he'd seen come through her bedroom door.

He stood below the window and faced the direction Liz looked out. A second-floor window, in the house he faced, looked right into her room.

Making his way back to the front of Liz's house, his body was stiffening. It needed movement. He shoved the flashlight into his pants pocket and felt to make sure the Leatherman tool was still there. He pulled out his cell phone.

Under light from the streetlamps, he followed the sidewalk.

He judged from the size of the Maple trees lining the street, that the neighborhood was 70 to 80 years old. The developer had maximized the property and minimized expenses. Whoever built the houses, used variations of a theme, on same-sized lots. He counted the houses until he came to the end of the block. He turned left and limped to the next street corner, turned left again and counted off the same number of houses he'd counted from Liz's house.

Michael stood in front of Eric's house and took a photo. He checked to assure his phone's camera captured the address in the porch's low light. It wasn't great, but it would do.

His right hand held the baseball bat, which made selecting his phone's voice recorder awkward. He spoke the address and described the evening's events.

As he began the narrative, he turned to walk back.

Eric was standing in his way.

His fists were flexing at his side. His head was lowered, and he was glaring at Michael.

This time, Michael had time to raise the baseball bat, with pain, but trying not to show it.

"Eric, you sure you want to do this?"

Eric's eyes opened wide and he stumbled back a step. "How do you know my name?"

Michael guessed him to be 18 or 19 years old. From his size, physique, and considering the force of his kick, Michael assumed he had played high school football.

"Eric," Michael said his name again, both to emphasize he knows it, and to assure the phone's recorder picked it up. "I heard Liz call you by name. And I saw your face as you charged and knocked me down the stairs.

"Why did you kill her, Eric?"

Michael's question caused Eric to retreat another step.

Eric looked at the sidewalk, then back up with his eyes narrowed and his upper lip curled.

"She had it coming. Most of my life she's been teasing me by taking off her clothes in front of her bedroom window."

He began to sob.

"She left the curtains open, knowing I was *watching*. This was the last straw. She had to pay for the misery she's caused me."

He screamed through his sobs. "She betrayed me!"

"So, you imposed the death penalty?"

Eric's body relaxed, his arms fell to their side, and he hung his head. "After seeing her cheat on me with another guy, I had to, I couldn't take it anymore."

"Cheat on you—?" Michael stopped.

He saw pushing him further, by confronting him with reality, wouldn't help. He changed the subject. "Eric, how did you get into the house without me seeing you?"

"Easy," he said, while still crying, "I've lived here my whole life, and the houses in this neighborhood are the same. All I had to do was climb over the fence and walk in through the kitchen door. I used a key I stole when I was a kid; it's been on my keyring ever since." He pulled the keys from his pocket and showed Michael, who sensed Eric calming.

"Behind like, a closet door in the kitchen, is a narrow wooden stairway that heads to the second floor. You can go out through a door on the second floor or keep climbing to the attic. I use the one in our house to get to my bedroom, or to the attic. It helps me escape when we have company."

"Have you used that key before, Eric?"

Eric looked at the keyring. "Yeah, lots of times. After everyone was in bed, I'd climb up into the attic and lay on the floor above Liz's room. Some nights I fell asleep there."

"What happens now, Eric?"

As Eric considered the question, headlights of a car turning into Eric's driveway shined on them. Eric wiped his face and turned.

The car door opened and a man, who Michael assumed was Eric's father, stepped out and asked: "Eric, what's going on?"

Eric turned toward the man. "Nothing dad, giving a guy direction."

When Eric turned back, Michael was 14 years away.

38

~

Friday, November 1st

A day... like no other. Will I ever stop thinking this?

Michael sat at his desk holding and staring at two documents Trevor had left for him to read, approve, and sign. But staring at them was not equivalent to considering them.

Stephanie was on his mind. At the same time, he wondered if Eric's family still live in the house he stood in front of last evening.

"Mr. Mays," Trevor said, through the phone's intercom.

Michael shook his head to bring himself out of his reflections. "Yes."

"When I returned to my desk, there was a phone message from Deputy District Attorney Hindler's Assistant. She said the information you requested will be ready to pick up at 3 P.M. She'll be there to meet with you."

"Thanks, Trevor. I'll be leaving soon—for the day. Anything you need from me before I leave?"

"No. I'll be spending the rest of the day doing research for the copyright infringement case we discussed."

"Great, thanks." That discussion was part of the meeting he had with Trevor just minutes before. Michael frowned and stared out his window.

I must have been on autopilot. I vaguely remember the discussion.

After signing the papers, he pulled out his cell phone, found the photo of Eric's house, and wrote the house number on a sticky note. He switched to the phone's recording app and listened to the recording he made while in front of Eric's house. When he came to the section where he spoke the street's name, he added it to his note. He sent the audio file and photos to both his work and private email addresses.

He returned the documents to Trevor and said goodbye for the day. In his car, he entered Eric's address into Google Maps.

It was 11:15 A.M. when he arrived at Eric's house. He parked his car in front of the house, while admiring the trees he'd seen only as dark outlines last night.

I'm stalling. Let's do this.

He knocked on the door.

It was only last night for me, but 14 years later for them. Maybe they've moved.

He was not sure if he was wondering or hoping.

A woman, in her mid-50s, opened the door. "Can I help you?"

"I hope so," Michael said, as he smiled. The woman remained stoic. The first thing Michael noticed was her brown hair. It was over-permed and gray at the roots. She wore a loose-fitting cream-colored sweatshirt with sequined flowers on the front, and blue sweatpants. Her house slippers looked comfortable. She had a book in her hand and removed her reading glasses as she looked up at Michael.

"I'm looking for someone who once lived here. His name is Eric."

She swayed. Her reading glasses slipped from her hand as she brought her fingers to her mouth. "Why, what do you want with Eric?"

Michael bent over and picked up her glasses. He handed them to her. "My name's Michael Mays. Are you related to Eric?"

"Yes, I'm his mother."

"Pleased to meet you. What's your name?"

"You didn't answer my question. What do you want with Eric?"

"I'm an attorney, and I'm a friend of Linda Curt, the sister of a young woman named Liz, who someone murdered 14 years ago—"

Before Michael finished his sentence, a man the same age and dressed in the same manner as the woman, minus sequins, joined them at the door. "I heard what you said to my wife. Why do you want to talk to us?"

"It's not you I was hoping to speak with, I want to talk to your son, Eric."

Utter sadness came over both of their faces. "We wish we could speak to him too, but we haven't in 13 years."

"I introduced myself to your wife. My name is Michael Mays."

The man looked at his wife before responding. She slumped, gave a heavy sigh and nodded.

"My name is Paul Anderson, and this is my wife, Anne."

"Paul, did Eric move away?"

His father stared off into space and sniffed. "No, he died."

"I'm so sorry, Mr. Anderson. This will be a difficult conversation to have. I take it you're Eric's father."

"Yes, I am." Paul said, and sniffed again.

Michael pulled out a business card and gave it to them. "Paul and Anne, can I come in and talk with you? I have a few questions regarding Eric's relationship with Liz."

Eric's father looked at Michael's business card, then at Anne. "Yeah, I guess that'll be okay."

Eric's parents sat on a sofa, leaning on one another; Paul put his arm around Anne. Michael sat in a love seat facing them.

"I'm so sorry for your loss. I hate to open old wounds, but how did Eric die?"

They looked at each other.

Anne took her husband's hand in hers and hung her head.

Paul's voice trembled. "He committed suicide."

"Oh no. I am sorry. I can't imagine the pain that's caused you. Which makes it harder to say what I have to say."

With resignation and his voice still trembling, Paul said, "Go ahead."

"I have a recording of Eric confessing to Liz's murder—" Anne broke down. Paul wrapped his arm around her and held her tight. Michael stopped and allowed them time.

After a minute, Paul looked up, eyes red and tears streaming from them. "Go ahead."

"Why did Eric take his life?" Anne got up and rushed off, sobbing. Paul watched her rush away.

"I'm sorry, Mr. Anderson, but I have to ask these questions."

"Why do you have to ask them, and reopen those wounds?"

Michael sought a gentle answer that expressed the injustice of the Russell's imprisonment. "Because there's a man who's imprisoned, for a crime he didn't commit."

Paul put his elbows on his knees and placed his face in his hands for a few seconds. He looked up at Michael and spoke just above a whisper. "The police told us Eric drove out, northbound," his voice faltering, "onto the Glen Jackson bridge. He stopped on the Washington side and parked his car.

"It was around 9 P.M. Two witnesses stopped to see if he needed help." Paul stopped and dried his eyes with his sleeve. "They told the police he got out of his car carrying a weight with a rope attached to it. We found out later it weighed 50 pounds. He tied the rope to his ankles, held the weight in his arms and tumbled over the side of the bridge," Paul gave a ragged gasp, "into the Columbia River."

Paul lowered his face back into his hands. "He did it so fast, they didn't have time to stop him."

I can't press this poor man for more information.

Anne reappeared holding a piece of paper. Her left hand covered her mouth and her right hand shook as she held it out for Michael to take. Only able to whisper, she said, "Read this, please." Her face was drawn. Tears streamed through creviced skin leading from her eyes to dripping on her sweatshirt.

Mr. Anderson said, "We've lived with this for 13 years. When they convicted Linda's husband for Liz's murder, our love for our son kept us from coming forward. We refused to believe Eric killed her."

The piece of paper was yellowed, wrinkled, and the ink—over the years—smeared from being re-read by grief-stricken parents.

Not waterproof ink.

Michael read:

"Mom and Dad please forgive me for what i've done and for what i'm going to do i love you so much but i can't stand the pain i'm in i killed Liz the girl i've loved since i was a little boy i didn't mean to kill her i just lost control and it happened if i could go back and change it i would right after i killed her i talked with a man who told me i carried out a death sentence on her that's true but i didn't mean to now i have to do the same thing to myself and join Liz
Goodbye and please don't hate me i'll love you forever
Eric"

With tears brimming his eyes, Michael looked up at Anne. She was weeping. He stood and hugged her.

Michael released his right arm and turned to Paul while continuing to hold Anne with his left. Her head laid against his arm. "Paul, do you still believe Eric didn't kill Liz?"

"No," he looked at Anne, "I'm not sure we ever did."

"Five years before he died, I found Eric sitting in the dark, watching Liz through his window. As I talked with him, I looked over to Liz's window. I saw her—naked—unashamed. I closed the curtains and asked Eric what was going on. He told me it happened most nights, and that he loved her. He was only 14, what did he know about love?"

"How did you handle it?"

"The next day I confronted her father. He refused to believe his daughter could do that and accused Eric of being a Peeping Tom. I told him it was obvious she was putting on a show for Eric. I told him to tell Liz to close her curtains.

"He became angry and said, 'Oh, so you stood there and watched a naked 16-year-old girl? The acorn doesn't fall far from the tree, does it?'

"I shook my head, and as I walked away, said, 'Tell her to stop.'"

Paul looked at Anne. She pulled away from Michael and hugged her husband. "Honey, we have to make this right, we can't allow Linda's husband to stay in prison for something Eric did." She let go of Paul and faced Michael. "What do we do, Michael?"

"Are you willing to meet me at the Multnomah County District Attorney's office at 3 o'clock this afternoon, and bring this note with you?"

Anne looked at Paul and nodded. He said, "Give us the address and we'll be there."

Michael gave them Carrie's name, her office's address and her phone number. As Michael left, he hugged both, and said, "Thank you."

In his car, Michael sat until he'd composed himself, then called Carrie's office.

"Deputy District Attorney Hindler's office, this is Shawna, how can I help you?"

"Hi, Shawna, it's Michael Mays. You left a message for me this morning."

"Yes, Mr. Mays. Ms. Hindler is able meet with you at 3 P.M."

"Shawna, does Carrie's schedule allow me to bring in a couple who want to talk to her? It will take, at most, an extra 15 minutes of her time."

"Let me check—yes, I'll add that to her schedule."

"Thank you, Shawna."

"You are welcome."

Ending the phone call, he noticed it was 12 P.M.

There's time to run errands.

He Googled Fred Meyer store locations, chose the Hawthorne location, then selected, Get directions. When Google Maps asked for his location, he entered the name of the pizza restaurant where his team held the after-game Little League party. Google calculated the restaurant was 2.2 miles from the Fred Meyer store. Michael figured it would take him half an hour at his walking pace.

He took a screen shot of the route Google maps displayed.

GPS may not work there.

From a grocery bag, Michael pulled out the clothing he'd worn on his previous trip to the pizza restaurant. He looked around to make sure no one was close; he changed clothes.

He removed the book, closed his briefcase, and opened the photos app on his phone.

"There she is," he said, when he found the picture of Jen, the Little

League team sponsor. He opened the book to page 70 and looked at the photo.

He was looking at Jen. He'd replaced himself. She was saying, "That's the smallest camera I've ever seen."

Michael couldn't remember what he said in response.

She won't know the difference.

"Yeah, it's great. The manufacturer hasn't released it yet, but they're a client. They gave me one to test."

"Never seen anything like it. I look forward to seeing you next season."

"Thanks, Jen. I look forward to it too."

Michael followed the route shown in the screen shot. Uneventful walk, it took him half an hour which allowed him 40 minutes to shop.

He walked into the store and headed to the sporting goods section. There were only a couple backpacks to select from, both designed for kids.

I'll pass.

Next, he went to the clothing section and found two Tommy Hilfiger Polo shirts that fit well, one white and one blue. Next, two pairs of 501 Levi's.

If there's a difference, I doubt anyone will notice. But just in case.

In the shoe section, he found a pair of Adidas; white, with blue stripes. Next was a lightweight, black, North Face jacket to keep in the backpack.

He checked out, paying with cash. Done shopping, he left the store and turned right on Hawthorn Street. Two blocks down the street, there was a small restaurant with a menu posted on the door. He checked his phone's timer; there was time for a quick lunch.

While ordering, he handed a $10 bill to the server. "I want to pay for my order before you submit it. I may get paged and have to leave quick."

The server smiled. "No one's asked me to do that before, but sure, I'll do that."

Michael put the book in his shopping bag. He ate his clubhouse sandwich and fries with his right hand. He held onto the bag with his left hand in case time ran out, which it did.

Back, sitting in his car, the bag was in his left hand and the second half of his clubhouse in his right. His fries were still on the table, over 30 years ago.

As he sat in his parked car and finished his sandwich, Daniel Wygal came to mind. Michael wondered if he knows Katrina is dead.

It had not been two full days, but Daniel did not strike Michael as a patient guy.

It was 1:30. His mind moved like a pinball bouncing from bumper to bumper. He thought of Stephanie and looked forward to seeing her tomorrow. Then Linda came to mind.

How will she receive the news of Russell's imminent release from prison?

He sat for half an hour, sorting through his plan to put Daniel Wygal *back* in prison.

A little after 2 PM, Michael headed to Carrie's office to pick up the police reports and meet with the Andersons. He recalled there being a sporting goods store along the way and made a quick stop.

Michael walked out of the sporting goods store with Smith & Wesson expandable 26-inch tactical baton, two canisters of police grade pepper spray with a quick-detach keyring connector, a compact pair of binoculars, a small tactical flashlight, a Leatherman tool and a black tactical backpack.

Ready for my next adventure. Now on to Carrie's office and the Andersons.

39

Katrina's unanswered phone threw Daniel to voice mail again. "Pick up, Katrina."

He grabbed his laptop and googled Helen, Georgia. He came across the Alpine Helen/White County Convention and Visitors Bureau site and called their 1-800 number.

"Alpine Helen, White County Convention and Visitors Bureau, how can I help you?"

"Hi, my name is Dan. I have a question and I don't know who to call, so I'm trying you."

"Sure, I'll do my best to answer your question, Dan."

"I live on the west coast. My sister and her husband are in Helen on vacation. I've been trying to contact her without success. Has there been any reports of serious injuries, killings, those kinds of things, in Helen? I'm worried sick."

"I don't think I'm supposed to give out that information. That's something the police handles."

Daniel pleaded. "I appreciate your confidentiality, but I'm 3,000 miles away—I have *you* on the phone—I'm going crazy with worry, and who am I going to tell?"

"Dan, I don't know much—oh, I hope I don't get fired for telling you this—but the police here in Helen shot and killed a woman. My understanding is there was a gun battle between the police and her. The rumor is that she was holding someone hostage."

Daniel chuckled. "That's not my sister, unless her husband was the hostage."

The woman laughed. "No, I heard she was holding a *woman* hostage."

"I appreciate your help; makes me feel better. I'll keep trying to get in touch with her, thank you."

"You are welcome, I'm glad I could help put you at ease."

"Michael, what did you do?" Daniel said, as he closed his computer and dialed his cell phone.

"Hey boss."

"How's your throwing arm?"

"I'm ammodextrose. I can manage."

"It's *ambidextrous*, BTH."

"I like mine better."

Daniel sighed. "Anyway, I've got a job for you."

"Great, I was worried that I'd made you too mad to give me another chance."

"Yeah BTH, I was almost there. Don't screw this up. Do you still have your weapons source?"

"Yep, he's still active."

"Good." Daniel explained to BTH his next assignment.

* * *

Michael walked into the District Attorney's office. The receptionist directed him to Carrie's office. Mr. and Mrs. Anderson were seated in a waiting area.

"Paul and Anne, thank you so much for coming. I'll try to make this as easy as I can for you."

Before they could answer, Carrie's assistant, Shawna came out. "Ms. Hindler can see you now," she looked at her watch, "that is if you're ready. It's ten minutes earlier than scheduled."

Michael looked at the Andersons, they nodded yes. "Okay, we're ready."

As they entered her office, Carrie stood. "Hi, Michael, good to see you. Casual Friday?"

"Good to see you too, Carrie. No, I took the afternoon off and changed out of my uniform. I hope you don't mind, but I asked Mr. and Mrs. Anderson to join us."

"Mr. and Mrs. Anderson, welcome."

Michael sensed they did not know how or where to start.

"Carrie, I'm sure you recall me telling you that Linda Curt's husband is in prison for the murder of her sister, Liz."

"Yes."

"Mr. and Mrs. Anderson have something they want to tell you, and something they want to show you."

Carrie stood. "But first," as she shook Paul's hand, "is it okay if I call you by your first name?"

"Sure. My name is, Paul, and this is my wife, Anne."

"Thank you," she said, and shook Anne's hand, "again, nice to meet you, Paul and Anne." She gestured toward two chairs facing her desk. "Please sit."

Michael sat in a chair against a wall that provided a view of both Carrie and the Andersons.

Paul and Anne told the story of their son's suicide, his history of obsession with Liz, and showed Carrie the suicide note. They explained why they didn't come forward years ago.

Paul said, "It's awkward for me to even offer that excuse."

"I understand," Carrie said, "but please, continue."

Anne placed her hand on Paul's. "We can't go on knowing an innocent man is in prison."

By the end of their story, Paul and Anne were weeping.

Carrie offered both a tissue. "Thank you," they said.

"Paul... Anne... I have a son, an only child. I can't imagine what you've went through. I can't imagine losing—" Carrie stopped and grabbed a tissue.

She stood, walked to the Andersons, leaned over and hugged them both. She moved to her office door. "Paul and Anne, do you mind stepping out for a few minutes while I talk with Michael?"

They both stood. "Sure," Paul said. They walked out holding hands and using their tissues. Carrie put her hand on Anne's shoulder as she walked by.

She closed the door. "Michael, where'd this come from?"

"I've joked that I'm good at what I do, but joking aside, I am. I nosed around in Linda's parents' neighborhood, which led me to Paul and Anne.

"After meeting with Linda's ex-husband, I asked her if she's okay with me investigating Liz's murder. She was reluctant, but trusts I'll do the right thing.

"Linda loathes her ex-husband and still believes he killed her sister. But, she hasn't heard about the Andersons and their son Eric. She told me if Russell didn't kill her sister, she wants us to bring to justice the person who did. Which, we find is impossible."

"Wow. I'll take this to my boss to get her take on it," Carrie said, "I'm not sure she will go ahead with only the suicide note."

"There is another piece of evidence I haven't brought up yet."

"Okay…"

"I have a recording of the Andersons' son, Eric, confessing."

"Do you have it with you?"

"No, but I'll bring it to you on Monday. The kicker is that the voice of the person talking with Eric is altered. They want to remain anonymous."

Carrie gave a slight head shake. "This is so unusual. But after you bring me the recording, I'll take it all to her."

"Thank you, Carrie. I'll thank the Andersons and let them leave. They're devastated by this."

"I *can't* imagine," Carrie said. "I'll walk out with you to say goodbye and thank them.

Back in her office, Carrie walked Michael through the police reports of his mother's murder. He was not prepared for what he saw. His mother was laying on the ground, her dress soaked with blood from a stab wound.

She looked at Michael. "Are you okay? Do you need to stop?"

Michael let out a heavy sigh. "No… let's keep pushing through."

Carrie pointed out that an early morning walker found his mother's body in Woodstock Park. That jolted Michael. "I played baseball in that park."

"I'm sorry, Michael. That information spoiled a good memory."

"Yes, it does. But it may help find the killer."

Carrie then discussed Daniel Wygal. "A real charmer and all-around nice guy. The Parole Board shouldn't have released him. The police suspected him of several other murders, but it seems they, *and* the District Attorney, chose the path of least resistance.

"Because the murders took place on August 8th, over five successive years, in five different parks, a local journalist dubbed the killer: The 'Portland Parks Ripper.'"

Michael put out his hand, palm up. "And the killings *stopped* with the arrest of Wygal."

"Yes, but without substantiating evidence—"

Michael shook his head and picked up the files from her desk. "I get it."

Carrie said, "He's a bad guy. You promised you'll be careful and not be a hero. Please, let the police do their job."

"I promised, and I will keep that promise. Thank you again for talking with Paul and Anne. They're dealing with the reality of what they've known in their hearts for years. This news will be hard on Linda too.

"After meeting Russell, I'm convinced he's not a good guy. Let's push aside what we think of his testimony. Crazy or not, he didn't kill her."

"Well," Carrie lifted her hands and shrugged, "we'll see where the District Attorney wants to take this." She dropped her arms. "But I believe Russell will be a free man, soon."

"That's my hope, not that I want him released, but it's the right thing to do. I'm headed home for the day. Thanks again and tell Matt and MJ hi for me."

"Will do. See you later, Michael."

40

~

At home, in his office, Michael wasn't ready to jump back into his mother's case files. Viewing the photos of his mother shook him, he needed a diversion.

On-line, he found a voice-altering program that offered a 10-day free trial download. While it downloaded, he watched a 'How To' video on YouTube.

Not too hard. Even I can do this.

Within minutes, his voice on the new recording sounded like a robot. He saved it in an Mp3 format and attached it to an email to Carrie, saying:

"Carrie, I got home earlier than I expected, so I'm sending the recorded confession to you today. Will you need the Andersons to verify the recording is their son's voice? Thanks again for your help."

Still avoiding the case files, he put his backpack together. He washed his new, old polo shirts, then the Levi's.

He un-packaged the items he'd purchased at the sporting goods store and found places for them in the backpack. Before stowing the tactical baton, he practiced extending and swinging it a few times.

Wouldn't want to be on the receiving end.

It fit perfect in the side-pocket designed for it.

He used the quick-detach keyring connector to attach the pepper spray canister to one of the backpack's shoulder straps.

The book fit well in the front compartment. He remembered the flash drive Stephanie's father gave him and put it in one of the backpack's small compartments, along with a protein bar, a small spiral notebook, a pen, and a pair of vinyl gloves. He placed the binoculars and the Leatherman tool in a compartment at the top of the backpack.

A bottle of water fit in one of the side pockets.

After trying on the backpack and making two minor adjustments, he removed it and placed it on the floor, next to his desk.

Plenty of room for the shoes and the clothing when they're done washing and drying.

Next, he organized the police reports from Daniel Wygal's expandable folder. He placed them in piles of relative information and lined them up on his desk, beginning with Daniel's personal information.

He pulled out his phone and created a contact for Wygal, including both the phone number Russell gave him, and Daniel's 1986 address. Placing the organized stacks back into Daniel's folder, he locked it in his briefcase.

Before getting too deep into the next phase of research, he needed an early dinner.

His stomach growled.

I haven't eaten since 1986.

He drove to North Mississippi Avenue. There was no parking available near his destination, but he found a parking spot three streets behind his favorite southern food restaurant: Miss Delta.

Worth the walk.

Mississippi Avenue is eclectic, vibrant, and busy. Restaurants, food trucks, and coffee shops line the street. A variety of retail storefronts are peppered in, along with a performing arts venue and a bicycle shop. At the south end of the street, there's a popular rescued-building-supply warehouse.

After an excellent Chicken and Waffle dinner, washed down by unsweetened iced tea, he entered Daniel's 1986 address into Google Maps. It was fifteen minutes away, depending on traffic.

Michael pulled up 14 minutes later and parked across the street from Daniel's former house. The owners of the 1930s era neighborhood homes maintained the houses and the landscaping well. And the trees were beautiful.

There was a man raking leaves in the front yard of Daniel's former house. Michael removed the spiral notebook and pen from his backpack, then locked his doors. He approached the man while calling out, "Hello. You've got yourself a career there."

"Man, it's work trying to keep up with the trees, but I love it."

Michael handed him his business card while introducing himself.

The man removed a leather glove and shook Michael's hand, surprising him by the strong grip the man's small hand delivered.

He leaned on his rake and read the business card. "Nice to meet you, Michael," he looked up, "unless you're here to sue me."

They both laughed; one was a nervous laugh. "No," Michael said, "but do you have time for a few questions?"

Michael guessed him to be in his early 70s. He was balding, had a wiry build, and was eight inches shorter than Michael. His faded jeans had grass stains on the knees, and his t-shirt read: "Old Guys Rule."

"I'm retired, so fire away. By-the-way, my name's Gus."

"Thanks, Gus, nice to meet you. I'm investigating a man who once lived here—"

"Daniel Wygal?"

"Yes." Michael said, as his head jolted. He raised his right-hand waist high. "Do you know Daniel?"

"No, but my wife and I bought the house from the Wygal Family Trust after the court sent him to prison."

"So, that must have been around—"

"1989." Gus jumped in again. "They arrested Wygal in the fall of 1987 and sent him to prison a little over a year later.

"May I ask why you're investigating." Gus gave another nervous laugh. "Does it mean I might lose the house?"

"No danger of losing your house, that I'm aware of.

"Gus, someone murdered my mother in 1986. The murder was never solved, although Daniel Wygal was a prime suspect. To my disappointment, the system recently paroled him.

"I'm talking to anyone who may have known him or is connected to him. Other than a convict, you're the first person I've talked to who has a connection."

"Sorry to hear about your mother, Michael."

"Thank you, Gus."

"You mentioned you're disappointed they paroled him?"

"Yes, I suspect Wygal killed my mother, and that he's still willing to kill at his convenience."

"I can understand *why* you're disappointed."

"It'll be dark soon; I don't want to keep you from your job."

"Like I said, I'm retired, and not concerned if the leaves get raked tonight or not. I'd be happy to help you, Michael, but other than the house, I have no connection with him."

"I understand, but even becoming familiar with how and where he lived, may lead me to another piece of the puzzle."

"What do you want to know?"

"Did any of your neighbors live here when Daniel did?"

"Yep, two I know of. The Smiths, across the street. You parked right in front of their house. I assume that Mini Cooper is your car. And, it's not just another Mini Cooper is it Michael."

Michael looked where Gus was pointing. "Yes, that's mine. And you're correct, it's fast, with first-rate handling. You must be a car guy Gus."

My whole life. Even had a Mini Cooper when I was a kid. I'd love to drive *that* car Michael."

"That can be arranged. Who are the other people?"

"The Benedetti's. They live three houses down on *this* side."

Michael wrote the names in his spiral notebook. "Great, thank you. Gus, is your house, other than paint and maintenance, the same as when you bought it? Did you remodel or make any modifications?"

"Over the years, we've painted inside and out. The only significant modification was a new roof and more insulation blown on top of the existing insulation."

"Is there storage in the attic?"

"Not to my knowledge. Since purchasing the house, I've only poked my head up through the scuttle hole a few times. I need to climb up, stand on the washing machine, and pull myself up to do that, so," Gus smiled, "it's not something I've made a habit of."

Michael finished writing his notes. "Gus, thank you for the leads and information. Nice to meet you."

"Nice to meet you too, Michael. I'll talk to my wife about our conversation. Maybe she'll remember something that might help you."

"Great. Thanks again, Gus." Michael shook Gus' hand. "Oh, one more thing."

"Sure, what do you need?"

"Can I take a picture of your house?"

"Take as many as you need."

Michael took several pictures and thanked Gus. As he walked away, he heard Gus say, "Michael."

"Yes," Michael said, as he turned.

"Do you think Daniel buried someone on our property?"

"I doubt it. I believe Daniel was smarter than that."

"Thanks, just wondering."

Michael walked to the Benedetti's house, then to the Smiths. Both were not home. He left a business card, on the front door of each house, with a note on the back asking them to call him.

His cell phone rang before he was halfway home.

"This is Michael."

"Michael Mays?"

"Yes, speaking."

"Mr. Mays, this Bernie Benedetti. "You stuck a card on our door?"

"Mr. Benedetti, thank you for calling."

"No problem, but please call me, Bernie. Sorry I missed you, but I took the missus out to dinner. Friday night ya know. What do you need, Mr. Mays?"

"And, Bernie, you can call me Michael. I just finished talking with your neighbor Gus about Daniel Wygal. Do you have time to talk? I can turn around and be there within minutes."

Bernie said, "Only if you've got a bottle of wine in your hand" then laughed. "Yeah, I knew Daniel. I'm okay with talking about him."

"Great. Red or white wine?"

"We're red people, Michael."

"I'll be right there."

41

"Hey," Bernie said, as he opened the front door and saw a man standing on the porch, holding up a bottle of red wine in *each* hand, "you must be Michael. You're not going to get us drunk and trick us into making you the sole beneficiary in our will are you?"

"Well, I am an attorney, and it's been said we have no boundaries."

Bernie laughed. "But I suspect *you* do, Michael. Come on in."

Bernie could play the quintessential Italian grandfather/restaurant owner in a movie.

His wife joined them, holding a corkscrew and three wine glasses. "Michael, meet my wife, Gina."

Gina could be the Grandmother hosting the restaurant's family table. Even gray hair pulled back... all she needs is an apron.

"Hi, Gina, so nice to meet you."

"You too, Michael." She picked up a bottle and opened it. After removing the cork, she placed the bottle and corkscrew on the coffee table. She gave Michael a hug. "Sorry for ignoring you, but *I was* focused." She poured three glasses of wine and handed one to Michael.

"Thank you. I didn't take it as ignoring me, maybe a little rude," Michael joked, "but not ignoring."

Gina smiled, and Bernie said, "I'm used to it, Michael." Gina elbowed him. "Ow," Bernie said, "I'd rather be ignored."

Michael held up his glass. "Apology accepted."

Bernie also raised his glass. "Thank you for providing the wine, Michael.

Now, what do you want to know?"

Gina said, "But first, have we met, Michael? Bernie, does Michael look familiar to you?"

"Yeah, now that you mention it, yeah."

"I sure feel like we've met, Michael?"

"Not recently, Gina."

"Hmm? Okay," Gina said, but continued to study Michael, "go ahead and answer Bernie's question."

"Earlier this evening, I was talking to your neighbor, Gus. We discussed the house he owns, which a man named Daniel Wygal once owned."

"Yes—Gus is a good friend—but we haven't seen Daniel since they sent him to prison."

Gina added, "But Daniel didn't own the house. His family did."

Michael took a sip of wine and wiped his mouth on the back of his hand. "That's what Gus told me. He said he bought it from the Wygal Family Trust in 1989."

Bernie looked at Gina. "That sounds right, doesn't it, Gina?"

"Yes, that was the year. And, there was no family. The Trust was only Daniel. We were told his father established it for him years before."

Bernie took a drink and looked at Michael for a few seconds. "Why are you interested in Daniel's house?"

"It's Daniel I'm most interested in. Gus told me you lived here when Daniel was arrested and sentenced to life in prison."

"Yes. We moved in about the same time as Daniel."

Gina corrected him. "We moved in six months before he did."

Bernie raised his glass. "Mother knows best."

"What you may not know is they paroled him a few weeks ago."

Gina again looked at Bernie. "No, that we haven't heard."

"He was the primary suspect in the death of several other women, my mother being one."

"Oh no, Michael," Gina said, "I'm so sorry you lost your mother. How old were you?"

"I was only 12."

263

"That means she was young. How tragic. That breaks my heart. Who would do such a thing?"

"Daniel Wygal would. I only recently learned of him, but I'm convinced he killed my mother. I'm looking for memories that may lead me to evidence the police can use."

Bernie said, "We'd love to help you, but, how can we?"

"Tell me about your relationship with Daniel?"

"I couldn't call it a relationship," Gina said, "he didn't have a relationship with *anyone* in the neighborhood. We held neighborhood get-togethers, here at our place, every three months. We always invited him."

"So, you invited him, but he didn't attend?"

Gina looked at Bernie. "He was here half the time, but he wasn't very social." Bernie added, "He wasn't rude—"

Gina jumped back in. "He was here, but it was clear he didn't enjoy being around people.

"Near the end of every get-together we took a group photo. Bernie set up his tripod and used the self-timer on his camera." She looked at Bernie and said, "Daniel never smiled in even one of those pictures, did he, honey?"

"No, I always felt sorry for him. It was like he never learned how to be a friend or act around others."

"Gina, you mentioned group photos," Michael said. "Have you kept them?"

"*Kept them*," Bernie laughed, and slapped Michael on the shoulder, "heck, she's kept every one of them. Catalogued and dated, along with the rest of our photos."

"Oh, Bernie…" Gina's face reddened. "We retired years ago, Michael. I keep things organized. That's who I am."

Michael tried not to let his excitement show. "Can I look at them, Gina?"

"I'll see if I have a flash drive. If I do, you can have all of them."

"What?" Michael's excitement began to show.

"I was an Administrative Assistant for years and began using PCs when they first came out. I believe it was in 1983, at least that's the year my boss gave into me pushing him for one. So, I'm good with computers. Again, it came natural for me to digitize our old photos and categorize them."

"Wow, Gina. I'm impressed. *I have* a flash drive in my backpack. It's in my car. I'll be right back."

"Okay, we'll be here enjoying *your* wine," Bernie said.

Michael walked back in with his backpack slung over his shoulder. "Here we go."

He set the backpack on an end table and pulled out the flash drive.

"Follow me," Gina said, as she took off down the hall. Michael and Bernie followed.

She entered the second door on the left. Michael followed her. Bernie moved at a slower pace, enjoying his wine.

Gina turned after walking into the office. She faced Michael, spread her arms, and turned back and forth. "Bernie converted one of our bedrooms into an office for me. What do you think?"

Michael looked at the file cabinets, the wall mounted flat-screen TV, and the bookcase. "What a great office." He walked to the bookcase and ran his hand along the edge of a shelf. "Where did you get these, they're beautiful."

Bernie walked in as Michael was asking. Gina pointed to him. "There's my carpenter. Bern's a superb wood worker."

"I say he's a craftsman."

"Yes, he is," her pride showing, while Bernie took a sip and waved off the compliments.

She thrust both arms to her right. "He made this desk for me too."

"I was so caught up with the bookcase, I didn't look at your desk. It's magnificent—understated beauty—great work, Bernie."

"Thank you."

"Is that cherry?"

"Yes, Gina loves cherry, so that's what I used. It was fun to make for her."

As Gina sat behind her desk and worked. Michael looked at Bernie who was beaming with pride and asked, "Bernie, how long ago did Gina save you from a lifetime of loneliness?"

Gina looked up, laughing. "Bernie Benedetti, you better get this right."

Bernie paused, put his wine glass on the corner of a small table, and made a show of using his fingers to count. "Sixty years, next year, but it only feels like a hundred." He ducked as she threw a pencil.

"Incredible. That's a rarity these days."

Bernie looked at Gina, then back to Michael. He walked to the desk and stood next to her. He rested his hand on her shoulder. "It's not fashionable to talk this way now days, but there's no doubt in our minds God has kept us together. And, that He's made us better at being a husband and wife, and parents and grandparents."

Gina added, "Without a doubt," as she placed her hand on top of his. "Not without struggles and tough times, but we kept our vows in focus, and God brought us through."

"You're right, Bernie. I don't hear that much... except from my grandmother."

"Grandmothers are smart, you need to listen to her, Michael." Gina said, with a smile and a finger wag.

"She tells me the same thing, Gina. I love her. She raised me and influenced my life in ways I can never repay."

"*Tell her* you love her Michael. Sit across from her. Look at her straight on and tell her you love her."

"Thanks, Gina. I *will*."

She nodded in approval as she handed him the flash drive. "Here you go."

"Thank you both for the help you've given me tonight. I'll let you know where it leads me."

"Please do," Gina said, "we have your business card. I'll invite you to our neighborhood get-togethers."

"You invite me, and I'll be here."

While walking back into the living room, Bernie said, "Have a seat, Michael. Finish your wine."

"I'd love to," as he held up the glass, then set it on the coffee table, "but I'm driving. Thank you again, you've been *so* helpful. And, it feels like we've been friends for years."

Gina said, "You can count us as friends, Michael."

Bernie handed Michael his backpack. "Thanks again for the wine. And remember, you're now officially a friend."

Michael hugged them both, then opened the door. Bernie slapped him on the shoulder and smiled. "See ya, buddy," he said, while closing the door behind Michael.

In his car and heading home, Michael's thoughts went first to Bernie and Gina.

What a great couple. I hope to see them again.

Then to Daniel.

Not a good guy… there's danger there.

Back in his apartment, he removed the notebook computer from his briefcase, pulled the flash drive from his pants pocket, and inserted it into a USB port on the computer. Too excited to even take off his backpack or sit, he clicked on File Explorer.

Gina did a great job of archiving these photos. 1986, let's see what's there.

He clicked the July sub-folder.

I'll try 07-04-86.

When the photo came up, he zoomed in until he found Daniel.

Yep, that's the guy.

He dropped his right arm out of the backpack and unzipped the compartment holding the book.

Thirty minutes should do it.

He found page 30 and looked at his computer screen.

Michael was standing in Bernie and Gina's back yard, 20 feet behind the camera. His backpack hung from his left arm, which struck him as funny.

So excited, I forgot the strap.

He closed the book, put it in the backpack, zipped the pocket closed, and secured the backpack in place.

42

After watching Michael approach his apartment building's front door, BTH waited until Michael entered, and the front door closed. He slinked to the door and picked the lock. He moved into a shadow and watched Michael climb to the top of the stairwell.

After Michael walked into his apartment and close the door, BTH ran out the front door and to the side of the apartment building. Before climbing the exterior stairs, he called his boss.

"Yeah?"

"Boss, he's back in his apartment."

"No better time than now, BTH."

"Will do, boss."

BTH climbed the old wooden exterior stairs, that were probably meant to be used as a fire escape.

At the top of the exterior stairs, he listened as he looked into Michael's kitchen through the glass in the door.

Man, they didn't consider guys like me when they decided on what kinda door to install.

BTH looked around. Seeing no one, he picked the lock and pushed on the door. It opened with a groan, causing him to stop. He knew Michael was in there but heard or saw no one. Without letting go of the door, he gave it a quick shove, eliminating the groan.

Before entering the kitchen, he visualized the apartment's layout. He remembered it from when he was last there. There was a doorway that led from the kitchen to the living room.

If I go straight through living room to the hallway, two grenades tossed from there will take out the living room and Michael's office.

At the living room doorway, he stopped, still hearing nothing.

Maybe he's taking a nap.

There was a canvas bag hanging to the left side of his body. The bag's strap rode on his right shoulder.

From it, he pulled out an M67 frag grenade.

He placed it in his right hand and removed the pin while holding a firm grip on the lever.

Pulling out a second M67 from the bag, he applied pressure to the lever.

With his right-hand index finger, he removed its pin.

I have less than five seconds to get out of here.

His breathing and his heart rate both raced.

He worried about being able to toss the grenade far enough using his right arm, which was hindered by the cast.

He walked to the hallway that lead to Michael's bedroom.

Straight ahead of him was a bathroom.

To his right, Michael's office.

BTH visualized his movements, walked a few steps forward, and let loose both grenades.

One toward Michael's office.

The throw towards his bedroom, due to the cast, dropped more than rolled.

BTH turned and ran like somebody was chasing him.

The first grenade exploded as he exited the kitchen door.

The sound of the explosion, along with the fragments of the grenade destroying the apartment, was deafening.

BTH fell forward and hit the second-floor landing as the second grenade exploded.

He covered his ears and waited a few seconds for the sounds to stop.

With a limp, he climbed the stairs and entered the kitchen. He stopped at the doorway to the living room. He pulled a handkerchief from his back pocket and covered his nose and mouth.

The grenades must have scattered his body everywhere.

He made a quick check of the living room. A golf bag lay on the floor next to Michael's office door. Golf clubs were bent, and several were missing heads. He checked the bag's pockets.

Not in there.

He checked the office and found Michael's briefcase. It was heavily damaged, but still closed.

Might be in this.

BTH looked at his watch and realized the cops would be there soon.

I'll take it with me—open it later.

He ran to Michael's bedroom and checked it without success. But it brought the painful memory of a baseball bat hitting his right forearm. While walking out of the bedroom, he scowled, scrunched his left hand, and cussed Michael.

Sirens warned him police and fire were getting close.

He made another quick pass through the office and the living room.

The sirens grew closer, causing him to abandon his search.

He hurried through the kitchen and ran down the fire escape.

Someone yelled, "Hey, what are you doing up there?" Without stopping, BTH yelled back, "I was walking by, heard the explosion and ran up to see if I could help. Nobody home; must have been a gas explosion." He kept running.

* * *

Michael stood watching the group break from the photo taking session. A man approached him. It was Bernie, much younger, but without doubt, Bernie.

"Hi," Bernie said, "I don't think we've met, but welcome. Come on in and get something to eat. My name's Bernie, what's yours."

"Michael. Glad to meet you, Bernie. I'm looking at a house in the neighborhood that may become available soon. I was drawn in by the voices and laughter. I couldn't resist crashing the party to meet potential neighbors."

"Which house, Michael?"

"They haven't made a final decision, and don't want to cause a stir, so they asked that I not tell anyone."

"That's okay. Anyway, get something to eat and drink, and meet the folks here."

"I'll do that, thanks."

Michael walked around, talking with neighbors, while keeping Daniel in sight.

He saw a much younger Gina. "Hi, you must be, Gina."

"Yes, have we met?"

"No, we haven't." Michael told her the story he had told Bernie.

"Well, I hope it works out for you. Do you want me to walk with you and make introductions?"

"Sure. Let me grab something to drink first."

"Go ahead, come find me when you're ready."

Michael turned. Daniel was standing right in front of him.

He leaned in till his face was inches from Michael's. With malice leaching from his entire being, he said, "I know you… don't I."

"This is my first time here, so I doubt we've met."

"I don't forget faces," Daniel said, glaring at Michael.

"If you figure out where we've met, let me know," Michael said, as he turned and walked away.

Daniel called out, "OMSI, wasn't it. You're good at jumping out of the way of VW buses. But don't give me a next time. I won't miss again."

Michael didn't reply. He scanned the gathering, found Gina, and headed for her.

"You found the drinks."

"Yes, fantastic punch," as he held up the plastic cup in salute.

"Thank you. You were talking with Daniel. Do you know him?"

"No, but he thinks he knows me."

I'm getting too comfortable lying.

"It surprises me he talked to you. He seldom talks to anyone at these gatherings."

"I guess I have one of those familiar faces."

"You're far from average looking, Michael."

"Why, Gina, you're embarrassing me."

"I'm harmless, Michael, I love that old man over there and wouldn't trade him for anything."

"I hope you get 50 or 60 years with him."

"A hundred, I hope."

"Me too, Gina. I appreciate the hospitality, but I must get on the road. I'll say goodbye to Bernie on the way out."

"You're always welcome. Come back again."

"I promise I will."

Michael stopped, told Bernie goodbye, and left through a backyard fence gate, near where he had materialized. He walked toward Daniel's house, crossed the street, and stood behind a maple tree, which he knew would grow much larger and contribute to Gus' raking chore.

After taking several pictures of the front of Daniel's house, he moved to the next tree and photographed the garage side of the house. He walked until he had a full view of the opposite side. He took one photo before the warm wind took home.

"*What?*" Michael said out loud, as he looked around at splintered wood, ripped leather and broken glass.

He heard someone yell, "Hey." He turned and saw a firefighter in protective clothing and a filter mask. "How'd you get in here? No one's allowed to come into this scene yet."

"Scene? This isn't a scene. It's my apartment."

43

"I'm sorry sir, but I cannot allow you to be here."

"Listen," Michael said, "I'm not trying to be a jerk, but who are you—yes, I see you're with the fire department—and why can't I come into my apartment?"

"Sir, my name is Jenkins, Susan Jenkins. I'm a Deputy Fire Marshal with the Portland Fire Bureau. There are *two* reasons you must leave. First, this is a crime scene and we're trying to protect evidence. Second, it's unsafe for you to be in this atmosphere without proper respiratory protection."

"Okay, I get that. But I need to grab my computer. I'm an attorney and I have to protect the files on it, if any are recoverable."

"I can't allow you to take it, sir. As an attorney, surely you understand protecting the chain of custody of evidence."

Michael leaned back against his desk while resting his right hand on the edge of what once was a beautiful desk. He was looking for a chance to remove the flash drive from his laptop. He looked around at the destruction. "Okay, and yes, I understand."

"Susan," her co-worker called out, "come over here, please." The Deputy Fire marshal looked at Michael as if to say: 'You haven't left yet.'

Michael raised his left hand in surrender. "Ok, I'll leave."

She turned and walked away. He found the edge of the computer and slid his fingers along its side until he felt the flash drive. He removed it and put it in his pocket.

As he was leaving, he interrupted Susan and handed her his business card.

"Please call me when it's safe to return?"

"I will." She looked and found his name on his business card, "Mr. Mays, I apologize if I was harsh, but my motivation is protecting you."

"Thank you, Susan. I appreciate that." He shook her hand and left.

Where do I go? What do I do now?

He walked down the stairs and opened the front door.

Wish I could have grabbed my umbrella.

To his right was a local TV station's mobile satellite unit. A reporter in a blue, hooded raincoat was standing with her back to him, talking to the camera.

Michael turned left; thankful he had parked his car a block down the street.

While taking off his backpack and getting into his car, his phone rang. After closing the door, he looked at his phone's screen and answered.

"Hey, Linda. How are you?"

"No, how are you? I was just watching the news and saw a reporter standing in front of your apartment building describing an explosion. It's so good to hear your voice."

"It's good to be heard," he said, with a laugh. Then he became serious. "It was *my* apartment."

"But, you're okay?"

"Yes, I wasn't home."

"What are you going to do? Where are you going to stay?"

"I just asked myself those questions."

"Michael, we moved back into our house today. Come over. Let's get you out of the rain. You can tell me what happened."

"I'll be there in two minutes."

Linda opened her door and hugged Michael. "So glad to see you're not hurt."

"Thank you."

She closed the door and walked to the living room. As they were getting ready to sit, Michael looked around. "Two things, your house looks beautiful, they did an excellent job."

"Yes, they did. They even brought in a house cleaning service and cleaned the entire house, top to bottom. May be the cleanest it's ever been."

Michael lowered and tilted his head. "Right."

Linda mimicked his movement and added arms waist high and palms up. "Well, I am who I am. Please, sit, Michael. What's the second thing?"

He took off his backpack and sat. "You moved back in and didn't call me to help?"

"Our move back was easy. Jacob and I only had clothes and toiletries to bring with us. It didn't require extra trips or heavy lifting, and you're busy so, why bother you?"

"Good. I would have had to send over my assistant Trevor to help. I had a golf tee time to keep."

Linda stood, walked over, and slugged Michael on the shoulder. "I've missed resetting you, Michael."

He rubbed his shoulder. "Felt more like abuse."

"So, what are you going to do? You can't go back to your apartment... can you?"

"No, too much damage. And, the police and Deputy Fire Marshal won't allow me in. They're treating it as a crime scene."

"Wow, any thoughts on who might have done this?"

"I know who did it."

"Who in the world would do that?"

"Remember when we discussed my upcoming meeting with Russell?"

Linda leaned forward and her hands shot out. "Yes, and I expressed anxiety and doubt, because I've *experienced* Russ' lies and deception."

Michael leaned back. "And I suggested someone in prison believes Russell's story."

She leaned farther forward. "Yes, but they'd be crazy too, right?"

"I'm not sure how to define crazy anymore—we're all a little crazy—but it's clear he's a ruthless sociopath. He wants the book, and he'll do anything—and sacrifice anyone—to get what he wants."

Linda leaned back. "Did you see him near your apartment after the explosion?"

"No, I haven't seen him since the Coffee Shop, when he asked for directions."

"Michael, if it's the same guy, a witness saw him hobbling away on crutches after he crashed into my house. Do you think the crash injured him to the extent he can't walk? Maybe he's having others do his dirty work?"

"You *may* be onto something Linda. A man calling himself Curtis shot my grandmother—"

Linda leaned forward and her hands shot out again. "What? When did that happen?"

"Linda please. Sit back and allow me to explain."

She sat back in slow motion. "I'm sorry Michael. With everything that's been happening, I'm on edge."

Michael looked at her, stood, held up his index finger, and walked toward the kitchen. She heard the refrigerator door open and close, and few clinks and splashes. Michael walked back in with two glasses of wine and handed her one of the glasses. "I hoped you had some wine."

"Carrie sent the half-full bottle of Chardonnay home with me the night I first met them."

Michael raised his glass. "I'm glad she did."

"Me too," she said, and raised her glass. "Okay, go ahead, Michael."

"The shooting happened last Sunday. I'm sorry for not calling you to tell you, but I've been crazy busy. She's doing okay. A wound to the shoulder is tough at any age, but at 90, I was... I am worried. She's recuperating at a friend's house; a retired physician."

"I'm glad she's okay, Michael. And I guess I'll forgive you. But I owe you a shoulder slug. Back to this Curtis character."

"Yeah, bad guy. He said he gave me fair warning about giving his boss the book. You remember I mentioned Stephanie?" Linda tilted her head, put her fingers on her lips and frowned. "A friend of mine—Coffee Shop— professional photographer."

"Oh yes, now I remember."

"And then, I'm losing track of time, what was it two—three weeks ago— a guy broke into my apartment? And, thanks again for helping me clean up the mess."

Linda laughed. "It was a mess, no doubt."

"It's a bigger mess now!" Michael said, as he took a sip of wine and set his glass on an end table. "After breaking into my apartment, he visited Stephanie's parents' house. He introduced himself as Bob and told Stephanie's mother I was critically injured in the same accident that broke his right arm. He claimed he knew Stephanie's a good friend of mine, so he wanted to get in touch with her and let her know.

"Stephanie's mother gave him the information he needed to locate her. I have no doubt Bob works for a man named, Daniel Wygal. The man Russell fears will kill him.

"Linda," Michael hesitated, "a woman, kidnapped Stephanie, and made demands that either I *met*, or Stephanie died."

"Seriously? What happened? Surely you meet her demands?"

"She's dead, the hit-woman's dead that is. She died in a shootout with the police."

"Here in Portland?"

"No, in a small town in Georgia, two days ago."

Michael paused for a few seconds to allow Linda to process his burst of information.

"Are you with me?"

Linda nodded. "I've got it. So, you believe Bob, the hit-woman, and Curtis work, or in the woman's case, worked for Daniel Wygal?"

"I do. Now, go back to where you and I began our relationship and agreed to join forces. Daniel Wygal is the white-haired man who tried to run over me and then destroyed your garage sale."

Linda looked at Michael and shook her head. "This is a crazy story. I've heard said, 'you can't make this kind of stuff up.'"

"It is the strangest thing I've ever faced," Michael said.

Linda set her glass on the end table. "What does he want?"

"Let me hold off a few minutes before answering that."

Linda angled her head to the right and frowned. "Okay, but is Russ helping him?"

"He better *not* be."

"That's an odd answer, Michael. I don't understand."

Michael ran his hand through his hair. Then placed his hand behind his neck, stretched his head back and gave a heavy sigh. "Linda, Russell didn't kill Liz."

Linda raised her voice and jolted forward with her arms out. "What? How can you be sure? And, if you are sure, who did, and what makes you believe Russ didn't?"

"That's a lot of questions Linda, let me explain my 'odd answer' first."

"Okay, but—"

"No, let me get through this, it's tough information to give."

Linda gave a heavy sigh as she leaned back and placed her head on the sofa's rear cushion. She closed her eyes and listened.

"When I met with Russell, I made a deal with him. If I discover who murdered Liz, and clear him, he will never contact you or Jacob again."

She opened her eyes and leaned forward. "I like the sound of that, Michael, but how can you guarantee it?"

"This is where it gets tough. You're convinced Russell lied during his testimony, right?"

"I do."

"This is difficult to say, but I've discovered *everything* he claimed is true."

Linda jumped to her feet.

"*No.* He's sucked you into his fantasy world. Maybe you should leave, Michael."

"Linda, please sit."

She looked at him, started to say something, but changed her mind.

She sat on the edge of the sofa, one leg forward, the other against the bottom edge of the sofa, preparing to strike.

"Linda, have I given any sign that I'm crazy or dangerous?"

"Neither did Ted Bundy."

Michael avoided snapping back at her.

Let that lie.

"Linda, please listen. This is not something I wanted. It took me by surprise, and I still can't explain it, but it's true."

"How can it be true? I can't—" she broke down and wept, face in hands.

"Linda, I will leave, if that's what you want. But there's a saying, 'The best predictor of future behavior is past behavior.' I'm asking you to give me credibility based upon my past behavior, please. I'll finish, then leave and you'll never see me again, if that's what you want. But you need to hear this."

Linda kept her elbows on her knees, face in her hands, but nodded.

"I told Russell that I have the book and discovered how to use it. The *'odd answer'* I gave you relates to the conditions of my promise. I told him I have the power of the book to put him back in prison. And, if he ever contacts you—or Jacob—I will use that power to put him back behind bars. Also, I'll use it if he helps his crazy prison buddy Daniel. He agreed to those conditions.

Linda, please look at me." She raised her head enough for her eyes to peek over her hands. "I discovered the person who killed Liz. It was the kid who lived behind your family's house—"

Linda's eyes came alive as she bolted up straight. "No, not Eric. He adored Liz and cared for her so much." She collapsed back into the sofa and became quiet while looking into the distance.

"And that was the motive, he became enraged because Liz left the curtains open as she and Russell—" Seeing the heartbreak on her face, Michael couldn't finish the sentence.

"I talked with Eric's parents. They showed me a suicide note he wrote, in which he confessed to killing Liz—" Michael hesitated.

"Suicide?"

"Yes, a year after he killed Liz."

Linda lowered her head and messaged her temples.

"The Andersons and I met at the District Attorney's office and presented the evidence, including a recording of Eric confessing to the murder. It was Carrie Hindler who met with us. She'll present the evidence to her boss, but believes they'll release Russell soon."

"Michael, I have so many questions. I don't know where to start?"

"Let me start for you. I'll fill in the blanks I'd want to know if I were in your place. If I miss something that you're trying to understand, ask me. Will that work? Will that help?"

"Yes," she said, "and I'm sorry for the Bundy comment."

"I understand and accept your apology. I cannot imagine what you're going through, but I did what was right, not because I have sympathy for Russell. Do you trust me when I say that?"

"I want to, but you've come along and demolished all that I thought was true, *for years*."

"I don't want to upset you, Linda. There's no benefit for me to harm you and Jacob, or to betray our friendship. The only reason I promised Russell I'd help him was to get the name of the man threatening us.

"He wouldn't give it to me. He believes Daniel will kill him if he finds Russell gave up his name. So, I had to bargain something. Getting him out of prison was my only bargaining chip."

Linda's expression changed. Michael sensed she understood his predicament.

"We have to stay united on this, Linda. Daniel will not abandon his quest. I don't think he knows we're friends, yet. You and Jacob haven't been targets and I want to keep it that way."

"*Me too*. You've answered *some* of my questions, but I'm still struggling with the book working as Russ claims."

"I assure you it does. I discovered its powers accidentally." He told her the story of answering the door to talk with his neighbor Tony. "Closing my front door, I remembered a photo of my Little League team that hung near my front door—"

"I saw that photo when Jacob and I helped you clean up the mess."

"Good, you have that in mind. As I looked at it, I sensed a warm wind blowing me from all directions. Next thing I knew, I was standing in a park watching my mother taking that photo."

Linda shook her head. "That's not possible, Michael."

"If I hadn't experienced it, I'd agree. You'll never accept it until you experience it yourself."

Linda scrunched her face. "How do I do that? You're right, I won't believe it. I'm talking crazy here, but I don't see how we can move forward until I experience it myself."

"You sure you want to do this?"

"No, but I will, if it helps me move on."

"Is Jacob home?"

"No. If he were, he'd have heard you and been down here by now. He's spending the night at the Hindler's, hanging out with MJ."

"I'm not sure this will work, Linda. But everything he claimed, including holding onto things and taking them with him, is true. I didn't think to ask him if that includes people."

As Michael was telling this to Linda, he removed the book before strapping on his backpack. "Once you've read the entire book, you can choose how much time—up to four hours—you want to spend in the past. So, I'll open the book to page 15, that's enough time to allow you to discover whether I'm crazy. First, are you thirsty?" Michael smiled. "Need to use the bathroom?"

"Yes, both." Linda said, and walked away.

When she returned, she picked up her glass of wine and tipped it back until it was empty. Michael smiled. "Hold my hand; you washed your hands, right?

Linda gave a guarded laugh and slugged his shoulder.

"I've missed your laugh. I still do."

"That's the best I've got."

"I understand. Again, I haven't tried this with a person, so if I disappear… I'll be back in 15 minutes."

Linda took his hand. He set his phone's alarm for 13 minutes, opened the book to page 15, and found the picture he'd taken an hour ago. He looked at Linda. "Ready?"

She looked up at him and nodded.

"Okay. Here we go."

Linda's home phone rang till it went to voice mail.

44

Linda wobbled.

Michael caught her arm.

"Thanks. I'm okay, it's so much to take in. We were just in my living room, now we're... where are we, Michael?" her head jerked side to side, and up and down, as she looked for a familiar landmark.

"It's July 4,1986. We're on a sidewalk, across from where Daniel Wygal lived. But," he pointed to the Benedetti's, "we're headed to that house."

Michael held her hand as they walked to the entry gate that led to the Benedetti's back yard. As they closed the gate, they heard Gina call out, "Michael, I thought you'd left?"

"That was my plan, Gina, but my friend wanted to meet you and Bernie first."

Linda looked up at Michael, with lips parted, and eyes squinting.

Michael leaned over and whispered. "Play along, I'll explain in about 34 years."

Gina got within five feet. "Gina Benedetti, meet Linda Curt."

"Great to meet you, Linda," Gina said, as she held out her hand. "Get something to drink, and there's plenty of food."

"Nice to meet you too, Gina. Thank you for your hospitality."

"I bet you'd do the same thing for me, Linda."

Linda smiled. "Of course, Gina."

"Well there ya go, enjoy yourself. Michael, go find Bernie, he'll want to meet Linda."

"We're on our way, thanks." As they walked toward Bernie, he stopped and put his arm in front of Linda.

Linda stopped and looked at Michael. "What's wrong?"

"I won't point to him, but the little guy, walking 20 feet in front of us?"

"Yes, he's on a mission."

"That's the weasely guy who broke into my apartment."

"Are you sure?"

"No doubt."

"Then he's the one who threatened Jacob?" Mama bear kicked in and Linda took off toward him.

Michael caught her arm. "Yes, but remember, that's way in the future."

Linda stopped and looked at Michael. "Preemptive strike." Michael detected her lips hinting a smile. She lowered her arms, relaxed her fists, and let out a sigh. "Okay, back to my question. How do you know these people?"

"I was just here."

"Seriously—?"

"Hold on, let's see what he does."

The little guy walked up to Daniel and pulled him aside.

Michael leaned into Linda. "That Daniel, AKA, the white-haired man."

Daniel and the weasel turned their backs on the party and moved close to the fence. Their discussion became intense. Daniel's temper flared. The little guy dropped his arms in resignation, shook his head in agreement, turned and walked away, heading for the drink table.

Michael took Linda's hand, walked to the table, and stood next to him. Michael reached in front of the weasely guy to grab a cup. "Excuse me."

The weasel arched back. "No prob."

Michael turned to face him. "Have we met here before? You look familiar."

"I've been here before, but I don't remember meeting you."

Michael remembered Stephanie's mother said she was visited by a man who called himself, Bob. "Is it Robert... or Bob?"

Surprised, he looked up. "Yeah, it's Robert, but I go by Bob."

"I've lost your last name, Bob?"

"It's Gruen. I still don't remember you."

"Hmm, must've been in passing. I noticed you talking with Daniel. Is he a friend of yours?"

"Yes, and I do odd jobs for him."

Michael noticed Daniel walking toward them.

"Nice to see you again, Bob. Excuse us."

Michael took Linda's hand and walked toward Daniel.

Daniel sauntered toward them. "I thought you'd left."

"I missed you and couldn't leave without coming back and introducing my friend, Carol."

Daniel looked Linda up and down, then at Michael and pointed to BTH. "Why were you talking to him?"

"I told him it was good to see him again; just getting to know him better."

Daniel looked lustfully at Linda. "I'd like to get to know Carol a *lot* better." He looked at Michael. "Why don't you go make yourself a sandwich, while I show Carol around? Maybe I'll take her to OMSI for a tour, then go out for a bite."

Linda said, "No thanks, Mr....?"

"Wygal, but you can call me Daniel."

"No thanks, Daniel. There's nowhere in my future for you."

Great. Michael thought. *I hope I can keep it that way.*

Michael's phone's alarm sounded. He removed it from his pocket and turned it off. When he looked up, Daniel was watching him and opened his mouth to speak.

Michael interrupted, as he placed his phone in his pocket, "I'm glad you had this opportunity to talk with me again, Daniel. I figured you were missing me."

He took Linda's hand, turned and led her to the gate. After walking halfway down the block, they were taken back to Linda's living room.

Linda fell onto the sofa. "Worldview shattered—in 15 minutes—to the extent you *renamed me?*"

"Daniel's a smart guy. I didn't want to give him your name. Russell may have mentioned it to him, and it seems Daniel has a good memory. Are you convinced? Ready to help me solve this puzzle?"

"Yes, and more than ready. What can I do to help?"

"Okay. We must divide and conquer. I'll do the time traveling."

"Thank you. What do you want me to do?"

"Can you find out if a Portland hospital treated a Daniel on the day he crashed into your house? I believe he's smarter than that, but it doesn't hurt to check."

"I'll find out."

"Daniel's on parole. He must check in with his parole officer. I'll get Trevor, my assistant on that. Also, find out if someone treated a Robert Gruen the night my apartment was broken into. Someone set his arm and cast it. I doubt he sought help in Portland. He may have driven to Vancouver, but more likely Salem."

"I work tomorrow. I'll get into my hospital's computer system and see what I can find out."

"Great. Our goal: get Daniel Wygal *back* in prison."

"Okay, Michael," she paused and held her hands out. "I'm waiting."

"Now what did I do?"

"You promised you'd tell me what was going on, and why you were recognized by the Benedetti's?"

"I was there earlier this evening. That's where I was when someone blew up my apartment. You and I went back a few minutes later, using a photo I took across from Daniel Wygal's house before the book brought me home."

"I'm sorry, Michael, but my head is spinning. My brain is refusing to compute this."

"Linda, it still shakes me each time I travel back, but it's more from excitement and anticipation than anxiety. You mentioned not computing. Something happened on my second visit to my Little League game. It makes no sense."

"What happened?"

"I walked 30 yards away—golfer, that's how my mind calculates distance—and sat on the grass watching my mother. I noticed a man taking photos. It was

Daniel, but he was still a stranger to me. Out of nowhere, a man appeared behind him. The man was carrying a rifle. As he moved to shoulder his rifle, he looked at me. I was sitting beside a Douglas Fir tree. I fell back while tucking my knees into my chest and rolled to my left and behind the tree."

"Are you sure he was aiming at you?"

"No doubt in my mind. He fired two shots. One bullet hit the ground behind where I was sitting, the other hit the edge of the tree."

"And you haven't seen him since that day?"

"No. Here's what I'm trying to wrap my mind around. The shooter appeared behind Daniel, just as *I've appeared* behind the photographer of the photos I've used."

Linda picked up on it. "How did the shooter get the photo from Daniel?"

"Yes. And that means someone else has the same book—or somewhere *in the future*—he gets my book."

Linda paused and considered the implications. "I hadn't thought of that."

"Either way, Daniel gave the photo to the shooter. That's what's puzzling me, Daniel didn't know me. Why give the shooter that photo?

"Maybe the shooter stole the photo."

"How could he know Daniel had a photo of me? Or, even who Daniel is?"

"Or, where he lived?" Linda said.

"Too many questions. I may have to wait until the shooter tries again."

"Dangerous game, Michael."

"What are my options?"

"None that come to mind."

The ring from her home phone jolted her; she looked at Michael. He nodded toward the phone. "You should take that in case it's Jacob."

She answered the phone. "Hello... hi, Jacob. How are you doing, honey?"

"I'm okay, mom. But was worried about you."

"I'm sorry. Michael and I stepped out for a few minutes and missed your calls—"

"I called three times."

"Again, I'm sorry and appreciate your concern, but I'm okay. Michael is here—"

"Can I talk with him, mom?"

"Sure. But first, are you doing okay?"

"I'm having a great time, but I was worried about you. I'm glad to hear you're safe."

"Thanks Jacob, I'll talk to you later; here's Michael."

Jacob wants to talk to you." She said and passed the phone to Michael.

"Hey, Jacob, your mother's doing great, but I appreciate that you were worried about her."

"Thanks, Michael."

"Are you and MJ getting along well?"

"MJ's a cool guy, I enjoy hangin' out with him."

"Good to hear; he's a good guy. I haven't forgotten your golf lessons, but someone destroyed my golf clubs. I'll explain later… hold on—"

He covered the phone and asked Linda, "Any plans for Jacob tomorrow?"

"The Hindlers asked him to stay tonight and tomorrow night. Why?"

"I'm going shopping for new golf clubs. Why don't you and Jacob come with me tomorrow?"

"Jacob going with you is a great idea, but I'm working tomorrow, Michael."

"Oh yeah, you told me that didn't you?" She gave him the look.

"Jacob, I need to buy new golf clubs tomorrow. Do you want to go with me?"

"Really, that would be great. Is my mom okay with it?"

"Yes. And tell Matt and Carrie I'll be there by 9:30. And, Jacob, MJ's welcome to come with us."

"Awesome. I'll ask him. Before you hang up, Carrie wants to talk with you."

"Great, talk to you tomorrow."

"Okay, here's Carrie."

Michael could hear Jacob telling Carrie about going with him the next morning.

"Hey, Michael."

"Hi, Carrie. What's going on?"

"I wanted to see if you wanted to have breakfast with us tomorrow morning. Jacob told me you're coming at 9:30 to pick him up. Can you make it at 9? I'm making *waffles*."

"Nine o'clock, I'd be there at 5 AM for your waffles. And I'd stand in line. I love them even more with chunky peanut butter and real maple syrup."

"I only have creamy style peanut butter, and we usually use a fruit compote for topping, so you'll need to get both."

"No, problem. I'll stop at the store on my way. I'll pick up chunky peanut butter and syrup."

"Great. We'll see you in the morning. Love you."

"Okay, love you too. Looking forward to it."

Michael turned. Linda stood with her head to the side, brow scrunched, and a slight smile. "I get the maple syrup, but peanut butter… on waffles?"

"Please don't tell me you've never tried it. That might end our friendship."

"Well, you got me to try time travel, I guess I'll trust you with this too."

"You will love it. Well, 9 AM will come quick; I better find a hotel. It'll be a short night."

"Michael, I have an extra room with a full bathroom, stay here."

"I appreciate that, Linda, but I don't want to contribute to neighbors spreading rumors about you. Is that too old-fashioned, Linda?"

"No, it's admirable. I appreciate your thoughtfulness."

"Thanks, Linda, but I am *not* a knight in shining armor. Something's been bred into me that helps me resist what my mind is considering."

Linda smiled and tilted her head slightly. "Michael, I guess you *better* leave."

Michael raised his eyebrows, pressed his lips together, and shrugged his left shoulder. "I'm being honest Linda. You're a very attractive woman. So, I agree. I should leave.

"I'll talk with Matt and Carrie tomorrow morning to find out what time they want Jacob back. He's great company. I look forward to taking him around with me. He can also come with me as I get my apartment issue, or lack of an apartment, straightened out."

"Jacob's yours tomorrow," she said, as she hugged him good night.

45

While walking to his car, Michael pondered all that had become his life.

What did I do with my evenings and weekends before the book came into my life? This past four weeks has been—

"The Files!" He blurted out loud.

The files on Wygal and my mother are in my briefcase.

Michael rushed past his car, to the road fronting his apartment. He stopped and surveyed the street.

Good, the news media left.

As he approached his apartment building, he scanned parked cars for occupants, and watched the sidewalks on both sides of the street.

Near his apartment, three men stood looking at the building. One was pointing and talking. Michael came within hearing range at mid-sentence. "… yeah, I told the cops a guy ran down the fire exit stairs. He yelled something about a gas explosion and kept running."

Michael approached the group and asked the man who was speaking, "Excuse me, did you say you saw someone running away from this building after the explosion?"

"Yeah, I did."

"Did you get a good look at him?"

"Are you a police officer?"

"No, the explosion was in my apartment."

"Wow, that's a bummer man. It was too dark to make out his face enough to describe him."

"How big was he?"

"At first, I thought it was a kid, until I heard his voice. It was a man."

"Do you remember anything else?"

"He was carrying something, but it was getting too dark to tell what it was. He was a small man, short and thin."

"Thanks for your help. I appreciate it."

"Sure, glad to help."

The Deputy Fire Marshal's car was still parked behind a police car, near his apartment building's entrance.

"Siri, call Carrie Hindler."

"Carrie, Michael here, sorry if I woke you, but I forgot to tell you something. I need to give you a heads-up."

"Sure, go ahead, Michael. MJ and Jacob are entertaining Matt and me, so there was no waking up involved."

"Good. Carrie—*crazy news*—someone blew up my apartment. I'll explain in the morning."

"What, are you okay?"

"I'm fine. I tried to get in to check it, but a Portland Deputy Fire Marshal won't allow me access; protecting evidence, chain of custody."

"They're doing the right thing, Michael."

"I understand, but I need your help with an issue."

"Okay...?"

"The files you gave me, earlier today, are in my home office. I don't want to leave them lying around unprotected. I'm going up to talk to the Deputy Fire Marshal again, to try to convince her I need to protect the file folders. If she refuses, I'll give her your work number and ask her to call you. Can the caller still choose call forwarding?"

"It isn't automatic, but the caller can press 2, and leave an urgent message for me. I check them an hour before bedtime. I seldom receive urgent requests."

"I'll text you when the Deputy Fire Marshal is calling. Talk to you tomorrow morning. Say goodnight to Matt and the boys for me."

"Will do, Michael. Goodnight."

"The investigators had locked his front door. Michael knocked.

On my own door.

The Deputy Fire Marshal opened the door. "Mr. Mays, I'm sorry, but your apartment is still closed and under investigation."

"I hate to bother you, Susan, but I remembered two files I need. They're part of a murder investigation. They're in my briefcase—"

"I'm sorry, Mr. Mays. Your apartment is a crime scene. You still can't come in."

"Do me a favor, Susan, please?"

She pursed her lips and paused before speaking. "What is it."

He opened his phone and brought up Carrie's office number.

"Please call this number; ask her about the files."

"Deputy District Attorney," Susan looked at Michael. "She works this late?"

"No, but while you leave her a message, I'll text her and ask her to check her voicemail."

"You have her personal number. Why don't you give it to me, and I'll call her direct?"

"Because—she gave it in confidence—I won't betray her trust."

"Show me her office number again." Susan left a voice message asking Carrie to call her back, "ASAP."

Michael sent a text to Carrie. She returned Susan's call within a minute.

After talking to Carrie and ending the call, Susan looked at Michael and shrugged her shoulders. "I guess it's okay for you to enter the crime scene." She bowed and swept her arm in front of her, palm-up, directing Michael into his office.

"Thank you."

He rushed into his office and looked where he left the briefcase.

"Hmm," he said out loud, "was it knocked to the floor?"

Nope.

He checked the entire office.

Nothing. The "something" the weasel was carrying was my briefcase. Wygal either now knows, or will soon know, that I know who he is.

* * *

"Boss, it's Bob."

"Did you get the book?"

"No, it's not there."

"Did you take out Michael?"

"I didn't waste time looking for his remains. Your directions absorbed me on finding the book, until the sirens got too close, I had to get out of there rapidly. But I found something you need to look at tonight."

"Okay, bring it."

"I'm in the parking lot, outside your place. I didn't want to waste any time getting it to you."

BTH checked in at the nursing home's front desk and made his way to Daniel's room.

Daniel looked up as BTH walked in. "What do you have for me?

BTH placed the briefcase on Daniel's bed, opened it and handed him the files.

After studying them, Daniel let his arms and the files fall to his lap. "He knows who I am. There's only one person who could've told him." He reached for his phone and placed a call.

"Billy, Daniel here. I was hoping they hadn't discovered your cell phone. I've got a job for you."

* * *

Michael found a room in a motel near his house. The room included a queen-sized bed, a bathroom, a sitting area with a sofa, and a writing table and chair.

What more could I need?

He threw his backpack on the bed and realized he does have more needs: toiletries, a change of clothes, a writing tablet and pen, a book to read, and peanut butter and maple syrup. He headed out to shop.

46

Saturday, November 2nd

Michael left his hotel and made it to the Hindlers' by 9 A.M. He had done his shopping for breakfast supplies last night, so he slept in until 7:30.

As he reached for the grocery bag in the passenger's seat, his phone rang. There was no caller ID. "Michael here."

"Oh, I'm so sorry, Michael. You won't enjoy hearing what you've done."

"What?"

"You might check the status of your good friend Russell Curt." The call ended before Michael could respond.

He did not recognize the voice.

The status of Russell?

He went cold. Chills ran through him.

Russell's dead.

He felt it to the depth of his soul.

The weasel got the files to Daniel.

Russell warned that Daniel would kill him if he found out he had helped Michael.

Carrie answered the doorbell. "Michael, so good to see you," as she hugged him.

"Here, let me take the bag."

She looked at him. "Michael, what's wrong?"

He hesitated, then said, "We need to talk."

Matt joined them at the door. "Don't just stand there Michael, come on in."

Carrie looked at Matt and shook her head.

Matt said, "Michael, come in, please."

Michael looked up. "I fear something terrible has happened."

Carrie took his arm and led him toward the living room.

Michael asked, "Can the three of us talk in private?"

"Follow me," Matt said, as he led the way to the study.

He closed the door behind them and motioned for Michael to have a seat. When he sat, he put his elbows on his knees, clasp his hands and hung his head. Matt and Carrie gave him time to gather his thoughts. When Michael looked up, Matt asked, "What's going on, Michael?"

Michael's speech faltered. "As I... pulled into your driveway... I received a call, from someone who's voice I didn't recognize—without saying Jacob's father is dead—the caller said he's dead."

"Are you sure?" Carrie asked.

"No, but in my heart, I know that's what the caller meant. Carrie, do you have a contact at the Willamette State Penitentiary? If you do, please call and find out if someone murdered Linda's ex-husband, Russell Curt? His trial was in Portland. It must have involved the Multnomah District Attorney's Office."

Carrie responded, "Yes. And we have a vested interest in knowing if someone killed a person we prosecuted."

"Would you check please?"

"Give me a few minutes." She moved to the study's desk.

When someone answered, Carrie introduced herself and said, "Put me through to the on-duty supervisor, please?"

Carrie looked at Matt and Michael. "I may be on hold for a few minutes."

Within less than a minute, she said, "Hello, James, I didn't expect you to be there on a Saturday morning—"

"That's related to why I called you.

"Is the prisoner's name Russell Curt?

"Yes, our office prosecuted him.

"What's the prognosis?"

Carrie's face became ashen, "Okay—you're busy, so I won't keep you—"

Michael interrupted. "Carrie, can I talk with James?"

"James, a friend of ours, also an attorney, is here with us. He'd like to speak with you."

"Okay, here he is," she said, as she stood and handed Michael her phone.

"James, we haven't met, but I visited Russell Curt last Tuesday. From the look on Carrie's face I sense Russell is dead." Michael looked at Carrie who was shaking her head no.

"He's not?" Michael said, in surprise. "I heard Carrie ask what the prognosis is, but I'd locked my mind onto Russell being dead.

"Thanks, James. I have information for you.

"As you and Carrie talked, I remembered a prisoner named Billy Chapman. I suggest you consider him as your primary suspect. He may have a cell phone. If you find one, check the recent calls and look for this number." Michael gave James his phone number.

"Someone called me minutes ago and said, 'I'm so sorry, Michael,' then added, 'you won't enjoy hearing what you've done.' He told me I should 'check the status of Russell Curt.' James, I hope that helps you."

"You're welcome. Do you need to speak with Carrie again?" Michael looked at Carrie, she shook her head, no. "Okay, you have my number; we should talk. I'll explain why I suspect Billy Chapman. You too, thanks."

As Michael ended the call and handed Carrie her phone, he looked at her, then to Matt. "What do I do with this? Linda's working, but I have to tell her. And she'll want to break the news to Jacob herself, and help him work through it."

"Have her come here. Let me fix breakfast, and we'll eat; by then Linda should be here. She can meet with Jacob here in the study," Carrie said, as she looked around. "We've allowed Jacob and MJ to use this room to play video games. They enjoy being able to close the door and be on their own. Jacob's comfortable hanging out in here."

"I agree, Michael," Matt said, "you and Carrie can come in here and talk with Linda before she meets with Jacob. I'll keep the boys busy while you do."

"Thanks, good advice. I'll text Linda to see if she can take a call."

Carrie said, "Michael, as soon as she reads your text, her mind will go to: 'Something's happened to Jacob.' Include assurance he's okay when you text her."

Michael gave her a thumbs up.

"Hey, Linda, thanks for the quick response."

"You said, ASAP." She laughed. "What's going on?"

"Linda, there's no easy way to tell you this—"

"Go ahead."

"Someone attacked Russell in his prison cell last night. He's in critical condition and prognosis for recovery is not good."

"Oh no, what happened?"

"Carrie, Matt and I were together when we heard. Can you get off work and come here—to their house—to discuss it?"

"I'll be there as soon as I can. It'll take a while for the hospital to find a replacement."

"Okay, see you soon."

Carrie began getting the waffles going while Matt and Michael went upstairs to check on Jacob and MJ. They found them in the family cave. MJ was adjusting Jacob's grip on a golf club. "Try that, take your left arm back as I showed you. You've almost got it, Jacob."

Jacob took a swing and hit the ball well. Matt and Michael clapped while Michael said, "MJ, Jacob doesn't need my coaching. You're doing a great job."

"Thanks, Michael. But I've shown him all I know."

"Well, thanks to you, Jacob crushed that ball." Which brought smiles to both MJ and Jacob.

Jacob hit more golf balls while Michael gave him pointers and suggestions.

Carrie came up into the room. "Okay guys, breakfast is ready." As they were walking down the stairs, she asked MJ and Jacob, "Did you guys learn something this morning that will help your golf game?"

Jacob said, "I'm not sure *anything* will help me." Everyone laughed.

"Welcome to the world of amateur golf," Matt said. "We all feel that way."

MJ added, "Jacob, you're doing great. You're catching on fast." Michael, Matt, and Carrie nodded their heads in agreement.

Carrie had set up a buffet style serving. Michael was behind Jacob, and joked, "Peanut butter and real maple syrup on waffles, it doesn't get better than that." Jacob looked back at Michael, one corner of his mouth up and his eyes squinting.

"Jacob, you've never tried peanut butter and maple syrup on waffles? When I told your mother about peanut butter on waffles, she had the same reaction. It almost ended our friendship."

"I guess I better try it then," Jacob said, as he looked at Michael and smiled.

When finished, everyone helped Carrie clean off the table. Linda arrived as Jacob and Michael were placing the rinsed dishes in the dishwasher.

They heard Carrie say, "Hi Linda, I'm so glad you could get off work." As she hugged Linda she whispered. "I'm so sorry, Linda."

"Thank you, Carrie," she said, as Jacob collided into her.

"Hi mom." He hugged her. "I thought you had to work today?"

"I did, and I'll explain, but give me a few minutes, okay?"

"Sure, I have to finish the dishes," he said, as he ran off.

Linda threw her arms out in front of her, while shaking her head and blinking.

"I know," Carrie said, "It's amazing what they'll do for someone else, yet won't even consider doing the same for us."

"If nothing else, it gives us hope," Linda bent her knees and fist pumped.

Carrie laughed. "Yes. We need all we can get. I'll get Michael and Matt, and meet you in the study," she said, while pointing to a doorway off the entryway.

While taking off her coat, Linda said, "Thanks," and headed to the study.

Michael followed Matt and Carrie. Matt turned and looked at Michael. "The boys don't need me to entertain them, so I'm coming in too."

"Good," Michael said, putting his hand on Matt's shoulder as they entered the study.

Michael said, "Hi, Linda." She hugged both Matt and Michael.

"Let's sit," Carrie suggested.

Michael took a seat facing Linda. "Linda, while we were on the phone, I didn't give you specifics. We thought it would be better to do that together."

Linda made eye contact with each one, as she said, "Who told you guys about the attack on Russ?"

"Let me start, where it started," Michael said.

"Which is always best," Linda said, with a weak smile, then looked at Carrie and Matt. "But first, let me say something. I've told this to Michael, but I want you to understand too.

"I have no love for Russ. He hurt me in the worst way, betrayed me through my sister. He was a thief and hurt people, not a good man. I wish him no harm, let alone death. There is no hurting or grieving in me for him. But I'm not rejoicing, a human life is at stake.

"My only hurt and concern is for Jacob. He was born after they took Russ into custody… he never knew his father, other than meeting with him in a prison visitor's room. Still, Russ *is his* father. I don't…" Linda broke down. Carrie came alongside her, put her arm around her shoulders and leaned her head against Linda's.

Linda looked up at her. "I'm not sure how hard he'll take this," as tears began to flow, "but I want to be strong for him. My fear is he'll sense I have no compassion for his father. That might hurt our relationship."

Michael asked, "Linda, what will you say if he senses that. How will you answer him?"

Her voice trembled. "I have no idea."

Michael said, "Yes—you do—tell Jacob the truth. Tell him, while he was an infant, you divorced his father. That his father is no longer the man in your heart; he is the man in your heart. Tell him your heart is breaking for *him*; that *he's* the one who has your heart, but you're sad a person may lose their life. Tell him that's all you have; there's nothing left for his father; but you're here, loving him."

Michael paused, stood, and walked to where Linda sat. He kneeled and hugged her. "I've come to know you well Linda. That's your heart. And Jacob owns your heart. You can't excuse that or say otherwise."

Michael looked at Carrie. She was weeping. Matt had tears running down his cheeks. Linda looked up at him, weeping, trying to give a smile, but failed. She attempted humor. "Could you write that out for me?"

"Speak from your heart, Linda. Jacob is so smart and perceptive. He'll recognize the truth and *see* your heart and your love for him; he'll love you for it."

"I'll try, but I'm not as strong as you think I am."

"You're stronger than you think you are. So, we're at loggerheads."

She smiled. "I guess we are."

Michael looked at her for a few seconds and hugged her again before speaking in a voice hushed by emotion. "Okay, are you ready to move on to how we found out about Russell's injuries?"

"Yes, go ahead."

The conversation began slowly while they recovered. Carrie and Michael told the story. Michael explained how whoever blew up his apartment, stole his briefcase, which triggered the attack on Russell.

"Russell told me if Daniel found out he gave up his name, he'd be dead by morning. Daniel's smart. When he opened the briefcase and saw that I had his case files, it pointed him to Russell."

"Wow, and I think *Russ* is a bad man," Linda said. "Daniel's got him beat. Okay… I get it. And I thank you for calling me and for supporting me through this."

Michael couldn't help himself. "We knew how hard it would be for a hard-working, single… Ow," he said, as both Linda and Carrie stood and slugged a shoulder.

They laughed, as best they could, then Linda said, "Okay, I'm ready. Please send in Jacob."

Half an hour later, Linda came out holding Jacob's hand. "Jacob and I are heading home to lie low for the rest of the day." Michael, Matt, and Carrie nodded in understanding.

"Jacob, go round-up your stuff while I talk with Michael, Matt and Carrie."

"Okay, mom."

They sat in the living room. Carrie, Matt, and Michael were quiet, waiting until Linda was ready to talk.

Linda looked up, "He took it well. His first reaction was to hug me and ask if I'm okay. Michael, I borrowed your idea and spoke from my heart, substituting my words for yours. Jacob understood and appreciated what I said. At one point he cried, but I sensed it was more for me than for his father. Thank you, guys, for your support and encouragement—it means the world."

Carrie put her arm around Linda. "You mean the world to us, Linda." Matt and Michael smiled in agreement.

"Okay," Michael lowered his head slightly, and his forehead creased, "The gloves are coming off. Daniel Wygal *must* be stopped. Carrie, I see it all over your face, you're concerned I'll do something crazy. And it may *take* some form of crazy to stop him, but I will honor my promise to turn over to you, and the police, whatever I come up with. I intend to keep that promise, but I *can't* promise I'll be careful. You're all too important to me to make that promise."

Carrie didn't respond, nor did Matt or Linda.

Michael looked at each of them while maintaining his look of lethal seriousness. "Daniel will not stop. He will come from every direction and use any means to force my hand. That puts us—everyone in this house—in danger.

"Even if I give him what he wants, he will kill me to assure I can't contribute to repeating the history he wants to change. There's no playing nice with this man. I'll do whatever it takes to put Daniel Wygal back in prison."

* * *

Daniel tried to find if anyone died in the apartment blast, but no one would release information. He picked up his phone and called Curtis.

"Curtis, at your service."

"Curtis, you back in town yet?"

"Yeah, got in late last night. You woke me up."

"You'll survive. I'm going to text you the address of a coffee shop. Michael Mays hangs out there on Saturday mornings. Stake it out. If he comes in, trail him until you find an opportunity to take him out. Don't forget the book. He *will* have it."

In a voice reminiscent of Lord Voldemort, Curtis said, "That will be my most sincere pleasure."

47

After Linda and Jacob left, Michael hugged and thanked the Hindlers. "Michael," Carrie said, "I understand what you said earlier, but please be careful, and *keep* your promise."

Michael covered his eyes with his hands, then dragged them down the side of his face. "I'm sorry Carrie, but I can't be careful, there's extreme danger in this man. And he surrounds himself with danger, and he has the resources to call in more danger if needed. I won't be foolish, but there's only one way I can play this out, and it's not by playing nice. But I will keep my promise to turn over to you and the police what I find."

Carrie hugged him again. Michael smiled a half-hearted smile, nodded to Matt, picked up his backpack and left.

He looked at his watch while walking to his car.

It's only 11:30? Two-and-a-half hours?

It seemed to him more like two-and-a-half *days* since he drove into Matt and Carrie's driveway.

He needed a place to sit, strategize, and collect his thoughts. With his apartment out of the picture, he headed for The Coffee Shop.

Michael arrived, ordered coffee and a chocolate croissant. He found a table, set his backpack on the floor between him and the window. He talked tough back at the Hindler's house, but sitting in The Coffee Shop, he wondered if he was tough enough to do what he had been pondering. It would require a cold resoluteness.

But he had no choice. Michael knew Daniel would not soften or stop. He had come to the point of realizing Daniel hated him enough to be merciless. And, that he would not survive unless he was reciprocal and preemptive.

His phone vibrated and shook him out of his thoughts. "Michael here."

"Where's that dinner you promised me?"

"*Stephanie*. It's so good to hear your voice. You must be home."

"Yes, I'm home with my parents—who are doting on me like crazy—which I've accepted." She said, with a laugh.

"Let me take you to dinner *tonight*. What do you say?"

"I say, a good steak and great wine is in order."

"Perfect, I know of a place for both. Will six o'clock work?"

"Yes. How should I dress? It sounds like it's a restaurant with cloth napkins."

"It is nice, but business casual is what you see there."

"I can do that, and I have something I need to discuss with you. See you at six. I'm looking forward to it."

"Me too, Steph. See you later."

Michael sat thinking about Stephanie while finishing his croissant and coffee. He couldn't shake the foreboding feeling he had.

He removed the note pad and pen from his backpack and mapped out his strategy to take down Daniel. Parts of it were gruesome.

His challenge was balancing his plan with his law practice and related commitments. He had no choice but to keep up with pending cases.

Fortunately, I have a brilliant assistant.

Michael also had the flexibility of being a Partner in the firm.

He tore out the pages on which he had made notes, and referred to them while outlining his plan. Brainstorming what he had learned over the past four weeks, he came to believe Linda was correct. The crash must have injured Daniel, and he was recuperating somewhere. Michael added that to his notes.

Michael's first thought was to find where Daniel was recovering. But he had no solid evidence to confront him with.

A visit would have only antagonized him and escalated his efforts.

I need to work in the past. That's where my future is.

As he sat pondering and calculating what he must do, a thought came out of nowhere.

Business casual?

Even if he could get into his apartment, he realized he would find only clothing that were Weasel fragged, with a hint of acrid smoke.

He packed his things and headed to downtown Portland, not noticing the Black Escalade pulling away from the curb behind him.

An hour and a half, and several hundred dollars later, he headed back to his car. In the parking garage, as he neared his car, a voice called out in a sing-song style.

"Michael," as it echoed in the concrete parking structure.

He reached back and drew his baton from the backpack.

Again, that strange sing-song voice, "Michael... Daniel will give you another chance to do the right thing." The voice changed to one Michael recognized. "Just wondering, did granny survive my warning shot?"

"Curtis, it's awful to hear from you. I've tried to put my finger on that accent, help me out."

Curtis sang, this time in a falsetto voice. "Cape Town born and bred."

"That must be why you're so angry and hateful."

Curtis said, in his normal voice, "Because I'm from South Africa?"

"No, Curtis, because your voice is terrible. Attempting to sing without a shred of ability must be a terrible disappointment to you."

Curtis went back to sing-song voice. "That was not nice, Michael."

"Please, Curtis, if you're going to kill me, do it now. Don't continue torturing me."

Because of the echo, Michael had not pinpointed Curtis' location.

Voices rang out from the parking garage stairwell.

"Curtis, here's your big chance, an audience. Come on, give us another creepy tune."

Michael caught Curtis' movement to his right. He guessed Curtis was trying to position himself so the group coming up the stairs could not see him.

As Curtis watched the group of people approach, Michael placed his shopping bags and backpack on the concrete floor in front of a red SUV. He detached the pepper spray and put it in his front pocket and stuck the baton in the back waste-band of his pants.

On all fours, he crawled between the vehicles and the concrete wall, stopping about 30 feet down the line of vehicles, across from where he estimated Curtis stood.

He hoped the group's car was not far from him. It wasn't.

The shoppers loaded their packages into the trunk, closed the trunk lid, got in the sedan, and closed the doors. Michael used the echoing noises to mask his movement.

When the driver started the car, Michael moved closer.

As the driver pulled out and drove away, he moved closer still.

He made it to a concrete pillar ten feet behind Curtis.

He waited.

"Michael, come out, come out wherever you are."

Michael picked up a broken CD case, which lay at his feet.

He drew out his baton and readied himself.

He threw the CD case like a frisbee.

It landed near the line of cars, opposite Curtis, making the noise and echo Michael had hoped for. "Michael, come ou—"

The noise alerted Curtis. He stood still, staring toward the direction the sound came from.

Michael saw a knife in his hand.

He sprang from behind the column.

When he got within five feet, Curtis turned.

Michael flicked the baton, extending it to full length. He drew back.

Curtis charged.

Michael hit his knife hand as hard as he could.

The knife flew from his hand.

Curtis screamed.

Far more pleasant than his singsong voice.

Michael's arm came back up, hitting Curtis backhanded across the side of his head.

Curtis fell hard.

"Stay put Curtis. You won't get up from the next hit."

Curtis looked up at Michael in a dazed rage, blood flowing from the side of his head, he tried to stand. Michael pulled out the pepper spray and gave Curtis a shot to the face.

He cried out in agony and put his hands to his eyes.

Michael used his foot to hold him down.

He dialed 9-1-1. The service was sketchy, but the call taker understood him.

Within two minutes, two police cars came up the concrete lane, lights flashing. Michael had his foot on Curtis' back, and his baton arm cocked and ready. The officers in the first car opened their doors, crouched behind them, pulled their guns, and told Michael to drop his weapon. He threw it ten feet to his right side. "The pepper spray too," an officer said. Michael threw it to his left side and raised his hands.

They approached him. "Do you have any other weapons sir?" Michael pointed to the knife on the ground. "No, that's his. It flew from his hand when I hit him."

"Please step back, sir."

Michael obeyed, but said, "Contact Sergeant Romero, and give her my name. Your department has been looking for this man. He shot my grandmother. I'm the attorney whose apartment was blown up night before last. This man may have been behind that too. He was here today to kill me. Can I reach in my—I forgot—my backpack and shopping bags are five or six cars down," as he pointed to the red SUV."

The officer Michael was talking to—the officer in charge—looked at an officer who arrived in the second car and nodded in the direction Michael had pointed. He returned carrying Michael's backpack and bags. "Check in that top front compartment, you'll find my business cards. Can I reach behind me and get my wallet and hand it to you?"

"Yes. But do it slow." He looked at his partner and nodded toward Michael. While his partner took the wallet from Michael's hand, the officer in charge kept his gun trained between Michael and Curtis. His partner pulled

Michael's driver's license from the wallet and gave it to the officer in charge. The other officer handed him one of Michael's business cards.

"Please cuff this man," Michael said, "do not trust him. I don't mean to tell you how to do your job, but I know what he's capable of doing."

The officer in charge told his partner, "Cuff him."

"You're cuffing *me?*"

"Until we get this sorted out… yes."

As his partner walked behind Michael, Curtis lay on the concrete moaning and rubbing his eyes. The officer in charge looked back at the officer who had retrieved Michael's backpack and bags. He pointed to Curtis. "Cuff this guy." Curtis made a leap to the knife and threw it backhanded at Michael.

The officer who had been sent to cuff Curtis, jumped on him. His partner joined him in subduing and cuffing Curtis.

The knife missed Michael but struck the leg of the officer cuffing him. Michael turned, the handcuffs dangling from his left wrist. He grabbed the officer to help steady him.

The officer in charge spoke into his lapel mic. "We have an officer down, dispatch EMS. We have two suspects in custody." He moved into his car and spoke on his phone for a few minutes.

One of the officers helped Michael lay the wounded officer on the concrete. They elevated the wounded officer's leg on a concrete parking curb and covered him with a blanket.

After he finished his phone conversation, the officer in charge approached Michael. "I spoke with Sergeant Romero. She vouches for you, and wants you to come into her office," he said, as he removed the handcuffs. "She'll take your statement there." He returned Michael's wallet to him. "Thanks for helping care for Kyle," as he looked at the officer laying on the concrete, He handed Michael his backpack, pepper spray and baton. Michael nodded.

As he turned to get his shopping bags, Curtis lay close to his feet. Michael tensed, squeezing his fists tight. He fought to keep from kicking him in the face. He glanced at the officer who'd given him his belongings. The officer sensed what Michael was feeling and shook his head in warning. Michael turned and kicked an empty plastic water bottle instead.

He gathered his shopping bags, found his car, and headed for the Captain's office.

48

"Mr. Mays, what is going on? First someone shoots your grandmother—" The Captain realized her callousness. "How's she doing?"

"I think she's good. She's recuperating at a doctor friend's home. They're long-time friends and he's caring for her. She's on a self-imposed retreat which, as you've seen, is for her safety's sake."

"Then your apartment, blown up, now this?"

"As I told you, someone's out to hurt me. But I have no evidence linking him to any of this. The guy you just arrested, he calls himself Curtis, maybe you can get him to give up his boss."

"We'll try. Follow me, we need you to give your statement to one of our officers."

Michael shadowed her. "I'm *happy* to help get this guy out of my life."

He gave his statement, thanked Sergeant Romero, then headed for his hotel to shower and change into his new clothes.

On the way to pick up Stephanie, he called the restaurant and moved the dinner reservation to 6:30.

He made it to Stephanie's parents' door with only minutes to spare. "Michael, welcome. Come in, please."

"Thank you, Mrs. Stephens."

"Really, Michael. Please, it's Karen, we're beyond formal greetings, aren't we?"

"Yes, we are, Karen," as he hugged her. He turned as Stephanie and her father approached. Stephanie hung back, allowing her father to greet him first.

"Mark, so good to see you again."

"You too, Michael, and you're always welcome here."

"Thank you. Who's this beautiful young lady behind you, Mark?"

Stephanie rushed up to hug him. "So good to see you, Michael."

They talked for a few minutes, then Stephanie said, as she put on her coat, "Mom, Dad, we have restaurant reservations, so we need to run."

"We understand," Mark said, "have a great time and we'll see you later."

The restaurant seated them upon arrival. Michael ordered a bottle of white wine. "Stephanie, I am so glad you made it home safe."

"Me too, Michael, me too."

"Are you up to talking about the experience?"

"Yes, it's good for me; helps with the healing."

She recounted the entire story. Marked by multiple "Wows" and "Incredibles" from Michael.

After finishing their main course, they ordered a dessert to split. While each savored small dollops of Chocolate Mousse, Stephanie said, "Now, tell me what's going on with you?"

"Stephanie, my life has become a nightmare. It's as if I'm living someone *else's* life. Last night, while heading home I thought, 'what did I do with my time before this started?' It astounds me when I consider how much has happened since you left."

She tilted her head and placed her hand over his. "Tell me what's been going on, Michael?"

He went through the entire story while Stephanie annotated it with the same words he'd used.

When he finished, she said, "But you've come this far through the nightmare. You saved me... *you* saved me, Michael!"

"I appreciate that Steph. I will get this guy. My concern is collateral damage to my friends and my grandmother. You were almost killed—"

"But I wasn't, and I have you to thank."

Michael smiled and nodded.

Stephanie placed both hands on the table and leaned forward. "Let's move on, okay?"

Michael smiled. "Good idea."

She placed her elbows on the table and wrapped one hand over the other and lifted them to underneath her chin. "I have a question."

Michael sat back. "I hope I have an answer."

"Me too because it's got me baffled. How did you find me? How did you get the police to my cabin?"

"Did your parents mention the photographs they gave me?"

"Yes, but I didn't push them, I wanted to discuss it with you."

"One photo you took—the one with the butterflies near the cabin's front door—you remember taking that shot?"

She tilted her head. "Butterflies near the cabin's front door—? *Yes*, yes I remember that. It was the clue I gave you."

"Exactly. There was an address on the wall next to door, 14A.

"The style of the door and the surrounding wood suggested it was a cabin. I contacted White County Emergency Dispatch, and we figured it out. There aren't other cabins with the address 14A, in Helen, Georgia."

"But how did you know it was Helen, Georgia?"

"Your parents gave me several photos. I pieced it together. There's no other Bavarian town in Georgia, with an Oktoberfest. And, one of your photos was of a bakery with a sign that read, 'Helen's Bakery.'"

"Wow," she said.

"That's a popular punctuation tonight."

"It is." She said, as they both laughed. "Thank you, Michael," she said as she stood, leaned over and kissed his cheek.

"*That* made it worth it. Well, that and the fact that you're safe and alive."

She smiled.

"Michael, there's something else I need to tell you."

"I'm listening."

"You and I have flirted around the fringes of our relationship."

Michael raised his eyebrows. "Maybe, a little."

"I learned, or it may be better to say, I realized something during my terrifying ordeal. I wished my husband was there to protect and save me. Which tells me I haven't recovered from his loss as much as I'd thought."

"That's understandable, Stephanie. You loved him."

"I did, I mean, I do. And I realized I'm not ready to start a relationship."

"I understand—I hate it—but I understand." They both smiled. Michael's was saddest.

"Michael, there's something else. I stopped in Washington DC on the way home to meet with National Geographic representatives. After seeing samples of my work, they wanted to talk."

"I don't think I'll like this."

Tears formed in Stephanie's eyes. "No, I don't think you will. They made an offer of employment. I asked for a day to think it over. They called me today, on a *Saturday*, and I accepted their offer. I'll be on assignment in Europe, for at least three years."

"Stephanie, I am so proud of you—National Geographic—here it comes again, wow."

"Thank you, Michael."

Attempting to conceal his sadness, Michael smiled.

A chapter of my life just ended.

49

Monday, November 4th

Michael could not concentrate on the contract he was reviewing for a client. He had spent Sunday running errands and sleeping. Though recharged physically, the news he had received Saturday night from Stephanie, hurt. He no longer looked forward to his coffee and chocolate croissant Saturdays.

His cell phone rang. There was no caller ID. "Michael Mays here."

"Is this the Michael who's my favorite grandson?"

"Grandma," Michael blurted out, "Perfect timing. I needed to hear your voice. How are you?"

"I'm recovering well. Around-the-clock medical attention helps."

"Marvin is good for you, that eases my mind."

"Oh, Michael, you made it about yourself didn't you."

"I can't help myself, grandma, but I learned from the best."

"I'm glad you've finally come to that realization, Michael."

"Grandma, has Dr. Malcom asked you to marry him yet, or are you going to continue shacking up with him?"

"Michael Mays, shame on you! If I could send you to your room, you'd be in there until next Monday."

He knew better than to tell her someone blew *his room* to bits.

"Grandma, I appreciate Marvin taking care of you."

"Me too, Michael. But having said that, it's the perfect segue into something I want to tell you."

313

"Go ahead, Grandma."

"Marvin and I *are* getting married."

Michael heard her giggle. "What, seriously?"

"Yes, Michael. I've known Marvin for many years and we're not getting any younger. He's always been so kind and shown concern for me. And, he's darned cute too!"

Michael stifled a laugh.

"So, we'll get married as soon as my strength returns," she said, as her voice increased in volume. "The wedding will be at our little church, and I want *you* to give me away."

"Wow, grandma, of course I'll give you away. I've never heard of a *grandson* giving his grandmother away, but it's an honor."

"Thank you, Michael. Other than my wound, we're both healthy, but at 90, who knows for how long?

"I'm so excited, Michael, I can't wait. We'll travel by cruise ships, and we've booked a cruise to Hawaii this coming February."

She's like a kid telling a friend about their upcoming trip to Disneyland.

"Warmth for our old bones. Marvin, and my surgeon, Dr. Haskel, both believe I'll be strong enough by then. They agree I'm healing much faster than either expected."

"I'm happy for you guys. You're thrilled aren't you. I can sense it."

"I am, Michael. We'll talk more later. Marvin's making breakfast for me, so I better get off the phone. But it's so good talking with you."

"Again, grandma, thank you for calling me. I've missed talking to you too. And please, tell Marvin I thank him for making an honest woman out of you."

"Michael, does anyone even say that anymore?"

"Me, but only because you've said it—more than a few times—talk to you later. I love you, grandma."

"And I love you, Michael."

"*Grandma*, before you hang up."

"Yes, Michael."

"There's something I want to tell you."

"I'm listening."

Michael took a deep breath. "Okay, my mother, was my mother, and I loved and adored her."

"Me too, Michael."

"But I consider you to be my mother. I call you grandmother, and what I mean by that, is that you are a *Grand*-Mother. I was lost when mom died. You didn't hesitate or question. You took me in, loved me, and raised me. I don't say thank you enough. When that bullet hit you—" Michael couldn't finish, emotion stifled him.

"Michael, you're making me cry; now stop it." She gave a choked-up laugh. "You are my son, and you are Deborah's son, she'd be so proud of you."

"Thank you, grandma. There is one more thing."

"I'm still listening."

"A while back, you mentioned you thought I had issues, feelings about my father I needed to work through. You were correct. I wish I could have had a relationship with him. He abandoned me, and I don't understand why?"

Grandma's voice softened. "When we can sit and talk, I'll give you information I've never shared with you. I believe you're ready."

"I'd appreciate that, grandma."

"Goodbye, Michael. I love you, but you know that."

"Yes, and I love you too, grandma. Enjoy your breakfast. Say hi to Marvin and I'll talk to you later."

"Okay, until then."

Michael finished reviewing the author's contract and took it to Trevor to retype with the changes and send it off.

"Will do, Michael. Deputy District Attorney Hindler's assistant called. Your replacement files are ready."

"Thanks, Trevor. I'll pick them up after lunch. If she's available, I need to spend time with her discussing a different issue."

"Should I assume you'll be out for the afternoon?"

"Yes, and I'll be leaving for lunch early," he looked at his watch, "in 30 minutes. I'm meeting with my realtor to look at two houses."

"I hope you find a house."

"Me too, Trevor."

Michael called his realtor to confirm the meeting. She gave him the addresses of the two houses and told him to meet her at the first address she had given.

Michael didn't care for the first house. The second one he loved. Both were within a quarter mile radius of his apartment.

This may be a home run. A house I love, in my favorite part of Portland, on my first day of looking.

"Let's discuss this one," he said, after touring, and re-touring the house. "I did *not* expect to find a house I'd love the first time out."

The realtor said, "Sometimes that happens."

They discussed the price, which Michael thought was too high.

"Michael, I agree. But in a market as hot as Portland's, it won't last long." She suggested a strategy and he agreed. Michael met her at the real estate office and signed paperwork to put his offer in motion.

"I'll let you know as soon as the seller's agent gets back to me."

"Great, I hope it comes together, I love the house."

Michael realized he was hungry. He drove to his go-to food truck and ordered a grilled marinated-chicken burrito. After eating lunch in his car, he went shopping for more clothing. Clothes purchased and wallet much lighter, he headed to Carrie's office.

When he arrived, Carrie came out of her office to greet him with a hug. As he walked into her office, she handed him the files and motioned for him to sit. "I've included your mother and the three other women our office suspected Wygal of murdering. You need a better sense of why he was a prime suspect.

The police could only tie him to one murder, the fifth victim. I'm giving you her file too. The murderer killed four victims in the same manner, but not your mother. The killer stabbed her once in the stomach."

"He's beyond being a bad-guy, Carrie. When I interviewed Russell, he told me Daniel ran the prison. Russell claimed even guards helped Daniel, but only because they feared for the safety of their families.

"Daniel managed by intimidation. He'd place pain in the life of anyone who didn't meet his demands."

"Speaking of Russell," Carrie said, "James, the man we spoke with about the attack on Russell?"

"Yes, I remember James."

"He's the Deputy Director of the Willamette Department of Corrections. He called to let us know they searched Billy Chapman's cell and found a cell phone. When they checked the numbers listed under recent calls, guess whose number was called at 9 A.M., last Saturday morning?"

"Mine, by chance?"

"Yes, *and* they found a thin shiv they suspect Billy used to stab Russell."

"We know who put him up to it."

"That's my take on it too. Billy confessed and said a guard let him out of his cell. He claims he didn't see the guard's face."

Michael gave a slight head tilt and raised his eyebrows. "I'm sure everyone believes that."

Carrie shrugged as she smiled. "He confessed that he went to Russell's cell, pretending he had something important to tell him. Russell leaned into the cell bars to better hear Billy whispering. Billy reached through the bars, wrapped his left arm around Russell's neck and pulled him hard against the bars.

He had a message to deliver before killing him: 'Russell, your only job was to keep an eye out for the book,' as he used the point of the knife to gouge Russell's left eye.

"He told the police investigators Russell screamed and push away with everything he had, causing Billy's grip to slip.

"Russell had almost broke free, but Billy made a quick jab to his throat, then released him. Russell clutched his throat and stumbled toward the rear of his cell. Guards heard the scream and within minutes they'd opened his cell and found him on his knees, leaning against his bunk. He was in shock, but still breathing.

"Billy failed in his attempt to stab Russell's carotid artery. The investigators speculate that the slenderness of the shiv's blade, and Russell jerking away, caused him to miss his target. The doctors believe Russell will recover—he'll be blind in his left eye—but alive."

"Thanks for updating me, Carrie. Further evidence that Daniel is despicable. I'll let Linda know how Russell's doing. Once Daniel got those files, this is the best outcome Russell could have hoped for."

"I agree. I wonder if Billy will survive Daniel's disappointment."

"Don't bet on it. Any word on Curtis?"

"The police are questioning him. They found his car, and a gun hidden in the trunk. It's the same caliber of bullet that passed through your grandmother's shoulder.

"They found the bullet lodged in the wood siding of the restaurant. We should have the ballistics test results tomorrow. That will probably cause him to give up Daniel in trade for a deal."

Michael looked at Carrie. "We can't afford to wait for Curtis. None of us are safe. He's kicking into high gear. I'm shifting to overdrive."

"Remember your promise, Michael."

Michael looked at her. "I'm trying to, but it's getting tougher and tougher each day. I appreciate the files, Carrie."

"Michael, before you go, I have to ask you, how are you holding up after seeing the photographs of your mother? You may never get them out of your head."

"I'm doing okay. As I told you earlier, if I learn something that helps me resolve her murder, and bring closure for my grandmother, what choice do I have?"

That evening, after an early dinner, Michael chose the most recent picture in the series of photo files the Benedetti's gave him. The title of the file was '9-5-87.' Michael remembered that the police arrested Daniel in late November of 1987, for a murder he committed on August 8th of that year.

He set his timer for 88 minutes and opened the book to page 90. Michael's goal was to determine how long Daniel stayed at the Benedetti's party.

As soon as Michael arrived in the Benedetti's backyard, he spotted Daniel and backed toward the fence's gate. He wanted to leave before being noticed, but didn't make it.

"Michael, I haven't seen you in a long time," Bernie called out.

He hoped his disappointment didn't show. "Too long, Bernie," he said, "it's been a year."

"That is too long, Michael. Let's find Gina, she mentioned you the other day, wondered if you bought that house."

"No, wasn't the right time." He realized the irony of what he said.

As they walked, he removed his backpack, placed the book in its pocket, and put it back on.

"Gina, look who I found."

"Michael, get over here and give me a hug." She hugged him like a long-lost relative.

"Where's your friend…"

"Linda?"

"Yes, Linda. She's not with you?"

"Not today."

Bernie said, "You better hold on to that one, Michael, she's a babe."

Gina gave Bernie a small shove. "And, a very nice young woman."

Bernie placed his hand on Michael's shoulder, leaned his head near Michael's ear, and spoke out of the side of his mouth. "*And*, she's a babe."

Michael laughed. "I agree with both of you. Bernie and Gina, it's great to see you, but I must get going. I'm meeting Linda and her son Jacob, but I was in the neighborhood and had to stop and say hi."

Bernie said, "Michael, don't wait another year before you come back. You're always welcome here."

"Yes, you are," Gina added, "I'm so glad you stopped by."

"Thank you both. I'll see you next time."

Michael walked down the street to Daniel's house and crossed over to the opposite side. He took a picture of Daniel's house from that vantage point. He walked to the end of the block, sat on a low stone wall and waited.

Several times, he stood, and stretched. After an hour, and stretching for the fourth time, he bent to sit.

"*Stop following me*," someone behind him yelled.

Before he could straighten and stand, something came down hard on Michael.

It hit his backpack first, which lessened the impact to his head. Still, it was enough to make him fall forward.

In a daze, he tried to roll over, but his backpack stopped him.

He blinked trying to focus as he turned his head and saw Daniel raising a 2x4 to swing again.

Michael's impaired cat-like reflexes were too slow to dodge the second swing.

He blocked the 2x4 with one of his hands. But not enough to keep the 2x4 from making solid contact at his hairline.

Daniel stomped on Michael's side.

"Next time... you die." He hit him again with the 2x4, this time on his left hip. The same hip injured when Daniel ran into him with van over 30 years in the future.

Michael heard a man ask, "What's going on here?" Michael could hear him shuffling toward him and Daniel. "I told my wife to call 9-1-1," the man said, as he stopped. "Daniel, what are you doing?"

"This has nothing to do with you, Smith. Get back in your house."

"I won't get back in the house; stop hitting that man, he's not getting up. If he was a threat to you, he no longer is."

Daniel raised the 2x4 to hit Smith. "I said, back in your house." He stopped, shook his head, and walked off toward his own house.

Smith asked, "Are you all right? I'll have my wife call 9-1-1 back and ask for an ambulance."

Michael extended his hand toward Smith. "Please, no. Just help me stand."

"You should stay down. You may have serious injuries."

Michael began to get up. "Please help me stand." Smith looked at him and began to turn away.

"*Please* help me up."

Smith huffed, turned back, and grabbed Michael's hand. "I give up."

On his feet, Michael said, "Thank you." As he hobbled away, he stopped and checked to make sure his phone was still in his back pocket.

"You should wait for the police," Smith called out, as Michael continued hobbling away.

"Thanks again for your help, but I have to go."

Michael walked three blocks and fell onto someone's front yard. He lay there until the warm wind took him back to his hotel room.

He sat on his hotel room's bed, his head throbbed, and his ribs were sore from Daniel's stomp. His hip had stiffened to the point it was difficult to walk. The injuries from Daniel's attack added to those he received in his bout with Eric.

Michael decided it was time to go to the Legacy Emanuel ER. As he was leaving, he opened his briefcase and grabbed the replacement files Carrie had given him, thinking he may have time to review them while waiting in the ER. Removing his backpack, he squeezed them into the backpack's largest pocket. His bruised hand made it difficult to hold the backpack while pushing in the files.

He knew he shouldn't, but he drove himself to the ER, while hoping Linda wasn't working. Michael wasn't in the mood to have anyone remind him he needs to be careful.

50

Michael limped into the ER. After a few standard questions, the receptionist asked, "Why are you here this evening, Mr. Mays?"

"I live in a third-floor apartment. As I climbed the stairs this evening, my neighbor's Golden Retriever heard me coming.

"As I stepped onto the 2nd floor landing, he got excited and jumped up to say hi. I fell backwards and tumbled down the stairs."

"Did the fall cause you to lose consciousness?"

"For a moment... I'm not sure. I laid there in a daze for a few minutes, assessing myself. I stood up and decided to come in and be checked by a physician."

"Good decision, Mr. Mays. Please have a seat and fill out this questionnaire."

"Mr. Mays," the receptionist called out. Michael waved and was slow to stand and walk.

A nurse said, "Please, this way." As Michael hobbled toward her. "Hold on, Mr. Mays." She stepped around the corner and came back with a wheelchair. "This will make it less painful."

"Thanks, my body *is* getting stiff."

After more questions, x-rays, and an overall exam, the ER doctor walked in while reviewing Michael's chart. "Mr. Mays, my name is Dr. Bill Langdon."

Michael offered his hand. "Nice to meet you, Dr. Langdon. Please, call me Michael."

"Thanks, Michael. We're taking you to a room where we can keep you overnight for observation. Is that all right with you?"

"If you judge it's best for me to stay, I'd be a fool to not follow your advice."

"Good." Dr. Langdon looked at Michael's chart. "You may have a mild concussion, and you're beat up. There are no broken bones, but I'd prefer to error on the side of caution. Someone will be here soon to take you upstairs."

"Thank you, doctor."

After settling in his room, Michael called his grandmother.

"Hi, Grandma."

"Michael, are you all right, or are you calling because you miss me?"

"No, I don't miss you," he joked, "I wanted to catch you in a sound sleep and wake you."

"Sleep? At 90? I don't sleep well anymore. I *wish* waking me up was an issue. Marvin and I are playing gin rummy. He's being embarrassed by my superior skills and being beat by a little old woman. What are you doing, Michael?"

"Well… I'm lying in a hospital bed, under observation for the night."

"Oh no, what happened?"

"Fell down a stairway which knocked me unconscious. The doctor said I may have a mild concussion."

"Where are you?"

"I'm at Legacy Emanuel Hospital—"

"Hold on, Michael," he could hear her talking with Marvin.

"Michael, we'll be right there. Marvin will bring me."

"No, grandma, please, there's no reason for you to come. I just didn't want you to hear about it later and heap guilt on me." Michael chuckled.

"Michael, we're coming—that's it—"

She ended the call.

I shouldn't have called her.

Less than a half hour later, wheeled by Marvin, Michael's grandmother came rolling into his room.

"Grandma, I'm *not* happy you came, but thanks for being here for me, as you've always been."

"Did you doubt I'd come? Even if they wheeled me in on a hospital bed, I'd be here."

Michael told his bogus falling-down-the-stairs story. Then moved the focus from himself to discussing the wedding, cruises, and how they first met. When the conversation lagged, he braved a question. "Grandma, is now a good time to tell me about my father?"

She looked at Michael, then to Marvin. "Give us a few minutes please." Marvin smiled, nodded and stepped out of the room.

Before she spoke, her eyes began brimming with tears. "Michael, I've never told you how sick your mother was when she was murdered."

"I don't understand, grandma?"

"Your mother had advanced liver cancer. The doctors told her she had, maybe, four months to live. The prognosis for her quality of life was miserable. We were heart broken. That was a week before someone murdered her."

Michael closed his eyes for a few seconds. When he opened them, tears seeped out. "Why was I never told this, grandma?"

"Because there was something else. Something happened that devastated your father, but when he tried to tell me, he broke down in tears and left. That was the last time I saw him. There were rumors of his drinking and depression. When he died... do you remember his funeral?"

"No."

"There wasn't one, that I know of. A former friend of his sent word of his death. I didn't ask him how he knew.

"Michael, I couldn't bring myself to pile more miserable information on top of your mother being murdered."

"Understandable, grandma."

"I guess I'm also a *Grand* mama bear." She said, while smiling through her tears.

"Yes, that's an understatement." Michael said, while struggling to smile. "I need time to process this—before I can respond—but appreciate you telling me."

"Michael, your father didn't leave you because of something you did. He left because he couldn't face you. Your mother's death saddled him with grief and guilt."

"Again, grandma, this will take time to digest."

"I understand, and it's best Marvin and I go, so you and I can rest and recover from this conversation. A conversation we had to have.

"If I waited too long, and only caused you more grief, I apologize, Michael."

"There's no need to apologize. I can't imagine how difficult it must be for you to discuss this. I know you'd much rather remember your daughter as a cheerleader singing the pony eating macaroni, giving mashed potatoes to an alligator, song."

She laughed. "Yes, that is a wonderful memory. I prefer to focus on those types of memories, but you deserved to know more about your mother and what happened in your father's life."

"Goodnight, grandma, thank you… I love you."

"I love you too, Michael."

Marvin called out from outside the room's doorway. "I love both of you."

They laughed and said goodnight.

Tuesday, November 5th

Linda came in early, dressed in blue scrubs.

Michael was reading USA Today and drinking coffee. He heard footsteps and looked up. "*How* did you know I'm here? Um… I meant that to come out: Linda, it's so good to see you."

Linda laughed. "Good to see you too, Michael. I'm glad you're okay.

She spread her arms and swung them from side to side. "This is my domain, they can hide *nothing* from me."

"You know, I don't doubt that. No matter how you found out, I'm glad you're here. When you walked in, I was reading about a PGA golf tournament and thinking about Jacob's golf lessons. This will set them back a few weeks."

"He'll be okay. Every time he's at the Hindlers', he and MJ spend time in the Hindler family cave. He's found a sport he loves."

"That's great." Michael folded the newspaper and set it on the bedside stand. "I've never asked you this, but what does Jacob do while you're working?"

"He spends his day with the friends who put us up while our house was being repaired. They're retired and love having him. If I work a weekend shift, he'll spend the day at one of his friend's house, but now, more often than not, he's at MJ's."

"He could do way worse than spending time at the Hindlers'."

"I agree, aren't they wonderful? Carrie and I are developing a good friendship."

"Fantastic, she's a great lady."

"Okay, tell me how this happened. I read your chart and talked with the doctor; I'm not buying 'the dog pushed me down the stairwell' story."

Michael told her what happened. "What are we going to do Michael? It's obvious he will not stop."

"You're right, he won't stop. He's smart, and cold-blooded."

Linda hesitated, looked down in thought, then back at Michael. "I want to go with you next time and—if nothing else—stand guard."

He stopped and considered that. "Maybe, but I fear for your safety."

"Michael, I don't feel safe the way things are. I want to help stop this guy."

"Okay, master of your domain, in your expert opinion, how long before I can get back at it?"

"If it's a minor concussion, and the doctor releases you today, we can start this weekend, but you *will* be sore. No fights or falling down the stairs, allowed."

"Or, slugs by two angry women, AKA, you and Carrie."

"No, I asked the doctor. He said as long as they're not head shots, shoulders are okay."

"But my head sits on my shoulders. Whiplash could put me back in here."

"Okay, I'll confine them to your stomach until I receive the doctor's approval to resume shoulder slugging."

Michael leaned his head slightly and gave a lopsided half-smile. "I appreciate your concern."

"I pride myself in that regard, Michael."

They both laughed. Michael pointed at her. "On a different note, I have exciting news. I made an offer on a house yesterday, even better, it's in *our* neighborhood."

"That's wonderful, Michael. What will you do in the meantime?"

"Find a nice hotel. While signing the paperwork in her office, my realtor reminded me I can bill it to my insurance."

"No, that's ridiculous. I told you we have an extra room. And there's safety in numbers. If the danger's as big as we think, there's wisdom in keeping the three of us together. To ease your concern that my neighbors might judge me, I'll mention your *'accident'* to my neighbor next door."

Michael smiled, and Linda said, "I'll tell her you're staying with us to recuperate until the purchase of your house closes. By telling *her*, the *entire* neighborhood will know." They both laughed.

Michael looked out the window, then back at Linda. He placed his right arm across his chest, placed his left hand on the side of his face, and nodded his head. "Well, it *would* give us time to strategize and get you up to speed on my action plan."

"Let's get this guy, Michael. He belongs in prison."

Michael looked at Linda while considering her statement. "We're on then."

"I have to get back to work. If the doctor releases you, there's a spare key under a rust colored stone in the planter on the front porch. The spare bedroom is on the second floor, to the right of the stairs."

"Thanks, Linda."

"You're welcome. See you later."

* * *

BTH answered Daniel's call. "Hey, boss, do you need me to come to the nursing home?"

"No. But I need you to do some investigating."

"How can I contribute to you?"

"BTH, throw the dictionary away!"

"But, I'm liking the tutelage more every day."

"Never mind. I'm having a memory today of me beating up Michael with a 2x4 and kicking him. If the memory is correct, it must have just happened. He was hurting. I've had a few vague recollections, but this one's clear. I want you to check hospitals, beginning with those near his apartment. Work your way out until either you find him or run out of hospitals within Portland."

"What should I do when I find him."

"Call me and I'll decide. I only want you to find out if they have a Michael Mays checked in."

"Okay, boss."

51

Michael called his office. He told Trevor his fake story and that he is in the hospital. After answering a few questions, he moved to hang up. "Mr. Mays, one more thing."

"Sure, go ahead."

"A woman named Leanna Jones called and asked if you were available. I told her you weren't but promised to pass her name and number on to you."

"Yes—Leanna Jones—from Vinyl Grooves. She'd slipped my mind. Text me her number, I'll call her."

"Will do, Mr. Mays. Take care."

"I'm in the *right place* for taking care. Talk to you later."

Michael received Trevor's text and called Leanna.

"Hello."

"Hi, Leanna, Michael Mays here. My assistant told me you called. I'm glad you did."

"Hi, Mr. Mays—"

"Please, Michael."

"Okay. Michael, I was wondering if I could buy you a cup of coffee and you could give me the advice we discussed?"

"Sure, but first, is there an issue?"

"No, no. I appreciated your offer to help me understand the legal issues related to songwriting. I called to see if it's a good time to meet."

"Leanna, it couldn't be a worse time. I'm in the hospital recovering from an accident."

"I'm sorry, Mr.… Michael. Are you going to be okay?"

"Yes, I'm doing great. But I'm behind on a case."

A nut case, who's trying to kill me.

"I need to beg off until I get through that. But I will contact you as soon as I can."

"No worries, Michael. I look forward to hearing from you."

"I promise I *will* get back to you."

"Thank you, and I hope you get better soon."

"Thanks."

No sooner had he hung up than his phone rang again. It was his realtor.

"This is Michael."

"Michael, this is Mel, they accepted our offer."

"Wow, that's great. What's your sense on why they didn't counter our offer?"

"The broker told me the owner's company promoted her and transferred her to the East Coast. The company included in her contract that she must get the house appraised by a certified real estate appraiser. If the house didn't sell for the appraised amount, they'd make up the difference.

"She's moved to the East Coast and started working; she just wants to get this behind her."

"So, what's next?"

"We need to get together to sign the paperwork. Your lender will call for a home inspection, and if everything checks out, you'll be in by January 1st."

Michael told her his story and where he was. She said, "Oh, no. How are you feeling?"

"Good, and I want to get out of here. The doctor gave me hope that he may release me before noon."

"Which hospital are you in?"

"Legacy Emanuel."

"I'm nearby. If it's okay, I'll stop by. I want to get the signed agreement in ASAP."

"Great, I'll be here." He gave her his room number and ended the call. *This is moving way faster than I imagined.*

* * *

"Boss, I've found him. He's in Legacy Emanuel hospital. Do you want me to take him out?"

"No. Nose around some. Find out how long he'll be there."

"You got it, boss."

* * *

Michael grabbed his backpack from the side table. He removed the file folders on Daniel Wygal and his mother's murder investigation. He began reviewing them.

Half an hour later Dr. Langdon came in. "Mr. Mays, how are you this morning?"

"Doctor, I'm doing great, other than my hip and my hands being *sore*. But, no headache."

"That's a good sign. Are you doing work, catching up?"

"Yes, reviewing a case."

"You're an attorney?"

"If I say yes will you hold it against me, and poke and prod me with enthusiasm?"

"Well, I just went through a divorce, so my exam may reflect my feelings toward divorce attorneys."

"Whew," Michael said, as he breathed out hard, "my scope of practice is Intellectual Property Law."

Dr. Langdon smiled. "Good, you're safe. Let's try a few tests."

As the doctor went through tests to check Michael's vision, pupils, and blood pressure, Michael asked, "I didn't think emergency room doctors do patient room exams?"

"They typically don't, but I'm not an ER doc. I'm an Orthopedic surgeon, but after my divorce, I like to keep busy. I was a Paramedic before I became a physician and surgeon, so I occasionally fill a vacancy in the Emergency

Room to keep in touch with my roots."

Michael smiled, while shaking his head. "Are you punishing yourself for the divorce?"

Dr. Langdon laughed. "It would seem so, but I do enjoy emergency medicine."

"I admire you, doctor."

"Thanks, Michael. Your tests look good. You're going home today. There's no evidence of a concussion, but I still want you to take it easy for a week. If you notice any evidence of confusion, memory loss, or balance issues," he handed Michael a business card, "give my office a call. They'll get you in at once. I'll tell the nurse to process you out."

"Thank you, doctor."

* * *

BTH sat in a waiting room. Every few minutes he stood and walked to a hallway corner that served as a vantage point to watch Michael's doorway. The fourth time he peeked around the corner, a nurse was pushing a wheelchair into Michael's room. He held his position and waited.

* * *

The nurse brought a wheelchair and asked if he needed help to get dressed. "No thanks, I can do this."

He had just finished and picked up his backpack when the nurse returned. "Uncanny timing."

"I've done this a few times," as she motioned to the wheelchair.

"I bet you have." Michael looked at the wheelchair, then back to the nurse. "I don't think I need that."

She cocked her head and gave him a look as she patted the wheelchair's seat. "Okay," he said with resignation.

* * *

BTH ducked back into the waiting room and watched from behind a magazine as the nurse wheeled Michael by. He followed them to the elevator, then dashed down the stairwell to the ground floor. He ran to the hospital's front entrance. He pulled out his phone. "Boss, I'm waiting outside the hospital. Mays is being released. What do you want me to do?"

"I want to know where he's staying. So, follow him and check in with me when he gets there."

"But I've got a clear shot to the front door from where I'm concealing." Daniel slapped his forehead, but let it go.

"No. That shot's *mine* to take. Just follow him and report back."

"Okay." BTH said and kicked the tree next to him.

* * *

As they were wheeling out, the automatic door that led to the covered pick up area opened. Michael's realtor rushed in. Surprised, she said, "Michael, I caught you in time."

"Yes, perfect timing, Mel." He looked at the nurse. "Do you mind if I sign this contract? It'll only take a minute."

"Sure, no problem."

The signatures done, the realtor thanked the nurse. The nurse pushed the wheelchair through the front door. Michael stood and the realtor restated a few details, thanked him again, and said goodbye.

He was hungry.

I should have stayed for lunch…

That thought evaporated when he saw his favorite burger joint coming up on the right. As he was parking, his cell phone rang.

"Hey, Linda."

"Hi, Michael."

"I'm doing an investigative trip this evening. You *sure* you want do this?"

Michael heard her sigh hard. "That's why I'm calling you, Michael. I've been reflecting on our discussion regarding me going with you. I've realized I'm being irresponsible."

"About Jacob?"

"Yes… you knew?"

"Yes, and I trusted you'd make the right decision. Your anxiety caused you to get caught up in the moment. But I would have stopped you if you continued in the direction we discussed."

"Thank you. The risk of me disappearing and abandoning Jacob is too high. I'm the only person he has."

"I'm proud of you, Linda. But please understand, if something happened to you, I would not desert Jacob. Nor could I allow the State to place him in foster care. That is if you'd be okay with me being his guardian."

"Yes. And I'd be willing to put *that* in writing."

"And I'd sign it. I appreciate your trust."

"I have to get back to work, but I wandered over to your room and found you'd left. Your doctor, Bill Langdon, was coming out of the room across the hall and saw me looking in the room. He updated me. I've seen him before, but it was the first time I've talked to him. Nice man."

"I agree, I liked him. He's recently divorced. He gave me his card, so I'm going to give him a call to see if he's a golfer, maybe get him out on the course."

"You won't be golfing for a while, Michael."

"And, I have to get past this Daniel Wygal thing first anyway. I'll see you at your house."

"Later, Michael."

Michael pulled into the burger joint. The counter line was only three-deep. He ordered and found a booth.

Taking off his backpack, he removed the folder containing the files of the women the police suspected Daniel of killing. It was gruesome stuff. He pulled out his mother's file and read the Cold Case write-up.

His order arrived, but he'd lost his appetite. He smashed the cheeseburger and fries into a front compartment of his backpack.

I'll eat it later.

He drank his iced tea while continuing to review.

It mentioned she was terminally ill. A discussion of the stab wound was followed by a comment: "The deceased had a high level of methanol alcohol in her blood."

He checked the files of the other four women. There was no mention of methanol alcohol.

Why methanol alcohol Daniel?

52

Back at his hotel to gather his belongings and check out, Michael strategized his next trip back in time.

His plan was to pick up where he had left off—but before Daniel attacked him—and find a gap when Daniel was not home. Time enough to search his home for evidence linking him to the four women police suspected he killed.

On his previous trip, an hour had elapsed between him leaving the Benedetti's and Daniel's attack.

Michael wondered how long Daniel would have stayed at the party if he hadn't showed up?

His things gathered and loaded, he checked out.

On the way to Linda's, as he considered his next move, it struck him that as soon as he materializes, the same thing will happen, Bernie will see him and call out to him.

Michael could go back to the previous month's gathering, but if there was evidence in Daniel's house, Michael wanted to increase his chance of finding evidence from all August 8th murders. Including Daniel's fifth and final victim; the murder that sent him to prison.

Bernie's 9-5-87 photo was his only, pre-beatdown by Daniel, option. Michael needed to conceal his identity and get out of their backyard fast.

He thought of wearing a mask, or a bandana, but brushed them aside. Glancing at his aviators clipped to the sun visor, he had an idea. Before going to Linda's, he stopped by his storage unit. His kayak leaned against one of the corrugated steel walls. Inside the waterproof compartment, behind the

Kayak's seat, was his kayaking hat. A eucalyptus colored Adventure Hat©. Wide, down-sloping front and side brims, and a floppy back neck-cape, which did not interfere with his backpack. Perfect for camouflaging him.

Michael locked his storage unit and headed to Linda's.

The key was in the planter, just as Linda said.

He put his belongings in the spare bedroom.

I can sit around here… or…

Michael opened the photos app, found the 9-5-87 photo, put on his backpack, sunglasses, and his Adventure Hat©. He looked at the floor, closed his eyes, and pictured the latch on the gate that would be behind him.

* * *

"Boss. I've got the house. Mays took his bags in a few minutes ago. It's the brat's house."

"The brat's house?"

"Yeah, you know, the yard sale brat."

"Well, well. Michael hit it off with Russell's wife. This will be fun."

"I'm hungry, boss. I'll get something to go and eat it while I observe for Mays."

"Make it quick. Get back there."

* * *

The warm wind took Michael to September 5, 1987, the Benedetti's back yard. Keeping his head lowered, he backed up, found the latch and quickly exited, closing the gate behind him. He hurried down the street toward Daniel's house, occasionally looking back to see if anyone opened the gate to check on the stranger who had intruded.

Two blocks beyond Daniel's house, Michael found a spot that allowed him to view three directions.

A towering maple tree provided cover that allowed him to shift views yet stay concealed. A stone wall protected him from behind and provided a backrest.

He had opened the book to the last page, giving himself the maximum time, and set his timer at 3 hours and 45 minutes, a 15-minute buffer.

While removing his binoculars from the backpack, he found the smashed burger and fries. He removed his sunglasses and hat and stashed them in the backpack. He tried the burger, not bad—not hot—but not bad. He tried the cold fries.

No thanks.

He washed the burger down with half of the bottle of water stashed in the side pocket. Each time there was movement around the Benedetti's house, he pulled up the binoculars and checked it out. After an hour and twenty-five minutes of seeing couples and groups leaving, a lone person walked out through the backyard gate.

A cold wave ran through Michael as he pulled up the binoculars and saw Daniel.

Michael kept the binoculars trained on him as he walked to his house and entered.

Several minutes later, his garage door opened, and a VW bus backed out.

Michael moved to kneeling behind the tree. He winced in pain as he bent to the side to follow the VW bus.

He took photos until Daniel arrived at the intersection and turned left, away from Michael's vantage point.

Michael shifted to a clearer view. He continued photographing until Daniel was out of sight.

Michael stood.

Oh man, I've stiffened up.

He needed to stretch and exercise, so he walked up the street, away from Daniel's house. After six blocks, he came to a corner market.

Time and weather had blistered the white paint on the old shiplap siding, revealing the variety of color changes over the years. Two neon beer signs lit up the windows and a large 'Drink Coca-Cola' sign hung high on one end of the building. Decades of exposure to the sun faded the sign from red to pink.

The jingle of the old shopkeeper's bell being struck by the door made him smile.

He walked the three traffic-worn linoleum covered aisles. He took a second lap. Food was his goal. Nothing struck him on his first lap.

Not much to choose from.

A Snickers display box caught his attention. It offered two options. He selected the largest bar and grabbed a can of ginger ale from the soft drink cooler.

He approached the counter and heard the man in front of him talking with the store clerk.

The clerk asked, "How are you doing, Bob?"

The customer—a small man—said, "I'm doing okay, just got off the bus, headin' home."

"Man, I think of how Daniel took you in last year, that was good of him."

Michael moved his head to the left to get a better look at the small man.

Bob, the weasel.

"Ain't that the truth. Not easy being an ex-con, trying to turn yourself around. Won't many people give us a chance or give us a hand."

"Don't I know it, especially an old con like me. You're still a young man, Bob. You weren't in but only a couple of years. It's good to see someone's on your side," the clerk said, as he handed Bob the bagged six-pack and cigarettes.

Michael had closed his eyes and pictured Bob when the clerk spoke, and the clerk when Bob spoke. Bob had far more swagger in his voice, while the gentle voice of the clerk betrayed his appearance.

"Thanks brother. I'm going home, kick back, have a beer, and watch some football, unless Daniel calls me and needs help."

"Have a good one, Bob."

"You too."

Michael chuckled to himself looking at the contrast between the two ex-cons. Bob could have been a skinny school kid next to the clerk. The clerk had two teardrop tattoos under his left eye and EWMN—Evil, Wicked, Mean and Nasty—tattooed on the knuckles of his right fist. Plus, sundry tattoos on his arms and neck.

If there were sumo cage-fighters, he might have been one.

As Bob turned, Michael said, "Hey, Bob." Bob's head tilted and his eyebrows squeezed.

"Last year, the Benedetti's backyard party?"

"Oh yeah—you said you knew Daniel—but I gotta tell you, he wasn't happy that I was talking to you."

"Yeah, Bob, I don't know what he has against me. I've done him no harm. I remember you told me you did odd jobs for him. What jobs do you do?"

"Daniel's been good to me, and I don't feel comfortable talking to anyone he don't like; especially about his private life."

"Okay, Bob, just making conversation." The young weasel turned and walked away.

Michael paid for his candy bar and drink, while the clerk eyed him with suspicion.

While walking back to his vantage point, he ate his Snickers bar. Bob was only a few blocks ahead.

From his Maple tree vantage point, Michael watched BTH approach the walkway to Daniel's front door. He pulled out his binoculars and continued to follow him as he turned onto Daniel's walkway, then up to the door.

He didn't use a key. Daniel left the front door unlocked for him.

Michael sat and calculated the time between Daniel driving off and the Weasel walking through the unlocked front door. It was about 30 minutes.

He finished the candy bar and drank the ginger ale as he reviewed his overall plan. At one point he dozed, but the distinctive sound of a VW engine woke him. He looked at his phone, Daniel was gone just over an hour and a half.

Michael watched him pull into his garage.

Done here. Might as well walk and try to limber up before I'm taken home.

After 15 minutes, his phone alarm sounded, as did the pain in his hip.

So much for muscles loosening.

He found a park-styled bench on the front lawn of a small church. Taking a seat, he considered what he'd learned from this exploratory trip.

I have less than a half-hour between Daniel leaving and Bob arriving. But Daniel left the front door unlocked. That makes easy work of entering.

Michael looked up at the church reader board's weekend message: "Remember those who fight and labor for us.

Worship the One who gives us rest from our labors and fights our battles."

He sat and pondered that point until the warm wind took him back to Linda's house.

Back, sitting on the edge of his bed, he found a note: "If you're hungry, food's ready."

Sounded great. He sent a text to her, "Got your note. I'll hobble down in a few minutes." She answered by texting a thumbs up Emoji.

Earlier, while at his vantage point, he thought of Daniel's recent lack of communication. It was an unnerving silence.

So, Michael poked the bear.

'Hey Siri, call Daniel Wygal."

The phone number that nearly cost Russell his life.

"Yeah, who is this?"

"Hey, Daniel, Michael Mays here. I haven't heard from you in a while, so I thought I'd call to find out how you're doing."

Daniel's throat rumbled. "Sure, I bet you were worried sick and losing sleep over me."

"Well, you got one word right: sick. I'm sick of your threats and intimidation."

"It's just getting started, Michael. You can't imagine what I have in mind for you."

"Let me see, Daniel. Katrina's dead and Curtis is in custody. And Billy, your former cellmate, the investigators found him out. He has confessed to attempting to kill Russell; how long before he turns on you? The District Attorney's office and the Oregon Department of Corrections are associating your name with all the above.

"So, tell me again, Daniel, how will you intimidate me? And, I know who Bob Gruen is and what he's done. The noose is tightening, Daniel."

Daniel remained quiet.

Michael said, "How long will it take the joint effort of the agencies I mentioned to find out which hospital or care facility you're in."

Michael was quiet. *Let him stew.* The phone went dead. Michael could imagine Daniel panicking with a sense of urgency to get out of town.

* * *

Daniel sat up, turned and sat on the edge of his bed.

Okay, don't panic. I need to contain this situation. I've paid for my medical bills with cash, so no government care to trace back to me. The only way to find me is through my Parole & Probation Officer. But even she has no idea where I'm staying—only my phone number.

He picked up his phone and dialed.

"BTH, it's Daniel, come get me now."

"I thought you wanted me to scrutinize Mays?"

"Change of plans. I need you here, now!"

"I'll be right there, boss."

"On your way to my room, confiscate a pair of crutches."

"You got it, boss."

Daniel packed his belongings into a duffle bag.

Sum total of my life.

After an hour, BTH walked through Daniel's door. "Hey, boss, look what I found orientated against a bed down the hall. Poor old dude crumbled to the floor when I mis... appro... priated 'em."

Daniel looked at the ceiling and shook his head.

How much of this can I take?

"Always the gentleman, BTH. That's one thing I admire about you. Let's go before the old guy's able to raise a fuss."

As they got into BTH's car, Daniel looked around at the empty beer cans, candy bar wrappers, and fast food bags scattered everywhere." We need to get you a different car, BTH, this thing's a piece of crap."

Adding worse to bad, the ashtray was overflowing, and the smell of stale beer, tobacco smoke and mold flooded the interior.

Dust gripped everything except BTH's driver's seat, the steering wheel, and gear shift lever.

Daniel wiped his finger on the window, looked at his finger, then at the smudge he'd caused. "You're a pig, BTH. Forget getting a different car, it wouldn't do any good. You'd trash it within a month."

BTH laughed. "It's the way I like it. Reminds me of growing up with my mama."

"Yeah, she was a jewel, BTH. A great role-model."

"Hey—" BTH thought twice and didn't finish.

"What's next, Boss?"

"Kill Michael Mays and get the book. Nothing's changed, same thing we've been trying to do for weeks. But first, I need a walking cast."

"I can help with that, boss. I have a guy."

* * *

Finished with poking the bear, Michael took off the backpack and made his way downstairs. Linda and Jacob were still eating, and a place-setting awaited him. Linda wiped her mouth with her napkin and started to stand.

"No, Linda, please stay seated. Tell me what I need to do, and I'll get it. I don't want your house to become a bed-and-breakfast… but I do appreciate your hospitality." Jacob looked up from eating and smiled at Michael's appreciation of his mother.

Linda pointed to the stove. "Casserole and bread are in the oven. Salad and dressings are on the table."

Michael opened the oven door. "Oh, man that smells good." That brought a smile from Linda.

Back at the table he asked, "Jacob, how are you doing?"

"I'm *really* good, Michael."

"Tell me why you're *really* good."

"I've got a great mom, a new best friend—"

Michael stopped buttering his bread and turned to look at Jacob. "MJ?"

"Yep. And I'm happy *you're* staying with us."

"I appreciate that, Jacob. I'm fortunate to have you and your mother as friends."

343

Linda said, "We feel the same, Michael."

"I've told Jacob about the man who's responsible for the attempt on his father's life. I told him the man won't stop until he gets the book."

Michael frowned as he considered what she said.

"Michael, Jacob deserves to know what's going on. He needs to be diligent at being aware of his surroundings, no matter where he is, or what he's doing."

Michael took a bite of bread and considered what Linda said. "I agree with your mom, Jacob. You're smart and I trust her judgement. You need to have that awareness.

Michael removed the cap from the salad dressing and poured. "I can't stress enough how dangerous this man is," he said as he screwed the salad dressing cap onto the bottle. "I just spoke with him."

Linda said, "Where? When?"

Michael set the bottle on the table and looked up. "Right after I sent you the text. I called him and told him he's well known. The DA's office knows what he's doing, as does the Oregon Department of Corrections. I told him Billy has confessed that he attempted to kill Russell—"

Linda jumped in, eyebrows lowered, and hands spread shoulder high. "How do you know that, Michael?"

Michael's jaw went slack, his head jerked back, and he closed his eyes. "Oh, Linda… I apologize." He looked at her. "Carrie told me just before Daniel attacked me. I assumed she told you."

"No, she didn't."

"My injuries scattered my mind, but I should have told you."

"Yes, you should have," she said with a heavy sigh. "But I can understand how sidetracked your mind was. Apology accepted."

"Thank you."

"I'm not sure calling him was a good idea. Aren't you concerned that what you told him will ramp up his efforts?"

"Yes, but I believe you're correct. The crash into your house injured him and he's recuperating. He will panic and make a mistake—"

"Or do something stupid," Linda said, "something catastrophic, which will hurt more people."

"He won't risk doing something catastrophic. The grenade into my apartment is the most collateral damage he's willing to risk. He doesn't want to damage the book."

"You're right," Linda conceded.

Michael looked at Jacob. "What do you think?

"Well, Christmas is coming up, and I always look forward to watching Christmas movies with mom."

Linda and Michael looked at each other's confusion, and both said, "Okay—"

"We should 'Home Alone' him."

Michael wiped his mouth and fingers on his napkin. "What do you mean, Jacob?"

"How the Home Alone kid thought of all the ways the robbers could get in the house, then set traps for them."

Michael looked at him, then at Linda, who was smiling, then back to Jacob. "Jacob, you're on to something."

53

After dinner, Jacob and Michael helped Linda clean up and put away leftovers.

When finished, Linda suggested they move to the living room. They sat and Linda looked at Michael. "Now, what do you sense Jacob is on to?"

Michael looked at Jacob. "I loved your suggestion and how you illustrated it by using the Home Alone movie."

Jacob beamed while brushing his hair out of his eyes. "Thanks, Michael."

"But we need to approach it from a broader perspective."

"How's that?" Linda looked over to Jacob.

"I liked the movie. The difference is that Kevin, that was the kid's name right, Jacob?"

"Yes."

"The movie script limited Kevin's world to his family's house and yard."

Jacob sat up and leaned forward. "But he'd go out to buy groceries and do other stuff."

"Yes, but it was during the day. He knew the burglars only came after it was dark, right."

"Oh yeah, that's right."

"But our world is much bigger. You go to school during the week, and sometimes on the weekends spend time at other people's houses. Your mom goes to work and runs errands. I go to work and... spend time in the hospital." Linda and Jacob shook their heads in agreement and laughed.

"So, *we* must brainstorm how Daniel and his henchman—the bad guy equivalents of the Home Alone burglars—might attack us?"

Michael hesitated. Neither Linda nor Jacob responded. "He'll attack our heart."

Linda pondered that. The understanding and realization crept up on her and hit her hard. "No." She turned her face toward Jacob. Wide eyed and lips parted, she gasped and looked back to Michael. "What do we do?"

Jacob watched his mom look to Michael for an answer.

Michael leaned forward, looked at Jacob, and gave a sigh. "Jacob, he will most likely come after *you*. If he kidnapped you, it would break our hearts." Michael glanced at Linda. "If Daniel Wygal doesn't know who you and your mom are yet, sooner or later he will. It feels awkward to tell you this Jacob, but you need to know so you can be on guard."

Jacob said, "I don't want it to surprise me; I'd *rather* know what might happen." Linda leaned over and hugged him.

They brainstormed how to best protect Jacob. They divided duties:

Michael and Linda will share the responsibility of taking Jacob to and from school.

Linda will meet with the school Principal and Jacob's teachers, to discuss the danger Jacob may face.

Michael will meet with Matt, Carrie, and MJ, to alert them.

There was a lull until Michael turned to look at Linda. "Tomorrow, I'll contact the security alarm company I used. I'll have them install a system here. Is that okay, Linda?"

"Yes, ask if they can bill me."

"No, it's on me; consider it my rent payment."

"Thank you." Linda nodded her head once as she smiled.

Jacob said, "Why don't you guys get guns?"

Michael looked at Linda and detected a slight shaking of her head. "Jacob, the State requires a lengthy process to get a gun; time we don't have. And they require a class to get a concealed weapon permit."

"Oh, I didn't know that."

"But I have something else we can use. I'll be right back." He attempted to run up the stairs, but his body protested. He returned with his backpack and removed the pepper spray canister.

"I used this the other day on one of Daniel's henchmen and need to replace it. But I bought two. This one hasn't been used," Michael said, as he handed it to Jacob. "It's for you to carry."

"*All right*. Thanks." Jacob turned it in his hands, looking it over.

Michael showed him how to use it. "Tomorrow, I'll get more so we each have one, plus a spare. Simple to use, and effective."

Michael sensed Linda wondering why he'd used the pepper spray. "Linda, let's discuss that later."

"Let's discuss it now. We agreed to keep Jacob informed."

"You're right, I'm sorry, Jacob. I'm not accustomed to talking about these things—"

"In front of a 12-year-old?" Jacob finished Michael's sentence.

"Yes, but I forget that you're not just any 12-year-old."

"That's because I'm being raised by a hard-working single mom."

Linda leaned her head forward, while her forehead met the heel of her hand. "Jacob."

Michael laughed. "Linda, do you expect less?"

Linda smiled, and looked at Jacob, who was grinning. "No, he can't help himself."

Michael explained his history with Curtis and described his most recent encounter. He finished up with, "One more of Daniel's henchmen taken down."

"Linda, tomorrow, I'll research on the other front." She nodded in understanding that he planned to use the Book. "Well, I have a few things I need to review for a case I'm working on, so I'm going to my room, which," as he looked at both, "I'm very thankful for.

"Also, the Deputy Fire Marshal called my office today to let know me I can enter my apartment."

"What does that mean?" Jacob asked.

"It means I can sort through the mess, salvaging what I can, and put it into my storage unit. The rest goes to the dump."

Completely unrelated, Jacob said, "Hey," as if he was revealing the best idea he'd ever had, "we could have waffles with peanut butter and maple syrup tomorrow morning."

"I'm in. Linda, do you have the ingredients we need?"

"I have peanut butter and syrup, but the ingredients will come from a bag of premixed pancake mix. They won't be up to Carrie's standards."

"It'll still be great, so it's a go," Michael said, "I'm making waffles."

Jacob noticed his mom pressing her lips tight and give a slight head shake. "You'll love them, mom."

"I'll try a bite of yours first."

They discussed schedules, decided on a time for breakfast, then went their separate ways for the night.

Wednesday, November 6th

Fueled by the peanut butter and waffle breakfast—which Linda tolerated—Michael worked with Trevor on case preparation. He met with his two partners and told them he was taking a week off to deal with his apartment and his new house. They agreed he needed time off. They also agreed with Michael bringing in a remodel company to strip the wood paneling from his office and paint the walls while he was out.

He met with Trevor to discuss his time off and the current caseload.

"I have plenty to keep me busy, Michael."

"And I have confidence you'll do it well, but I'll be available by phone if something comes up." He mentioned his office remodel. "Trevor, I'd like you to keep track and answer the remodeler's questions while I'm gone. If it's something you're not sure about, give me a call." He gave Trevor the list of changes he had worked out with the remodel company's owner and discussed what he was having done.

"I appreciate your trust, Mr. Mays."

Okay… I give up. He can call me whatever he's comfortable calling me.

He gave Trevor Linda's address. "Call the alarm company you recommended. I want to meet and discuss an alarm system installation at this address."

"I'll get right on it."

Michael spent the rest of the day contacting a moving company, renting a larger storage unit, updating Carrie Hindler, and buying the pepper spray cannisters.

That evening after dinner, he gave Linda a pepper spray cannister. He described what he had observed when he used it on Curtis, then excused himself. "I have research to do. Do I need to take Jacob tomorrow?"

"Nope, I've got it covered."

"Great. Good night guys."

"Be careful, Michael." Linda said, causing Jacob's head to flinch while his eyes narrowed. Michael looked at him, smiled, winked, and shrugged his shoulders.

Michael changed clothes, put on a ball cap, and took two Ibuprofen. After assuring his period-correct money was in the book, he placed it in his backpack. He attached a new pepper spray cannister, then put on the backpack.

He opened the book to page 60, pulled out his phone, and found the picture he'd chosen.

Familiar warm wind, and he was standing behind the tree watching Daniel drive out of sight. He crossed the street and made his way to Daniel's house, then in through the unlocked front door. Michael smiled at the realization his body was loosening. He still hurts, but at least he's moving better.

"Who the hell are *you* and what are you doing in this house?" said a massive man as he extracted himself from a leather recliner and stood defiantly in front of Michael. He had huge ears, wore a wife-beater t-shirt, and jeans that needed to be at least a 15 inches bigger waist size if he hoped to pull them up to his waist.

Has himself convinced that he still wears the same size pants he wore in high school.

"Who are *you?*" Michael said, as he looked up at big-eared wife-beater. "Daniel didn't mention you. I'm here to wait for him and Bob."

Big-eared wife-beater said, "Don't give me that. I lived 25 years behind bars with *world-class* liars, I can smell a lie from a mile away."

Big-eared wife-beater lunged. Michael's only hope was to use the massive man's weight against him.

He spun sideways, while moving backwards to avoid big-eared wife-beaters right arm.

With one hand Michael grabbed one of the wife-beater shirt's shoulder loops.

Using the other hand, he grabbed the seat of big-eared wife-beater's pants.

He continued to turn with all his might.

Big-eared wife-beater rammed headfirst into a credenza.

The impact knocked pictures from the wall and caused the television to fall on big-ears' head and shoulders.

He was knocked out, but Michael wondered. *For how long?*

Down the bedroom hallway he discovered Daniel's door on the second try. He pulled drawers out of the chest-of-drawers, dumping each one.

Nothing.

There was nothing under the bed or mattress. Next, he opened Daniel's closet door and pulled everything from the shelving above the clothing.

Nothing.

Michael stood back and looked around, then turned back to the closet. Something visible through a small gap between two hanging shirts caught his eye. He pulled out clothing, throwing them behind him.

He stopped—frozen—overwhelmed by what he saw.

Daniel had mounted a large cork board on the rear wall of the closet.

Polaroid pictures, attached by thumbtacks, covered the cork board.

Pictures of the five victims—lots of pictures.

Taken while Daniel was stalking them, and after he had killed them.

What a sick ego this guy has.

The ones that caught Michael's eye were selfies.

Polaroid selfies.

Daniel's face was predominant in the selfie. In each selfie, the dead woman lay on the ground behind him. Michael grabbed those five photos. Plus, he chose one photo of each victim lying on the ground.

This should put him back in prison.

Each photo had a date written on the back, the most recent '8-8-87.' Less than a month ago.

The murder that put him in prison.

As he looked at his mother's collection, something struck him as odd. Someone had taken two pictures of a woman *and* a man. He grabbed them but did not have time to study them.

I'll check them when I get home.

He removed his backpack and placed the photos in the front pocket. He finished zipping the pocket, and heard what sounded like a raging, charging bull.

He spun around as big-eared wife-beater hit him full force, causing his backpack to fly from his hands.

The big-eared mammoth landed on him, crushing the wind out of him.

Big-eared wife-beater wrapped his huge hands around Michael's neck and spit out a deluge of obscenities, causing his spittle to shower Michael's face.

In his peripheral vision, he caught sight of his backpack to his right.

No way to reach it… is this where I die? 1987?

He was twisting his head while trying to pull big-ear's hands from his throat.

There was no way he could overcome the big man.

He sensed his level of consciousness fading.

Mustering his remaining strength, he made one final attempt to twist out of his hold.

It didn't work.

But while attempting, he saw the tactical baton.

The impact knocked it from the backpack's side pocket.

It was lying on the floor to his left.

He let go of big-eared wife-beater's arm.

His reach was less than an inch short of the baton.

He rocked repeatedly until he had moved enough get his middle fingertip on it, dragging it back a fraction of the inch

With all the strength he could muster, he rocked again.

Two fingertips touched the baton and dragged it back to the point he did not have to rock again.

With his fingertips, he swept the baton's handle toward him until he could grip it.

Flicking it open, he hit big-eared wife-beater on the side of his head, over, and over again.

Not powerful hits, but enough to cause serious pain.

Big-eared wife-beater yelled and put his hands up to cover the side of his head.

That caused him to get off balance enough for Michael to roll into big-eared wife-beater's off-balance side, which toppled him off Michael.

Big-eared wife-beater was in pain and dazed but managed to stand.

Michael switched the baton to his right hand.

Drawing back and using all his remaining strength, he gave three whacks to big-ears' head.

Forehand, back hand, then forehand again.

The behemoth fell hard.

Michael would never know if big-eared wife-beater gets back up.

He grabbed his backpack and hat and kept the baton at ready in case he ran into Bob, the weasel. The irony of the situation being reversed struck Michael.

As he turned to leave the bedroom, he saw on Daniel's dresser a large spring-type binder clip clamped onto a thick stack of credit card receipts. He shuffled through the receipts and found three dated 8-8-87. As he bent over to pick up one of the tossed shirts, he stopped, stood, and removed the 8-8-87 selfie from his backpack. He surveyed the pile and chose one to hold up, side-by-side with the photograph. It was the same shirt.

Daniel's hairbrush was on the dresser. Michael removed hair from the brush bristles and put the hairs in the shirt's pocket along with the credit card receipts. He stuffed the shirt into his backpack's center compartment, and the 8-8-87 selfie back into the backpack's front pocket.

At the front door, he stuck his head out and checked the sidewalks.

No one in sight.

The Benedetti's house was his next destination. There, he photographed the gate to their backyard.

As Michael continued walking, he looked back toward Daniel's house and saw Bob in the distance, carrying his bag of beer and cigarettes.

Michael sped his pace, waiting for the book to take him home. He imagined Bob's reaction to finding the damage done to Daniel's home photo gallery, and to the big-eared Goliath's fall.

54

BTH stood in the front doorway as Daniel pulled up to the curb.

Halfway up the sidewalk Daniel said, "What's the emergency?"

"Follow me."

As they entered the house, Daniel saw the smashed credenza and broken TV on the floor. He walked closer, then looked at BTH. Through gnashed teeth, he said, "Who did this?"

"You ain't seen nothin' yet boss."

BTH stood with Daniel at his bedroom door considering the scattered contents and the heap-of-a-man on his floor. He walked over and looked in his closet. BTH could see the flexing of muscles in Daniel's jaw, and his fists clenching and unclenching.

Daniel's face reddened as he ripped off and threw the remaining Polaroid photos from the corkboard. "Throw them in the fireplace. Burn them all, until they're nothing but ashes; then dump the ashes somewhere miles away."

"Okay, boss."

As he picked them up, BTH asked, "You're destroying your collection?"

"This is just part of my collection. A thief has the rest of it. But I'll get more BTH," Daniel turned toward BTH," and I'll be hanging my first photo of a dead *man*."

As BTH finished picking up the photographs and was walking away, Daniel pointed to big-eared wife-beater. "And do something with this mess,"

"I can't carry him by myself," BTH whined.

"Do what you have to do, but put visqueen down first." Daniel said, as he walked out of his bedroom.

* * *

Wednesday, November 6ᵗʰ

Michael arrived back in his bedroom. He showered and changed his clothes. He checked his phone for the time. 6:43 P.M., still time for research.

As he headed to the front door, he saw Linda sitting on the sofa with her legs curled to her side and wrapped in a blanket. She was reading a book while having a cup of tea.

"Hey, Linda."

"Michael, are you okay?"

"Yeah, but I had a run-in with someone nearly twice my size. There was a point where I wasn't sure I'd survive."

"Michael, maybe you shouldn't be doing this."

"Either I take chances and suffer *some* consequences now, or wait until the bad guys initiate *dire* consequences."

"I know but—"

"Linda, I'm willing to take these chances; there's too much at stake. I'm heading to talk with the couple who purchased Daniel's house back in 1989. If you're still up when I get back, I'll update you. If not, I'll catch up with you tomorrow."

"Okay, but please be careful."

"Thank you, Linda, I'm glad you keep reminding me. I keep forgetting."

She waved her hand toward the front door and laughed. "Get out of here."

Michael knocked on Gus's door. "Hi, Gus, remember me? Michael Mays. I stopped and talked with you a week ago."

"Yes, good to see you again. What's going on, Michael?"

"Sorry to bother you, but I have a question."

"Go ahead, but first," Gus said, as he stepped aside, "please, come in."

"Thank you."

"How can I help you, Michael?"

"Gus, this may be a stretch, but I'm wondering if you took photos of this house while you considered buying it, and if you did, do you still have them."

"That's a question above my paygrade. Honey, can you come here please?" Gus' wife came bustling out. "Yes. What's going on?"

Michael's first impression caused him to chuckle to himself.

Modern day Aunt Bea from Mayberry RFD.

"Honey, I met this young man a week ago. Someone murdered his mother when he was…"

"Twelve years old." Michael said.

"Yes, 12 years old. But her murder was never solved… Michael, why don't *you* tell her."

"Sure—"

Lois looked at her husband, then at Michael. She extended her hand. "Michael, my name is Lois. I remember now, Gus mentioned his conversation with you."

"Nice to meet you, Lois."

"Very nice to meet you too."

He told Lois his story.

"Michael, I'm so sorry."

Aunt Bea's sympathy and understanding.

"Thank you, Lois. I'm hoping you and Gus might help me."

"We'll try."

"When you bought this house, did you take pictures, and, if so, do you still have them?"

Lois looked at Gus. "Didn't Johnny take pictures when we first looked at the house? Johnny's our son—grown—but I still call him Johnny." Gus looked at Michael, smiled, and shrugged his shoulders.

Gus said, "I know he gave them to us, but who knows what happened to them?"

Lois lowered her chin, then brought her hand to the side of her face, then looked at Michael and Gus. "Maybe I do. Let me check." She turned and disappeared down a hallway.

Michael could hear an old file cabinet drawer scraping along drawer-glide rollers, long past worn out. She re-bustled back in with a thick file folder.

Looks more like a giant, over-stuffed soft-shell taco.

She walked to the dining room table and removed items one-by-one. Gus could not help himself. "Honey, try the back of the folder, where the oldest ones would be."

"Well," Lois smiled and laughed, "I could do that, couldn't I."

"Won't you look at this," she said, as she held up a plastic baggie full of photos. She handed it to Michael.

He asked, "When did you take these?"

Gus said, "I imagine it was January or February, 1989. We bought the house in early spring of that year."

"Gus and Lois, will you allow me to borrow these? I promise I'll return them."

Gus looked at Lois, who nodded yes. "If it's okay with Lois, it's okay with me."

"Thank you so much," Michael said, as he hugged them both, "I *will* get them back to you."

"That works for us, Michael. We hope they help you," Lois said, with her Aunt Bea smile.

Michael drove off thinking, I *love it when a plan comes together.*

A-Team's swaggering and cigar smoking, Hannibal Smith strutted through his mind.

Next—Coffee—could be a long night.

He sat in the parking lot of a vintage trailer turned coffee shop, coffee in hand. He studied the photos Gus and Lois gave him. After deciding on a photo of the front of the house, he sat, finishing his coffee and reviewing his plan. His phone's timer set to 58 minutes, Michael opened the book to page 60 and looked at the photo.

He was standing across the street watching Johnny taking pictures, as Gus and Lois watched.

Michael walked to the corner market where he had encountered Bob.

Wow… what a difference two years made.

Someone painted the store off-white with dark red trim.

Nice.

He smiled as he walked in.

Bell's still on the door.

He picked up a box of Zip-Lock sandwich bags and a roll of packing tape.

At the front counter paying the clerk, he looked past her and saw quart-sized Styrofoam containers. The clerk used the containers for soup-to-go from the big pot on the counter behind her. "Can I have, or buy, one of those large soup containers?"

"I'm sorry, only sell them with soup."

"I understand. How about this, I'll pay you the price for one of those containers of soup, but hold the soup?"

"Isn't that a famous movie scene?"

Michael smiled and gave a slight nod. "Something like that."

"*Okaaay,*" as she turned and grabbed a container.

"Lid too please."

As she handed him the container and lid, she asked, with a hint of mockery, "Anything else I can *give* you?"

Michael pointed. "I noticed that can of paint on the windowsill?"

"Yeah, the owner used it to mark off an area outside the front door for the plumber. The boss suspected that's where a pipe was leaking. The can's been sitting there for over a year."

"Will you sell it to me? Give it to me?"

She smiled, and said with saccharin sweetness, "Because you're such a valued customer, I'll throw it in as my way of saying thank you.

Michael held up the can as a toast to her. "Thank *you.*"

55

After paying for his supplies, Michael hurried back toward Daniel's house. He stopped along the way and sat on a mossy stone wall which bordered, and contained, a wall of arborvitae.

Michael removed the vinyl gloves, photos, and Daniel's shirt from his backpack. He pulled out his phone and photographed the fifth victim's picture, then shoved the phone back into his pocket.

After putting on gloves, he cleaned the surfaces of the photos by wiping them on his pant leg. In separate Zip-Lock bags, he dropped in the selfie Daniel took, respective to each of the first four victims. Before zipping up each baggy, he removed a few hairs from Daniel's shirt pocket, and dropped them in. When Michael picked up the photo of his mother he paused. Already at emotional overload from bagging the first three photos, he could no longer choke back the tears.

For a minute, he sat holding his mother's photo against his heart. Not only because his heart was breaking, but from the rage coming over him. An anger he had not experienced before, which steeled him to continue his mission. He placed her photo, along with Daniel's hairs, in a baggie. It was a struggle to put a piece of Daniel alongside his mother's photo. A snarling moan came from the depth of his being as he pressed and sealed the baggie and placed it with the other three.

Michael put the photo of the fifth victim in another Zip-Lock bag, along with Daniel's selfie/victim shot and the three credit card receipts. He stuffed the baggie into the shirt pocket.

After placing the first four bagged selfies into the Styrofoam container, along with a few more hairs, he put on the lid. He did not know if the packing tape's adhesive would survive 30 years, but by using the entire roll he sealed it as best he could.

He dropped the remaining photos into a Zip-Lock bag, then put it and the shirt into his backpack and headed for Daniel's former house.

Approaching the house, he walked past the for-sale sign then turned onto the walkway which led to the front door, which was ajar. He heard people talking, so he knocked and entered. The realtor was in a bedroom discussing the house with Gus, Lois, and Johnny. Michael walked toward the voices.

The bedroom where I almost died.

They turned as he approached. The realtor asked, "May I help you?"

Michael had his hands in his pockets to conceal the vinyl gloves he wore.

"Yes, I saw the for-sale sign and came in to look around."

Gus said, "It may be sold." Lois' head flinched and spun toward Gus, while her eyes squinted.

"Okay, sorry to trouble you. Good luck with your purchase. I'll find my way out."

He exited the hallway that led to the bedroom area and kept moving until he was out of the line of sight. Near the rear of the house, he found the laundry room.

All right, the scuttle hole Gus mentioned.

Michael set the sealed soup container and spray paint can on the washer and removed his backpack. He placed the tactical flashlight in a front pocket of his jeans, then stuffed the backpack into the highest shelf of a wall mounted utility cabinet and shut its door. He climbed onto the washer, stopped, and listened.

Still checking out the back rooms.

Gently removing the attic access door, he set it off to the side, then placed the Styrofoam container and spray can on top of it.

He began pulling himself up.

One foot kicked a cabinet door—he hung midway, listening—they stopped talking for a few seconds, then continued.

Once up, he replaced the door.

He shoved the paint can in his waist band at the hollow of his back, then picked his way across the ceiling joists. With the flashlight clenched between his teeth, he headed for the exterior wall farthest from the scuttle access door.

He fought to maintain balance as he shuffled from joist to joist. Each step searched for an insulation covered joist.

Paint can in my rear waist band, stooping, while holding the soup container in one hand, the other grabbing rafters for balance—from behind—I must look like a crab taking dinner back to its lair.

At his destination, he scooped handfuls of insulation from an area two-foot in diameter, leaving a 2-inch layer on top of the lath and plaster ceiling. After checking the soup container to assure it was still well-sealed, he laid it on top of the layer of insulation. He scooped insulation back around and over the container, leveling it to match the surrounding insulation. Carefully stepping on joists, he considered the insulation from three sides. He was convinced it would go unnoticed.

He pulled out the spray can, and while doing his best to muffle the rattle, he shook it up. With the can upside down and angled toward the exterior wall, he sprayed a vertical line on the plywood above where he had buried the container. He imagined in thirty years it would look like just another construction marking.

Satisfied with his work, he made his way back to the attic access door. On the way, he stopped six joists back to bury the can of paint under insulation. He first rubbed the spray can against his sleeve to wipe it clean of fingerprints left from when the clerk gave it to him.

Back at the scuttle hole, he did not hear voices. Michael removed the scuttle hole door and listened for 10-15 seconds. Still no voices. He lowered himself to the washing machine, replaced the scuttle door, recovered his backpack, sat, and slid off the washer.

As he left the house, Michael re-locked the front door from the inside.

While removing his gloves and shoving them in his pocket, he walked away as if he were out for a leisurely stroll. Until the warm wind hit him.

Back in the coffee-trailer's parking lot, he didn't waste time getting back to Linda's.

As he walked in the front door, Linda was still in the same position reading.

Don't women's legs cramp from sitting like that?

"Hey, Michael. You remembered my advice."

"Yes, back safe and whole."

Michael explained what he accomplished.

"Wow, great idea, but do you think they're still okay after all these years?"

"Before I answer that, do you realize what you asked?"

Linda tilted her head, pondering that, then her eyes flew open wide. "Again... wow. You were there—just minutes ago—and now we're sitting here discussing it in a historical context."

Michael said, "It's still hard for me to accept it as reality." He looked down. "But, then there's insulation on my pants legs, which I thought I'd brushed off."

"I was going to say—" she said with a laugh.

"Back to your question. The photos should hold up. They're inside zip lock baggies and sealed in a Styrofoam container, surround by insulation, which *should* maintain a stable temperature. I don't know how the hair samples will hold up for DNA evidence, but the selfie photos tell story."

"I agree. You've been busy, Michael, what's next?"

"You sure you want to know? It's gruesome."

"I'm a nurse in a Level I trauma center. My world can be gruesome."

"I can only imagine." He explained his next move, and how he saw it playing out.

"You're right, that is gruesome... horror movie gruesome."

"It's also dangerous. I should describe where the police will find the evidence. Is there pen and paper nearby?"

Linda pulled out a drawer in the end table next to her and removed a writing tablet and pen. "I don't like what you're suggesting, Michael."

"Linda, I think I'll be okay."

She looked at him as she handed him the pen and tablet. "You *think* you'll be okay."

He ignored her and began to write. "When I'm done, hide this somewhere, in case."

"In case of what Michael?"

He looked at her. "Okay, I get it. Though I'm not inclined to acknowledge the possibility."

"Understandable," she said.

"I'll sketch a map too, can't hurt," he said as he drew.

"There, that should do it," as he handed the pen and tablet back to Linda.

She read it and said, "Makes sense." She folded the note and set it on the end table. "Before I go to bed, I'll hide this."

"Bed is still years away for me."

"Doesn't that sound crazy?" Linda said. "I mean... I've lived the last twelve years assuming Russ was crazy."

"To the uninitiated, no doubt it sounds insane. Linda, before I get back at it, something has been eating at me since our first conversation."

"What's that?"

"When you told the story of Russell, his trial, and your father, I asked about your mother."

"I remember that, yes."

"Could her illness have resulted from her discovering the book? Might she have used it to travel back in time to foreign countries, which resulted in her contracting malaria?"

Michael saw a look of surprise and realization come over Linda. She sat in silence, staring off into the past. "Michael, that must be it. Since I didn't buy Russ's story, I never considered it.

"The Center for Disease Control didn't believe she hadn't traveled." Tears ran down her cheeks. "That must be what happened. I know this may sound odd but thank you. I've lived with this mystery for years. Her death still breaks my heart, but you've given me resolution. Even, closure."

"That's how I hoped you'd receive it. It seemed so clear, but I looked at it through a different lens."

Michael said good night. Linda stood. "Wait," as she walked over and hugged him, "Thank you again for being my friend, Michael. And being here for Jacob and me."

She let go. His eyes watering, he smiled. "Okay, I must have insulation in my eyes. I better get back to work. Goodnight Linda."

"Goodnight Michael and be careful."

"Again, I'm glad you keep reminding me. Goodnight."

56

Showered and fresh clothing, Michael appeared ready to face this phase of his plan. But his facade did not reflect his emotions.

His hands trembled as he opened his bedroom door and headed to Linda's basement.

Yard sale boxes lined one wall. In the corner opposite the boxes, there was a partial roll of black visqueen vapor barrier sheeting leaning against the wall. He picked it up and brushed off the dust and cobwebs.

There was a small workbench sitting against an outside foundation wall.

At one end of the workbench there was a mayonnaise jar lid containing a few old cigarette butts. Above the jar was a small window in the concrete foundation.

Ashtray and ventilation.

Linda had avoided emptying it for over 12 years.

A pair of scissors hung from a pegboard panel above the workbench.

Using them, he cut out a three-foot square section of visqueen. There was also a partial roll of duct tape on the pegboard. He set it, along with a Q-tip he had brought from his bathroom, on top of the visqueen. He left them on the workbench.

On his way back upstairs, he returned the visqueen roll to where he had found it.

Back in his bedroom, he picked up the backpack and put it on. Next, he pulled up the 8-8-87 photo on the phone's screen.

He opened the book to page 10 and looked at his phone's screen. Warm, omnidirectional wind took him back over three decades to the evening of Daniel's fifth victim.

Michael stood about five feet behind a large Douglas Fir tree. Dusk was giving way to dark. He saw Daniel's silhouette as he photographed the murder victim.

The Polaroid's flash lit up the area, momentarily illuminating a woman lying on the ground with Daniel standing over her.

While moving closer to the tree, Michael stepped on a dry fir cone.

Daniel called out, "Who's there?"

As he walked toward the tree where Michael was hiding, his feet ruffled the grass and fir needles.

After a few seconds, the ruffling stopped.

Michael stood frozen with his breathing stilled, but his eyes moved side to side.

The ruffling of grass and fir needles restarted, but the sound steadily diminished.

After a few seconds, another flash.

The selfie.

Daniel's footsteps quickened. They turned from ruffling the grass to crunching on gravel.

He's running away.

After 20 seconds, a door slammed, and a VW engine started. Daniel drove away.

Michael waited.

He told himself it was to assure Daniel had left.

But it was more about mustering up courage.

Michael pried himself from behind the fir tree barrier.

Each step felt as if grass was wrapping tentacles around his feet, trying to stop his mission, but he plodded on.

At the body, Michael stood staring as twilight surrendered. Tears welled in his eyes.

She may have a family who will wake up tomorrow morning missing their daughter, sister, wife, or mother.

That thought steeled him and gave him resolve.

From the backpack, he removed Daniel's shirt. He kneeled and wiped the woman's blood with the front of the shirt. He pulled a few hairs from her scalp and placed them in the shirt's pocket. As he rolled up the shirt, something compelled him to pray for her family. Tears flowed as he prayed.

While saying, "Amen," the warm wind took him away.

Michael was a wreck as he stood at the foot of his bed, rolled-up shirt in hand. But he could not quit now.

In the basement, at the work bench, Michael unrolled the shirt and saw the blood. He became nauseous but choked back the emotion. With the Q-tip, he smeared blood on one of the sales receipts in the shirt pocket. Behind the receipts, were the Polaroids of the murder victim. He smeared a drop of blood on the selfie photo Daniel had taken with her.

Also, in the pocket was a picture of Daniel's VW bus, taken as he drove away from his house. The license plate number was clear and readable. Hair from both Daniel and the woman were in the pocket.

He began to wrap the shirt but stopped.

I can't seal this up while the blood's still wet, it's supposed to be a month after the murder.

On the right edge of the pegboard, hung an old hair dryer. He remembered his grandfather using one on electrical heat-shrink tubing. Michael feared degrading the DNA, so he set the hair dryer to warm. After plugging it in, he turned it on while holding it approximately a foot away from the shirt. He swiveled his wrist to move the hair dryer back and forth. That, and the distance, caused the air to cool. After five minutes the blood was dry enough. He feared pushing it any farther.

He wrapped the folded the shirt in the visqueen and sealed the edges with duct tape. With the hair dryer still on the warm setting, he used it to set the duct tape's adhesive. He smoothed the duct tape with his fingers as he checked it for seal. Satisfied, he headed to his room.

Back upstairs, he opened the Photos app on his phone and found the photo he had taken of the Benedetti's gate after he had left Daniel's house, and the big-eared wife-beater on the floor of Daniel's bedroom.

As he began to open the book, there was a quiet knock on the door. Michael said, "Come in."

Linda opened the door. "Are you okay, Michael? I heard sounds coming from the basement."

"I'm okay. Have a seat."

They sat on the bed. Michael told her what he had done. At one point the emotion hit him hard again. He had to stop.

"Michael, I can't imagine. I'm a nurse and I could not have made it through that."

"Hardest thing I've ever done, Linda."

He told her of how his realization that the next day her family would begin missing her—for the rest of their lives—had strengthened him.

"But, why do this? The authorities convicted and sent Daniel to prison for this murder."

"But *would he have been caught,* if I don't get this evidence to them?"

"What do you mean?"

"What if, after discovering someone found the pictures in his closet, Daniel destroyed the rest of the photos as a pre-emptive measure? And," he held up the visqueen wrapped bundle, "what if these photos were the evidence the police used to convict him? If I *hadn't* discovered the photos and not sent this package to the police, how many *more* women would he have killed before he was found out?"

"That's why you're an attorney. My mind doesn't work that way."

"That's not a bad thing. Sometimes it makes me—and those around me—crazy."

"Well, I'm glad it works that way. Michael, something puzzles me?"

"Okay, maybe I can *un-puzzle* you?"

Linda gave a half-smile. "Rather than go to the trouble of hiding evidence in the attic of Wygal's former house, why didn't you put the evidence for the five victims in this one package?"

"That's a good question, Linda, and one I wrestled with. Here are my thoughts: There's no statute of limitations on murder. I'll play 'what-if' again.

"What-if we can't tie any of Daniel's current crimes to him? If I had put the evidence for all five victims in this one bundle, it's possible they would have paroled him after 30 years. I can't imagine that happening, but what-if?

"By presenting the evidence in this manner, it removes the what-if."

"But isn't that selfish on our part? The families have suffered unresolved grief for over thirty years."

"As a member of that group of families, I'm acting as the spokesperson for them. I'd rather assure my mother's killer spends the rest of his life in prison, than take the chance he's released to continue his havoc. I'm sure my grandmother and the other families would agree."

"Okay, I get your point; it still troubles me, but I get it. So, what's next?"

"I hate to rush off, but I have to get back to September 5th, 1987."

"Alright," she said, while shaking her head, "still sounds crazy."

"As it does to me too. I'll see you in the morning. Maybe over waffles?"

Linda smiled. "Maybe over waffles. Goodnight, Michael."

Michael remembered that he needs Jimmy Feller's business card. It was in his briefcase. He rushed down the stairs and grabbed a tape dispenser. Back in his bedroom, he placed the business card on the package and taped it to the visqueen.

He opened photos and found the gate photo. He opened the book to page 15 and looked at the photo.

While opening the Benedetti's gate, Bob came to mind. He was walking into Daniel's house to find the mess Michael had made.

To make sure nothing changed, Michael looked around carefully as he stepped through the gate. No change, Daniel had left.

Bernie and Michael spotted each other. Bernie called out, "Michael, did you forget something?"

"No, Bernie, but could I have a word with you inside the house, in private?"

"Sure, Michael." Bernie said, as he placed his hand on Michael's shoulder and walked him to the sliding glass door.

In the Benedetti's living room, Bernie said, "Have a seat, Michael. What's going on?"

"Bernie, I need a favor."

"I'd be happy to help."

"Great. Bernie, I told you I'm an attorney—"

"Yeah, I remember that."

Michael held up the visqueen wrapped package. "In this package, I have evidence in a criminal case I need to get to the police officer whose name is on this business card," as he pointed to Jimmy's business card. "This isn't breaking the law—I promise you that, Bernie—but I cannot have my name associated with what the package contains. It might hurt the case and the bad guy would get away with a horrible crime."

"Michael, I'm honored you trust me. If there's danger with your name being associated with the case, I have a concern."

"What's that, Bernie?"

"Fingerprints. This is plastic and you're carrying it without gloves. We need to wipe-down the outside."

"Bernie, you are a smart man. Do you have experience with cleaning up evidence? You know… with a name like, *Bernie Benedetti?*"

"You *never* know, Michael," Bernie said, with a smile and a wink. "But *I will* get this to the police."

Michael could not tell him the 1987 Michael Mays is only 13 years old, with no fingerprints on file to trace back to him.

Bernie went into the kitchen and used Windex and a towel to wipe the package. Michael leaned against a kitchen counter. "Bernie, that business card is from a few years back, Lieutenant Feller may be a Captain, or higher, now."

Bernie turned his head toward Michael. "Whatever Mr. Feller's rank is, I'll get it to him."

Michael glanced at his phone. He had a minute left.

"Bernie, please tell Gina hi for me, and that I *will* stop by again soon, but I have to go."

"Sorry you have to run, Michael. She'll be disappointed she missed you."

"Please apologize to her for me, Bernie."

"Okay, Michael," he said as he shook Michael's hand, "don't be so long next time."

"I promise I won't be," Michael said, as he was heading to the front door. Closing it, the warm wind swept him away.

57

Michael materialized back in Linda's spare bedroom and heard, "Well, look at that, BTH. It's Michael Mays in the flesh."

"Yeah, boss, just like you said—makes me feel better—you're not crazy."

Michael saw Linda and Jacob, still in their pajamas, with guns to their heads. Daniel holding Linda, and BTH holding Jacob.

Michael stood there, glaring at Daniel. "What's the matter, Michael, no cocky comebacks, or cutesy threats?" Michael did not say a word. "Now, Michael, you know what I want, and when do we want it BTH?"

With a bitter laugh, BTH said, "Promptly boss, we want it promptly."

Daniel looked at BTH. As if he was thinking, I'm just going to shoot him too.

He looked back at Michael. "You bet your life we want it *now*, no wait, Michael's betting the lives of mom and the brat. Still nothing to say, Michael?"

"Daniel, what guarantee do I have you won't kill us, whether you get the book or not?"

"There are few guarantees in life, Michael, but I'm sure I'll find the book in that backpack, whether you're alive or dead."

"Let me ask you this, Daniel."

"Make it quick."

"Are you sure you can use the book once you have it in hand?"

Daniel's demeanor changed to that of a daydreaming fourth-grade kid whose teacher interrupted him with a question.

"Don't give me that. Anyone can use it," he said, but his confidence was slipping.

"So, Russell didn't tell you that not just anyone can pick it up and use it?"

"He didn't because you're bluffing," Daniel waved the gun, then put it back to Linda's head, "stalling for time."

"Stalling for what time, Daniel? There's no hero coming through the door to rescue us. What's my motivation for bluffing?"

Daniel stared at Michael for a few seconds.

"Okay," he said, glancing at the ceiling. "Let's say you're telling the truth, what's the special trick?"

Michael laughed. "Seriously, you think I'll *give* you the solution?"

"You *better* give me the solution or he," he nodded toward toward BTH, "spreads the kid's brains all over this room." BTH cocked the gun's hammer.

Michael looked at Jacob and noticed his hand was by his pajama pants pocket and his index finger was wiggling.

Michael looked closer. Jacob was sliding something held by his thumb and middle finger. He slid it half out of his pocket, then back down.

Pepper spray canister, he takes the pepper spray to bed with him. You gotta love 12-year old's.

Michael said, "Hold on, Jacob. Be brave."

Daniel's head swung toward Jacob, then back to Michael. "What are you doing, I'm talking."

Michael's face reddened and he glared at Daniel. "Look, he's 12-years old and frightened. I was trying to reassure him and calm him. Let's make a deal. I have two questions for you. You answer them, and I'll tell you what I know.

"I'm not in the habit of making deals,' Daniel said patronizingly, "but because we're close friends, I'll make an exception." Switching back to threatening he blurted, "What are your questions, Michael?"

"First, since discovering the photos hidden in your closet, I've wondered. You killed all five women on August 8th—different years—but why August 8th?"

Daniel slumped. "Since you'll take it with you to the grave, I guess I can tell you. I was a Senior in high school and worked at one of our family's grocery stores. My dad was a great businessman and owned several different businesses. I came home early one day. I wasn't feeling good.

"Thinking no one was home, but hearing noises coming from my parents' bedroom, I opened the door. My mother was in bed with another man. She screamed at me to get out and threatened me to not tell anyone.

"I had to tell my father. I loved and admired him; he was a great man. But she destroyed him. He was never the same after that.

"He divorced her but couldn't recover. By-the-way, I testified against my mother at the divorce hearing.

"When I was 25, I came home from work and found him in our garage... with a knife through his heart. There was a suicide note apologizing to me and explaining his choice to put his broken heart out of its misery. It was August 8th."

"And that's why you use a knife."

Daniel gave a twisted smile. "Appropriate isn't it. And I used the same knife my dad used. You can't trust women. If I found myself attracted to one, I channeled that attraction into stalking her until August 8th. Then I destroyed *her* heart.

What's your second question?"

"I want you to think back to when you were stalking my mother—"

Daniel cut Michael off, "That's a pleasant memory, Michael."

"Enough, Daniel. Do you want me to tell you or not?"

"I'm sorry, Michael, I didn't realize how *sensitive* you are. Go ahead."

"You were stalking my mother in Woodstock Park during one of my Little League games. It was the first time you noticed me. I sat on the grass to watch my mother. Someone appeared, or a better descriptor, materialized behind you and fired two shots at me."

"That wasn't one of my people, Michael."

"I believe you, Daniel. But there must have been a connection. You gave him the picture you took that day, didn't you."

"That was a long time ago."

"Not that long ago to me. Why did you give him the picture?"

"As I recall, he came to my house the next day and told me he knew I collected and kept pictures of women I'd stalked. He asked me if I had a picture of you. I told him I had one, but I wouldn't give it to him, and that he needed to leave.

"My refusal didn't make him mad or fluster him. As I began closing the door, he grabbed me, with the speed and strength of a professional, probably military.

"He threatened to call the police and hold me until they arrived. I couldn't break free; there was nothing I could do. I had no choice but to give him the picture. He took it and left."

"He didn't tell you why he wanted the picture?"

"No. I never saw him again. Now, I told you the truth. I gave, now you give me the book and tell me what you know that I don't."

Michael looked at Jacob and nodded his head.

Daniel looked down at Jacob, who was whimpering. Michael looked at Linda and shut his eyes tight and opened them. He nodded at her, clenching his eyes tight again. She got the message and closed her eyes tight.

Michael looked at Jacob. "Now."

Jacob pulled the pepper spray from his pocket with his finger on the actuating button.

He lifted his arm, turned it toward Daniel, and pushed the button.

It was a bullseye face shot.

Jacob raised his hand above his head and sprayed in an arc, saturating BTH's face.

Both men howled in pain.

Linda broke free, wrenched Daniel's gun from his hand, and shoved him back.

His walking-cast caught on the leg of a decorative chair.

Falling, he first hit the bedroom wall, then crashed to the floor.

Jacob twisted free and moved behind Michael.

Michael grabbed BTH's gun.

As Michael shoved him, BTH squeezed the trigger. In the confined space of the bedroom, the shot was deafening.

Michael wrestled the gun free from BTH's hand and slammed him into the wall.

He and Daniel lay on the floor cursing and yelling in agony.

The pepper spray in the confined space was affecting them. "Linda, open the window, let's get fresh air in here."

She sprang toward the window. "Got it."

Michael opened the bedroom door.

As he turned back, he saw Jacob walk over and give Daniel and Bob one more shot each to the face.

He cannot help himself.

Jacob looked at him and smiled. Michael chuckled out loud.

Michael dialed 9-1-1, then handed the phone to Linda. "It's 9-1-1. I need to tie up these two."

"Okay. Michael, there's blood coming from your right shoulder."

He looked at the blood. "I know where I can find a good trauma nurse. But first, I have to get these two tied up first."

Linda looked at the blood, and started to say something, but the 9-1-1 call taker coming online interrupted her.

Michael took out two neckties from his closet and used them to tie Daniel and BTH's wrists behind their back. Both lay whimpering, with an occasional curse and hollow threat.

Michael remembered his promise. "Daniel, I promised I'd tell you something you didn't know, so here it is, you're going *back* to prison... for the rest of your life."

Daniel could only grunt vague threats. Bob only whimpered.

After the paramedics and the police left—with Daniel and Bob in handcuffs—Linda, Jacob and Michael sat in the living room.

For a few minutes, they sat quiet.

Jacob was the first to speak. "That was *awesome!*"

"Jacob, *you* were awesome. The pepper spray—I mean come on—brilliant."

"Thanks, Michael."

Linda said, "Jacob, I am so proud of you." Jacob sat there beaming.

Linda stood. "Stand up, guys." She gathered them together for a hug.

Michael said, "Watch the gunshot wound."

Linda lowered her head and looked at him with a smirk. "The Firefighter Paramedics, *official agents of the government*, called it a 'graze.'"

"And what caused the graze…?"

They broke from the hug and she again gave him the look, that turned to a smile. "It's over."

"Not quite," Michael said.

Linda tipped her head to the side. "What do you mean?"

"I have one more thing I *must* do."

"Tonight?"

"No. First, you, Jacob and I need a good night's rest."

Jacob smiled, raised his arms to shoulder height, then clinched his fists. "Waffles in the morning?"

Michael and Linda looked at each other.

Linda looked at Jacob. "It's waffles in the morning."

58

Thursday, November 7th

Jacob and Michael finished setting the table for breakfast. Michael called out, "Linda, what else can we do for you?"

"I've got it. You guys hang out and catch up."

Michael took a seat across from Jacob. "How's school? Anything new and exciting?"

"More exciting than last night?"

"No, that's hard to beat."

"Yeah, it was awesome."

"I agree. But looking back, I was most impressed with how you handled yourself. The whimpering was priceless; award worthy."

Jacob grinned. "Thanks, Michael."

"So, anything else going on?"

"Well, school's okay, but kind of boring."

"It gets better. Once you get to the level where you get to choose the subjects and courses that interest *you*, you'll enjoy it much more. How are you and MJ doing?"

"*Great*, he's become my best friend."

"I'm glad, MJ's a good kid."

Jacob nodded his head. "And, mom and I are going to *church* with the Hindlers."

"Your mom hasn't mentioned that. Do you listen to the Pastor or sit there daydreaming like I used to, a lot?"

"No, I've been listening to him, but it's new and causes me to think."

"That's a good thing, but I sense it's confusing you."

"A little, yeah."

"Jacob, my grandmother raised me. As a kid, church was a big part of her life, so it became part of mine. But I retreated from it as I got older. Lately, I've sensed there's a hand knocking on my head, maybe my heart, saying, 'Hello, I'm still here, can I come in.'" They both chuckled.

Jacob looked at his plate, then at Michael. "I might be sensing that too."

Michael leaned forward. "What do you think of this, I'll talk to your mom, if it's okay with her, and if *you're* interested, I have a journal; I'll buy you one. We can record our thoughts and discuss what we're sensing. If we hear something we question or don't understand, we'll note it in our journal and discuss it."

"That sounds good."

"We're on. Maybe we bring Matt and MJ into the conversation. In Law School, Matt never wavered in his faith."

"Knucks," Jacob said, as he held his clenched fist out.

Michael fist bumped Jacob's. "Knucks it is."

Linda walked in with a platter of waffles and a side plate of bacon. "What are you guy's knucking about — is that a word — *knucking?*"

"It is now," Michael said, as they laughed.

"Michael, what's on your agenda today?" Linda asked, as they served themselves.

"My priority is marking salvageable items in my apartment before the moving company arrives."

"Need any help?"

"No, it's a slow job. I need to decide what to keep. There *is* something you could do if you have time."

"What's that?"

"Take Carrie Hindler the note and drawing I made last night."

"I'd be happy to do that, Michael. I'll call her to find out if she's available for lunch."

"Great idea. How long before Jacob has to leave?" Michael asked.

Linda looked at her watch, "Half an hour, why?"

"If Jacob's willing," Michael said, as he looked at Jacob, then back at Linda, "I'll ask him to re-write my note and re-draw the drawing. Carrie might recognize my handwriting. What do you think?"

"It's a good idea, if Jacob's willing."

Jacob spread his arms, with palms up. "I'm right *here*… you guys can ask *me*."

Michael and Linda laughed. Michael said, "Jacob, are you willing to do that?"

"Sure, where's the note?"

"You finish your breakfast," Linda said, "and I'll round up the note, some paper and a pen."

Linda was off to find pen and paper.

Jacob said, "Michael, I've been wondering about something, but afraid to ask."

"You can ask me whatever you want, Jacob."

"Last night, while mom and I were being held by the bad guys, out of nowhere you appeared. Right before our eyes. It was like a Star Trek movie."

"Here you go," Linda said, "sorry to interrupt," as she handed Jacob the note, the pencil, and the paper.

Michael presented Jacob's question to Linda.

Linda sat, resumed eating, and listened.

"Jacob," Michael said, "that involves a story much longer than the time we have before you leave for school. But I promise I will tell it to you." Michael looked up from his plate to Linda. "That is, if it's okay with your mother."

"Jacob, *together*, Michael and I will explain. How does that sound?"

"Sounds good. Tonight?

Linda laughed. "Let's wait till this weekend."

Jacob gave her a thumb's up and finished eating.

"We need to get going, Jacob. Grab your stuff," Linda said.

Without looking up, he reached beside his chair and lifted his backpack from the floor. "Got it right here. Hold on, I'm just about done with the note."

"While you finish, I'll grab my purse and jacket."

"Okay, I'm done with the note and the drawing." Jacob said, as his mother returned. He handed it to her. She looked at it and put it in her purse. "Looks great, Jacob, thanks. Let's go. See you later, Michael."

Michael walked to his apartment. Standing in the apartment's hallway, he made a slow survey of the damage, then did the same for the rest of the apartment. After marking the salvageable items by priority, he went into his office.

Can't avoid this any longer.

He picked up his backpack, he brushed dust and debris from one of the two, now perforated, overstuffed chairs. As he sat, the front door opened, and Linda called out, "Hello... Michael are you here?"

"Hey, Linda, I'm back here, in my office."

She walked in and gave Michael a hug. "It's been so long." They both laughed.

"I'm sorry to interrupt you, but can we talk for a few minutes?"

"Here." He offered her the overstuffed chair. "It looks ragged, but it's still comfortable."

"Thank you, Michael. This morning when I asked if you needed help, it wasn't about helping."

Michael chuckled. "Whatever I did wrong, I apologize."

Linda smiled. "You did nothing wrong, you've done everything right."

Michael saw that Linda was serious-minded, so held his tongue.

She looked down at her hands in her lap, while pausing, then raised her head. "Michael, where are we in our relationship?"

"Wow, I wish I would've asked that first."

Linda raised her right eyebrow and smiled. "But you didn't."

"Let's start with friendship. Linda, you've become one of my—no— you've become my best friend. Now you. Where are we on *your* friendship spectrum?"

"I agree. I've never had a better friend than you, Michael. What are your expectations from our relationship?"

"You mean romantically?"

"Yes… I guess that's what I mean."

"I have no expectations. I don't think we're there yet. Can we get there? I don't know, but I'm willing to jump in and take this ride with you."

"Michael, I'm so happy to hear you say that, because that's how I feel. And I'll get in the car and ride with you. We can navigate this together."

"I get to drive."

"Typical man."

Linda gave Michael a long hug. "Thank you, Michael, I'll see you tonight." Michael walked her to the door and hugged her again.

Back in the overstuffed chair, Michael removed the Zip-Lock bag of photos from the backpack. He found the one he wanted, Daniel, at least he assumed it was Daniel, taking a picture of a man and a woman in what appeared to be a park.

Michael found a small magnifying glass in his desk drawer. He could make out his mother's face, but the face of the man holding her was turned away.

Is it my father… or…?

Low light, almost dark, but I must do this.

He opened the book to page 30 and looked at the photo.

Warm wind took him to a spot about 20 feet behind Daniel, who was leaning out from behind a tree.

The Polaroid camera made its signature whir. Michael stepped behind a tree to his left but kept his eyes on Daniel.

Daniel pulled his head, his arms, and the camera back behind the tree.

The man who held Michael's mother, swung his attention toward the sound of the camera. He stared that direction for a few seconds.

It's my dad!

Michael realized he wasn't hugging his mother. He was holding her to keep her from falling. His father was weeping. "I'm so sorry, Deborah, I can't take watching you in this pain."

"What did you do Garret... Garret—" She couldn't get the last words out.

"I love you. Please forgive me, Deborah. You shouldn't have to suffer with this pain. There's no end to this—for months—unless I help. I can't let you go through it."

Michael turned, slid against the tree trunk. He sat, weeping with his face in his hands. He remembered what his grandmother had told him while he was in the hospital.

"Your mother had terminal liver cancer, and the prognosis was a terrible and painful several months leading up to her death."

"My dad killed my mom," Michael sobbed.

He could only sit, broken hearted.

Daniel's voice calling out brought Michael back to the moment. "You think you've ruined my fun? You can run, but you have not deprived me."

Michael heard the terrible sound of Daniel plunging a knife into, Michael assumed, his father.

Then seconds later the whir of the camera, then another.

Michael gathered himself, wiped his eyes, and stood.

He stepped out from behind the tree.

He could see the dark silhouette of Daniel was standing with his back to him with a knife in one hand, camera in the other.

"No...!" Michael screamed and ran toward Daniel.

Michael's toe caught on an exposed root, causing him to tumble.

Daniel looked at him with the evilest smile Michael had ever seen.

"It's *you*," Daniel mocked, "I hope you enjoy the gift I left you."

He turned and ran.

Michael got up, rushed to his mother, fell to his knees, and hugged her.

Overwhelmed with emotion, he said, "Mom, I never got the chance to know you, or tell you how much I love you."

Her body jolted.

He pulled back to see her face.

Her eyes floated open.

She whispered, "I know Michael... I know. And... I love—" her eyes drifted closed. She left him.

He continued kneeling and hugging her until the warm wind took him back to his overstuffed chair.

He sat sobbing but managed to smile through his sorrow.

I got to say goodbye to my mother and tell her I love her. Somehow, she knew it was me. She recognized me!

It took a half hour to compose himself.

What happened to my dad? He must have dropped my mom and ran away, frightened by Daniel. Dad—?

Michael wept again, as he dealt with the realization his father left his mother lying on the ground, vulnerable to Daniel's knife.

I can't excuse that. But now I know why there was a high level of methanol alcohol in her blood. He mixed it into her drink.

His grandmother once told him his mother did not drink much, but occasionally had orange juice and vodka with his dad.

Michael believed if he went back and investigated restaurants near the park, he would find that his mother and father had dinner and drinks.

Somehow his father substituted the methanol for the vodka. Even if she had been healthy, a person her size couldn't handle the methanol.

Michael could not imagine the guilt and shame his father had owned.

No wonder he didn't come around, he couldn't bear to face my grandmother or me. He drank himself to death.

His father did something unconscionable.

I can believe he thought he was doing the right thing, maybe even a good thing. But still... running away?

A thought came to him.

Did my dad kill my mom? Would she have died that night if Daniel hadn't stabbed her?

The truth could not be found, but he chose Daniel as the person who took his mother from him.

Carrie had pointed out his mother was not stabbed in the heart, as the other four were. Because Michael had no interest in ever seeing Daniel again, he would ponder that the rest of his life.

But Michael got to say goodbye to his mother and tell her he loved her.

She knew me. And, she tried to tell me she loved me.

59

Saturday, November 16th

"I can't believe I've never been here," Linda said, as she and Michael walked toward the entrance to VanPort Acres. "For two years, I drove past here five days a week on my way to and from Clark College."

Michael said, "I've lived in Portland my entire life. My first time here was just weeks ago... in 1982." They both laughed. "Still sounds crazy doesn't it."

Linda turned her head toward him. "*Yes,* and I will *never* get used to it. You mentioned you planned to go back and repay the money you won. How did that go?"

Michael smiled. "I wish you could have seen the cashier's face when I bet that stack of money on one horse to win."

"No pun intended," Linda said, "but I *bet* she was shocked."

"She was. What if she'd known I purposely picked a loser?"

"She would have thought you were nuts and called security."

"Well, there's truth there, but I couldn't think of a better way to return money. With the $20 I began with and the money I won using Jimmy Feller's betting method, I was only a few dollars short. I see it as the racetrack's contribution to fighting criminals in their city."

"Michael, any regrets related to what happened between you and Daniel?"

"No regrets—well to be honest—part of me wishes I would have shot him. But Daniel got what I hoped for. The rest of his life in prison, with no chance of parole. And, the justice I had hoped to give the families of the victims.

"I do have concerns, Linda. We discovered he's *very* wealthy. What will he do with that wealth? Does he have any people left on the outside, or did we take them all out of the picture? Can he still reach out and hurt us? Those are my concerns."

Linda stopped and turned. "Carrie promised she'll work on that. Let's trust that she can control his use of the money."

Michael gave a half-smile and a shrug. "That's my hope."

"What about the shooter in the park?"

He shrugged again. "What can I do? There are no leads. No motive that I can see, and it hasn't happened since. I'm baffled."

"Me too." She said, "Michael—" then hesitated.

"What is it? You can ask me anything."

"I feel like I'd be prying, but I'll ask; if it's too personal just tell me."

Michael gave a slight nod and smiled. "It's okay."

"Weeks ago, you mentioned you saw a counselor. Has there been any follow-up?"

"I saw her last week. We discussed the journaling she assigned, and it was enlightening."

Linda glanced at him, turned, and began walking.

Michael pivoted and caught up. "Aren't you curious?"

"Yes, but—"

He took two long strides, turned and stopped in front of her. "But I want to tell you. I'm excited about what I'm discovering."

Linda stopped, smiled, and said, "Then I want to hear it."

Michael looked down and watched a scrap of paper tumble between them on the asphalt. "This past six weeks, as I've journaled my relationships, I've realized that I have four good friends. You," he looked up at her, "Matt, Carrie and—some might find it odd—but I count Jacob as one of my best friends."

Linda smiled. "He certainly sees you as his friend. And I'm happy you guys have that friendship."

"Me too. My relationship with Matt and Carrie dissolved after Gwen and I divorced. But we've picked up where we left off.

"But I have two *big* realizations, First, I've betrayed my upbringing."

Linda turned her head as she lowered her eyebrows. "Explain that?"

Michael said, "Maybe the term '*betrayed*' is too strong, but over the years, I've drifted away from an important part of my heritage. My mother and grandmother were both involved in a church, and the related activities that brings. My heart is being tugged back in that direction."

Linda stopped and turned toward him. "Jacob and I go to church with the Hindlers, join us."

"Jacob told me that a week ago; I just may do that."

"Okay, what's your second big realization?"

Michael placed his hand on Linda's back as he turned and began walking. "My first year in college I began hiking and camping with classmates. That continued through law school, I loved it. *Gwen* didn't. I gave it up for her, which translated into giving up my outdoor oriented friends. I love golf because it's outdoors and it's challenging—and because I'm good at it—but *Gwen* hated that too.

"Linda, after my first marriage, one of the things I've hoped to find is someone with interests similar to mine; specifically, the outdoors.

"So, my second big realization is, I look forward to finding that person and being married again."

Linda took Michael's hand. "I'll start gathering resumes from single nurses at work."

Michael clutched his chest. "Wow, a dagger… right to the heart."

Linda leaned her head against his upper arm and put her hand on his heart. "Michael, we both agreed we are best friends. And, that we'd continue being best friends and see where it leads. Do you sense it's leading to something else? Because I don't."

"I agree. I love our relationship; maybe I should start introducing you as my sister."

Linda looked up. "I'll take that."

Michael stopped and hugged her.

They continued walking.

Michael looked down for a few seconds. He stopped and turned to face Linda. "I have a business trip to Los Angeles next week. An attorney I met a few weeks ago, gave me her business card and asked me to call her if I'm ever in LA. I did. She's picking me up at the airport. We're having dinner—*she's* buying—then dropping me off at the hotel where my meetings will be held."

"I am so glad to hear that, Michael. But that's a *long-distance* relationship."

"There's no relationship yet, but who knows? I believe there was attraction the moment we met."

As they entered the racetrack, Michael pointed left to trackside. "Let's head over there, I want to check out something." After walking 100 feet, he stopped. "No way."

"What?"

"Bear with me. Let's go to the concessions stand."

After buying seven beers, Michael and Linda walked toward a group of five men in their mid-sixties. "Excuse me," Michael said, as they approached the group. "We're looking for the Jimmy Feller School of Horse Race Betting?"

They looked at Michael; one of them yelled: "Michael… *beer*." Michael laughed so hard he slopped the beers.

"Well, not the same Michael you met years ago. But because you *are* detectives, I'm not surprised you remembered."

"Are you his son?" Jimmy asked.

"It's that obvious?"

"Spitting image," Jimmy said, and his friends agreed.

"Here, have a beer," Michael said, as he handed them out. He and Linda took the last two.

"All right," they shouted.

Michael scanned the faces of the five friends, then looked at Linda and smiled. "Gentlemen, meet my best friend, Linda."

"Hi Linda," each said, while shaking her hand, then Jimmy raised his cup. "Here's to, Michael and Linda." The five friends agreed as they touched cups.

"Michael, is your father still alive?"

"Sadly, no."

"I'm sorry. I've hoped I'd someday be able to thank him for, somehow, providing me with evidence in a murder case the bureau was investigating."

"Are you sure it was him who provided the evidence?"

"What I know is that on the back of my business card, taped to the package I received, was written: 'From a student who graduated with honors from The Jimmy Feller School of Horse Race Betting.'"

Michael said, "Sounds like something he'd do."

"Say, Michael, did your father teach you my method?"

"Can't say that he did, Jimmy, but he said if I ever go to VanPort Acres on a Saturday, buy five beers when I got here. And," Michael pulled a bag from his jacket's pocket, "take a bag of Peanut M&M's with me."

Jimmy looked at one of his buddies. "Hold this," as he handed him his beer.

He put one arm around Michael's shoulder and the other around Linda's. "Step over to my classroom. I'm admitting you into the Jimmy Feller School of Horse Race Betting. School is in session."

Jimmy's four friends moaned and yelled: "Noooo... run away. You don't understand what's about to hit you."

Michael looked back with a smile and waved. "Gentlemen... I believe I do."

Epilogue follows

Epilogue

Grandma's Church, Portland, Oregon - Saturday, December 28

Grandma's Church, Portland, Oregon - Saturday, December 28th

"Can I have your attention please," Michael said into the microphone. He was standing at the front of the church's basement community room. His grandmother and Marvin sat at the head table, along with the Pastor of their church.

"You'll have an opportunity to say a few words to, or about, the bride and groom. But first, I'm going to tell you something you may not know.

"Someone murdered my mother when I was 12 years old—my *grandmother's daughter*—was murdered." He said as he looked over at his grandmother.

"I owe this woman so much; it is impossible to repay her. And Marvin, I can never thank you, or repay you, for having pity on this poor, helpless woman." Everyone laughed as his grandmother shook her fist at Michael.

"But Marvin I pity you because you will find she is anything but helpless. And when she decides—please, get out of her way. You and I together cannot stop her when she sets her mind to do something.

"She took in a young boy, whose life was shattered. Mind you, her life was shattered too. She lost her daughter and watched her grandson be broken. But she pushed her pain and her hurt aside, determined to see her daughter's son raised in such a way that he has no doubts he's loved. In such a way that his mother would be proud of the man he became; that goal is *still* in question." He looked at his grandmother who raised her eyebrows, lifted her right hand, and with fingers spread, rotated her wrist back and forth.

"She raised me to love and adore her in return—that love and adore thing—probably wasn't her goal, but she achieved it."

He looked at his grandmother again. Tears ran down her cheeks. Marvin was hugging her, with his head against hers, his eyes watering. "Thank you, grandma."

"Michael."

"Yes, grandma?"

She stood, used a napkin to dry her eyes, then walked to Michael's side and put her arm around his waist. She motioned for Michael to give her the microphone.

"Michael didn't tell the whole story. He has always been very smart. As a child he amazed me with his ability to put together information and come to a rational conclusion. Even in the board game Clue. I never won that game when playing against him. I wanted to ground him till next Monday for embarrassing me over and over again."

Everyone laughed as Michael hugged her.

"Michael gave me the greatest gift I could ever receive on this earth. He put together clues and brought the man who murdered my daughter to justice. He is behind bars for the rest of his life. In no way does that equal what he took from us, but it brings resolution. Something I thought I would never see. Thank you, Michael."

She handed Michael the microphone, then put her hands to her face and wept. Michael held her until Marvin came over and walked her back to her chair.

Everyone in attendance stood and applauded.

"Now…" Michael said, as he dried his eyes, "Let's see if I can recover from that. Truth is, I'll never recover from that; thank you, grandma."

"Okay… I've wrestled with this, what do I give two 90-year-olds for a wedding present?

I mean… a 20-year bond or annuity… wouldn't be appropriate, unless grandma determines that she and Marvin will live another 20 years, then—?"

Michael said, as he shrugged his shoulders and raised his arms half-way.

"I could go on and on with age related jokes, but why waste what precious time they have left?" His grandmother gave him the look only she can give.

"A while back, I was in the hospital recovering from injuries. Grandma told me over the phone that she and Marvin were getting married and planned to travel while they still can. She mentioned that they had booked a cruise to Hawaii, and as it turns out, it will be a honeymoon cruise.

"So, Marvin and grandma, what I give you, besides my love and support, is this, I upgraded your cruise ship cabin to a stateroom suite—it's beautiful— with amenities you'll love.

"I booked several excursions for you. Surfing Waimea Bay, zip-lining above a tropical forest canopy on Kauai, and cliff diving on the Napali coast."

Marvin jumped up, clenched his fists, and threw his arms in the air while yelling, "Yes!" He fell back onto his chair, pretending to be out of breath while grandma fanned him with her hand. He brought down the house.

After the laughter died down, Michael said, "Actually, I booked four very nice guided tour outings for you."

"Thank you, Michael," grandma said, echoed by Marvin.

"When my grandmother asked me to give her away, she honored me. I knew this would be a wedding for the ages… wait… wait…" Michael glanced at his outlined notes. "You may have never done this, but sometimes *my* fingers miss the letter key I *meant* to hit, and spell check doesn't pick up the mistake. Well, the 's' and the 'd' are side-by-side on the keyboard. That should have read, 'I knew this would be a wedding for the aged…,' I love you, grandma." Michael looked at Dr. and Mrs. Marvin Malcom, smiled, bowed, and extended an open hand to them.

After the laughter subsided, his grandmother stood. "Michael."

"Yes, grandma,"

"If I could still ground you, where would you be?"

"In my room until next Monday, Grandma."

While I have your attention, please take time to leave a brief review on Amazon. Reviews from other readers attract potential reader's more than any other factor; especially for an author's first novel. You would help me, and I would appreciate your support. I look forward to us taking Michael Mays on many more journeys!

Thank you,

Acknowledgements

"Every good gift and every perfect gift is from above, and comes down from the Father of lights, with whom there is no variation or shadow of turning." James 1:17

Thanks to:

My family and friends for their support and encouragement, Jerry Jenkins Writer's Guild, Mark Dawson – Self Publishing Formula, Cousin Don Gallian for his legal insights, Damonza Cover Design, Polgarus Studio – formatting, and My eight great Beta readers: Larry Spielman, Jim Bally, Rosalie Oekerman, Alyssa Zimmerman, Peggy Spielman, Larry Boehm, Stephanie Kender, and Dianne O'Havre.

Made in the USA
Middletown, DE
24 October 2020

22696960R00239